THIRD CONTACT

THIRD CONTACT

ENVOYS, BOOK 1

PETER J ALDIN

Editing by Alliance Book Editing (US) www.alliancebookediting.com

For those who risk their own wellbeing
while protecting the rest of us ...

AUTHOR NOTES

At the back of this novel you'll find a ***short lexicon***. It's there to explain the colorful terms you'll find in the story. Also, there's a ***guide*** to Human-settled Space to help with the various human factions and locations mentioned.

An astute reader will note that human characters sometimes get Tluaan terms wrong—this is only natural for people still learning those terms ... who don't have the benefit of a universal translator!

A quick but heartfelt **thanks** to my beta-readers Andre Jones and Sean Brien: your time and effort will always be appreciated.

Silvia Brown translated Jogianto's scrawled message into idiomatic Spanish. *Estoy agradecido.*

Alexandre Rito created the magnificent book cover.

And, of course, I'm always, *always* grateful to you, Neen ...

CAST OF CHARACTERS

Diplomatic Staff & Crew (Confederation)

Chris Gregory, Ambassador
Grace Renny, Diplomatic Assistant / Bodyguard
Piers Luigi Vido, Diplomatic Yacht Pilot

Tactical Fire Team (Xerxes)

Enforcer Antonia Jogianto
Enforcer Hecate Morales
Enforcer Olesco
Enforcer Umbrano
Enforcer Dayang
Enforcer Manolo
Colonel Andre Fowler

Peacekeepers (Confederation)

"Chipper" Tukimatu, Corporal, Blue Squad
Lyford Stines, Corporal, Blue Squad
Pandora Chandrasekhara, Corporal, Blue Squad
Denise Westermann, Corporal, Blue Squad
Eddie Wepps, Sergeant, Blue Squad Leader
Anthea Ouw, Sergeant, Red Squad Leader

Bradley "Widowmaker" Bradstock, Corporal, Red Squad

Mickey Kumar, Corporal, Red Squad

Tluaanto ("Domain Space" Personnel)

Buoun: Curator-Chief of the *Human Exhibition and Research Facility*; Envoy

Pi: Auxiliary Councillor, Domain Space

Naat: Grand Councillor, Domain Space

Ahn: Senior Registrar of Suuchaat Orbital, Buoun's sister

Vazak: "Commander-of-Sixteen," a senior officer of Suuchaat Orbital's warrior guard

Important Crew Members of the Confederation Naval Vessel *Assured*

Pan Xinchun, Captain

Wisdom Chinyama, XO

Henry Sintopas, Ensign, Chief Comms Operator

Renee Lindberg, Chief Petty Officer, Systems Oversight

Lieutenant Milena Berderhan, Pilot, *Devilfly* Space Fighter

PRELUDE

Buoun

The object had entered the star system a mere two cycles before Surveyor-Chief Buoun's small craft pulled alongside it.

It had to be a construct. A vessel of some kind. Buoun's superiors had suspected this when it first appeared on sensors a half-cycle ago, making course adjustments that steered it toward Suuchaat.

Now that Buoun could see the thing with his own eyes through the windows of his survey skiff, those suspicions were confirmed. Twenty arm-lengths long and cone-shaped, the object appeared composed from a composite of metals, ceramics and synthetics.

What is it? *he wondered and scratched at his throat fur.*

Near him, the skiff pilot made quiet noises in her own throat, indicating a mounting anxiety. The vessel—if that's what it was—gave off zero comms signals, nothing to indicate life aboard. Unlike his pilot, Buoun felt excitement rather than concern. There was a small chance that the original clans now forming Domain Surface had launched some kind of secret vessel, back before Domain Space's *monitoring became as robust as it was now. Perhaps a vessel sent beyond the solar system for data-gathering. If* that *were the case and if it were returning with Domain Surface research—illegal research!—then such a discovery would earn Buoun great prestige. Through the excitement came a twinge of fear: the craft would also be dangerous if an enemy crew existed aboard it.*

And then, another thought.

What if it is aliens?

His hearts beat hard at the prospect.

Non-Tluaan life!

They had presumed such beings existed because of long-range observance of the planet Kh'het 3, almost five light-years distant. But he'd heard nothing about orbital activity around that distant world. And if it had launched craft in the direction of Suuchaat, then surely that would have been detected—there would be panic over such a thing.

Besides, *he thought,* this object came from a different direction to the Kh'het star system.

And now it was here in Chaatu system, decelerating but only two and a half cycles from reaching orbit around Suuchaat.

"Closer to it, Surveyor-Chief?" the skiff pilot asked him.

Buoun shook himself. He had been so engrossed in possibilities and questions that he'd forgotten where he was. The skiff had two seats, one behind the other, and barely room to move around them. For the short trip between the asteroid mine and the passing intruder-craft, Buoun had chosen to stand stooped at the silver-furred female pilot's backrest. That way he could see better through the forward window. Now he was glad that the angle of the glass prevented a reflection in which the pilot might see the anxious twitching of his ears.

Keeping his voice steady, he said, "Of course we get

closer. The orders haven't changed. Find a way to dock with it ..."

"... and board it," she finished, the tremor in her voice obvious. Her ears also twitched.

"Yes."

"Liberty Habitat were unclear as to whether that order applied to both of us," she started, and he cut her off with an impatient hiss.

"I'll go alone." If we make it that far without it firing at us. *"I'll spend one fifteenth aboard, collect what I can and return."* As long as some scaly-skinned, multi-eyed alien doesn't tear off my head for a trophy.

"Docking in twelve two-hundredths," she said. Now that she wasn't boarding with him, she sounded cheerier.

The accord had been in place for thirty-eight orbits. Thirty-eight orbits of relatively peaceful exploration and expansion for the entire species, finally relieved of the compulsion to destroy, freed from millennia of war and infighting. Domain Surface were free to explore beneath the planet's mantle, to improve agriculture and renewable energy above it. Domain Ocean developed underwater habitats and commerce, learning to coexist with semi-intelligent life down there and to farm the oceans' resources rather than abuse them. Domain Moon, though largely beholden still to both Surface and Space for resources, were nevertheless thriving in their own way, settling an airless rock and making it sustainable.

And Domain Space were expanding the boundaries of the species, growing rich on the bounty of an entire star system ... and soon another system if current plans fared well. Decades of peace, stability and development.

And now, this object. From *outside* our system!

It was fascinating! Astounding! And if it proved to be

alien, then it had to be braked to a complete stop and soon, before the other domains noticed it.

As he crouched in his skiff's mating arm, Buoun watched comms chatter scroll across his wrist device. Some of the Council suggested it could be a bomb. Others that it might be a lost artifact, a boon, something they could reverse engineer to travel fast and free among the stars. If it were the latter, it might accelerate Domain Space's Kh'het Project, vastly reducing the nine orbits it would take to fly there.

What if it holds the secret of FTL travel? *Buoun wondered.*

"You think it does?" asked a voice in his ears.

The pilot.

Buoun must have spoken the thought aloud.

She added, "What if Surface wants it and comes for it?"

"They no longer possess ships capable of that. Not after their ridiculous skirmish over the moon being classed as 'land'."

The pilot chuckled in Buoun's headset. "They are *idiots; it's true."*

When he'd been eighteen orbits-old—still a child, really! —Buoun had gambled his entire future on becoming a surveyor, expecting to spend the next ninety orbits sailing among the asteroid fields and small satellite mining operations. After just six orbits of exactly that kind of work, his promotion to Chief had been a welcome surprise, bringing him more intellectually challenging work along with greater status in his clan.

And now, *he thought as he awaited the opening of the mating arm's sphincter,* it has brought me into danger. *Locking clamps scraped and clunked and whirred, seeking purchase on the object's non-compatible hatch, while sealant guns hissed and hummed to establish a viable join. When that sphincter opened, anything might await him. Belly-crawling bugs with acid-breath. Poison atmosphere. Domain Surface warriors with long knives. An automated security system set to incinerate intruders. Anything.*

But. Orders are orders.

As a senior staffer working closest to the object's route, Buoun had been the only one in a position to intercept the thing quietly—before it came in sight of the other Domains' orbitals and satellites.

And so it falls to me to investigate it. To make contact with any creatures that might be on board. Or with automated lasers, poison gases, electric shocks, acid-breathers ...

"Or perhaps," he whispered aloud, "to find opportunity."

"I didn't catch that, Chief," the pilot said.

"Talking to myself. Strategizing."

"Some news, sir. The object is decelerating further."

"Stopping?"

"If it continues at this rate, then yes, it will. In about three two-hundredths."

And being attached now, we are slowing also.

It was time. The only noise coming from beyond the sphincter were the creaks and clicks of straining metal and plastics.

"Is the join viable?"

A pause, then, "Should be."

"Open the sphincter."

There were no belly-crawlers, no acid-breathers, no electric shocks, long knives or automated security lasers. There was *atmosphere—though it was stale and under-oxygenated. Buoun kept his suit on while the skiff repressured the compartment beyond the sphincter, and while the sensors on his wristwrap tested for toxins.*

At twenty arms in length, the object was a little shorter than his skiff. This compartment took up perhaps one third of that length, sitting between whatever drive housing lay at the rear end and the vessel's thick and enclosed nose section. There were recognizable details, particularly a central square console welded to the "floor". Everything seemed oriented with reference to this central chin-high pillar and to this this floor, indicating the makers thought in terms of up and down like Tluaanto did. If he turned off his helmet-beam, illumination was minimal, leaking from tiny globes scattered here and there along walls, the ceiling, the central console. Many globes weren't working. No windows or view-ports either. There were screens on the console, four of them, one each side. Another was set into the wall between the cabin and the vessel's drive or engines which had powered down now.

Buoun noted all of this during a slow circuit of the cabin, relying on his magnetic boots to anchor him. Writing abounded, on labels, signs, even on the floor. The figures were different to the various rune-systems used by the Domains. But there was a lot of repetition, and he thought with a few months of work he'd be able to make some sense of them. He'd always enjoyed language-learning, had once thought of training as an envoy, a diplomat.

He was about to call to the pilot to relay his initial findings when a small silver panel set on the console's flat top drew his attention. Or rather, it was the imprint upon it that drew his attention—a crafted depression in the shape of what had to be a hand. Five digits, one opposable. Narrower than most Tluaan fingers, shorter than crafters', longer than warriors'. But the palm was about the same size.

"Remarkable!" he gasped and had to force himself to control his breathing as he began to hyperventilate. There could be dozens of reasons and purposes for that handprint. A sign of the builders' nature to curious finders like him. A personalized control for the missing owner of the vessel. Or a generalized control of some kind.

His gloved hand hovered above it. The idea was dangerous, but someone had to put their hand there.

"I don't," he whispered, quietly enough that the suit wouldn't interpret it as a message for the pilot. He thought, We can have engineers over here soon enough to investigate and see what it's connected to. *Again he thought of explosives, electric shocks. Perhaps, if he touched it, it would release a kind of robot from a hidden alcove to kill him. Or restart the engines and send him hurtling through the system and out the other side.*

"It's an invitation," he told himself, following some intuition, some instinct, his hand closing toward the panel. "They wanted the finders to put their hands there."

He was right.

Beneath the pressure of his palm, the panel immediately glowed purple. He felt a humming through the deck as power came on around the small chamber. Yellow lighting flickered to life along the roof. And then a ball of light bloomed from the top of the console, rose into the air and hovered there, sending Buoun staggering back into a wall, his hearts racing, mind babbling shock-induced nonsense.

"What is it?" the pilot demanded in his ears. "What's happening?"

"It's—" he started, then his breath caught as the ball of light resolved and morphed into an image.

"It's ..."

A three-dimensional image of another creature.

"It's ..."

A creature not from his star system.

"It's magnificent," he finished and ignored the string of questions coming from the pilot after that.

It revolved slowly, but otherwise, the image didn't move. This meant he could stay where he was and still study it in detail. The creature was beautiful. Bipedal. Roughly Tluaan-shaped. Clothes covered its torso, neck, upper arms, legs, and feet. It was impossible to tell if it was actual size or a representation; if to scale, then the creature would stand no higher than Buoun's waist, but he suspected it must be taller to have hands the size of that palm print. Light brown and mainly-hairless skin showed on its exposed surfaces. A curly thatch of dark fur upon the scalp. Its teeth were bared, and they were very white, mainly the flat molars of a herbivore, though there were also meat-teeth top and bottom. Like Tluaanto. After three revolutions, the image came to life, but languidly, its arms rising to chest height, palms turned upwards. It spoke. The voice was deep, and the language flowed, words merging together like the language of the Harimirim clans who now comprised Domain Ocean. It looked a little, he realized, like the tree-dwelling and fruit-eating bubunuims who had lived in a colony near his home village when he was a boy, just before the establishment of Domain Space. Gentle, playful creatures he had all but forgotten, so long had he been off world.

Images appeared and flowed in a crescent around and over the creature in a rainbow of data. Flying vehicles. Buildings. Different versions of the creature's face in pale skin, dark brown, black. Long scalp hair, short hair, no hair, curly, straight, wavy, light-colored, dark-colored. Hands appeared bearing writing implements to sketch figures in the air. The main creature shrank to a smaller size, was joined by one with different clothing and hair and skin; they embraced, separated, stood together with teeth bared, staring toward Buoun's belly. They joined hands. And then they faded away, leaving him with an instant and profound sense of loss. He wanted them back. He wanted to see—

A screen on the console came to life, divided into a grid of squares containing various icons. Buoun was not ready to touch any yet—though he would and soon—he was still absorbing everything he'd just seen.

These aliens were advanced and therefore powerful, but if they were not obfuscating, then they seemed peaceful, as befitted the bubunuims they resembled. And if they had sent this envoy craft, this negotiator vessel, especially to make contact, and if it carried no biological weapons, no disaster, then the craft would definitely benefit Domain Space.

Buoun had begun a career in space survey, had risen to a supervisor rank faster than his peers. But even at this young age, it had become a boring life. Now he had an opportunity indeed. A new career loomed, possible, tantalizing. Buoun could become an expert in the alien language and technology. His childhood fancies of being an envoy could be realized in becoming an envoy to aliens! He would craft a message to send back, invite them here, establish a relationship. Having been the first point of contact, and having learned their language and their ways, he would be the chief conduit of commerce and learning. Buoun might become the most important Tluaan ever born.

"Pilot, a change to the plan. I'm staying here a little longer."

A pause, then, "How much longer?"

"How much food do we have?"

"Enough for three or four cycles."

"Then there is your answer."

Buoun switched off his communicator. "Yes," he told the screen full of icons. "You are both the opportunity and the challenge I've always wanted. I will learn to be the envoy you need and my people need. I will learn your beautiful language and learn it fast. And when your *envoys come here in an orbit or two, I will be ready."*

An orbit or two, *he thought.* Plenty of time to learn a language.

He returned his hand to the purple panel, and the hologram shimmered and reset, and it started its message from the beginning.

FORTY-TWO YEARS LATER ...

March 11, 3014, Old Earth Calendar

1

CROUCHED IN THE ROCKY TUNNEL, Xerxian Tactical Enforcer Antonia Jogianto wriggled her nose as sweat ran down from between her eyes. She kept both hands on her pulse rifle, refusing to show weakness by wiping away the offending droplet, no matter how much it itched and tickled.

Worse than the sweat was the lack of visibility, the fact that she couldn't see out of the tunnel and into the asteroid's interior cavern. She was stacked two back from her commander who'd put himself up front of the strike team's line. Even crouching, Colonel Fowler was a head taller than her. The Confederation Peacekeeper sergeant stacked between them was shorter, sure, but he was broader. From her position, only a tight wedge of cavern was visible through the tunnel mouth. She would be running into an area she hadn't been able to scope personally.

This is bullshit, she thought. *Nah, it's worse than bullshit, coz bullshit don't get ya killed.*

Sure, she had Fowler's eye-feed playing in the corner of her *retinaid*, but it wasn't the same as seeing something for yourself. The transmission lacked depth. And it was tiny.

The bead of sweat reached the tip of her nose. She tried to blow it off quietly, without alerting the woman behind her in line. The drop just sat there, irritating her. Torturing her.

It was goddamn hot in the tunnel, and in her body armor.

And Ana was nervous as hell.

Her clan trainer's number one motto had been, "*True Tacticals are not afraid.*"

But the guy was a moron.

Nothing wrong with a few healthy nerves, she told herself. *It's a sign of intelligence in a dangerous situation. And when you're jammed between a wuss of a Peacekeeper in front and a dog's wife behind you ...*

As if reading her thoughts, Tactical Enforcer Hecate Morales muttered an insult at her back. Ana didn't give her the pleasure of showing she'd heard it.

Goddamn this.

If she'd been *second* in the queue, she'd have a better view over Fowler's shoulder—and she'd be in the position rightfully hers, the one she'd occupied for her past five live-fire missions. But the Confeds didn't want to watch Xerxians fighting through Eye Cam Feed; they had insisted on sending some of their dumbass troops along. She should be staring at the back of Fowler's hair. Instead, she was staring at a Confed Peacer helmet.

What was this idiot sergeant's name? Wets, Wex ... *Wepps*. That was it. Stupid name for a stupid *tulalâ*.

It was all politics is what it was. Directly behind her were her five Tactical comrades. Behind them, several more dark-blue Confed uniforms made up the end of the stack. Blue uniforms and weakling helmets like Wepps's in front of her. It was frustrating, hacking frustrating.

Never know, she tried to encourage herself. *Wepps might catch a laser round that would otherwise hit me.*

Maybe the extra firepower would be worth having. And the extra targets ...

The thought cheered her up, allowing the knot in her gut to unwind a little. The bead of sweat dropped from her nose, relieving her ...

Then Hecate nudged her in the small of her back. And the knot in Ana's gut wound tighter.

Hecate had had her eyes on Ana's 2IC position for months. Two more promotions and both of them would have their own team. But Hecate was three years younger than Ana's twenty-five—

Nowhere near the veteran I am.

—and possibly hungrier for honor and glory. Hecate had taken advantage of every opportunity to needle and undermine Ana. For months now. It was reaching a point where Ana would have to do something about it ...

For now, she had to satisfy herself with the mental image of punching her teammate in the throat. But maybe during dinner, she'd slip this bitch a goofie and perform a little minor surgery on her when she'd passed out. Nose job? Lip job? Ear job? Ana smiled: it was sure fun to think about.

"Sorry to bump you," Hecate murmured. She was leaning too close, her voice too loud. "Hope I didn't distract you."

Ana's smile evaporated. This time, she did turn her head slightly. Enough to murmur back, "Distract this" as she flipped the bird.

Hecate laughed a low laugh.

Concentrate, Ana told herself.

She had to focus. Forget Hecate. Any second now, they'd be out in the cavern. Any second now, the shooting would start.

THE STARSHIP *ASSURED'S* bridge was crammed. Standing room only, and even *that* was hard to find. Ordinarily, less than a dozen personnel would staff this room. Today eight technicians had crowded in as well, updating modules, running diagnostics, even taking snack orders—any excuse to be here for the action!

There was also Ambassador Chris Gregory, serving as observer. And he was not enjoying it.

The lack of seating and the constant ebb and flow of busy crewers had forced Gregory to the very edges of the rectangular room. Accustomed to the comfort of his diplomatic yacht—and to sharing it with a personal crew of two—Gregory muttered curses as he pressed himself into the nook between a sensor station and the back-corner data-library station. It was hot in here, stuffy, and tangy with electrical tastes and body odor. Those *Assured* crewers wearing lighter-colored uniforms had dark sweat patches creeping from their armpits. They all smelled like they needed showers—badly!

One technician avoiding another coming the other way pressed against Gregory for a few seconds—completely obstructing his line of sight to the forward viewscreen where the day's important action was depicted. No apology was offered. The bump of a shoulder, then a hard weight pressing into his ribs, before the woman moved on and left Gregory rubbing his chest and breathing through his mouth. The close proximity of so many bodies was unsettling, claustrophobic. Whatever happened to the generously expansive starship bridges from fictional nanobooks? On those, nobody jostled, everyone was provided with a chair or stool, and people's grooming was impeccable.

It was so crowded today that his assistant had been forced out into the short corridor between the bridge and the lifts. Gregory huffed a humorless laugh at the memory of Grace Renny's pissed-off expression as she'd moved outside. As a veteran "minder", losing sight of her boss never sat well with her, even if that boss was standing in the heart of a starship surrounded by the safest people in the Confederation.

A male crewer hurried past, his body odor pungent enough to wrinkle Gregory's nose. The crewer quickly exchanged money with the communications officer. They were betting, no doubt, on the outcome of the mission playing out on the screen ahead.

Betting, Gregory thought darkly. *And we're all meant to be on some kind of noble endeavor here. The* Assured *is the Confederation's beacon of moral authority, and her crew are gambling on who or how many will die today.*

Commissioned almost seventy years earlier, the *Assured* had been one of the first starships departing Foucault's Moon with a double-barreled brief: pare back the scourge of Xerxian piracy, and rebuild ties with Foucault's sister planets after humanity's greatest dark age. Those sister planets had been separated for centuries by the devastation of the PBT pandemic, then by centuries of local quarantine, of societal and technological breakdown, and in some places —such as the Xerxes system—of feudalism and lawlessness. *Assured* and her sister ships had been designated *Reconcile*-class. In those days, they'd carried over two hundred and fifty crew, more than twice as much as *Assured* now carried —and if Gregory thought the bridge was congested today, his mind boggled at how much more crowded and stinky ship-life must have been in his grandfather's days.

He glanced left past the doorway to where the stocky Red Squad Peacekeeper on bridge duty was squashed into an alcove of his own. He appeared stoic about it—but then as a soldier, he was no doubt accustomed to conditions like these.

Peacekeeper marines, Chris Gregory thought. Seventy years ago, the *Assured*'s marine complement had numbered four times her current ten. Back then, she'd also carried two fighter-interceptors whereas now she only carried one. Utilitarian in shape and design, *Assured* was nowhere near as graceful as the larger and younger Escort Carrier *Bountiful* sitting six kilometers above her and to starboard. But both ships shared the philosophy of interior design that discouraged people sitting when they could be standing. While *Bountiful*'s bridge was a spacious crescent-shape winding around the forward edge of the ship above a massive open-mouthed hangar deck, *Assured*'s bridge was this blocky six-by-four-meter box buried deep in the center of the ship where it was hardest for a particle-beam or missile to reach.

It had been ten years since anyone had fired anything at this particular Confederation ship. The offenders back then had been a swarm of smaller Xerxian pirate vessels from the Star Killer faction who, at the time, had been harassing Centauri system for over a century. There was nothing left of the Star Killers, nothing beyond the debris clouds they had been blasted into.

Today's mission was intended to neutralize the pirate menace forever, eliminating the final rogue warlord and allowing Xerxes itself to come under the civilizing influence of the Democratic Confederation of Human Colonies.

At least that was the hope.

It wasn't Ambassador Chris Gregory's hope.

Chris Gregory had his doubts.

He craned his neck around the streams of crewers manning and tuning sensors and weapons controls so that he could keep watching the forward viewscreen wall. The multiple video streams were even more unsettling than this overheated room. Through the eye-cams of the raiding party, the tight tunnels and uneven features of Asteroid CP11X's interior kept jerking and bumping around. Each time Gregory focused on one of the Eye Cam Feeds (ECFs), he felt his lunch rising. But he had to watch. He had to bear witness to this. As an ambassador, it was his duty, no matter how much violence sickened him.

Too small to read from his position at the back of the bridge, information dribbled in letters and symbols across half the ECFs—those of the ship's "Blue Squad" Peacekeepers. No words or symbols appeared on the other seven feeds, those belonging to the Xerxian Tacticals nominally in charge of the mission. The final feed was from the chest-cam of an *Assured* medical corpsman bringing up the rear.

Two meters back from the forward screen, a long operations board allowed for monitoring and control of the ship by her captain, her two helmsmen, and her XO. With all the data streaming to that board from the other workstations, Captain Pan Xinchun and Commander Wisdom Chinyama should have been as frantically busy as most other bridge personnel. But the pair stood watching the screens like Gregory did, occasionally pointing or murmuring with their heads together. Chinyama, being the taller of the two, had to stoop a little to achieve this. Gregory wished to hell there was space for him to be over there with them; whatever they were discussing was definitely his business too; he'd be the one coordinating the follow-up negotiations with the ruling "Sevens" Party back on Xerxes.

A console operator called, "Away team approaching red zone," as various ECFs showed the stack of soldiers turning a corner in the narrow tunnel. The space there might have been pitch-black since the feeds were uniformly vision-enhanced, tinged with green.

A woman working the sensors beside Gregory offered him a brief grin. "Kill-or-capture mission. Don't get many of these, eh? So exciting."

Gregory returned her smile politely and thought her naïve. She was easily his age, mid-forties. She should have had a little more perspective. And maturity.

He sighed and fidgeted, trying to get comfortable.

Perhaps he was being unkind toward her, labeling her *naïve.* He was stressed, that was the problem. He would no doubt witness a person die via that screen soon, and the idea was making him crazy.

Kill-or-capture mission, he thought. *An excuse for the Xerxians to ignore the 'or-capture' clause and focus on the 'kill' part.*

"Away team *reaching* red zone," called the console operator.

At the same time, three ECFs showed the Xerxian Tacticals leader, Colonel Fowler, squatting and raising a closed fist for the fireteam to stack behind him and wait.

"Quiet on bridge," Captain Pan hollered. Light gleamed from his oiled-back hair.

Noise on the bridge fell away. Those crewers without actual stations scurried out into the hallway where they piled around the doorway to watch. Grace would be further irritated with them being between her and her boss.

Onscreen, Colonel Fowler said softly, "Team in place. Hostiles ahead: two at my one o'clock and six at ten o'clock." Fowler's ECF showed him looking into a wide cavern, flaring with lights and rimmed with cabinets, trestle tables, camping cots, and carry-cases. Gregory could make out the eight people in two clusters across the cavern, forty or so meters away from Fowler's position.

"Here we go," Gregory whispered, and hoped to God he really wasn't about to watch someone die.

TWO AT TEN, *six at two.* Ana repeated Fowler's words to herself.

The colonel would head right toward the group of six. The next in line, Sgt. Wepps, would go left. Following alternating procedure, Ana would head after Fowler. Fast. The pressure was on her to get in behind him immediately, to protect him and add her firepower to his.

Her hands squeezed tight around her PR19's firegrip and foregrip. What was taking so goddamned long? What was he waiting for? The enemy were right there.

Wepps extended an arm out past her so his own troops could see his signal—a gesture she couldn't decipher.

She cursed under her breath. She was no stranger to firefights. But this was the first time that anyone—to her knowledge—had ever vidded her before. Maybe *that* was the main reason for her nerviness.

Godrotten Confeds. Why they gotta do this?

Later, some DCHC key-pusher would play back her record, going over and over it, adding notes for some bureaucrat's file. Prissy old men and women might analyze every step she took today. Little weaners who didn't know the killing end of a pulse rifle from the tip of a dessert fork.

Concentrate, idiot, she thought and once again wished Fowler would just move and get this over with.

She wriggled her nose again, rolling her shoulders under her ballistic vest. Their target—Warlord Luján and his remaining crew—were feisty bastards with great reflexes. Their pirate weapons only had one setting: kill. Ana's new Confed PR19 was set to stun.

The problem with stun is that it doesn't always stun. So her original Tactical Trainer had told her. *"Peacekeeper" marines used them a lot when they were taking Nakayama Station off of us. For a lot of our guys—when the Confeds didn't hit them just right—stun only made them madder.*

The Trainer had laughed at the end of that little speech. Ana could only hope he'd been joking.

THE TEAMS HADN'T MOVED YET. What the hell was

Fowler waiting for, Gregory wondered. A clean kill shot? Was he imagining all the children he'd leave fatherless and enjoying the fantasy?

Stop it, he reprimanded himself. Such cynicism toward a representative of the ruling Xerxian faction was unbecoming a diplomat. If only it hadn't been a Xerxian who'd killed his predecessor. Sure, it wasn't one of the Sevens faction. But really, in his very private opinion, all Xerxians were the same, regardless of faction.

Besides, the team's weapons were set on stun. No one was dying today.

Fowler's helmet jostled, jerked forward. His right hand came up with three fingers extended.

And Chris Gregory's breath caught in his throat.

FOWLER RAISED A GLOVED HAND, three fingers extended.

Part of Ana was immediately relieved at the sight. But her heartrate sped up, nevertheless.

Fowler dropped the first of the three fingers—

Three ...

The second—

Two ...

And put his hand to his rifle as he charged forward.

Go!

Ana surged forward after him, ready to cut right. Her rifle tracked toward a surprised-but-moving target across the cavern, her finger curled over the trigger.

She fell, sprawling.

Her weapon discharged twice before she got her bearings enough to get her finger off the trigger. One of the stun bolts kicked up dust near her; she had no idea where the other one went. Hecate clambered over her, stepping on her thigh for leverage. Ana caught a gleaming smile before Hecate focused on the people she was trying to shoot, and was gone, running past.

The bitch. The *bitch!*

Ana hadn't tripped.

Hecate had pushed her.

2

PEACEKEEPER CORPORAL CHIPPER TUKIMATU rushed along the tight asteroid tunnel. Despite hunching over, his helmet scraped the ceiling a couple times. He kept his weapon angled to the floor, trying to see ahead of him, trying to move without stepping on the heels of Peacekeeper Westermann in front of him.

Already, shouts rolled out from the cavern ahead, accompanying the dull crack of stun-bolts. It was pandemonium out there, and he needed to be in amongst it, helping the team.

He hustled toward the opening, last in line except for the corpsman. At the opening, just as he was raising his weapon and seeking a target, Westermann fell with a surprised yelp. It took him a second to analyze: a burn to her thigh, the pain just registering in her eyes as he drew alongside. Chipper juked right, making it harder for her shooter to hit him too. He hoped the corpsman would help her without injury to himself.

Weapon up, Chipper kept his big frame moving, glad of the lower artificial gravity on the asteroid. His gaze swept the wall opposite him. The shot had come from high

—he'd just made out the laser flash as it hit her. Where...? *There!* The sniper was ten meters up, crouched on a rock ledge, his muzzle tracking Chipper. As if dodging a rugby fullback, Chipper dove left for the doubtful cover of a wooden crate. Light flashed over his shoulder, and he smelled ozone. In midair he turned, twisting his rifle. A millisecond before his shoulder hit the ground, he squeezed off his shot. Impact: both his body impacting against the ground, and his stun pulse impacting the shooter. The sniper spasmed and toppled forward, rolling off the ledge. Chipper gasped.

"No! God!"

Going against his training, he squeezed his eyes shut before the man hit the ground. But even above all the shooting and shouting, even all the way across the cavern, he heard the sickening crunch of the body landing. Time continued to slow for him.

He collapsed onto his back, tinnitus ringing in his ears, nausea hitting him in the gut, guilt swelling up from his conscience. *Killed him. I killed him.* He'd never taken a life before.

His heard his father's laconic voice murmur in the back of his mind, *Shouldn't have joined the Peacers then, ey, boy?* But there was nothing joke-worthy about this.

And then he heard his Marine trainer yelling in his head. *Move move move move move!*

He obeyed, rolling on to his feet and coming into a crouch. Avoiding looking at his kill, he started scanning the scene. It was chaos. Peacers were in cover behind turned over tables or crates, or prone on the ground, or crawling for better positions. They were firing—occasional laser bursts lanced out from the enemy positions, but most of the fire was stun-bolts. A couple of pirates were retreating down another tunnel. Three, it looked like, were trapped behind boxes near another exit, pinned down. Three more were prostrate and unconscious. Apart from Westermann's injured leg, none of the other soldiers seemed hurt except ...

Wepps!

Oh crap! The sarge wasn't moving.

Four meters back from Wepps, another woman—a Tactical!—had fallen also. He vaguely remembered dodging her as he'd exited the tunnel earlier. The woman was getting up but carefully, and he wondered if she'd been hit, so he got up and jogged over, keeping low. He reached for her, asked if he could help—and winced when she bared her teeth at him.

Sheesh, I'm only trying to help, he thought. It was her turn to be up and jogging now, jogging away from him. Her angry rejection stung him. But not nearly as much as the guilt of killing that sniper.

Again he heard his father, this time from a memory, *Boy, a fella like you, the Peacers is no place for him. Stay here. Work the fish farm with the rest of us.*

His eyes found their own way to the crumpled body across the cavern.

"I wish I had, Dad," he murmured. "Right now, I wish I had."

MORE PEOPLE JOSTLED Ana with thighs and knees as they pushed past her coming out of the narrow entranceway. The dusty air pulsed and sizzled with weapons fire. A laser sliced into a Peacer woman a couple of meters ahead of Ana's position. The woman went down.

Shit, she'll lose that leg, she thought and started to belly crawl fowards. Goddamned Hecate. She'd screwed this up.

A navy-suited Peacer glared back at her from where he'd found cover behind an upturned table. "Nice one, pusbrain," he spat.

What?

Another Peacer loomed over her, startling her so that she almost swiped at his legs with her weapon to knock him down. Everything about this guy was big: body, thighs, upper arms, head, even those soulful eyes. His skin was a shade or two darker than her Filipino-descended skin. And if she'd thought Wepps had big shoulders, this guy's could prop up a roof! "Help ya?" he asked.

She snarled wordlessly and got to her feet, brushing by him, scanning for targets. She needed a target. *There!* Sixty meters from her position, one pirate was bolting between a line of boxes and a tunnel opening. She got off a shot. Missed. "Hack it!"

A pulse grenade went off—behind the crates the pirate had fled from. Two other hostiles staggered from their cover there to collapse in the dust, hands over their ears, writhing. Tacticals moved in on them.

"Hack it," she repeated. The firefight was over as quickly as it started. She'd missed the whole damn thing.

Because of Hecate. Where was she, where was that—?

Hecate was thirty meters away. Standing close to Fowler and deep in conversation with him. Their backs to Ana, they were apparently watching Tactical Olesco fumble his way through getting cuffs on a downed pirate.

"So that's your plan, bitch," Ana muttered. *Push me out the way to get closer to Fowler.*

Checking the state of her uniform, she brushed dirt from her chest-armor and forearms, then surveyed the rest of the cavern. There were three exits off the wall opposite, and it didn't look like anyone had gone chasing down those yet. Five pirates were down, it appeared, one of them dead judging by the angle of his neck. How did that happen? Another was on her knees in surrender; Tactical Manolo applied cuffs to her. Tacticals Umbrano and Dayang had their noses in a crate—Ana knew them too well. They'd be pretending for the ECFs, commencing a rough catalog of Warlord Luján's inventory; but the ECFs couldn't read their minds, couldn't tell *Assured*'s officers that Umbrano and Dayang were secretly deciding what was worth looting from these boxes once the ECFs were off.

Someone had to go guard those tunnels against possible reprisal.

I guess that's me.

She started forward and passed the Peacer team leader Wepps who was prone and unconscious. There'd been four Peacers assisting the Tacticals: the big guy with the little boy eyes was checking on a pair of unconscious hostiles, the woman with the lasered leg was groaning and swearing while the medic applied a burn pack, Wepps was down, and the flat-nosed one who'd called her *pusbrain* was caring for his fallen team leader.

"He dead?" she asked the man. Wepps didn't look dead—no blood, no visible laser scorching.

"You *brain*dead?" the man replied.

Screw him; she was only asking. Ana gave him the bird. She had plenty of bird to go round.

Fowler separated from Hecate, aimed at one of the tunnels. Hecate pirouetted, chin up, checking the ceiling for drones or cams. She lowered her gaze once to throw Ana a wink.

Ana saw red then. She changed course. She had the rifle up and centered on Hecate's back and her finger inside the guard when Fowler barked, "Jogianto! Stow that now along with the attitude. Your mistake. Your problem."

Reluctantly, Ana lowered her weapon. *She shoved me,* she wanted to tell him—and she would later.

"And that's not your worst problem," said Olesco in her ear.

The lean and curly-haired Tactical had come over from the crates he'd been checking. Olesco had been born in the same shanty town as her. She'd seen him around during their childhoods and educations. And then they'd ended up in the same Sevens Party Tactical class. Since then, he'd been someone she trusted—for six years now, he'd always been an ally. Also, he'd spent a few nights in her bed over those years, which had been pleasant too. His voice was half-sympathetic, half-amused as he added, "You realize who downed the Confed?"

She frowned and looked toward Wepps again.

The corpsman had moved to the prone sergeant now, injecting him with something. The Peacer who'd called her *pusbrain* was upright and sending Ana a withering look.

"*I* downed him? I ... didn't ..." But maybe she had. She'd fired twice. The first round had hit the ground, but the second—she had no idea where that went. "*I* stunned him?"

Olesco nodded sympathetically, patted her shoulder and pushed his prisoner past her toward the tunnel mouth.

"It wasn't me." Then louder: "It wasn't me. It was her!" She pointed across the cavern.

Hecate laughed. "Nice try."

People were staring at her. No one was buying it. Not her own people. Not the big Peacer with the little boy eyes. As far as they were concerned, she'd tripped and shot the Confed. Positioned now in a tunnel mouth, Fowler turned his back to it, his hard gaze raking the cavern. As it passed across her, it hardened further, narrowing like someone focusing a laser beam. Inside her soul, she burned with the touch of that gaze. It moved on, but the meaning stayed with her. She'd be disciplined for this. She might even lose ranking. Lose it to ...

She swore, locking eyes with the woman who'd caused this.

Nice and slow, enjoying it, Hecate flipped Ana the bird.

CHRIS GREGORY HADN'T REALIZED he'd come out of his alcove until he was halfway across the congested bridge and the firefight was halfway done. Now that it seemed to be over, he pushed his way to Captain Pan and asked, "What's happening? Luján is dead?"

Captain Pan acknowledged Gregory with a nod then pointed to a freeze-frame from someone's eye-cam. "Went down that tunnel."

"How do you know that?" Gregory asked. He hadn't heard any of the soldiers report that.

Pan quickly pointed to one of the feeds. "Saw it on *that* cam." Then he leaned toward his XO, resuming their quiet conversation.

Gregory waggled his fingers at a nearby crewer to get her attention, then asked her, "They'll give chase? You think they'll chase him?"

"Hope so," she said, grinning.

Hope so! She was another one who saw this as entertainment. "Well, why haven't they, do you think?"

As Pan had done, she gestured to the screen. "Check it out. Looks like a couple of them might be getting ready to do it now."

FOWLER HAD WAVED Ana over to his position. "You're with me."

"Sir, I—"

"Shut it, Jogianto. Luján went this way. Let's concentrate on that." He raised his voice. "Hecate, in Wepps's absence," a glance at Ana, "you're in charge here. Umbrano, you're with Jogianto and me."

"Sir," Ana said. "One of them went down that tunnel too."

He squinted at her. "You sure?"

She opened her mouth to answer, but Umbrano coming nearer answered for her. "I saw it too." Umbrano scratched at his beard; his eyes were a little wild, the pupils a tad too dilated; he was high again. And Fowler didn't seem to notice nor care.

"All right. Pick a buddy and go find her. Jogianto and I will take Warlord ourselves."

Umbrano grinned and hollered at Tactical Manolo to come join him.

"Should we take a Peacer?" Ana asked.

Fowler shook his head and strode away. "Tight tunnel. Two's plenty. Unless you doubt your own ability to walk competently."

She swallowed a curse and followed him. It wasn't right, Hecate doing that and getting away with it, making her look like a fool.

Maybe it'll show up on these ECF feeds.

Unfortunately, all Hecate had had to do was turn her gaze upwards for the split second it took to—

Trip me. Bitch!

The tunnel swallowed them like the mouth of some beast. She hated tunnels. Hated tight places. And this was tight, as he had said. At least this one had tiny light globes set regularly along it and she didn't have to switch to infrared. A dozen paces inside, Fowler stood aside and waved her past to take point. Was he going to shoot her? *Don't be stupid,* she told herself; *he's giving you a chance to regain status.*

They followed the twists and turns of the tunnel for what seemed like a kilometer. It seemed to be taking a long time, but when she checked the time stamp in her retinaid, it had only been five minutes since they'd left the cavern. Light bloomed ahead, indicating another open area. Perhaps one of this asteroid's hangar airlocks.

Something jostled the back of her rig. She startled, turning. Fowler's hand was moving back to his weapon.

"What did you do?" she asked.

He smiled. His smiles were so ghastly, Ana found she preferred him angry. He tapped his rig, then pointed at hers. "My comm has mysteriously stopped transmitting. And now yours has too."

Her hand went to her rig, but she didn't turn it back on. "Stopped..."

"Must be mineral deposits in the walls, or a magnetic field causing the interference."

"They ... won't buy that," she said carefully. "Sir."

He winked. "Normally. I prearranged some programming that will indicate interference in the feed signature."

"Clever," she said. "But *why*?"

"You have a chance to make up for your error earlier. Sometimes in mistakes there are opportunities."

"I didn't make a mistake. It was—"

"Jogianto, I don't care. The opportunity for us is that when you stumbled, after your weapon discharged, the rifle struck the ground and its selector accidentally switched to *AP*, to full power."

"But it didn't."

Fowler sighed.

They traded stares for a few seconds while her mind worked. Then she got it. "You want me to ...?"

"Yes. Problem?"

"No, sir." She edged toward the light showing around that corner ahead. It was no loss to the universe if Luján died. The guy was a devilish bastard who'd killed a lot of Tacticals in his time, along with innocent "collaterals." And if this was her chance to undo what that bitch Hecate had done ...

... then why did she feel so bad about doing it?

CHIPPER HELPED the corpsman get Wepps on his feet. The sergeant was groggy and mumbling about pins-and-needles in his extremities, but the medic seemed to think being upright was the best thing for him.

Standing nearby, Corporal Stines asked Wepps, "Permission to kick that woman's ass, sir?"

"Fine with me," called the Tactical designated as Hecate by his HUD. The woman had an ugly scar across an otherwise finely sculpted face. She was getting cuffs onto two groggy pirates. "She's always been a little clumsy."

Wepps rubbed at his arms as Chipper let go of him and swayed a little as he found his balance. "Inquiry will sort it out."

Stines growled, "Sarge, you're taking this well. She shot you."

"With a stunner." Wepps yawned.

"It could've been set on kill."

"And it wasn't." Wepps reached out and slapped the man's webbing. "Help the corpsman carry Westermann out of here, Peacer. Put your energy into useful things."

When the man had grabbed his end of the stretcher, Chipper told Wepps, "That woman, Jogianto, she said it was the other chick who stunned you, sir."

Wepps raised an eyebrow. "Chick?"

"Er ... lady. Woman. That one with the scar who was behind her in line."

"She said *she* shot me?" Another yawn.

"She actually said 'it was her'."

Wepps rolled his arms and took an experimental step, then had to grab hold of Chipper's webbing to stay on his feet. "Well, Corporal, whichever one of them did it, I can only hope Colonel Fowler will kick their ass for me. Coz this is truly an unpleasant experience."

"WHY HAVE those two feeds gone down?" Gregory called to Captain Pan.

Pan just shook his head, clearly irritated with the ambassador's interruptions. *Well, get used to it, Bubba. I'm meant to be in charge here.*

It was left to the XO to answer. Commander Wisdom Chinyama turned his ever-patient face toward Gregory and told him, "Signal reads as if it's scrambled. Might be a magnetic field. Or the pirates may have scramblers down there."

"So how do we find out what's happening?"

Without turning, Pan said, "The old-fashioned way, Ambassador. We wait. And they tell us later."

3

THE WELL-LIT AREA beyond the tunnel was a dock, a cube cut into the asteroid centuries ago. Blast doors had been set into both ends. The doors at Ana and Fowler's end were open, retracted into the floor. The ones at the far end were sealed, separating the business area of the dock from the giant airlock beyond it, a failsafe against exposing the asteroid interior to vacuum. The dock was largely devoid of cover—devoid of anything except for the two vessels in it.

Warlord Luján had lost most of his fleet in the cat-and-mouse engagements of the past year, some here in "home-spread"—as Xerxians like Ana thought of Xerxes system—and some outside of it. Upon entering the "east" dock at the asteroid's far tip an hour earlier, the away team had found and disabled a scout-ship. Here in the "west" dock, Luján had two ships waiting: a small, single-occupant fighter, and a larger Halcyon-6 freighter.

The latter craft was the center of the activity inside the dock, activity transmitted to Ana and Fowler's retinaids by the tiny roachbot Fowler had a minute earlier sent scuttling along the wall. She and Fowler were still tucked back around the curve of tunnel beyond the blast doors closest them. Luján had three of his people with him, all male. One was a pilot, visible through the freighter's cockpit windows as he powered up ship systems. Another was helping the warlord shift a repulsor-trolley laden with supply crates toward the freighter's ramp—they were still a good twenty meters from it, but once Luján vanished inside the Halcyon-6, Ana's rifle would be useless. She would have already tried for him, were it not for the third pirate who'd been posted as a sentry and held a grenade-launcher. Though the man didn't know they were there, his weapon was angled in their direction.

"Hack," she whispered, imagining a grenade detonating against the wall or ceiling near her. "He fires that, we're done."

"Then we don't let him fire it, do we?" Fowler whispered back. Crouched behind her, he fussed with the roachbot controls on his datapad. The tiny drone's camera tilted straight down toward the floor as it transitioned from wall to roof and continued toward the sentry's position. "You'll get about five seconds once this goes off. Make them count."

She nodded and pushed away from the wall, hidden by the tunnel's curve and shadow, but weapon up, ready to step sideways and start firing.

The roachbot was above the sentry now. It stopped moving.

"All right," Fowler whispered. "Arming now."

In her retina feed, a red blinking asterisk announced that the roachbot had been converted from mobile camera to grenade. Its legs detached from the roof. The feed from the camera plummeted toward the bot's target. The sentry let out a cry of alarm a second before the bot detonated with a *whump!* and a flash of orange.

Ana took two fast steps sideways then four forward, weapon angled toward Luján's position. She halted for a steadier aim. The rustle of clothing told her Fowler was doing his best to follow close. Across the dock, Luján's offsider wheeled around, one hand pressed to his ear in the aftermath of the explosion that had taken out his comrade, the other hand plucking at the handgun at his hip. The warlord had abandoned both the trolley of resources and the idea of fighting. He was sprinting for the ramp.

Ignoring the man with the handgun, Ana trained her weapon on her designated target. Ten meters from the ramp now. Eight. Six. A moment before squeezing the trigger, she shifted her aim a millimeter ahead of him. Ana fired into the gap between the ramp and Luján. The blue-white pulse streaked through the air space between them. In the space of a half second, the warlord went from running to collapsing. Though his body curled and folded unnaturally, Ana had already seen that he'd lost a chunk of his head.

Her attention shifted to the final hostile in the dock and she darted left, away from the direction she had heard Fowler moving behind her so as to avoid friendly fire. Her weapon tracked back toward the hostile. He had his pistol up. His focus was on her. It would be close.

Fowler fired first, his rifle barking from behind her right shoulder. Three stun rounds in quick succession. The pirate's arms spread wide as he toppled back, his handgun flying loose.

The colonel appeared beside her and gave her that demonic grin of his, pointing his weapon toward the fallen warlord. "Oops," he said.

She started forward again. "The ramp." A moment later, she was jolted backwards as Fowler tugged at her webbing. "What—?"

Then she saw it too. The ramp was rising. Beyond the freighter, a red light, a globe as big as her whole body, began pulsing. The signal for *airlock opening.*

"Helldamn," Fowler growled.

"The Confeds can mop him up," she said and then made a *yik* sound as Fowler tugged her backwards again and spun her to face him.

He jerked his head back the way they came. "We need to get that blast door closed in case the autos don't kick in. Pretty old asteroid, this one."

"What? Why?"

If the colonel thought the airlock would expose them to space, he was losing his mind. The outer doors simply couldn't open until the inner lock doors closed.

Unless ...

"The freighter has tri-cannons?" she asked.

"The freighter has tri-cannons," Fowler replied. "He shoots out those doors, this dock won't seal fast enough to save us. Or our comrades back there."

As they raced for the blast door controls back where they'd been sheltering along the tunnel, a burst of heated air rippled past them, a sign the freighter was moving. Clanks and deep gongs declared that the door mechanisms had engaged between dock and lock.

Reaching the control panel, Fowler struck the button as Ana skidded to a halt beside him. Nothing happened.

"They locked it off?" she asked. "Those bloody *bakas!*"

Fowler snapped, "Light!"

Ana flicked on her rifle flashlight and shone it on the panel. Fowler drew a smartwire from a pouch on his chest webbing, connected it to his datapad and stuck the other end into the port in the panel. He called up a hack-window and started some super-fast three-finger typing.

A loud clunk from the dock told them the middle doors were fully open. The freighter engines whined as the pilot steered it through, hovering above the dock floors.

"Hurry," she hissed, forgetting her place for a moment.

Fowler ignored her, bottom lip clamped between his teeth, typing fingers a blur.

A new whine, deeper than the engines, started up out in the airlock. Weapons powering up.

"Holy Mother," she whispered.

When Ana had turned fourteen, her grandfather had insisted she get a St. Mary tattoo on the back of her left hand. "I don't believe it, of course," he'd said, "but just in case."

She turned that hand over, kissed the tattoo, and raised her eyes to the roof. She had never believed either. But ...

"Yes!" Fowler gasped and joined Ana in the middle of the tunnel to watch the inner blast doors come to life. The ancient iron structures made as much ruckus as the others had.

In the airlock, something boomed. The hostile pilot had fired at the outer doors. Ana kissed the tattoo again. There was no point running. A moment later, she realized they were both still in place. No sudden vacuum sucking them out into the void.

"Didn't penetrate," Fowler said.

Another whine came from the other side of the rapidly closing blast doors. Another power up. Another attempt. It would be close. But even then, if the animal in that cockpit decided to rotate the ship one-eighty, fire at *these* doors ...

The inner blast doors clanged shut. Ana heard the whine of magnetics sealing them. Beyond them, another boom. Ana and Fowler held each other's gaze, both obviously awaiting the same moment. Again, she thought, there was no point in running. If he got the outer doors open and turned his cannons on these, the doors at the far end of the tunnel might seal, but she and Fowler wouldn't make it in time.

One more muffled boom inside the dock airlock. And then the whoosh of a ship leaving.

Ana sagged with relief.

Fowler, on the other hand, gave no sign of emotion,

returning to the wall, unplugging his datapad and stowing it. "The Confeds will no doubt get that guy. But at least he did us the favor of venting Luján's body to space."

"Oh," Ana said as his meaning hit her. "No one needs to know."

"Exactly. You stunned him, far as you know. I got the other two. Pilot screwed it up for his people before we could get them out."

"And if they recover the bodies?" she asked. "They probably will. Confeds are goddamn fussy about things like that. Their forensic tests will show I killed the warlord."

"Then I'll take the blame for lying. We'll revert to the original story, that your kill setting must have been selected during your fall. I'll say I was covering our asses, but in the end, we would have accomplished the mission anyway. One dead warlord isn't a bad thing, after all."

"And ... what about Hecate tripping me?" she asked.

He shrugged. "*If* she did, then maybe it'll show up on her ECF, or those of the people behind her. I'm sure it'll all become clear at the inevitable inquiry."

"Inquiry? What's an inquiry?"

This time, when he touched the webbing over her shoulder, it was almost sympathetic. "Something the Confederation is very fond of. When you arrive back on *Assured*, you'll get about an hour to shower, eat, and brush your teeth. After that, you'll find out exactly what an inquiry is."

March 12, 3014, Old Earth Calendar

4

"IS your name Tactical Enforcer Second Rating Antonia Jogianto?"

"No."

"No?"

"No. Antonia Jogianto is my name. Enforcer Second Rating is my ranking."

"Please refrain from semantics for the remainder of this inquiry."

"Not semantics. Specifics. Cultural differences. Can't help those."

A pause.

"Very well. You discharged your weapon into Peacekeeper Sergeant Wepps. Do you deny this charge?"

"Charge? Being tripped is a crime?"

"You were tripped by someone else?"

"As I've been saying for the past three hours, hell yes, I was tripped."

"This is why you shot Wepps?"

"I didn't shoot him on purpose. Blame Hecate."

"You are referring to Tactical First Rating Hecate Morales?"

"You mean Second Rating. Unless ... oh, shit, she's been promoted?"

"Please refrain from profanities."

"But she's been *promoted*, yes?"

"I don't know. The information in front of me states her rank as First Rating. Please allow me to ask the questions."

"Then ask your questions. Faster we're done, faster I get some shut-eye. It's goddamned one a.m. ship time, three a.m. by my body clock."

"You are claiming that Hecate Morales tripped you intentionally? And that this caused the weapon discharge?"

"Yes and yes."

"Are you claiming that she meant you to shoot Sergeant Wepps?"

"How would I know that?"

"Are you claiming that she meant you to shoot—"

"No, alright? No. I'm telling you she pushed me over and caused an accidental discharge of my weapon."

"Your finger was inside the trigger guard of your rifle?"

"It was."

"Why?"

"Why!"

"Why was your finger inside—?"

"I understand the question, dude. I don't think you get what it's like to be in a firefight."

"Procedures for both DCHC and Sevens Party state that an operative's finger shall remain outside the trigger guard before entry into a hostile enclosed area. Only when the operative in front of you has stepped aside shall you move your trigger finger inside the guard and onto the trigger."

"Didn't hear a question mark that time."

"The question is why did you move your finger inside the guard before Sergeant Wepps had stepped out of your way."

"And I'm telling you that he had stepped aside, and I was following my CO, and I had multiple hostile targets out in front of me, and I was prepping to shoot some of them. In other words, I was doing my job."

"You claim that Sergeant Wepps had cleared the way for you to step into the active zone?"

"Yes. And can you write down an accurate description of the pissed-off expression on my face at all these dumbass questions, please?"

"Please refrain from profanities."

"Oh, I am, trust me. I could get a whole more profane than this."

"How did Warlord Luján die?"

"Oh, we're finished with the Wepps thing? You believe me now?"

"How did Warlord Luján die?"

"Goddammit."

"Please—"

"He was sucked out the loading dock when his own pilot blew a hole in the outer airlock doors. I'm sure Fowler already told you this."

"We are asking you."

"And I answered."

"The Halcyon-6 pilot destroyed the outer airlock doors after you had stunned Warlord Luján?"

"Yep."

"How long after?"

"Yeah, sure, like I had time to watch the clock."

"How long do you estimate?"

"Here's the sequence of events for ya. You work out the times. We ran in. Luján and one of his guys were pushing a trolley onto the freighter's ramp. Another guy was halfway between us and the ramp. Fowler got the closest guy. I shot Luján. Fowler shot the last guy. That was, like, three seconds or four maybe. Before we could retrieve their unconscious bodies, the freighter engines started up, the pilot opened the center blast doors remotely, and we realized the bastard's ship was armed with tri-cannons."

"Please refrain—"

"So. Then we leg it back to the inner dock blast door control panel. We try it. It don't work. Our enemies disabled it, or recoded it, or something. And then it's a race for Fowler to jack it using his datapad before the pilot destroys the outer doors. Fowler won that race, by the way. In case you hadn't figured that out yet."

"You claim that the warlord and two of his men were alive after you shot them, but the actions of the pilot killed them."

"Stop this 'you claim' crap. I'm telling you in simple English. Want me to switch to Spanish? Will you believe me then?"

"Please refrain from sarcasm and hostility. We are simply acquiring information for the record."

"Sure. Record this."

"Please refrain from vulgar hand gestures."

"Can I take this goddamn thing off my face now?"

"Please, refrain from profanities."

"*Goddamn* is not a profanity."

"It is."

"Well, can I?"

"You cannot."

"It itches. It's like wearing a spider."

"We have several details to—"

"And the light is hurting my eyes."

"The reader does not cause pain. It has been thoroughly tested against—"

"I don't care. I'm taking it off."

"Tactical—"

5

PRESUMABLY, the spider-like device sensed the pressure of Ana's hands where she clutched at it. It came free immediately, its legs relaxing their grip, sensors withdrawing from her skin. As it dropped to the desk, Ana felt the prickle from tiny scratches along both cheeks and her left temple.

"Put that back on!" Peacekeeper Sergeant Anthea Ouw snapped from the far corner of the room. The team leader for *Assured*'s other squad—the one that had stayed behind during the mission—was dressed in Peacer navy-and-gray, her hair was buzz-cut, and her teeth were bared in fury. Ouw looked as pissed as Ana felt; anyone would think it was *her* who got stunned—or tripped.

Temper, temper, Ana wanted to say. Ouw wasn't the one who had to wear the suffocating thing. And no matter what the oily-skinned technician who'd been grilling her said, that light *had* hurt her eyes.

"Replace it now," Ouw repeated.

"Useless, Sergeant," sighed the oily technician. He was hunched over a small pad, but his eyes were raised in Ana's direction, glare as fierce as Ouw's. "She's broken the contact. It'd take another twenty minutes to calibrate and that's if her synapses cooperated a second time."

"I'm ordering them to cooperate," the Red Squad leader said.

"Out of her control," the tech replied. "Entirely subconscious."

"No," Ana corrected him. "Entirely *conscious*." She sent the apparatus skidding along the long conference table. Trailing wires behind it, it looked like a squimmid crawling back into the ocean after laying its eggs.

She stood, fingers brushing her medium-length hair back into place. "Not that I answer to you, Sergeant, but can I go now? I was serious about that shut-eye."

There came a moment's grinding of teeth from Ouw and head shaking from the tech. Then Ouw stabbed a finger at the door behind Ana.

"Get," she said, as if addressing an animal.

Well, Ana thought as she tapped the door button, *to the Confeds, us Xerxians* are *animals—barbarians and animals.*

The door retracted into the wall with a swish.

Hecate rested against the wall across the corridor. At the sound of the door, the woman's head snapped up. "Have fun?" she asked in the sickly-sweet tone used by Centauran actors in their soap-bubble-operas.

Affecting the same tone, Ana replied, "Up yours, sweet cheeks" and stepped aside for Hecate to enter the compartment. "The whole truth and nothing but," she reminded her.

The door shut, separating them again.

"Sea cow," she muttered and turned right ... almost colliding with a man-mountain of a Peacer on station outside the conference room. She backpedaled a little, realizing it was the big guy who'd tried to help her up on the asteroid.

"Sorry," he said, as if he had bumped into her and not

the other way around. And the *bulala* was actually smiling at her, shyly.

Jesus, he was a big unit. The guy probably stood at one-ninety centimeters and weighed one-twenty kilograms.

And he was apologizing to her for something she did.

"Grow a pair," she muttered and stepped around him.

The memory of his offer of help while she'd crawled in the dust of that cavern and missed the entire firefight was worse than embarrassing—it was humiliating. He'd treated her like a beggar, like a child in the gutter. As if things hadn't been bad enough.

As she marched away, she heard him say, "Have a nice day, miss." And from the tone in his voice, he meant it.

Ana was used to being treated like crap. With rare exceptions, it was the nature of life. Her family did it. Her clan-party did it. Even her home city did it. Tacticals like Hecate did it. Those interrogators had just done it.

In view of all that, the repeated kindness of the big Peacer back there was worse to her than a kick in the gut.

THE CAPTAIN'S Ready Room was a rectangle about a third the size of the bridge and it lay off the short corridor between the bridge and the elevators. A meter-wide slab of polished Castoran steelwood ran down its center, serving as a table. A flat disc sat mid-table, a hologram transmitter currently emitting a sphere of static but ready to connect to the Xerxian Capitol Building a half billion kilometers away.

As Gregory entered the compartment, his bodyguard slipped in behind him and took up a position beside the door, the way the Peacekeeper on duty on the bridge would. Grace was a centimeter taller than Gregory, lean and lithe. Her red hair was tied in a bun and her casual clothing allowed for freedom of movement. She wore a sidearm on one side of her belt and a flick-out baton on the other. The four existing occupants of the room shot her glances, but none objected to the ambassador having his own security. Pan, Gregory knew, actively approved of her presence since he trusted Xerxians less that Gregory did.

The compartment smelled of the coffee pot in front of Chinyama. Pan, Fowler, and the visiting *Bountiful* Captain Dilshad Farahaji all had steaming mugs in front of them. As junior-most crewer present, XO Chinyama gestured to the pot, offering Gregory a mug. The ambassador declined.

As he took his seat, Farahaji yawned. Then she smiled apologetically at him. "Sorry. One a.m. is way past my bedtime."

"It's the wee hours here," Gregory replied, "but it's late morning at the Xerxian Capitol building. They wanted contact at a civilized time."

"Sure," Pan said from the head of the table. "*Their* civilized time." He raised his eyebrows at Colonel Fowler. "Nothing personal, Colonel."

Fowler—as he always did when not on mission—wore a tidy black-and-gray uniform, a jeweled nose-ring, and an expression of smug self-assurance. He lifted a hand in a *no worries* gesture. "I agree, sir. It's always the politicians who get to work at convenient times, never us."

Farahaji chuckled politely at the joke.

Pan steepled his fingers in front of him. "Ambassador, are we ready to transmit?"

His gut tightened at the topic of the discussions they were about to have: the prospect of Xerxes joining the DCHC. His argument to the parliament committee had been that they weren't ready. Xerxes might outwardly demonstrate a commitment to democracy, but there was evidence to suggest it would take a generation or more before the "old guard" passed power to more educated and enlightened youngsters capable of better embracing and following Confederation values. His argument and his evidence had been shouted down. One committee member had called him "racist." He'd been ordered to lead the negotiations and to "do it with enthusiasm and without prejudice". The most sympathetic member of that committee had patted his shoulder privately afterward and told him, "The thing to remember, Chris, is that we're all better off taming the monster than fighting it. So, pat the Xerxian chancellor's head and coo and feed her sweet treats. We need her tamed —her and all her fellow inbred, Machiavellian, predatory freaks."

In answer to Pan's question he said, "Thank you, Captain. Let's proceed."

Chinyama had up until now been tracing circles with a lead pencil on a paper notepad. Now he lay down the pencil and cleared his throat. "We will need to wait a minute or so longer. The last communique we had from the Xerxian chancellor's office said she wanted Warlord Luján's Second to attend this meeting."

"Gods, she's parading the vanquished," Pan muttered. "It's like a Roman circus."

Chinyama said, "I've taken the liberty of having Sergeant Wepps bring her in." He checked his tab and added, "They're three minutes away."

Those three minutes passed without conversation. Coffee was slurped and mugs clanked against the table. Farahaji yawned again. Pan's breath whistled in and out of his nose. Chinyama sketched circles. Fowler tapped a finger against his cheek. Gregory worked hard to remain still and composed.

Eventually, the door chimed. Chinyama checked his tab again then called "Enter!"

The door slid open. A woman stood there. She had stringy hair and limbs that seemed too long for her torso. Her body odor wafted Gregory's way on the aircon's currents, and he started breathing through his mouth. Grace flashed him a *Wow she's ripe!* look and shuffled further from the doorway, grimacing.

Wepps had to prod the pirate to move her inside and let him in behind her. Her hands were cuffed before her, her expression one of detestation as she surveyed the people around the table. Another waft of body odor made Gregory wish they'd cleaned her up before bringing her in. Wepps guided her to a free chair and pushed her into it. She blew him a kiss as he moved back to stand near Grace.

"Your name is Antigua?" Chinyama asked her.

She hawked spit and Gregory stiffened, expecting it to sail across the table at the XO. But she swallowed it, staring sullenly at everyone *but* Chinyama and Gregory.

Gregory recalled then that some pirate factions historically had a thing against people with dark skin.

And the committee called me *a racist!*

"That's her name alright," Fowler said. The man was smiling. Gregory wondered how personal this was for him—the Xerxians had had centuries of inter-faction fighting, betrayals, family vendettas. Or perhaps the man was merely satisfied with seeing a generic enemy humiliated.

"We're good to go, then, Captain," Chinyama said.

"Your show now, Ambassador." Pan manipulated the controls before him and leaned back.

The holo field rippled with color for a few seconds before resolving into the head and shoulders of a woman in her late sixties. In her office, Gregory knew, Nguyen was seated on a rotatable stool in the middle of a holotube, a connected ring of screen-transmitters that enabled her to turn and look at all the players around this table as she desired. As the 3D image of her head resolved, Nguyen was staring directly at him. There wasn't a hint of emotion or reaction on her face, and it took Gregory a second to realize that she *could* see him.

"Chancellor," he said. "A good day to you from DCHC starship *Assured.*"

"And to you, Ambassador Gregory. It's good to see you again."

"And you," he lied. He gestured to his right. "For the record, with me in this room are *Assured*'s XO Commander Wisdom Chinyama and Captain Pan Xinchun, *Bountiful*'s Captain Dilshad Farahaji, Sevens Party Tactical Colonel Andre Fowler, Peacekeeper Sergeant Eddie Wepps, my assistant Grace Renny, and the outlaw pirate known only as Antigua who is our prisoner."

As he had mentioned them, Nguyen's head had turned toward each person, nodding in respect. When she reached Antigua, he could see her scowl, the first sign of emotion.

"A very special welcome to you, Antigua," she said.

Antigua still did not reply, but she dropped her gaze. A smidgen of fear had entered her expression. The Sevens promised incarceration for Antigua's crimes as with those of the other surviving factionists; perhaps Antigua didn't believe that to be her true fate.

Or maybe Xerxian political incarceration is worse than death.

Nguyen's head turned back toward Fowler. "A shame we lost the warlord to space, but no matter. We have a sizeable number of his followers in custody now, and this is a wonderful result. I believe this mission was the twentieth mission of your squad in its current composition? Excellent. I can only imagine how wonderful your twenty-first will be!"

Gregory repressed a groan. *Twenty-one missions. This superstitious fascination with products of the number seven.* He thought it was as childish as congratulating the man for his sneaky murder of Warlord. Because no matter how well Tactical Jogianto was doing testifying to this story in the inquiry room downstairs, Gregory was not buying it. She and Fowler had either killed the warlord themselves or left him to die at his pilot's hands. No doubt a narcissist—which he knew Nguyen to be after several meetings with her—had ordered the murder of an armed rival.

"Seven times three," said Fowler, bowing his head. "It will be glorious."

Returning attention to Gregory, Nguyen said, "The democratically-elected Xerxian government is grateful for the assistance of your military personnel and also your diplomatic support, Ambassador."

"Our efforts have been in support of peace and stability, Chancellor."

"As have ours. And with that in mind ..." She turned back to the captive pirate. "Antigua, will you capitulate?"

For the first time, Antigua stirred her vocal cords. "What is the point of that? You have killed or captured all of our fighters. We have nothing to surrender to you."

"You have your families, still off-world and hiding out there somewhere." There were Confederation agents hunting these very people now, Gregory knew, on Centauri and Pollux. Nguyen went on, "You still have the assets you have hidden with them."

"You want our husbands and wives and children in your dungeons too. Ha!"

"Not dungeons, Antigua. State-of-the-art humanitarian prisons. And so long as we have no evidence against your family members, the only time they will see the inside of a prison is when they are visiting you and your fellow raiders. They are offered amnesty and jobs on Xerxes."

"Jobs." Antigua snorted the word.

"Capitulation, Antigua. I must hear it before we can move on."

"What choice do I have?" she said quietly. "Against our very natures we do capitulate."

"Excellent." Nguyen's head revolved to acknowledge

the others. "Then, Ambassador, Captains, we are well on the road toward one unchallenged Xerxian government and therefore toward acceptance into the Confederation."

Antigua let out a theatrical cackle. "You Confeds have no idea."

Without looking toward the prisoner, Nguyen sighed. "I think we're finished with her now, Ambassador. Can we remove her from the room, please?"

Gregory nodded to Wepps.

The sergeant touched the commlink in his ear. "Chipper."

The Ready Room door opened and the biggest Peacer Gregory had ever seen entered. He reached for the prisoner, but she was already rising and she dodged his grip. Before he could usher her out, Fowler cleared his throat.

"Chipper. That's your name, Peacer? I watched the replay of your ECF feed. Excellent shooting with that sniper."

"Er, thank you, sir," the Peacer said simply. Gregory was surprised to see that he was actually blushing as he hustled the prisoner out of the compartment.

Fowler called after him, "If you ever want to join a real team ..."

Pan growled, "Enough, Fowler."

"A joke, Captain. I'm sure the corporal saw the humor. A little pleasantry between soldiers."

Although no one but Fowler appeared amused by his jest, Nguyen chose to take his side. "We can all use more pleasantries these days, can we not? Now that the enemy is out of the room, Ambassador, we can continue. I believe you'll want to come join me at the Capitol to discuss further negotiations."

"Indeed. We have the matter of a half dozen facility inspections to conduct, and then I'm sure—"

A gesture from Nguyen cut him off. The chancellor was

making a regretful face. "The thing is that while you might be ready for us, we still have one barrier to being able to fully focus on *you*."

Gregory glanced around the compartment. Both starship captains were shaking their heads tiredly—perhaps they'd expected game-playing like this. Chinyama as usual kept his expression neutral. Fowler's face was blank, but his eyes were alight with amusement.

Gregory asked, "What barrier are you referring to?"

Within the holo field, Nguyen's hand rose in a placating gesture. "There's just one final anarchistic faction to subdue."

"One ...?" Gregory got control of his voice, wondering what the Xerxian leader was playing at. "We were told that the warlord's faction was the last of the splinter groups."

"We never told you that," she said. Fowler shook his head to support his leader.

Gregory replied, "The communiques all stated—"

"I apologize for cutting you off, but all of our communications mentioned one last faction operating *within our own territory*. We did not mention the one that has recently reappeared to trouble our interests from outside our home system."

"Unbelievable," Pan muttered.

"I can see the perturbation this might cause you," the chancellor continued, "and my government apologizes if our representatives gave you the wrong impression. The truth is we hadn't mentioned them earlier because for years we thought them eradicated. It wasn't until recently that our agents discovered this faction had retreated into unsettled space for not only years but decades. Recently they have been absorbing some of the remnants of other defeated groups. It was a brave defector from one of these groups that drew attention to them."

"A defector?" Gregory repeated.

"That is correct. Trust me when I say, this is the group historically responsible for many of the early raids on both the Centauri and Oceana systems. They are one of the oldest pirate clans, and as such, they are quite set in their ways. Correct, Colonel?"

"Nowhere near as progressive as the rest of us," Fowler put in.

Nguyen continued, "They have recently signaled their intention to upset our union with the Confederation, angry at what they consider the loss of tradition. Which is code for them being upset that the DCHC's power is growing beyond their own power to avoid it. But be assured that they can cause us all a great deal of trouble, and with their numbers swelling lately, time is of the essence in squashing this threat."

"Squashing it," Pan said. He was staring at Gregory, demanding permission to enter the discussion. Gregory nodded slightly and Pan charged ahead. "If it's our assistance you are hinting at, then it'll require authorization from Naval Command."

"Of course. And thank you for offering."

"I didn't ..." Pan cut himself off, shaking his head. Both his fists were clenched together so tight, his knuckles were white.

"Give us details," Gregory said. "Please. The captains and I will report to our respective superiors and have an answer for you inside of two standard days." Sweat was building at his collar, threatening to trickle down his back. He would dearly have loved to reach around and scratch at it. But, unlike Pan whose disquiet showed openly, Gregory was a representative of government and didn't have the luxury of signaling his frustration.

"Excellent. We appreciate that. Very much. One of my aides will transmit some datapackets to you. Our intel places these throwbacks in the Pollyanna System."

Gregory had never heard of it, but the two captains certainly had.

"That's thirty-six light-years from here!" Captain Farahaji exclaimed while Pan shook his head again.

"I believe so," Nguyen replied. "Not so far."

"Far enough."

"And it's outside of settled territory," Pan added.

"Outside of official settled territory."

"Just how far did your raiders venture?" Farahaji asked. "In the dark times?"

"How many more pirate and insurgent groups are out there?" Pan added.

"Captains, please," Gregory intervened. While he admired their honest anger, he had to at least give the impression of keeping this solution-focused.

"It's all right, Ambassador," Nguyen said. "We're certainly not in denial of our history. And the short answer is that, from the information we have, this is the last of the groups we need to worry about."

"That doesn't answer the question," Pan muttered.

Like the politician she was, Nguyen went on as if he hadn't spoken. "So, yes, thirty-six light-years from here and travelling outward from the DCHC core. We believe they discovered and resettled an old Chinese black site created in the old times. They have a small fleet, one we'd be hesitant to confront on our own since Xerxes is only now assembling an official navy of her own under strict DCHC observations. Hence the support of *Assured* and *Bountiful* is, in a word, vital."

Pan had been tapping away at his datapad; now he passed it along to Gregory. "*That's* the Pollyanna system. No habitable worlds."

Nguyen said, "They don't need worlds, they have sealable asteroids and they have their fleet. Pollyanna is where they work from."

"The name of this faction?" Gregory asked.

Nguyen paused for a moment then she said, "Clan Lobos."

If Gregory had thought the room was wound as tight as he could get, he was wrong.

Pan barked, "What!"

Farahaji actually facepalmed.

Wepps and Chinyama both abandoned their usual professional stoicism to gasp. Grace swore colorfully beneath her breath.

"Clan Lobos?" Gregory asked, doling out the syllables slowly.

Nguyen said nothing. Fowler was nodding, watching them keenly like a Caultan snow wolf.

Pan was on his feet now, leaning on his fists on the table top. "Clan Lobos were wiped out during the Battle for Centauri seventy years ago. This very ship took out their last three vessels."

"So we believed too. However, we discovered that they didn't commit all their forces to that blockade. Enough remained in hiding that they have repopulated, built new ships, stolen others ..." She gave a shrug. "The worst thing is we now believe them responsible for the recent *Heavens Gate Adventure Cruise* massacre."

Farahaji groaned. "That was them?"

"Apparently, yes."

"My XO's mother was on that cruise," she said quietly. "Her and ninety-five other innocent people."

An ominous silence settled over the room for a long time, each person lost in their thoughts and Nguyen giving them the time to digest her revelations.

"You have proof?" Gregory finally said.

"I do."

"Send it. Please."

"If that last claim is true," Pan added, "then *Assured* would be happy to help you."

"*Bountiful* too," said Farahaji.

Gregory wished the two captains hadn't said that. As they'd already made clear, they couldn't make promises without official approval.

"Send the information, Chancellor," he said. "We will get back to you as soon as possible."

"A good day to all of you," Nguyen said, shortly before the holo field broke up into static.

In the moments that followed, nobody made to leave. Gregory put his finger inside his collar and scratched.

There was a lot to discuss here.

Gregory wished they could do it without Fowler in the room.

6

THE SLEEPING QUARTERS assigned to the Tacticals was a glorified passageway. It had a wash basin by the entry doors at each end and three double bunks along each wall—that was pretty much it. Above the existing bunks, the Confed Navy had pulled out two more tiers of them and replaced them with cupboards.

When Ana returned from her inquiry, Tactical Manolo was rummaging through one of these cupboards, standing in the narrow aisleway and forcing Ana to make herself skinnier to get past her. Shorter than the Peacer with the soulful eyes, Manolo probably rivalled him for weight. She maintained a lot of bulk—her calves were the thickness of Ana's thighs.

"Nothing but first aid gear," Manolo complained, her husky voice louder than it needed to be. "Could've at least chucked a little booze up there for us."

"Booze is at Caultan prices and you get it at the ship's bar," Umbrano's deep voice rumbled from one of the lower bunks.

"Unofficial bar," Ana said. "The one the officers don't know about."

"Caultan prices!" Manolo mock-spat and slammed the cupboard. "For what we done today, we should be getting a bottle each for free."

"Of whatever we want," Umbrano agreed. "Make mine Polluxan vodka."

"Scotch," Manolo said wistfully. "The really good stuff from Foucault."

They were the only two Tacticals in the bunkroom apart from Ana. Despite it being the early hours of the morning, everyone else was busy. Fowler was at some bigheads meeting center-ship. Olesco and Dayang were rostered on weapons-checks down in the hangar armory. And Hecate ... well, Hecate was no doubt sitting in that inquiry room lying through her teeth.

Ana's bunk was above Umbrano's. She hauled herself up and sat with legs dangling. "We'll get standard bonuses for yesterday's takedown. We can afford the booze."

Manolo gave her the evil-eye for a moment before climbing onto her own bunk. A lot bigger than Ana, she had to duck her head to sit up there. "Not enough for Caultan Scotch." Her dangling feet were bare.

Ana put a heel on the bunk base and started untying her laces; putting boots back on after her shower had been almost as annoying as having to go the damn inquiry. Almost.

Manolo was speaking again and it took Ana a moment to realize it was directed at her. "As long as you don't cost us that bonus."

Ana stiffened. "What's that supposed to mean?"

"There's talk the Confeds gonna tax us. As punishment for friendly fire."

"Helldamn," rumbled Umbrano.

"There's talk?" Ana said. "What talk? Who's telling you that?"

"Hecate said."

"Ah. Hecate. Of course she did. Well, sister, if our pay does get docked, you can blame Hecate and not me."

"What are you talking about?"

"Bitch tripped me. That's how I shot that Wepps guy."

Umbrano hooted a laugh.

"Ain't funny, Umbi!" Ana yanked off one boot, tossed it behind her, and started on the next.

"Looked pretty hackin' funny," he said, "you skidding through the dirt and firing stun bolts off."

Unamused, Manolo seized control of the conversation again. "Well, I was right behind Hecate and I didn't see nothing."

"That's coz you're blind!"

"What!"

That sent Umbrano into paroxysms again—and set Ana's bunk shaking. The big man's deep guffaws bounced around the small space like shrapnel. "Blind! That's ... that's a good one, Jogi! Remember ... remember that time ... that time she walked ... into that glass door?"

Manolo reached up, yanked open a cupboard, and threw a bottle of antiseptic at him. It must have hurt, but Umbrano only laughed harder, gasping for breath.

Small things, Ana thought, but she was glad that Umbrano had drawn Manolo's attention. She shouldn't have insulted her like that. With Hecate gunning for her position, Ana needed all the friends she could get. With both boots off now, she turned and lay back, hands under her head.

Friends. Sure. I got lots *of those.*

"So, what was the inquiry like?" Manolo asked her. She seemed to have forgotten the insult and the prospect of an impending fine. "They shoot you full of truth drugs?"

"They don't do that."

"Oh." She sounded disappointed.

"They fit this rig to your head—it looks a bit like a squimmid."

"Squimmid!" Umbrano barked. His laughter hadn't stopped yet, and now it morphed into a coughing fit.

Ana shook her head slightly. *And small minds.*

"What's the rig do?" Manolo asked.

"I'm guessing it measures brain activity, skin temperature, crap like that. They probably think it tells them if you're lying or not." Was it stupid that she hoped the rig hadn't worked for her but *had* worked for Hecate?

"So, did ya?"

"Lie?"

"Yeah."

"I didn't lie about Hecate, I'll tell you that much."

"Shit, Ana, she wouldn't trip ya."

"She did."

"Nah. And if she did, it was an accident. Maybe you moved too slow and got in her way."

Apparently, that wasn't funny, because Umbrano's laughter finally waned, his coughing passing too.

"I didn't move too slow. We've been a unit for years. Have you ever seen me move too slow?"

Manolo scooted off her bed, dropped to the floor, and started going through the cupboards above the next set of bunks. "No, but I never seen Hecate trip anyone neither."

"She's been giving me the evil eye for weeks. Ever since the talk of Fowler moving on. She wants his job."

"Who doesn't?" Umbrano said.

"That's why she tripped you? What makes you think you're next in line?"

"Er, a little thing called rank."

"Well, she's ahead of you now on that one alright," Umbrano said. "Promoted to First."

"Exactly. She planned the whole thing. She's been doing a bunch of ordinary stuff for weeks, same as me. Then she makes it look like I do one bad thing. Bam. She's promoted. I'm overlooked. Telling ya, she wants that job."

"Tell ya what I want?" said Manolo. "I want that Wepps guy you shot. Ya think ya can go past his bunk later and stun him again for me?"

From below Ana, Umbrano's hooting started up again.

GREGORY'S personal yacht was moored inside *Assured*'s hangar bay and he headed for it the moment the meeting broke up. He marched up the long entry ramp, turned left at the top, clomped through the yacht's circular lounge, and went straight for the drinks station in the corridor behind it.

Coming out of his small cabin, his pilot Piers stopped and stared at him. "Straight scotch? Must've been a crap meeting."

The statement made Gregory instantly cranky.

Crankier, he corrected himself.

Without turning, he said, "This would be a great time to give me some space, Piers."

Piers said nothing. Seconds later, Gregory heard his boots on the ramp, headed down.

Good. At least someone around here cooperates.

He moved out into the lounge, a compartment five meters across with a semicircular couch on each side of it and small tables fixed in front of those couches. Gregory leaned a hip against the portside table. He got one good sip of scotch before more footsteps sounded on the ramp, headed up.

"Ah, crap," he whispered.

A moment later, he found himself face to face with a very angry Grace Renny. She loomed in the access-way between lounge and cockpit, hands on hips, glaring daggers.

Gregory angled his glass toward her. "Scotch?"

"How 'bout I hold you down and tip it in your eyes?"

Gregory screwed up his face. "Rather you didn't."

"Nice trick, getting me stuck behind the officers while you do a runner for the lifts."

"I wanted some alone time."

She pointed at him, hard. "You get alone time in the shower, in your bed, and on the can. That's all. As I keep reminding you, you're a diplomat and your ass belongs to the DCHC—and because my ass does too, and because my job is following your ass around and keeping it safe, it *burns* my ass that you keep finding ways to give me the slip."

Gregory sipped whisky. "You said 'ass' a lot in that sentence. Long sentence, by the way."

"Thanks, don't need an editor. Need a boss who behaves himself."

"Grace. I've had one of the crappiest days in a long, long time. I need some space. I need a couple more of these." He raised the glass and sipped more scotch. "Then I need to think about how I'm going to talk my bosses out of signing off on something stupid."

She frowned. "Not happy about this Clan Lobos thing, huh?"

"Great deduction, detective."

"Tell me. Talk it out."

"Sure. Why not? In a nutshell, now we've cleaned up Sevens's rival faction—the rogue faction that was meant to be the final rogue faction—and we've killed several human beings for them, apparently there's a whole other rival group they want us to go neutralize, one that's no doubt twice the size of Luján's. And which is also thirty-something light-years from here in the wrong direction."

"You're pretty good at long sentences too."

"And," he continued, "the Xerxians have the gall to say *they* won't join the Confederation unless we help. As if they are doing us the favor by joining."

“In a way they are,” she said slowly.

“Wow. Helpful thoughts.”

“The Silvers have been—”

“Xerxians,” Gregory admonished her.

“The *Xerxians* have been the worst thing that happened to humanity’s interests in space since the PBT virus. Bringing them into a stable relationship with the broader society where they abide by our laws keeps us all safer long term.”

“I have heard this argument, you know.”

“And I happen to agree with it.”

“I happen not to. If the Xerxians become signatories to the constitution, they can vote on laws, suggest laws. Won’t that be fun? We’re bringing into our civilization a bunch of feudal-minded savages who put on educated accents and clean clothes and pretend to love peace but really just want power. And we’re handing it to them. On their terms.”

“And?” she asked. “What else is bothering you? You’ve been irritable for days.”

“What else? Oh, I’ll tell you what else. This right here is my life, Grace. My life’s work. And I completely and absolutely detest it. For eighteen years, I’ve been sucking up to tiny-brained despots and economic bullies, signing treaties that make me nauseous. And now, apparently my job is to support killing people on behalf of one of those despots. I became a diplomat to achieve important things. Noble, worthwhile things. But there are none of those left anymore.”

“For example?”

“For example, there’s no alien species around to build relationship with. I was born centuries too late to negotiate the personhood of the Anachromites. I hadn’t graduated in time for the mission to reestablish contact with the Jarinyi. So, I get to spend my time working with humans. And what fantastic work that is. Thirty years ago, my father got the meaningful and rewarding task of bringing Foucault, Pride of Mao and Centauri together to kick off the Confederation. *I* get to sanction murderous Xerxians committing more murder!"

He realized his voice had risen so loud, he'd been shouting at her by the end of his rant. He threw back the rest of the whisky, and turned his back, feeling guilty. He didn't like people who yelled at their staff. Especially when those staff were as close to him as Grace and Piers were.

"Very well," she said after deliberating a moment's thought. "I'll allow you two more glasses of scotch. You can have your pity party. And you can have your thinking time. As for giving you space, I'll lock down the yacht and nap in the cockpit. Anyone calls for you, I'll tell them to bite me. When you eventually need something or when you're going to bed, you buzz me."

He turned back and tried on a smile. "You're a good assistant."

"Better than you deserve, ya numpty." She began to turn and froze halfway with an amused sparkle in her eye. "Oh, and when you pour your next scotch, be sure and bring me one too. There's a good boss."

AT 0245 SHIP TIME, Gregory sent his datapack off to the minister back on Foucault. In it, he had copied all of Nguyen's data, the record of the Ready Room meeting, the various ECF recordings from the away mission, and his own strong recommendation that the DCHC immediately suspend Xerxes' pending signatory status with the Confederation Constitutional Committee. The recommendation was well-argued, well-phrased, and Gregory knew there wasn't a chance in hell that the minister would accept it.

7

CHIPPER and six other Peacers piled into an elevator, commandeering it. While Chipper repeatedly pounded the *close doors* button, three more Peacers raced past outside, headed for maintenance tubes and stairways.

"Why we're running, I don't know," Stines puffed from beside Chipper. "There's twenty callbooths. And ten of us."

"Then you won't mind if you're last one out of the lift," Red Squad's "Widowmaker" Bradstock said from where he was squashed against the back wall. Bradstock was older than the other Peacers, his buzzcut hair a steel wool gray, and it was said he'd enlisted twenty-seven years back to assist the Centauran government against sectarian violence on their smaller continent.

"Screw that," Stines scoffed. "And get the doors shut, will ya?"

"Trying," Chipper responded and pounded faster.

Just as the doors began to respond, an approaching ship's nurse appeared, wanting in. Snarls and swearing from the occupants made him change his mind. He, too, had turned for the stairs before the lift doors shut.

"I closed 'em, I get out first," said Chipper.

"The hell you say," Stines growled.

Others echoed Stines's sentiment, but unlike Stines, their comments were good-natured. They jostled Chipper for position, but he held his ground, breathing deep after the run from hangar deck. They weren't getting out before him. Today he got to call home for the first time in a month, talk to his parents for the first time in a month. Yes, sir. Once those doors opened, it'd be a sixty-five-meter sprint down C-Deck's main arterial corridor and thirty meters more across the recreation hall, and then he'd be in one of those booths, calling Oceana. Two minutes ago, at 1140 hours, they'd all been standing at ease in the hangar while Red Squad Sergeant Ouw issued them an access code for ten minutes callbooth privilege. And the moment she had uttered that wonderful word *dismissed*, all of them had set off running.

From behind him, another Red Squadder joked, "Hackin' unfair. I was first one in, I should be first one out."

"How's that gonna work, genius?" Stines said.

Blue Squad Corporal Pandora Chandrasekhara laughed. "Should've thought of that before you pushed in front of me."

"Yeah," said Stines. "They don't teach tactical thinking in Red Squad?"

The indicator pinged, announcing C-Deck. A half dozen fellow Peacers shoved and tugged at Chipper before the doors had even opened, but he held his ground, braced against those doors, feet planted firmly. The lift came to a stop. The doors opened. Chipper surged forward ... and felt a foot hook firmly around one of his insteps. The next moment, he was falling, twisting in midair so that he landed safe on shoulder and thigh.

"Crap!"

The others raced past him, ribbing him.

Stines, evidently wrong-footed, tried to vault him, but

snagged the back of Chipper's knee and landed across him. "Clumsy norf!"

While the two men disentangled, three more Peacers burst from a nearby stairwell and charged past them. Seven crewers—all in kitchen uniforms—had been walking calmly along the arterial before the Peacers converged on it; they wisely pressed flat against the edges as the tide of soldiers swept by.

"Buggers tripped me," Chipper said. He was up and running again, but at the back of the pack.

"Sure they did, *norf*," Stines barked over his shoulder. "You're as bad as that Xerxian Jogianto."

They came into the Rec Hall and skidded to a stop, mouths open in shock.

The hall was the biggest open space on *Assured* after the hangar. It contained a myriad of recreation resources and equipment: ping-pong tables, gym equipment, a small kickball pitch and basketball half-court, console games, card tables, even a wrestling-and-judo ring.

Twenty glassed-in cubicles stretched halfway across one wall, the ship's callbooths, only useable when crew members were issued access codes and permission.

All of the callbooths were in use.

Worse, there were queues, some of them four people deep.

"What the hack!" Stines yelled. A couple of heads turned his way, but the other Peacers were complaining also, so his shout was lost in the hubbub.

Keeping ahead of the kitchen crew who'd entered behind him, Chipper trudged across the hall in Stines's wake. They joined adjacent lines.

In front of him was a buddy of his from Red Squad, Mickey Kumar. Mickey asked a bearded Ensign in the next line, "Why so many people, guy?"

Chipper recognized the man from the times he'd been

on bridge duty. Ensign Sintopas, head comms officer. And here he was standing in line to send a message packet home. No wonder he seemed as annoyed as Stines did. Sintopas scratched his neck and scowled. "Non-shift personnel got permission, same as you."

"Same *time* as us," Chipper said.

Mickey gave Chipper a wry waggle of his brows. "That was well-planned, ey?"

"Dang."

Chipper scanned the three people ahead of him. If the woman currently in the cubicle had only just entered, she'd be a full ten minutes. It'd be forty before he got his turn.

Well, they've earned their turn too, I guess.

"If there's one thing we get trained real well to do," he told his Peacer colleagues, "it's waiting."

"Yeah, good point," Mickey sighed.

"Shut the hell up, Chipper," said Stines.

IN HIS YACHT, Chris Gregory had his feet up on the lounge coffee table, martini in hand. There was another waiting for him on the table near his feet and an empty glass beside that. It was now almost noon ship-time, nine hours since he'd sent his datapacket, one hour since he'd had "breakfast." Mozart played on the lounge speakers, while the lounge screen displayed a recording of an Oceanean beach with gentle waves lapping at impossibly yellow sand. He also had a little buzz going.

Across from him, Piers lay along one of the couches, reading a book on his pad and occasionally rousing himself to reach out for his mug of mocha. Piers had also risen late and the crumbs from his morning croissant were spread across his chest and the small table beside him.

Into this peaceful milieu, Grace came tramping down

the back corridor from her quarters. She wore green bell-bottomed sweat pants and a white sleeveless tee. Usually his assistant wore long-sleeved tops. The tee revealed her arms to be well-toned. Her hair was damp from her shower and loose. She didn't appear to be armed, but Gregory knew she'd have a miniature pistol of some kind holstered under one of her trouser legs. Spying her boss's glass, she gave him a half-hearted scowl. "It's evening somewhere, right?"

"Chancellor Nguyen on Xerxes will be drinking a night cap before bed about now."

"Right. Well, it's midday here. Do you need me to advise you to keep it to one glass?"

"That's his second," Piers said without looking away from his book.

She noticed the other glass then. "Right. Well, at least you've mastered self-control. So. I am heading down to the Rec Hall to read a message from my sister and send one back," she said. "Either of you buttheads want to come?"

Eyes still tracking the lines of his book, Piers said, "We're on a diplomatic yacht. We can send and receive messages anytime we want."

"And who would *you* call, Piers? Mistress 1 or Mistress 2?"

"I'm a happily married man. I only keep one mistress at a time."

"Your wife's such a lucky woman."

"He's right," Gregory said. "Just use the comms here."

"Maybe I want to get out of *here*. Maybe I don't like being cooped up in a yacht the size of my apartment day after day. Besides, I thought we could play some ping-pong or shoot hoops while we were up there."

"Thanks," Gregory said. "I'll pass."

"Boss. You need a change of pace. Come with."

"Grace, I'm quite safe in here with Piers."

"Yeah, Grace. Anyone attacks him, I know sixteen ways to kill them with my tablet."

"Come on, boss. Slum it with the little people. Use a comm booth to call someone. You have friends, right? College friends. You have a brother. Your Dad's still alive."

"Yeah, Dad's still alive."

She put a hand to her mouth. "Oh, I'm sorry. I didn't mean ..."

"I know you didn't. It's fine, Grace. You didn't make me think about the girls. Really. I was thinking more that calling Dad would unleash the advice monster ... as well as allowing him to run through a list of his latest health problems." He made a face. "I might stay here, enjoying a rare midday drink and listening to fine music."

"It's not that fine," Piers muttered.

"You can come back and do that later, boss. Come on. Call your friends."

"Kinda out of touch these days."

"So, get back *in* touch."

"Listen, Grace, I know you mean well, but I talk for a living. Reviving those old friendships will mean more talking. They'll tell me about their work, their hobbies, and their kids. How the kids are growing up. I won't have anything to talk about because: first, my work is confidential; two, my hobbies are strong drinks and classical music; and three, my kid *isn't* growing up."

"Three years, Chris," she said in a tone far gentler than he was used to her using.

"I did know that," he said.

"Leave him alone," Piers said and tapped his screen to turn another page.

"Shut your hole, Piers. Chris, please. At least come for a walk with me. I'll make my call, we'll shoot hoops, then grab some lunch and another martini at the officer's club. I'll buy. The ship's in downtime mode, so there'll be a movie in the cinema later. Or is it open mic night? I think it's open mic night. That'll be fun, right?"

"I'll pass. But thank you." He finished off his martini and leaned back, snuggling deeper into the couch cushions.

"You can't spend your whole life either working or bumming around in here ... with *him*."

"Or wandering around a starship with *her*," Piers said.

"At least I'm encouraging him to do something."

"He is doing something. Leave him alone."

Gregory cleared his throat for attention. "Mom, Dad, I appreciate your concern, both of you. Dad, concentrate on your book. Mom, go make your call. I am fine."

Grace's sigh was dramatic. "He doesn't leave the ship without you," she told Piers.

"And I'll make sure he has his pacifier and bottle," Piers returned.

"Moron." She stomped out of the lounge, opened the ramp, stomped down it, yelled from the bottom, "Close it!"

Piers reached up to slap the control on the wall behind his head. Over the grinding noise of the ramp's curling up, he asked, "Who's she think is gonna attack you on a Confed starship?"

"Xerxians," Gregory replied, stretching for his datapad.

"Oh. Well. She has a point."

Gregory muted his pad, tapped into his video files, and called up *the* video. The video he'd been watching over and over every day since arriving in Xerxian space. The video of *them*. Tabitha and Belle. Playing in the water at the Yajna Indoor Pools Complex. Careening down the water slides. Skipping through the splash pools. Ice cream ran down Tabitha's wrist. Burger sauce painted a clown smile around Belle's mouth. That same mouth formed the silent words, *I love you, Daddy* into the camera's eye. That day had been a great day. Perhaps, Gregory's best day ever. A day now six years in the past. A wife and daughter—a family—now three years dead.

No, I'm not very sociable at all these days, I'm afraid, Grace. The sad thing is that the people I enjoy hanging out with the most are these two ghosts alive only on a video file.

CHIPPER CHECKED the bank of clocks above the kickball pitch at the end of the hall. There was one clock for each DCHC planet set to the local date and time of their capital city, along with one for the large artificial habitat Bona Vista. The last and largest clock displayed local ship time. Before the PBT Crisis and the dark age that followed it, corporate space navies had been set to Earth's Greenwich Mean Time. To maintain a cultural connection with humanity's birthplace—even if Earth's few remaining nations were uninterested in any official relationship—the DCHC had voted early on to revive that practice aboard its naval vessels.

"1215," he read. "Mickey's got one minute left in there."

He and Stines had finally reached the front of their respective lines. A few more people had joined the queues, including the ambassador's assistant—who, rumor had it, was a kung fu killing machine—but it seemed like most people who wanted to call home had been and gone, at least until the current crew shift ended.

"Should've given us priority," Stines grumbled. "We're the hacking heroes, not these norfs." He waved a muscly arm at the crewers in the lines either side of them, some of whom shot him dirty looks for the comment but none of whom were game to argue out loud.

"A minute for me, two for you and we'll be in there, bro," Chipper comforted him.

Stines jerked a thumb behind him at empty space. "Yeah. At the back of the line. Last ones, we are. Hacking insult." He indicated three of the booths across to their left where they could see the black uniforms of Tacticals inside. Jogianto—the woman accused of stunning Sgt. Wepps—stood next in line for one of them. Stines said, "Look at that. They even let the bloody Silvers in ahead of us." *Silvers* was Peacekeeper slang for Xerxians, referring to an ancient pirate novel about Long John Silver.

Chipper decided to ignore Stines again. His teammate could be as sour as he wanted to be. Chipper was choosing to be cheerful.

The glass door in front of him burst open.

"Happy days, Chipper." Mickey Kumar came out with a big grin spread across his face. He slapped Chipper's left arm, latched on, jiggled it. "Happy *days*. Had a datapacket from my girlfriend. Only a day old. She's on Landfall Island. Did I already tell you that? Coz your parents are on Landfall, aren't they?"

As the only Oceaneans aboard *Assured*, Chipper and Mickey had become fast friends. Being separated into different Peacemaker teams and thus spending less time together probably helped that, since there was never any operational tension—or snoring!—to come between them.

Playfully, Chipper took hold Mickey's hand—the one latched on to his arm—applied an aikido grip to it and twisted. Hard enough to make Mickey let go with a light-hearted yelp, but not hard enough to hurt him.

"Okay, okay, I'll stop grabbing you," Mickey laughed.

Chipper returned his friend's grin, releasing him. Free now, Mickey's hand pressed above his heart as he pretended to swoon. "She misses me, bro. Misses me. Not as much as I miss her. But she was crying by the end of her message."

"Shouldn't you be sad she was crying?"

"No, bro. Means she loves me. She's waiting for me. I think we'll get married."

"Hey, schoolgirls," Stines groused. "If you're gonna stand there assing about, then I'm taking that booth."

Chipper shoved his pal aside. "Catch ya at dinner, Mickey."

"You bet. I'll tell you—"

But the end of Mickey's sentence was cut off as Chipper closed the booth door at his back. He slumped onto the stool and faced the console. "Access code Delta-Mike-one-six-Peacekeeper-Blue. Play new messages from home ID number twenty-twenty-sixteen, Oceana, Landfall Island, Margaret and Matiu Tukimatu."

A pause, then the booth told him, "One message, audio only, three minutes four seconds in length. Want me to play it now?"

"Absolutely!"

The message started. Chipper's father and mother talked over each other for all of those three minutes, a tangle of local news, family news, and questions aimed at him. He laughed constantly, and at the end, he felt his throat constrict with sadness at the distance between them. If only he could talk in real time to them ...

He checked the time: six and a half minutes left. "Booth," he said. "Run through every question asked and pause for me to answer them, then I'll record a personal greeting at the end."

"Confirmed."

It took the AI a half second to find and play his dad's first question: "You well, son?"

He swallowed and replied, "Physically, never better, ey. Emotionally, not so good. Had a ... an experience I'll tell you about when I'm home. Just send up a prayer or two for me, ey? Next question."

His dad: "How'd you spend your last birthday?"

"Mickey Kumar threw me a small party in our mess. No presents. Lots of drinking. And no, I didn't get drunk. Next question."

His mother: "What do you eat on them starships anyway?"

He laughed as he replied, "Oh, we eat better than Oceaneans do! Except we don't get fresh seafood. But there's some amazing cakes here. Trust me, I'm not losing weight, that's for sure. Next question."

His ma again: "All that traveling you're doing, you must've found a girl by now. *Have* you found a girl yet?"

"Sheesh, Ma. Girl? Woman, you mean. Like I keep telling you, I meet heaps of people, but I'm never around one place long enough to say more than hi. The only *woman* I've met lately is this Tactical—yeah, that's a Xerxian. Now, don't fuss out, there's definitely no romance there. But I kind of feel a bit sorry for her. She's not like the rest of her team. She ..."

He ran out of words to explain Ana Jogianto, so instead he told the booth, "Record personal greeting. Ma, Dad, I'm sending some more money home. I know you keep telling me not to, but since when did I listen to you two, huh? If you don't want to spend it, put it away for me for when I'm back. Also, I can't tell you about my current assignment, but it'll be over soon. I'm going to request that I see out my contract with a transfer to the emergency response brigade, you know, helping people during floods and wildfires and all that. I love you both. Heaps. Give Russell a kick in the backside for me and tell him to stop eating so much shellfish or he'll get fat. Fatter! And give the whole town my best, ey? This is me saying bye and I'll see you in a year or so. Message ends."

"Confirmed."

"Booth, using earlier authorization, transfer two thousand five hundred Caultan francs from my personal account to the message recipients."

"Confirmed. Transfer will take three ship-standard days."

"Cheers."

Exiting the cubicle, Chipper felt buoyant. Even though he hadn't been able to talk to them in real time, knowing his parents were out there and thinking of him never failed to provide relief and reassurance. They would be there to talk things through with when he returned. Just the reminder that they would love him no matter what—somehow it made everything a lot better.

Stines was still in his stall. His hands were flying about and though his words were muffled, whoever he was messaging seemed to be on the receiving end of a dressing down. Tactical Jogianto was stepping inside her cubicle—she glanced his way with a stony expression before slamming the door. What was the reason for this hostility, he wondered. Embarrassment over the stunning incident? A generic loathing for all non-Xerxians?

Back by the Rec Hall main entry, comms officer Sintopas and three other guys were starting up a poker game. Sintopas seemed to be providing the chips along with the cards.

One of the players was Mickey. He waved Chipper over.

Why not, Chipper thought. Chow time was an hour away. There was very little to do. He strode over and dropped into the last chair at the table. "Count me in, boys. Little Chipper's feeling lucky. May as well hand over your francs now."

Mickey laughed.

Ensign Sintopas scowled. Perhaps he was related to Stines.

WHEN UMBRANO CAME out of the booth, he held the door for Ana, a rare show of thoughtfulness.

Someone had a happy message or two, she thought.

Then he spoiled it by asking, "Calling a lover back home?"

She offered him a thin smile. "Two actually."

Umbrano guffawed and slapped her shoulder as she slipped past him.

The closed door shut out the voices from the gym. Facing the booth console caused memories to well up in her head. She didn't want to access any messages she had waiting for her. Any message for her would only be from her parents. And while she had an honor-duty to hear them and act upon them, the older she got, the harder it got to accept it.

"Booth," she said, hoping this thing worked like the ones back home, "how many messages do I have in Harrigan Services Tuckbox Number 111993, located on Foucault's Moon?"

"Code, please."

Right, no voice prints here.

"Access code Epsilon-Charlie-seven-seven-Tactical-Jogianto."

"Confirmed. Harrigan Services Tuckbox Number 111993 report eleven unplayed messages for Antonia Jogianto."

Hoping that Confed companies' guarantees of customer confidentiality extended to its military vessels, Ana pressed on. "Total duration?"

"Forty-one minutes, five seconds."

Well, I'm not gonna cram that into ten minutes, am I?

"Can you summarize subject matter?"

"Please say 'I authorize you to skim my messages'."

"I authorize you to skim my messages."

A pause before the booth replied, "Local weather, local currency fluctuations, the balance of your credit account, the two farmers, an incident in—"

"Play everything related to the two farmers," Ana interrupted, her shoulders slumped. She leaned an elbow on the console, her cheek against one fist.

Her father's voice came through the speaker, his tone upbeat as befitted one "friend" telling another some interesting news from their planet. Only the story about the farmers was not news, but a coded message.

In the story, the two farmers had moved from one continent to plant a new farm on another, leaving the original holding to their child. They had fallen upon hard times and asked the child to sell the farm and bring the proceeds to them. She hadn't, choosing to enjoy her own flourishing farm and refusing to share even its annual profits with them.

And on it went. Not too hard to decipher. And not at all subtle.

The hand against her cheek moved up to rub across her eyes. "Pause message," she said, cutting off her father's voice.

Over the years they had set up this system, this tuckbox, to pass messages through. Increasingly, their messages had consisted of accusations that she cared more about the corrupt Sevens Party than she did about her own flesh and blood who were political enemies of that party. That she was delaying her own defection to enjoy the exciting life of a Tactical and to amass wealth to spend upon herself and not her poor, long-suffering, political refugee parents.

"I'm so over this," she muttered.

A moment later, the booth said, "Message not recorded. Your access code does not permit you to send messages."

Yeah, I know, she thought. Fowler didn't want his team sending anything back home—or elsewhere. Right now, Ana was glad of it. The constant haranguing from her mother and father, their distrust of her—it had worn her down to the point she thought she'd explode.

Yes, she had a blood-duty to her own parents. Yes, she'd made them a promise at thirteen standard years old—*God, I was just a kid!*—that she'd take what she could and bring it to them on Foucault by the time she was eighteen. But they had abandoned her on Xerxes, fled to Foucault on refugee visas with no thought for her welfare beyond dumping her with an uncle as a mentor. No one, least of all her, had anticipated that mentor would convert *to* the Sevens Party less than a local year after her parents left her. To survive, she'd had to follow suit, to pretend allegiance and enthusiasm. And as her teens had passed and her twenties arrived, she'd found herself in a military career—and discovered that there might be something more important than fulfilling an immature promise to two toothless old clutchclaws. There was every chance that this party they hated so much could actually transition Xerxes from centuries-old barbarism back to civilization. And then they could return to Xerxes as free citizens, where she could set them up in a better life on the home world they belonged to.

Of course, they didn't see it that way.

This latest—what was that word? parable?—yes, their latest *parable* about the farmer's daughter was eating at her, so much so that if she'd been able to send a reply, Ana would have told them to go kill themselves and let her live, with much harsh language to go along with it. Who did these two strangers think they were, telling her how to live her life? These two assholes who'd abandoned a thirteen-year-old to save their own skins—

"Do you want to resume playback?" asked the booth.

"No," she said and reached for the door. "End session."

In a corner of the Rec Hall, a poker game had started

up. Ana raised her chin, pulled her shoulders back, and strode toward it. She needed to take this out on someone.

Dragging a chair over, she announced, "I want in."

An Ensign wearing comms officer badges sniffed as if she'd farted at him. "Game's closed," he said.

"Let her in, bro." The Peacer she now knew as "Chipper" shuffled his chair aside, making room for her. He gave her that goofy, chubby-cheeked smile of his. "Room for more."

She shoved her chair into the gap without replying or smiling.

"Yeah, her money's as good as anyone's," another Peacer chuckled.

The comms officer grudgingly reached beneath the table for a small case. He counted out chips, recorded her name on his pad. She watched the current hand play out before they could deal her in. The shorter Peacer and a ship's nurse folded as soon as they got their initial hand. Two maintenance techs folded midway through the betting. The comms officer stuck it out to the end, and he lost big. Chipper won it all.

"Good win," she told him as he raked in his chips.

And now it's my turn, she thought.

March 13-14, 3014, Old Earth Calendar

8

IF GRACE WAS self-conscious rolling around on a gym mat with him, she sure didn't show it.

Pinned beneath her—with her knee on his chest and her rubber knife at his throat—all Gregory could do was waggle his eyebrows and attempt a joke. "Best two out of three?"

"That *was* number three," she said and rose, allowing him to sit up and rub his chest. "You failed all of them."

He and Grace were around the same age, using the naval "Old Earth" calendar: forty-seven and forty-six, respectively. But she was *much* fitter than he was. Three times this past year—times when Grace had been asleep, when the yacht had been between stars, and when Piers had been bored—the pilot had brought up the topic of Gregory "making a move" on his minder. Gregory had laughed it off the first time, told him it was out of the question the second, and then the third had asked Piers what his fascination was with Gregory's love life.

"What love life?" Piers had replied. "I'm trying to help you here."

"This is none of your business."

"I'm just saying that you're hetero, she's hetero. You're a

man, and a man has needs."

"And a man has principles. Hetero or otherwise."

Piers had laughed.

Gregory had said, "You're only confirming Grace's picture of you as a two-dimensional lothario."

To which Piers had said, "Thank you."

Snatching his attention back to the present, he got up into a crouch and said, "I think my exercise for the day is over."

"Nah," Grace said, "you're just getting started. I'll lay off the grappling and floor work, okay? Instead, I'll teach you some simple punching and blocking."

"Oh, sure." He rubbed his chest again. "That can't possibly hurt me."

She lowered her voice. "You need this, Chris. The physical activity. And the self-defense."

Gregory got all the way to his feet with a groan of effort. "Don't see why. I have you for defense."

"Yup. Ya do. And I wanna know you can at least make a show of defending yourself. If the worst thing happens and we're ever the ones being boarded, or—" She raised a hand to forestall his scoffing. "—or we're on-world somewhere and things get glitchy."

Gregory turned a full circle, noting the other people in the Rec Hall: three techs shooting hoops, two hangar-workers lifting weights, two Tacticals at the climbing wall and ropes area. None of them were interested in what he was doing. There was no embarrassment in it. And yes, he thought as he shifted the rubbing hand down to his middle-aged paunch, he certainly needed the exercise.

"Show me some punches, then," he said. "Let's see if I can make black belt before this trip is over."

Grace laughed easily. "Let's see if you can make *any* belt before this trip is over."

"Thanks very much."

She came alongside him and started demonstrating stances and footwork. As she did, Gregory glanced at the Tacticals making ready to climb the ropes: one of them was the one named Jogianto, and he wondered how the inquiry into the friendly fire incident was going.

"You listening, boss?" Grace growled in his ear.

"Yes, I am. Put my feet like so. Hold my hands like so."

Another voice spoke up from behind his back. "Excellent. Never too old to learn to fight."

Fowler, Gregory thought, refusing to turn or to break the stance Grace had shown him. "Never too old to learn lots of things," he replied.

Chuckling, Fowler moved into eyesight. "Diplomats usually fight with words. Perhaps Ms. Renny will change that trend with you."

Coming out of the stance, Gregory hid his irritation with another attempt at humor. "Or perhaps the exercise will increase my lung capacity so I can fit more words into a sentence."

Fowler quirked an eyebrow at the joke, and Gregory had to admit that it hadn't been funny. "Well," the colonel said, "you never know."

He continued on toward the Tacticals now up on the ropes.

As Grace got him to adopt the position and began the next instruction, Gregory thought, *A kung fu ambassador. Not on my watch, sunshine.*

ANA WAS HALFWAY up a climbing rope—racing Olesco on his—when Fowler found her.

"Jogianto," the colonel called up. "News."

Her heart lurched. *News?* Had the Confeds snitched on her about receiving messages from her parents? She wouldn't put it past that rat-weasel Sintopas to trawl through her personal communications as payback for cleaning him out at poker. The Confeds all made themselves out to be noble and above such behavior, but she'd seen the animal hatred in his eyes and the desperation in the way he'd played. No, she decided, it wasn't that. Sintopas would be the type to blackmail rather than snitch. *Damn,* she thought as Fowler snapped his fingers in impatience, *it's the inquiry.*

Abandoning the race—Olesco was ahead of her anyway, and she could save face now by claiming interference—she scrambled down, dropping the last two meters to land in front of her commanding officer. She gave a relaxed salute. "Sir?"

He jerked his head to follow him and led her to the only quiet corner of the gym. "Inquiry verdict is in."

She sucked in breath to control her heart rate and her expression. "Yes, sir. And?"

"And you're out of their crosshairs, Second Rating."

Ana released the rest of the breath in a rush, wincing at the show of emotion. She covered it with bluster. "About hacking time. Waste of our time."

"True. We do have to go through the motions, though, if we want to look like good little Confed-wannabes."

She nodded. "I get that. Just burns my ass they tried to charge me with something under *their* laws that wasn't my fault."

"First, they weren't at the charging stage. Second, an inquiry's how they decide what happened and whose fault it was—or wasn't. And if we do get to join them, then we need to get used to their ways. Which annoys me as much as it annoys you, trust me."

A thud announced Olesco dropping to the mats beneath his rope. Ana glanced his way; the guy's skin was shiny with sweat, his gym clothes leaving his arms and legs bare. He really did have great arms and legs, she mused for a moment. Pretending disinterest, he moved in the opposite direction toward the treadmills.

She refocused on Fowler. "If we join DCHC, do we know yet if the Tacticals get disbanded? Do we all join Peacekeeper companies?"

"I don't know any more than I did last time you asked. My guess is still that we'll keep our own militia. But there'll be new regulations we have to observe." He grunted, impatient again. "You look like you have more questions."

"I do, sorry, sir."

"Ask them."

"The inquiry, Colonel. Did the ECFs show that Hecate pushed me?"

"They did not. Nothing clear showed up on anyone's feed."

"*Mierda.*"

Fowler glanced over his shoulder at whatever-the-hell-it-was that the ambassador was trying to do. "Voice down, Jogianto. Give me a smile and a nod. Far as the Confeds are concerned, everything is happy in Tacticals-land. Any more questions?"

Ana dropped her voice. "Colonel, do you believe me or her?"

Fowler's stony face tightened into a mild glare. "Now *that* sounds like a question a Confed would ask. I have no evidence either way. I don't believe anything either way. And I'm not basing anything on the incident if that's what you're worried about. Yes, I see you have more to say. Spit it out, just be quiet about it."

"Colonel, Hecate was promoted in the aftermath of the mission."

"She was. She had accrued enough points for that." By points, Fowler was referring to the unwritten ledger that all Tactical COs carried and updated in their heads. Ana had always hoped she'd be the one carrying one in her head, and that if that day came, she would be fair and conscientious about it. She had never been convinced that Fowler was conscientious about his.

"And my points? Sir."

"Are doing fine, Second Rating. Trust me when I say, you acquitted yourself well in the matter of Luján—enough to make up for the accidental shooting of Sgt. Wepps." He stepped a little closer, enough she could smell the cologne he favored. "And between us, I'm happy your finger was on that trigger when you fell. I'm happy you stunned that little Peacer mold-stain. That earned you a couple more points right there. Damned Confed team leaders always think regulation way is the right way. They look down on us. He's the same. I might have to find a way to get him *accidentally* shot again sometime."

She must have let some of her shock at this last inference slip because he gave her a wink as he stepped back. "Little joke there, Jogianto. On the topic of your points tally, you got nothing to worry about. Keep doing what you've been doing, keep following my lead and you and Hecate both will have a team of your own soon. Now give me a smile and a salute. I've just delivered you good news after all." He returned her salute, pivoted and left her standing there, staring at the mat.

Good news. It *was* good news. The Peacers had nothing to hang on her, and if Hecate had gotten away with it, it hadn't hurt Ana's promotion chances. Or so Fowler said.

The mission to Luján's asteroid may have been the last action she'd see for a while, so chances to earn points would come harder. She had no control over that. But she had control over her fitness. And fitness affected everything.

"Olesco!" she called across the gym. His head turned as he jogged on the treadmill. "Get over here! We got a ropes race to finish!"

9

THE NEXT MORNING, Gregory came out of his quarters in fresh clothing, toweling his hair dry, to find Grace standing at the galley bench, Piers at her shoulder. Both appeared keyed up. Gregory had a feeling he knew what she was about to say, felt himself tense, undoing the relaxing effects of the hot shower.

"Message from the bridge, boss. Captain Pan says, quote, 'Check your inbox. I just got the thumbs up from Fleet Command'."

Unnecessarily, Piers added, "We're going to Pollyanna to chase more pirates."

INTERLUDE

Buoun

More than sixty orbits ago, Surveyor-Chief *Buoun'nyimiun't had become* Curator-Chief *Buoun'nyimiun't, administrator of the* Human Exhibition and Research Facility. *That facility had been planted inside Asteroid 99001 and had grown over tens of orbits until it filled the asteroid.*

The first fifty-six orbits of his Curator-Chief tenure had been a luminous time for Buoun, a florescence of knowledge gathering.

But, as the Humans wrote in many of their literature files, all good things must come to an end.

The end of Buoun's good things *had started with a major change at the apex of Domain Space leadership.*

The old Grand Councillor, Minqaa, had died. Minqaa had been a humanophile, encouraging Buoun in everything he did, lavishing generous budgets and staffs upon the Facility, providing them this entire asteroid.

The new Grand Councillor, Naat, had been quite the opposite: scornful of the Facility's successes and aims, furious at the resources he thought were squandered by it, and of the belief that Humans were a creature of the distant past. Humans, he said, were extinct as a civilization and as a species. With Naat's ascendency, everything for Buoun and for his Facility had gone down the vacuum commode.

Councillor Minqaa had forgiven Buoun for allowing the Human probe's stardrive to self-destruct when the device had effectively eaten itself just two fifteenths after Buoun first boarded the probe. She had listened patiently and with interest to Buoun's two theories on that: firstly, that the probe was ancient, and his reactivation of its systems caused some kind of mechanical failure; second, that the Human makers had programmed this failsafe to prevent intelligent species reverse-engineering the drive. "Then I will grant you the resources to piece it together from whatever is left," she had told him, "and to learn whatever else you deem valuable from its remaining intact systems and hardware."

Councillor Naat had been stewing with anger over the loss of the stardrive for more than fifty orbits. When finally he came to power, he was anything but *forgiving at both that event and Buoun's team's inability to replicate the technology. Three cycles after his appointment, Naat had called Buoun to his chambers. "I am halving your budget, Curator-Chief," he had said. "In one orbit from today, I will halve it again. You see the pattern? The only way for you to reverse this pattern is to give me a working interstellar drive. I care nothing for the languages you have learned, for your theories on the composition of Human physiology, for your musings on Human philosophical paradigms. Your people, your domain, we are going to the stars. Without the technology gifted us by that probe—before you ruined it—such expansion will take us hundreds of orbits if not thousands. Make me that stardrive, Buoun. Or watch your Facility dwindle into nothing. And your reputation with it."*

And today, that threat had come true. Today his facility

was officially decommissioned. And Buoun was left to pack it up alone.

He dumped a box atop a dusty trolley and leaned on the box's edges, regarding the jumble of items inside it with the despair befitting a Tlu who was in the process of dismantling his life's work. Befitting a Tlu who would never again set his eyes upon these wondrous alien artifacts. The pile of circuit boards remained fascinating, even after all these orbits, the logic of their design so non-Tluaan—the sapphire-and-ruby-colored components arranged like artwork amidst the silver and gold soldering. An aesthetic that no Tluaan technician would have followed. They were delightful things, to be sure.

But no objects had been as captivating as the one he now hid in his left thigh pocket. The "picture book," *as Human English called it, was small as his palm, a mere ten pages thick, and filled with age-faded drawings of animals from the Human home world. Whenever he had felt depressed these last few orbits, whenever he had lost hope, it was this* book *he turned to, leafing through its pages with gloved fingers, drinking in the details, imagining the Human individuals who had created it, printed it. The* book *was beautiful. If Buoun had been permitted, he would have taken it home long ago to place beside his bed, and it would have been the last thing he saw each night before falling asleep, the first thing he saw upon waking. It would have been safe there, and no one would have competed with it for his affection. No mate lived in Buoun's home. No children. His joining was to this facility, and his legacy was his research. Well, the book was his now. No one would care enough about the inventory of Human items to miss it. This one thing, he would keep.*

"Fifty-six orbits of bliss," he muttered to himself, straightening. "I had fifty-six orbits of bliss. And then Naat's shrinking of my world. And then *..." He regarded the line of fourteen loaded trolleys with bared teeth. "And then,* this!"

There was no one about to hear him since he had lost his

last assistant a long time back. The task of packing the Human artifacts into a waiting cargo barge was Buoun's alone—and he had just five cycles to complete it before reporting to the mining corps for reassignment.

The mining corps. The job of his youth, but he would return to it at a much-reduced rank and salary.

"Not that my salary has been worth more than mlegeip'boug spit these past few orbits," he muttered. After a long stretch of his back and a quick sigh, he put his hands to a trolley's handles and started pushing.

His facility's research—the computers, data banks, lab and engineering equipment—had been taken away half an orbit ago. These last hundred and twenty cycles, Buoun had been a curator in deed as well as name, the custodian of a secret museum of esoteric things that interested no one and was visited by no one.

One of his feet trod on asteroid rubble, a pebble. He stumbled, lost grip on the trolley, and dropped to one knee. It hurt. He had bruised that knee, and bad. He raised his face to the tunnel ceiling and howled. He howled for heartbeat after heartbeat after heartbeat, the way the ancestors of his species had howled in the jungle homeland when one of their pack was lost to the predators below. With no one to hear him, Buoun howled like a Tlu at the end of his sanity, at the end of his hope, at the end of his life's prime and with nothing but misery and obscurity to look forward to.

When the howling was done and the pain in his knee faded to a dull ache, Buoun remained kneeling there, his face to the ceiling, his mouth open and spitless and empty of words to express his loss. For he had lost everything. Everything that could ever possibly matter to him. He had dreamed of being the first to meet the Humans, of forging unbreakable bonds between that people and his. And his dream was now revealed as the dream of a fool.

One orbit after the probe's arrival, Grand Councillor

Minqaa had permitted Buoun to send a simple message in the direction the probe had come from. A message that Buoun had placed much hope and much faith in.

The Humans had never responded.

Buoun rose slowly to his feet, put his hands to the trolley, and shoved it forward again.

Perhaps, he told himself, perhaps if the Humans were not a dead race, they would arrive here some time, meet the Tluaanto here among these asteroids as friends and trading partners, they would walk the fields and sail the oceans of Suuchaat, they would assist the Tluaan species to reach beyond their single puny star system.

Perhaps, in future, they would come.

But Buoun was now sure that he would miss that day. Indeed, that day was undoubtedly so far in the future, Buoun would never live to see it ...

March 16, 3014, Old Earth Calendar

10

THREE THINGS ANNOUNCED *Assured's* emergence from leapspace: a trill-chime from the helmpanels, the appearance of normal space on the main viewscreen, and an explosion of activity amongst the crew. Leaning against the bridge railing, Gregory found himself once again the observer and wishing there was something he could do to contribute.

Then again, he thought, *is this really the kind of mission I* want *to contribute to?*

"*Bountiful* has completed leap," a sensor panel rating reported. "Fifteen klicks off our starboard."

"Noted," replied Pan from his place between the two helm stations. "Other contacts?"

"None yet, sir. Sweeping deeper."

XO Chinyama raised his voice from Gregory's side. "Comms, sweep for buoy."

"No signal buoy detected," Ensign Sintopas replied.

"The pirates must've destroyed the CUSET-era one," Pan said with a shake of the head.

"Launch signal buoy," Chinyama called.

"Buoy away," Sintopas called back.

Gregory leaned close to the XO. "Signal boy?"

"*Buoy*. B-U-O-Y."

"I see. And why's that important?"

Patiently, Chinyama explained, "Every system needs at least one signal buoy to link that system with the FTL-leapspace signaling network."

"Ah. Of course. Apologies for interrupting. Still so much I'm ignorant about. And take for granted."

"Perfectly fine," Chinyama responded with a polite smile before moving across to one of the sensor stations.

"Other contacts yet?" Pan called again.

"Negative, sir," replied the same sensor operator.

Gregory sighed quietly. Perhaps the captain was right to be impatient. The quicker this was over, the quicker they could all get on to higher duties.

"If it's ever over," he muttered to himself. When had there ever been a time in human history without war?

THE POLLYANNA PLANETARY system had obviously been named ironically. It was lifeless and it was dull: a comet belt and two asteroid belts strung around a red dwarf; zero radio or leapspace comms traffic; no detectable artifacts. Its four planets comprised two long-orbital-period ice giants, one ice dwarf in the outer reaches, plus an uninhabitable rock-and-lava "super-earth" closer in.

Chipper had been reading this intel on the short walk from the lifts to the Mess shortly before *Assured* dropped back into normal space. Since then, he'd found himself a Mess booth right by a viewport where he could sit and stare at the system in real time.

Viewports like this had once been windows, he knew—they'd been real glass. Or hardened and tinted synthetic versions of it. For the last century, at least in those systems recovering enough to build star ships, most viewports had become electronic screens. They looked and felt like windows and relayed information in real time and at real distance, but the image was provided by cameras fitted to the other side of the hull. When the iron gray of leapspace had given way to the black of normal space, he'd been a little disappointed that nothing was visible out there but the pinpricks of distant stars. *Assured* simply wasn't pointed the right way for him to see anything of the Pollyanna system. He had to resort to using his pad for data on it.

They had reentered mundane space outside the orbit of the ice dwarf—the small planet labelled Pollyanna-D—seeking to avoid detection. Their quarry were thought to be based in one or both of the asteroid belts. They could certainly use those to shelter from radiation.

And why on earth was he preoccupied with such trivia? Why, he wondered, was he sitting here turning his cup of coffee around and around its saucer, flipping through screens of data on his pad, chewing on his lower lip, pondering such things?

Why? Because I'm nervous. That's why.

There might be action soon. If not today, ship-time, then perhaps tomorrow. And if not then, and if not here—if the action was cancelled—then something else would come up, in a month or in a year. Chipper was a Peacekeeper, with six and a half years still on his contract. He would be sent into a firefight again. What would happen then? Would he live? Worse, would he kill someone else?

He glanced around him. There were people at every table, some of them crewers, some military like himself. Stines, Chandrasekhara, and Westermann—the rest of his Blue Squad buddies—were across the room, giving him space. Three Tacticals—Umbrano, Dayang, and Manolo—had commandeered another port-side table toward the back and were playing dominos. The Red and Blue Squad sergeants had crowded into a booth with three medical staff playing a board game. Up near the servery windows, Red Squad member Bradstock arm-wrestled a brute of a mechanic—and was losing, from the sounds of the crowd chatter. Other crew surrounded them, and there was evidently some betting going on there. Chipper noticed that Ensign Sintopas hadn't learned his lesson the other day and was at it again, playing blackjack with three women crewers. A few tables hosted people staring out the viewports like he'd been doing, but to most people on this ship, star travel was humdrum.

Humdrum, he thought with a shake of his head. *When Dad was a boy, us Oceaneans were still finding it difficult to sail around the world. Fifty years later, we're out here in the stars.*

The next thought he had was not so cheerful: *And we're chasing down people I'll probably have to kill.*

As an Oceanean, he should have been happy to do it, seeing as it was Xerxian raiders they were after. The Xerxians had recovered interstellar flight earlier than other colony worlds. For two hundred years they'd used it to harass weaker communities, stealing resources and earning their nickname Silvers—pirates. Oceana had fared badly for a time. But the Oceanean way was to forgive, to move on. None of those acts had been committed during the past sixty years, the last one happening during his grandfather's youth.

Still, despite the Oceanean "way," there were plenty of people back home who'd pat his back and buy him a meal in gratitude for teaching some pirates a lesson for old time's sake.

He sighed and turned his coffee cup a full circuit again, turning his thoughts to the combined briefing the Peacekeepers and Tacticals had attended three hours ago.

Sergeant Ouw and Colonel Fowler had run the meeting

together. Intel was shared. Background on Clan Lobos. It wasn't certain yet that "ground" troops would be needed—it wasn't certain the pirates were even here. But plans were in place, nevertheless. To foster further cooperation between the military personnel on board, *Assured*'s two Peacekeeper teams had been turned into three ...

The ten Peacekeeper troopers had been reallocated and mixed in with the six Tacticals to form Alpha, Bravo, and Charlie fireteams. Away missions would fall under DCHC purview this time, so Fowler would remain on *Assured* during any action. All teams had been told that stun settings were preferred but lethal force was authorized.

That day back on Asteroid CP11X, doing what he'd trained to do, responding in a manner that had drawn praise from others, even from the Tacticals, Chipper had lost his innocence. It had gone from being an adventure, a game, the fantasy of a mind long overdue for moving out of adolescence—to hard, spine-chilling, gut-turning reality. Lives were at stake. Real lives.

There'd been battles on Oceana during the dark age of course—skirmishes between islands, and bigger ones with Xerxians. This history had fueled juvenile, simple-minded stories of heroism in battle, intimating that fighting could be exciting, fun, rewarding.

He saw the sniper falling from his perch again and thought that his job these last few weeks had been anything but rewarding. Chipper was one of the few Oceaneans to apply for Peacers who had passed the physical tests and the gene scans. He—

Relax, skittle-head. It probably won't happen in this system. Bountiful *is here with her fighter craft. Sergeant Ouw said the engagement will probably be ship-to-ship, forcing a surrender. You have time before you're ever needed again. You might* never *be needed again. You might be able to transfer to disaster relief. Besides, once* this *is over, there should be peace for reals. The pirates are the final enemy.*

Maybe. There was also the isolationist former-Chinese world Yun Dao. No one knew that world's strengths. Or their intentions.

Geez crummeze, get a grip, man.

Chipper went and got himself another coffee and bagel. The arm wrestle had ended, the combatants shaking hands. Judging by Sintopas's grumpy demeanor, he was on another losing streak. When Chipper got back to the table, Tactical Jogianto was there. He'd left his pad there and the detritus of earlier snacks. She had nothing, her hands clasped in front her.

"No other tables were free," she said and pushed his tab to his side. It wasn't quite true— there were seats at the others. Why hadn't she sat there? he wondered. Maybe she liked elbow room.

Maybe she likes me.

He shook his head at the thought and the way it had popped into his head, hopeful and hungry.

Juvenile.

"I don't mind company," he said, sitting. "I came to look out the viewport, but there's not much to see."

She grunted and turned her face to the port. End of conversation, it seemed.

She definitely does not like you, skittle-head. Which she's made pretty clear a few times now.

For thirty minutes, they sat that way, not talking, her literally staring into space, him trying to focus on his tab without stealing glances at her.

Then the four-meter-wide monitor above the serving counter flared to life. All conversation stopped. Heads turned. Captain Pan was broadcasting from the bridge. Behind him, the numbers of bridge personnel were back to regular lean levels and they were all quiet. At his shoulder stood XO Chinyama. Both of them had deadly serious expressions.

"We are reading hostiles at seventeen thousand kilometers," Pan said. "Three pirate corvettes, leftovers from pre-PBT times. But showing weapons signatures and maneuverability that's healthy enough. Both *Assured* and *Bountiful* are attempting to catch them."

Pre-PBT corvettes, Chipper thought. *Eight-hundred-year-old ships. No,* nine *hundred. And they're still working. Ships that size, that's a minimum of*—He did a quick calculation—*sixty crew spread across them.* Tough for less than twenty trained troops to fight hand-to-hand against that many if they boarded them all at once. It was doable, but they'd have to bring in *Bountiful*'s ship security officers who had zero combat experience. Or training.

Pan was still talking. "Currently, Ambassador Gregory is trying to communicate with them. If they refuse to negotiate, our strategy is to disable their ships and force a surrender, rather than destroy them outright. Fireteams, you may be needed as boarding parties, but it will be hours before we are close enough to confirm that. For the time being, fireteams are to continue to stand down. Ship-to-ship engagements will come first. If engagements take place, they'll be broadcast throughout the ship on this channel. May the Gods, ancestors, and powers of all religions be with us. And inspire our enemies to surrender quick. Captain out."

The screen went blank.

Conversation exploded around the Mess.

For the first time in a half hour, Jogianto met Chipper's eyes. "Stand down, he says. We should be running drills."

"He probably expects we'll only be needed for transferring unarmed prisoners."

"Then he expects wrong. He should ask Fowler what to

expect. Those Lobos *cabróns* aren't giving up their independence without some serious bloodshed."

"They're that dumb?"

"They're that committed." Her gaze ran up and down what she could see of him above the table; she looked like she was determining whether or not he was worth speaking with. She must have decided the affirmative. "Look at it this way. Someone comes into your house and says you have to abandon your way of life, start a new one that you'll hate, and maybe spend your life in prison too. You gonna let them take you? You gonna let them take your family? Your stuff?"

"I ... never thought about it like that."

"Hear me right. I want those *perros feos* gone. They ain't helping anyone's cause." She fished inside one of her thigh pockets and brought out a flat flask, unscrewed the lid. "They're kinda like these forest animals we got on Xerxes, pack animals that don't come near towns or farms for years. Then one day, bam! They attack a dozen or more at once before hiding where we can't find them again." She tipped the flask back, took a couple of swallows.

"Is it really a good thing to dehumanize the enemy?"

"I told you, they're *animals*," she said. "Wild animals." She swallowed more of whatever was in the flask, then put it away.

"They're human beings. Some of them *must* want a peaceful life. For their kids, at least."

"Helldamn, man, you ain't read a lot of history, have you? I thought you Peacers had to have an education to make the cut."

"I'd appreciate it if you'd stop insulting me."

"Hey, I don't *want* to think you're dumb. But you sure act like it."

"This is how Tacticals talk to each other?"

She shrugged. "If you can't take a little rough talk, guy, I'm not sure you're in the right job. You know we both got assigned to Fireteam Alpha, right? Talk is, Fowler and Ouw consider that team the cream of the crop. Word is, you took out a sniper on that 'roid with one shot *while* moving to cover." She nodded. "I respect that. But if we serve together, I gotta know that wasn't a fluke. Are you good, or are you some dumbass who got lucky?"

Squashing down all the things he wanted to say, Chipper took his datapad and slid out of the booth. With exaggerated politeness, he said, "I think a seat just freed up over there. I look forward to serving with you, Tactical Jogianto."

He could feel her eyes on him the whole way across the Mess to where he pushed in next to Westermann. He was careful not to bump the burn-cast still wrapped around Westerman's thigh where the sniper's laser had hit her.

"Fraternizing with the enemy?" she joked.

Chipper glanced back the way he'd come. Jogianto had turned back to the viewport again. Her fingers were drumming on the table. "Yeah," he said. "We were real chummy."

Westermann pinched his cheek between thumb and forefinger. "Naw, don't worry, big boy. You're back with the good guys now."

"Until we see action," Stines grumbled across the table. "Him and me are in Alpha team with her and another of them Tacticals."

Westermann released Chipper's cheek and reached for Stines's, but he butted her hand away. She grinned. "Then you Blue boys will have to watch each other's backs, wontcha?"

"Yeah." Stines nodded seriously. "That's right. You got my back, Chipper?"

"Of course."

"I got yours too. Gotta keep an eye on them Silvers in our team. All we know, they're in cahoots with the bastards we're chasing."

"I don't think—" Chipper started, but Stines waved him to silence.

"Just watch 'em. That's all I'm saying. I'm happy to go out and cook a few of their lot. But it burns me that we're doing it to bring their planet into the DCHC. Makes no sense."

They all slumped a little in their seats, pondering that.

Something Jogianto had said came back to Chipper then. The image of armed and hostile people invading a home, ordering people about, changing their lives against their will. It's what Xerxian pirates *had* done a dozen times on Oceana. It's what greedy, malicious human beings had done over and over again for all the millennia of the *Homo sapiens* story—Jogianto had been wrong about his ignorance of history.

A civilization, he thought, required some of its men and women to form police forces, militias, armies—to serve, to protect, to shield the other 99.99% so they could live peacefully in their homes. Hadn't he told his parents as much during one of their heated discussions about him signing up? *Someone has to do it, so why shouldn't it be me?* Until now, it hadn't fully hit him what that meant.

He straightened in his seat. *Yep. Time to grow up, Chipper. Grow up all the way. You want a universe where people can live safely without violence? Then it's gonna take a little violence to make it that way.*

"We're soldiers," he said quietly. "Soldiers follow orders and do their jobs." He had no glass in his hand and the others had coffee cups, but he mimed raising a toast anyway, the Peacekeeper toast. "To doing our jobs."

The others raised cups and completed the toast: "And coming back alive."

LESS THAN ONE minute into the chase, the three corvettes split off from each other, headed in different directions.

A short meeting was convened in *Assured*'s Ready Room, with Gregory, Pan, Chinyama, Ouw and Fowler present in person—also Farahaji onscreen from *Bountiful*.

"Three of their ships, two of ours," Pan said by way of kicking off the discussion. "Which two do we follow?"

Farahaji said, "We can chase all three. *Bountiful* can send one of our smaller ships after one of them."

"A fighter." Fowler didn't sound as if he liked that idea. "*Assured* can send their own."

"Not a fighter. We carry two Mumford T15 *Lioness* pursuit runners. Not quite as fast as larger vessels inside a planetary system, but with far better acceleration. They're long-range vessels too with tough, efficient sublight drives, a forward-firing laser emitter, and a ship-to-ship missile bank."

"And if they actually catch their prey?"

"They carry up to ten troops plus the pilot."

"They were made to catch smugglers originally," Pan explained.

Farahaji nodded. "We fly that to *Assured* and pick up one of your three fireteams—adding them to some masters-at-arms from our security team—then send it after one of the corvettes."

Chinyama cleared his throat politely and leaned forward when eyes turned to him. "Two of them appear to be running for separate areas of the outer asteroid belt. Let's send the *Lioness* after the furthest one. Assuming it's planning to eventually arc back into the belt, the pursuit runner could vector inside that arc, take a flatter trajectory toward an intercept. They might catch it before it gets inside."

"And if it gets inside?" asked Gregory. He had expected

to remain silent during this meeting. As a diplomat, there wasn't much for him to contribute on military tactics.

Chinyama replied, "The *Lioness* should break off pursuit."

"No, the *Lioness* stays on them," said Pan.

"Captain, with respect, I don't like heading among those rocks whether it's with the smaller pursuit ship *or* with one of our capitals. Asteroids force our vehicles into chokepoints and kill zones and we sacrifice maneuverability. Better to send missiles after them, or bomb the field to break it up and shake the pirates out."

Pan pursed his lips for a moment. "Perhaps. We'll consider that when and if we get to that point. Captain Farahaji, I agree with my XO that the pursuit runner goes after the bogey who broke to our starboard—after it stops here to pick up a fireteam. How about *Bountiful* chases the bogey that broke to port? *Assured* will stick on the one that was center of their original formation."

Farahaji agreed, Chinyama nodded, and Fowler shrugged. With that, the meeting broke up.

"Ambassador, why don't you stay in here?" said Pan.

"Here? As in this room?"

Pan's smile held a tinge of acerbity. "That's what 'in here' means. I'll get Sintopas to hail that middle ship and patch them through to you."

"Ah. I get to negotiate a surrender."

"Exactly."

"I'm up for that."

"Good. You are titular head of this mission whenever we're not in direct action. I'd say that gives you sixty minutes to convince them before the shooting starts. Good luck."

CHIPPER SAT ALONE on a bench at the edge of hangar deck while Fireteam Charlie donned their vests and headgear. Charlie comprised two Xerxian Tacticals plus all but one of *Assured's* Peacer team formerly designated "Red Squad". When Mickey Kumar noticed him, Mickey nudged the others to acknowledge him. They did so with grins made out of bravado and adrenaline. He snapped off a salute, wishing them luck. Chipper was the only other Peacer there to witness the fireteam get onto the newly landed *Lioness*—but two Tacticals had come to see them off too. Fowler and Jogianto stood in a huddle down along the wall. Neither were speaking. While Fowler's gaze swept across and around the group getting prepped, Jogianto seemed most interested in one of the Tacticals—a classically handsome guy about the same age as Chipper who he thought was named Olesco.

Did they have history, him and her?

So what if they do, boy? Even if Jogianto did like you, she's not exactly the kind of girl you'd take home to visit the folks. He turned his attention back to Charlie team and forced a chuckle at the thought, imagining the horror on his mother's face if he ever hooked up with a Xerxian. He then imagined Jogianto coming to their home, stealing his Dad's wristwatch, their best cutlery, their holopad. Kidnapping their dog for ransom. An Oceanean and a Xerxian. That'd be the day.

"Line up!" Charlie's team leader called. Sergeant Ouw had been—and would be again at some stage—*Assured's* Red Squad sergeant.

The *Lioness*'s ramp was lowering. Charlie stacked up ready to climb it. The pursuit runner's fuselage was five times the size and breadth of the average Sprite fighter or Devilfly interceptor; her sleek hull was adorned with outboard engine nacelles, a black laser emitter, a roof-mounted missile-pod, and mounds of shield generators fore and aft. Mickey flipped off a salute toward Chipper.

Fowler called out to his people, "Our twenty-first mission! Luck be with you!"

"Sevens party!" Tactical Dayang replied with a fist in the air.

Tactical Olesco craned his neck around and waved to Fowler ... or to Jogianto. Only Jogianto returned it.

ANA FELT bad about feeling bad. As a Xerxian, she should be proud to see her fellow warriors head out into the black to chase down an enemy. Only, she felt like she should be going with them. And she wondered if Olesco—maybe the only person she could trust—would come back. Not being there on that pursuit runner to watch his back—and to share in the glory of a win—it really burned her.

The *Lioness* pushed through the bubble of the deck's atmosphere shield and into the vacuum of space. A second later, the drives lit up, and the pursuit ship raced away.

GREGORY'S ON-AGAIN-OFF-AGAIN dialogue with the corvette commander had been going for fifteen minutes now. The patchiness of the conversation was not due to distance. Across a gap of sixteen thousand kilometers and closing, there was no noticeable delay in the exchange of video and radio signals. The problem was that every few minutes, the pirate commander would cut off the signal out of bloody-mindedness. Two or three minutes later, she'd reestablish it again, grinning her gap-toothed smile at Gregory from *Assured's* Ready Room's wall screen. And the corvette commander had just severed the connection yet again.

Fifteen damned minutes. All of it spent going in circles.

He now had forty-five minutes left to argue for surrender. Weary and frustrated, he signaled for Ensign Sintopas to take a break from operating the room's comms.

"Get yourself a coffee."

"Thank you, sir," Sintopas said, heading for the door.

"And one for me," Grace added before he made it outside.

Sintopas looked miffed at the request, but didn't argue.

Grace had been leaning against the wall whenever Gregory's dialogue was active, staying out of sight of the screen's cam. Now she dropped into the closest chair with a huff of breath. "Not such a good day at the office."

"They're toying with us," he told her. They were the only ones in here at present. The XO would no doubt return seeking an update. For a minute or two more, Gregory could relax. A little. He gestured to the screen with his water glass. "She's grandstanding for her crew. Showing them how tough she is. She's not going to listen to me."

"Of course not. You're making sense. And she's a psychopath."

Gregory offered her a wry smile. "Shall I write it that way in my report?"

Grace didn't smile. "You need to threaten them with the Mako missiles we're carrying."

"That's Pan's next step once my hour is over. He thinks they'll capitulate under duress. I'd rather appeal to reason while I can."

"Boss. Chris. Pan's right. This ain't trade; this is war. These are desperate and proud people. They only understand dire consequences. The longer we avoid conflict, the less of a threat we seem."

"But—"

"Your real skills will come into play when there's terms to be discussed. For now, you need to deal with these people as criminals on the run. When I was a cop, I dealt with the toughest street gangs on Theseus. Trust me ..." She pointed at the dead screen. "That commander gives in early because it's the *sensible* thing to do, and her crew will mutiny. Then you'll be talking to some new assface with something to prove. But, if you fire that missile and tell her she has twelve minutes till it reaches her, she'll have a reason to capitulate that her crew will understand. She surrenders, we disarm the missile, they survive."

Gregory found the fingernails of one hand were digging into the palm of the other. He spread both hands flat. "I do see your point, Grace. But what if she doesn't capitulate? What if she's that stubborn she tries to outrun the Mako?"

"Then she dies. Probably. Her crew too. Like I said, this is war. However. The other two corvettes will know. Whoever else they have hiding in this system will know too. They may be a little less inclined to tempt fate."

"And so now we're in the numbers-game of war. Kill a few to save a thousand."

Grace was nodding.

"God, I hate this."

"That's because you're not insane."

"Dammit." His fists beat on the table lightly. "Guess we better go ask Pan to arm a missile."

"This is why you're a good diplomat, boss. You actually listen to advice."

As they rose, the door opened. Sintopas froze there with two coffee mugs in his hands. "What?" he said.

"About face, Ensign. We're moving this to the bridge."

FOUR MINUTES LATER, after the corvette commander

had told Gregory to do some physiologically imaginative things, and then shut off communications again, *Assured* fired her Mako.

Gregory stood with Pan and Chinyama by the helm, watching the comet trail of the missile's exhaust arc away in front of them, pursuing the corvette.

"I hope they don't surrender," a crewer behind Gregory muttered to another.

The other replied, "This is for the *Heavens Gate* massacre, you rat bastards."

"Duties!" Chinyama barked, silencing idle chitchat on the bridge.

Gregory watched the countdown-to-impact clock with rising consternation. When the missile was six minutes from impact, he asked the comms station to hail the corvette. The enemy ship did not respond. He swore under his breath.

At five minutes out, Pan leaned close and murmured, "One down, two to go."

Gregory didn't respond.

At four minutes to impact, Sintopas called out, "Corvette's hailing us."

"Open channel," Pan responded.

The corvette bridge appeared onscreen, the commander in the foreground with her six-strong bridge crew arrayed behind her. She was ashen-faced. Her crew wore their fury in their expressions. All were dressed in shabby clothing and poorly groomed.

"We surrender," she sneered. "Call off your little attack dog."

Pan nodded to one of the weapons cons.

"Disarmed," the controller called. "Braking sequence initiated."

Gregory followed the captain's gaze to a monitor on the side of the helmsman's station where the flight path of the missile was displayed. For a moment, there seemed no change, and then the missile slowed. Pan had told him that it would soon come to a full stop and await later pick up; expensive munitions like this were not to be squandered. Disarmed, it could be brought back on board, refueled, and used again.

Onscreen, the corvette commander checked a monitor of her own, then nodded. "Safe," she told her crew. She appeared to be attending her own helm, making adjustments.

"Corvette slowing," Pan's helmsman announced.

"I want assurances we won't be harmed upon boarding," the commander said.

Gregory was about to give her those assurances when he noticed movement on the screen at the commander's back. "Behind you!"

It was too late.

As if choreographed, two of her crew had lifted handguns in unison, firing even as Gregory called out. Their commander had no time to turn or react. Her chest became a bloody pulp. Blood and flesh spattered against her comms' camera. She dropped from view. Shocked gasps erupted around the *Assured* bridge. Gregory felt his own teeth grinding as he tried to keep his shock under control. Chinyama murmured "Animals" and averted his face. Pan nodded as if he'd expected it—and perhaps he had.

On camera and visible between the spots of blood and gore on the lens, one of the armed men moved forward to fill the space formerly occupied by his commander. Actually, Gregory realized, he was standing a little to the left, no doubt forced there by his commander's crumpled corpse. The man's frown relaxed into an expression of derision. Without taking his eyes from his video audience, he reached forward to the corvette's helm controls.

"Corvette accelerating," *Assured*'s helmsman said.

"On your worlds," said the man onscreen, his voice calm, emotionless, "do your children play a game called Catch Me If You Can?" He winked, then reached aside to cut the feed.

"*Shārén bù zhǎyǎn,*" Pan cursed softly.

Gregory translated in his head. Idiomatically, the phrase meant *stone cold killer*. Gregory thought it was an understatement. He asked, "How long to reset that missile?"

"Too long," Pan said. He adjusted the forward screen to display the missile still firing bursts of breaking thrusters; a faint glow in the distance marked the corvette accelerating away. He turned to Gregory. "We'd have to decelerate to pick it up, bring it on board, refuel and reset it, reload it. An hour's work at best. The question now is, do we use our second and last Mako, or do we—?"

"Look!" Chinyama pointed to the screen.

Gregory and Pan both whipped their heads forward in time to catch the explosion. When it cleared, there was nothing left of the missile.

"What happened?" Gregory asked.

"Corvette lasered it," said Chinyama. He looked as though he wanted to say more—a lot more—a stark departure from his usual phlegmatic demeanor.

"Futile gesture on their part," Pan said. "But I'm sure they got a kick out of it. Comms, contact *Bountiful* and relay the events of the past minute to them."

"Aye, sir," said Sintopas.

"Launch second Mako, Captain?" Chinyama asked.

"Not wasting another one. Time to catch them?" Pan directed the question to his helmsman. To Gregory's knowledge, although the corvette had been slowing, *Assured* hadn't.

"Two hours, twelve minutes, sir."

"XO, use beams once we're closer." He took Gregory's arm and began steering him around the periphery of the bridge toward the exit, his voice lowered. "In two hours, we'll be close enough to fire particle beams with accuracy, try to cripple them." He stopped them to lean over a crewer's screen, changing the image to a slice of asteroid belt. Giant rocks tumbled about on their slow axes, appearing at distance like tossed gravel moving in slow motion. "Their current course brings them close enough to this edge of the belt that we suspect it's their destination. *Bountiful*'s corvette is headed for the shadow of the ice dwarf, Pollyanna-D. The ship that Charlie Team are chasing is pretending to go for the middle of nowhere, but its course will enable it to curve back toward a point further around this asteroid belt from our corvette's destination. I doubt these pirates are interested in heroics, and therefore they're not leading us away from their people."

"They're headed for assistance," Gregory said.

"Precisely." He straightened and gestured for the crewer to return to his task. "No doubt there's something hidden in Pollyanna-D's shadow and waiting for *Bountiful* —a small fleet, a gun-platform." He shrugged. "And there'll be people and automatic *somethings* in those asteroids. Gun emplacements. Combat vessels. In the late 21st century, the People's Republic of China used AI-drones in Earth-system skirmishes, so there might even be some of those."

"We're flying into ambushes."

Pan started toward the door again, and Gregory kept pace. "Not us or *Bountiful*. Our corvettes won't reach cover in time. The *Lioness*'s prey may well, so if there's anyone to be ambushed it'll be Charlie Team."

"But surely the other two corvettes know we'll catch them." Gregory then remembered Grace's words earlier. He glanced up to where she stood by the door alongside the Peacer on bridge duty. She raised a wry eyebrow. "Proud people," he said, shaking his head.

"Proud to the point of delusional narcissism," said Pan,

reaching the door. Pausing, he raised his voice so that the entire bridge could hear him. "Be ready for support vessels coming out of the asteroids. And from behind Pollyanna-D. XO, call me when we're close to our quarry."

"Aye."

In the corridor and headed for the lift, Pan said, "Ambassador, I suggest you and your assistant do the same as me for the next two hours."

"What's that?"

"Take a long nap. Because the hours after that are going to be very busy."

11

FIRETEAM ALPHA HAD BEEN CALLED to the drill center.

The drill center's moveable fittings had been arranged into the configuration of the compartments, hatchways, ladderwells, and passageways expected to lie beyond the old corvette's docking hatch. For the past half hour, Alpha had practiced room clearing and taking corridors. Chipper enjoyed the physical activity—although it indicated an increasing expectation that his boarding party would be launched, it also stopped him from thinking too much. After their fourth time assaulting the mock-up of the corvette's main deck, Chinyama's voice came on speaker to relieve them and order Fireteam Bravo to enter the center in their place.

Alpha team piled out into the anteroom, plucking towels from walls to wipe away sweat, sucking at water bottles and refilling them, silent in their own thoughts. Normally, Chipper thought, a team would be loud at this point, whooping it up, trading banter, or debriefing their experience seriously. This team was quiet. Was Wepps aware of its lack of morale and cohesion? It hadn't affected performance in the maze, but a real mission would test that and test it hard.

Hecate and Jogianto were on opposite sides of the room, Hecate sitting in the lotus position with her eyes closed and a frown wrinkling her scarred forehead, Jogianto a bundle of energy who bounced on the balls of her feet one moment, stretched her calves against a wall the next. Stines, like Chipper, kept looking between the two women, though unlike Chipper he was scowling at them.

"Alpha, huddle!"

Sergeant Wepps's order cut off Chipper's thoughts midstream. Wepps strode into the middle of the room and his new team formed a tight circle around him.

His new team. My new team. Stines, Jogianto, and Hecate. The two women stood beside each other, but stiffly. Considering their obvious antipathy, he didn't understand why Fowler had recommended them to serve together nor why Wepps had approved—*or* Commander Chinyama, who was *Assured*'s head of security.

"Our performance was at standard," Wepps said. "That's good enough to prevent any of us dying. I hope. If we get more time, we'll get back here and do it again. I'd prefer to be *above* standard."

"*If* we get more time?" Hecate asked.

Wepps showed her his wristpad. "Intercept distance in thirty-three minutes. By that time, we need to be assembling with Bravo on hangar deck."

"Oh," the woman said. "Good."

"Good? Any missions we undertake are not personal, Tactical Hecate. While you are working with me, we are professionals and everything we do is professional. Besides, we won't be boarding anything if the corvette gets destroyed."

"I hope it doesn't," Stines said. "I'd love the chance at bagging a few more Xerxians."

"Stines," Wepps warned.

Stines raised his hands, wearing his innocent-face. "I meant pirates, Sergeant. Silly goose. Always getting my words mixed up." He waggled eyebrows at the two Tacticals; they stared stonily back.

"If you don't mind me finishing my speech ..." said Wepps. He paused until both Hecate and Stines had nodded in apology. "Good. If we do board, we know what to do, and now we know we can do it well, as a new team. Fireteam Bravo will come in behind us to secure unconscious hostiles while we continue sweeping and securing all three levels. The corvette's corridors are tight, but unless these pirates did some heavy renovating, we know each deck has only one spinal or arterial corridor with two access corridors crossing it. Not many ways for their people to get in behind us if we deploy bots and drones and if we work our way through it methodically."

"Always a chance they'll hide people in cupboards," said Jogianto. "Under mattresses. They've done shit like that before."

Hecate nodded, although her agreement appeared grudging. "They can double back on us via crawl space too."

"Totally. So what do we do about that?"

"Last squaddie drags," all four of his troops said in unison, using Peacer lingo for walking backwards.

"And Bravo have our backs also," Chipper added.

"So, we've got that covered. We got this, but remember to stay crisp over there."

"Yes, Sergeant," said Chipper and Stines.

"From here, you go shower, get into fresh kit, and be waiting for me in twenty-five minutes on hangar deck. I only have one more thing to say—"

"Don't shoot me in the back," Stines murmured. Hecate snorted a laugh. Stines seemed surprised by her approval of his jibe, but grinned tentatively back at her.

Jogianto's skin flushed dark, her jaw working, her hands tightening into fists.

Wepps stabbed a finger at Stines, leaning in until the fingertip touched Stines's forehead. He dropped his voice so only his team could hear it. "One more bullshit comment from you, Stines and I'll be swapping you for Pandora from Bravo."

"Sorry, Sarge."

"And after that, you'll be leaving *Assured* the moment we get back to Foucault to see out your tenure on janitor duties."

"Won't happen again, Sarge."

"It better not." Wepps straightened, glancing at Jogianto. "Let's have this out in the open now that Stines has brought it up—and so diplomatically. I don't care how my accidental stunning happened. It did. It's done. It was deemed an accident. I hold no grudge. Every member of this team has an outstanding service record with their respective militaries. When we see action, we *will* work as a team, and we *will* work as a great team. We will protect each other. We will support each other. One hundred percent." He paused a moment then added, "This is where you all say 'Yes, Sergeant'."

"Yes, Sergeant," four voices responded.

Chipper found himself grinning despite the tension. Or maybe because of it.

"Hangar deck twenty-*four* minutes. Dismissed." Wepps stayed behind as they left.

In the corridor, the women went one direction, the men the other. Chipper glanced back. Jogianto and Hecate were keeping pace but on opposite sides of the corridor.

"Those two hate each other as much as I hate them," Stines said.

"How about we do what the Sergeant said and be a team?"

"What's up with you? You're normally the life of the party. Lately you're as sour as a Polluxan lemonapple."

Well, that's the pot calling the kettle black, Chipper thought. "Nothing wrong with me." He pushed ahead to enter the changing rooms first. "I agree with the sergeant is all. We're professionals. Let's act like it."

Stines blew a raspberry. "Fine, Lemonapple. Just remember what I said about watching my back out there. These Silvers—"

"These two *Xerxians* are now Alpha teammates. I'll watch your back, Stines. And I'll be watching theirs too."

As they started stripping off kit, Stines shook his head. "Kid, I think I get you. But I hope you hear me when I say this. You can watch their backs all you like. But watch their hands and their weapons too."

GREGORY HADN'T NAPPED. Neither had Grace.

They sat in the yacht's lounge, sipping Centauran coffee and watching the corvette draw closer on the wallscreen.

"Two hours gone," Grace said. "We're close now." She pointed up, indicating the bridge several decks above them. "They'll be warming the particle cannons now."

Onscreen, light flashed in the space between the two ships. Green. Now red. The flashes were there for a second and then gone again.

"What was that?" Gregory asked. He hadn't been able to tell which direction the energy had been traveling.

It was Piers who spoke, leaning on a wall but watching with them. "Corvette's laser array."

More light pulsed, this time a bright blue-white. Gregory thought he caught it coming toward them this time.

"Now an EM burst. They're trying to throw off our

sensors at close proximity, blind us. That works on fighters and freight and passenger ships. Won't work on us."

Gregory checked the distance counter in the bottom left of the screen. Less than three hundred kilometers between them now and closing fast. At that distance, neither ship could miss with lasers. "Why not keep lasering us? We can't dodge, surely."

"No, but we have superior shields," said Grace.

"And we're not firing at them yet because ...?"

"It's about accuracy," Piers replied. "They're moving on a corkscrew course with some random variations. Looks reasonably steady onscreen because our comms computers adjust to match them, but minor random variations would make it tough to target engines precisely. That's if Pan wants to disable, not destroy."

"That's what he ordered Chinyama to do."

Piers grunted. "At fifty klicks out, he'll match speed and have a clearer shot."

"Probably still kill 'em," said Grace. "Old ship like that."

Piers shrugged. "Mm. Maybe. Depends what strength particle beam we use. If *Assured* causes the corvette engines or reactor to explode then, yup, the rest of the ship goes with it. Same as ours would. But if we can damage them just a little, then they'll lose power and we'll have them. Ship'll be dead in the water, but the crew will be alive and well. For a few days, at least."

"Until battery power dies," said Gregory.

"Exactly. Then—"

Piers clutched at his throat and made gasping sounds while Grace wrapped her arms around herself and shivered in mock cold.

"Hypothermia and suffocation," Gregory sighed.

"Not nice ways to go," agreed Grace. She added, "We'll have a breaching party on them before that happens."

A comms signaled bleeped from the cockpit and Piers went to check it.

Gregory said, "I'm glad Pan ordered boarding parties to use stun settings as much as possible."

"The pirates won't."

"We need to be seen as using every means possible to bring the *Heaven's Gate* perpetrators to face justice in a lawful court."

"I get that. I *was* a cop, you know. I just think sometimes it's safer to fight fire with fire."

"Well, if we blow them to pieces, a discussion like this won't matter much. There won't be anything left to prosecute."

"Message from bridge," Piers announced, returning. "Firing on corvette in sixty seconds."

THE CORVETTE DID NOT GO down without a fight.

Standing with her new temporary team on hangar deck, Ana fussed with her Peacekeeper webbing while watching various views of the battle displayed across the chamber's eight wallscreens. Of the eight, she preferred the view as seen from directly below *Assured*'s bow. The corvette was fifty or so klicks away, but the camera had zoomed in closer, showing the ship as a blocky hunk of metal taking up maybe a tenth of the screen. Light lanced toward it as *Assured* fired three short particle bursts into the corvette's tail. Yellow-white flares showed a rear shield absorbing the bursts. The pirate vessel shuddered under the blows, but kept on, veering slowly to port as it continued corkscrewing, avoiding the fourth and fifth bursts entirely. It must have slowed a little as suddenly it loomed large in the display. Any shifts in speed and direction would be easy to match, Ana knew. Acrobatic dogfights—where vessels slipped out of their pursuer's sights—were impossible with large ships, especially at this range and these kinds of speeds.

Another trio of particle bursts streaked between the warships, longer ones this time. The pursued ship's rear shield glowed, visible now as a faint yellow shimmer literally covering their ass.

Stines gasped, "Christ Almighty!"

Ana saw them at the same time.

A cloud of the light gray spheres jetted from the corvette's sides.

Chase mines.

A 22nd century version of 20th century marine corvette depth charges.

"They still work?" she said to no one in particular.

"They've used all of 'em at once," Chipper said at the same time.

"Pointless," said Wepps.

Fireteams Alpha and Bravo whipped their heads around to watch the charges' passage on multiple screens. Some pattered against *Assured*'s forward shield. Most streaked by their flanks, tiny dots attempting futilely to lock and latch on. Even with their own semi-autonomous blast-drives to assist them, *Assured* was moving too fast for them.

"They weren't built to be used as countermeasures," Wepps finished.

More particle beams crossed the gap between ships, this time bursts of longer duration. Though the corvette attempted slow turns, climbs and dips, none of the latest beams missed their target. The rear shield grew brighter. And then—so quickly, Ana almost missed what happened—the shield flared white and vanished. The next particle beam after that punched directly into the white-hot exhaust. A second later, a gout of fire spewed from the hull beneath the exhaust cone, and the drive-glare snuffed out.

No more particle beams followed; *Assured's* weapons con had done their job.

Hemorrhaging fuel and chunks of steel, the corvette slid away and above them onscreen as *Assured* swept past it. The DCHC ship would be braking, Ana knew, as she commenced a gradual arc back toward her crippled prey, keeping a respectful distance for the moment.

"We going in, y'think?" Stines asked Wepps.

The sergeant merely shrugged without taking his eyes from the screens.

No point asking that, Ana thought. *We still have to wait to see if the ship explodes yet. Who knows how much damage we've actually caused?*

"We'll take out their cannons on the next approach," Chipper said, his big hands gripping his vest in a relaxed pose. He seemed far less antsy than he had been the last few times Ana had seen him.

"Duh," replied Hecate.

It was Chipper's turn to shrug. "Just saying. I wouldn't wanna be heading over there with them taking potshots at our skiff."

ACTUALLY, *I don't want to head there at all,* Chipper told himself. *But this is my job. I signed up for it. And there's not much chance I'll stun someone off a high rock shelf this time.*

"Well, I'm ready to kick some Lobos ass, and hard. How 'bout you sister?" Hecate asked Jogianto. "You ready?"

"Always," her fellow Tactical grated through clenched teeth.

Just what was their problem with each other, Chipper wondered. Or was it some nuance of Xerxian culture he simply didn't understand, this animosity?

Must be a helluva fun place for tourists if they're all like this.

LEANING OVER HIS PAD, Gregory sorted through the information streams coming to him from *Assured*'s various data feeds—and more distantly from *Bountiful*'s.

In the hour since disabling the corvette, *Assured* had circled around to target the enemy ship's gun mounts and pull alongside. Both ships still moved since the corvette's crew had not engaged braking thrusters. Sensors showed that damage to the pirate's sublight drive had not spread outside the drive compartment. While a handful of pirates may have been in the vicinity and therefore killed, most crew would remain unharmed as life support was still operational. There had been no comms traffic from them, but no doubt the remaining crew were digging in and prepping for boarders.

Ten minutes ago, *Bountiful* had fired on the second corvette. The damage she'd caused had spread to other compartments, sparking a cascading series of interior explosions. These left the hull largely intact but extinguished all life aboard.

Continuing to move along the planetary plane of the system, *Bountiful* had been able to peek "behind" the ice dwarf Pollyanna-D long enough and well enough to confirm there was indeed a weapons-platform lurking in orbit there. Their quarry had been hoping to make it in time for support. The station hadn't fired, and at a distance of almost three million kilometers, that was understandable. The carrier would complete a flyby to ascertain whether or not there were ships capable of fleeing the system near the platform, before returning to *Assured*.

Another bleep from the yacht's comms sent Piers

jogging forward to listen, then back again to relay the message. "Alpha-Bravo's skiff leaves in three minutes. Bridge says they'll cast the vision from the boarding party down here for you." He pointed to the lounge screen.

Where me and my disapproval can't be seen.

Gregory swiped his pad to *off*, rose from his chair, and stretched his back.

"Tell them no need. Grace and I will come up and watch it with them."

12

"OUR SKIFF IS CLOSE TO DOCKING," XO Chinyama told Gregory quietly. They stood with Fowler to the side of the helm and the forward hologram station while Pan manipulated data in the holofield.

"Once we take this ship, we'll turn our attention to those asteroids?" Fowler said. "Join the *Lioness*?"

"Yes," Chinyama said. "It's still likelier than ever they have at least one base in there."

"I agree. And we need to get in there and capture or destroy them."

"Preferably capture," Gregory said. "Wherever their base is, there'll be non-combatants there, Colonel. Children."

Fowler held his stare for a moment before lifting one edge of his mouth in a wry half-smile. "You haven't met Clan Lobos. My grandmother did—more than once. She once told me they don't know the meaning of *non-combatants*. The passengers aboard the *Heaven's Gate* would testify to that—if they weren't all dead. But I take your point. The Sevens Party respect and concur with the DCHC value on human life, even the lives of murderers."

That, I doubt, Gregory thought. To Chinyama, he said, "I discussed this with the captain yesterday: we *could* blockade the system now we know where the bulk of the faction are located."

"To what end?" Fowler interrupted. "You want to tie up major resources laying siege for an unknown time period? If we do trap them in there, they might have enough resources to survive comfortably for a century or more. The smart thing to do is to strike while we have them destabilized."

"Military action inside asteroid fields is fraught—" Chinyama started.

Fowler interrupted again. "Everything is *fraught.*"

Pan signaled and cut them both off. "The time and place for this discussion is later in the Ready Room, gentlemen." He flicked a hand toward the primary viewscreen where Fireteams Alpha and Bravo's ECFs were coming online. They showed the inside of an assault skiff's airlock. "They've reached the corvette."

Via Corporal Chipper Tukimatu's feed, Gregory watched Sergeant Wepps working the docking controls by the hatch. No one on board spoke, though their breathing was coming through loud and clear and heavy. Fireteam Alpha arranged themselves at the hatch while Bravo stood back. A smaller team of two medical corpsmen hovered nervously behind Bravo, back near the pilot.

No matter what Gregory thought of violence, he had respect for the courage of these people, for what they were about to do in the name of bringing humanity's worlds together into a peaceful union. They had little idea what waited on the other side of that hatch—except that it would probably involve people shooting at them. Fingertips brushing the tiny crucifix he wore beneath his tunic, he mouthed words, words he wasn't sure he believed in anymore, but words he could only hope would help this boarding party. "Protect these soldiers as they discharge their duties. Protect them with the shield of your strength and keep them safe from all evil and harm."

He glanced around him. In the lead up to the Luján mission, bridge crewers had been excited; this time they were tense, their actions muted. The bridge was also a lot less crowded, something he was glad for. Since all Peacekeepers were off-ship, no one stood on bridge duty. In such a situation—and unguarded bridge—protocol demanded the XO wear a sidearm. Chinyama had retrieved one from the nearby weapons locker.

Guns, guns, guns, Chris Gregory bemoaned. *Will there ever be a time we don't need them?*

ANA WAITED IN FORMATION, down on one knee at the left-edge of the hatchway. Hecate knelt over at the right. From beyond the hatch, a loud ratcheting noise communicated the shuttle's transfer tube feeling for a viable lock with the corvette's mating port. Stines stood behind Ana, Chipper behind Hecate. All had weapons up and bodies shielded behind the bulkhead in case of incoming fire—their vests couldn't protect them completely, and certainly didn't protect arms and legs. The face-shields and helmets they wore would provide some protection against ballistic weapons but little against energy ones.

Once Wepps finished programming the hatch controls, he stepped back behind Chipper, his rifle slung on his back and a cambot in his hands. These tiny Confed bots couldn't explode like Xerxian roachbots—but along with their camera, they did carry pulse-emitters for stunning hostiles.

Except for the slow rise and fall of their shoulders as they breathed, Hecate and Chipper were still as statues. In contrast, Stines whispered the same five cuss words in a kind of mantra. Bravo Team and their corpsmen had gathered out of the way near the pilot. Ana checked her selector for the thirtieth time: still on stun. A muscle kept twitching in her shoulder. She rolled it back to ease the tension.

Come on come on come on.

And then, a deep clunk and a series of clicks as the tube locked in place, pressurizing fast. The right side of the hatch cracked open a hand's width. Wepps tossed the crab-legged cambot into the mating tube beyond and flipped up a monitor-screen hinged to his vest.

"Clear," he said, a moment later.

Closest to it, Chipper smacked the hatch release, sending the door zipping fully inside the skiff's hull. Hecate moved first, hugging the tube's right side, with Chipper behind her. Ana and Stines took the left. The next hatchway—the one belonging to the corvette proper—stood open, revealing the soiled walls and threadbare carpet of the corvette's receiving compartment. Hecate swung right and into the compartment's nearest corner while Ana mirrored her on the left. No one awaited them.

Stines and Chipper headed directly across the four meters of open space to the next hatchway. This one had been sealed, Ana knew from briefing maps that beyond it stretched one of the two cross-passages that cut width-ways across this level. When that door opened, she'd be staring thirty-six meters along it toward its junction with the arterial corridor.

Chipper pulled out a hand-held cutting laser. The ceiling was around three meters high, and Chipper aimed the narrow beam near the very top of the hatch, marking a circle the size of a baseball, before commencing a slower run around it to cut on through.

No smells could reach Ana through her face-shield, but she imagined the compartment filling with the tang of burning steel, a new odor to overpower the pungent stench of mildew she knew must be "out there," since mold spots were in evidence everywhere. She'd lived in bad places, but how could these *bakas* live with *this*?

Wepps murmured commands into his wristpad. The cambot responded, scuttling up and into a ready position near Chipper's lasering. The sergeant said, "Stines. Grenade ready."

Stines pulled an anti-personnel version and showed it to his sergeant. "The bot probably won't zap all of them."

Wepps nodded.

Ana nodded too: in approval. The Peacers weren't taking any chances going through this first door. Maybe they weren't so dumb.

When Chipper completed his circle, he used the laser unit to poke the chunk of metal through the door, stepping back to make way for Stines. The bot raced through as Wepps watched his vest monitor. Shouts and shooting erupted the other side of the door; Wepps's scowl and glance at Stines told Ana the bot hadn't made it. Stines pushed the grenade through. More shouts, then the *crump* of an explosion, the pings and clatter of shrapnel.

Chipper slapped the door control. As it whisked open, he and Stines sprayed stun rounds through it. Then they stepped into the passageway, Ana and Hecate following.

No doubt there was mold and rust on the carpet and walls here too. But Ana couldn't see any of it for the blood specks and scorch marks left by the grenade. Ana registered the bodies: three definitely deceased, one screaming and writhing, one spread-eagled and moaning, all of them torn up in some way. Chipper and Stines each fired a stun bolt to put an end to the screams and moans, while Ana and Hecate raced through the middle of the mess. She made it to the single doorway along her side of the passage as Hecate reached the room on the opposite side. Neither had doors, the areas behind them being cargo holds. She leaned inside for an initial check, spotted no one, stepped inside and swept the room: a few piles of weathered crates against the far bulkhead forty meters away; a line of ten grubby cots down the middle of the space; nowhere for anyone to hide. There was one hatchway to the arterial corridor, halfway along the room's side wall—she monitored it until Hecate called "Clear" and Chipper and Stines both added "*Junction* clear." Ana left the cargo hold the way she'd come, then joined Stines and Chipper at the arterial junction.

"Bravo team," she heard Wepps call behind her.

The support team and corpsmen could now emerge and start securing prisoners. Not that they *had* living prisoners so far, Ana thought. The trauma of a close-range stunning had probably ended those two injured pirates.

As Wepps came up to join them, she looked past him to the airlock. Bravo emerged, led by a middle-aged Peacer nicknamed Widowmaker—a name she felt was better suited to a pirate or Tactical than a Confed. There came two of Wepps's original team behind him and then Tacticals Manolo and Umbrano. Umbrano stuck out his tongue as if trying to taste the air beyond his face mask. While the two Tacticals jogged past the carnage to join Alpha team at the junction, Widowmaker checked the pulses of all the enemy. He shook his head over all of them, then signaled for the corpsmen to follow him.

Two paramedics, Ana thought. *Probably gonna need more than that.*

THE MOOD on *Assured*'s bridge was grim. No one spoke. No one moved.

Via the ECFs on the main screen, Gregory watched the activity play out. He recalled a line he'd read in a classical novel, something about a character having their heart in their mouth. He now understood its meaning. At any moment, these soldiers onscreen might get cut down or carved up like the first five pirates had been. His fingers went to his crucifix again as Wepps sent Manolo and Umbrano through the intersection to clear the cargo holds to either sides of the accessway over there. There, the Tacticals' ECFs showed piles of captured contraband and consumables. It took both a full minute to ascertain no hostiles were hiding among it.

While Wepps held the junction facing aft, the rest of his team went forward to clear the next crossway and the compartments beyond and along it. There were no further contacts.

The next step in the plan was *not* to take the next levels immediately. Instead, Alpha Team would secure the auxiliary CIC at the aft end of the bottom level, where they could hack in and seize control of all onboard systems. And that meant ensuring no attackers came down the lifts or ladders at them.

The corvette had a personnel elevator forward, a goods elevator astern—one Peacer from each team kept an eye on those for the time being. It also had four ladderwells joining all three levels and extending into the crawlspace below the lowest level. Rather than committing personnel to those ladderwells as easy targets for snipers or grenade-droppers above, it had been deemed best to place autonomous Spitter drones in each of them. Bravo team member Westermann—limping because of her previous leg wound—carried a drone under each arm to the forward ladderwells while Chandrasekhara took two aft with Manolo and Umbrano guarding her.

As the first drone activated, flying silently up its ladderwell, Chinyama broke the silence on the bridge, explaining for Gregory's benefit, "The Spitters will take position at the very top of the well, above the topmost hatchway and facing down. Any hostile poking any part of their body in there will immediately regret it. Even if they're down at the crawlspace end."

"Why 'Spitters'?" Gregory asked, suspecting he knew the answer.

"They 'spit' ballistic rounds. From a magazine of fifty 10-mm bullets."

"And they couldn't be equipped with stun emitters?"

"Not if they want to hit someone coming out of the crawlspace," Pan replied. "Trust me, Ambassador, this is best for the safety of our—"

Pan broke off as fresh violence erupted on two of the ECFs.

WEPPS HAD RETURNED to the skiff briefly for the tank of siesta gas before accompanying Ana to the corvette's stern. Like the other interior compartments on this level, the Auxiliary CIC there had no door or hatch, just an entry gap from floor to ceiling. Ana could see nothing beyond it but for the control desk that sat in the middle of the room. Again, from briefing maps, she knew there were two floor-mounted stools either side of the desk, and the room opened out to the sides for about three meters beside them.

At the sergeant's signal, Ana entered right and he to the left. The compartment was empty—nothing but the light from a single overhead bulb and the glow from retrofitted modern displays, handpads and keypads along the desk. Ana frowned at them: they were very new, shiny, with a few scratches and not a few gaps around their edges where they'd been forced to fit into the desk.

Stolen from Heaven's Gate? she wondered.

Both used their rifle straps to slide the weapons around and onto their backs. Wepps stayed left, placing the gas cannister upright against what Ana thought must be an air filter. When he twisted a node atop the cannister, a tube snaked out and up along the air filter, its tip coming apart into a mass of long cilia that caressed the filter housing as they sought a way in. Ana stayed right, bending over the desk. She pulled a small datapad from her vest, sat it down, and slipped the free end of the pad's smartwire into an empty data point on the console. Corvette systems icons popped into existence on her pad screen; she touched the one for *engineering* then tapped in the release code for the subversion-protocol she'd created.

Three seconds later, she told Wepps, "I'm in. I have control of air supply and filtration." She clicked on another submenu and tapped in code. "Elevators too; shutting them down."

"I'm not in," he replied tersely, watching filaments attempting a way into the air filter. "Damn this old tech. I might have to cut—"

Movement cut his sentence short. Back beside the entrance, a bulkhead panel was shifting, coming off the wall.

With no time to swing the rifle from her back, Ana quick-drew her sidearm as Wepps went for his, EM-pistols with no stun setting. The first man out of the hidden compartment fired at Wepps, shooting from the hip, an ancient-looking ballistic pistol; the noise of the shot would have deafened Ana in the confined space were it not for the sound-dampeners in her Peacer helmet. She fired too and the man dropped, crying out in anger or pain or both. To her dismay, Wepps fell too. No time to check him. A second shouting man was emerging from the wall, but clumsily; his shoulder caught as he tried to extricate himself, and Ana hit him twice before he got a shot off. She stepped around the desk and ended the first man's yelling with a round to the forehead.

Then she checked on Wepps, ignoring the shouted inquiries coming from the comms speakers in her helmets.

Wepps was on his ass, his pistol hanging from his index finger by the trigger guard. Behind his faceplate, he was swearing quietly, grimacing. He tapped his vest; Ana saw the scuff where the bullet had hit him. Then he gave her a thumbs-up and reported in to the rest of the team, insisting they hold their positions. Ana kicked the two pirates, making sure both were dead, then booted their handguns into a corner, before offering Wepps a hand up.

He nodded his thanks and turned back to the siesta gas cylinder. The feeler-tendrils had finally latched on to a particular spot on the air filter, working themselves inside. A green light flashed on the cannister.

Wepps said, "Ready." He stroked a control on the gas supply, then tapped his comms again. "*Assured*, Wepps. Releasing siesta now."

"Good work," Ana heard Pan reply.

"THAT WAS CLOSE," Pan told Chinyama who nodded grimly.

The bridge fell silent again as all watched the next ten minutes play out on the various ECFs.

Gregory had been told the siesta gas would render the remaining pirates unconscious. It was odorless, harmless, and extremely fast-acting, a mercy tool first employed against violent religious agitators on Centauri.

The effectiveness of both the gas and the tactic was proven after Alpha team used ladderwells to climb to the corvette's middle level. The floor there was littered with unconscious bodies.

Nevertheless, as they checked the area, the team

watched wall panels as carefully as they watched doors and corners—just in case.

Bravo came behind them, collecting enemy weapons and applying hand- and ankle-cuffs, corpsmen assessing and treating minor wounds sustained while falling, reporting numbers of Lobos pirates accounted for so far—twenty-three.

No deaths on the center deck, Gregory thought with relief. *At least that's something.*

And then, Alpha climbed to the top deck, regrouping outside the ladderwell. And there, they encountered their next problem.

THE NEW LOBOS commander had pulled a number of his people into the bridge and sealed it off. Somehow, he or his crew had also found a way to seal it from the rest of the corvette's airflow.

While Wepps, Hecate, and Stines swept the rest of that level, Ana and Chipper had been charged with guarding the blast door sealing off the bridge from the arterial. And it was that door Ana was staring at now in bewilderment, grinding her teeth.

"It's transparent," she said for the third time. "Why is it transparent?"

"It's called clearsteel," Chipper muttered from across the way. "Lots of CUSET-era ships used it. Usually for exterior windows."

"But why? Why make a blast door clear?"

"Why'd they do anything back then?" He'd had his rifle leveled at the people milling beyond the door since approaching it. Now, he lowered it. "Can we talk about the more important issue? What do we do about *them*?"

His nod, Ana knew, was aimed at the three pre-teens

pressed against the glass—*clearsteel!*—in front of ten adults. They appeared to be two boys, one girl, but their long and matted hair and skinny bodies made it hard to tell, not to mention the dirt on their faces. And the hatred contorting those faces! Most of the adults held modern-era pulse rifles along with a couple of birdguns—what CUSET people would have called *shotguns*. The kids had machetes.

"Yeah," she muttered back. "That door comes down, this won't be pretty."

"No," he replied. "I mean the kids." His eyes were glassy as he glanced across at her. "I can't shoot them."

Ana checked over her shoulder, Wepps was returning, still halfway back down the deck, jogging.

"They ain't kids, Chipper. Pirates call 'em *prentices*. Blood 'em young. Commit 'em to the life ahead."

Just like my parents did to me but in a political way.

She returned the murderous glares of those three prentices as they banged machete handles against the clearsteel and bared their yellow teeth to shout what looked like obscenities. It was hard to think of them as 'kids,' children. As Wepps joined them, Chipper turned the wall, struck it with the meat of his fist, put his forehead to it.

Man, he is really *burned up about this!*

"Okay, Chip?" Wepps asked.

The big man's reply was mumbled, unclear.

Ana said, "It's the pren... It's the kids there."

Wepps sighed. "Yeah, that's an issue, all right." He scratched the back of his neck. "I'll ask *Assured* for orders. Meantime, we need to withdraw to the first crossway."

Ana shook her head. "They're not coming out. They'll make us come *in*. When they see us prepping for breach, they'll all take cover and make us work hard for it."

More neck-scratching from Wepps. "*Assured*, you seeing and hearing this?"

Ana didn't hear the reply this time, broadcast only to

Wepps's comms as he listened with lips pursed and face blank. "Copy, *Assured.* Chipper, eyes on that door. Hold here until the others are down the ladder."

"What's happening?" Chipper asked, getting control of himself.

Wepps's wince was slight, fast. Ana almost missed it before he answered Chipper. "We're to evac prisoners and both fireteams over the next hour. *Assured* are moving closer to improve turnaround times. I'll redeploy two Spitter drones once you two withdraw."

"And then?" Ana asked when he paused.

"They're launching an interceptor. There'll be a surgical strike on that bridge."

Ana nodded approvingly. Chipper swore beneath his breath.

"Do I need to send you down the ladder first?" Wepps asked him, tone hard.

Chipper straightened his shoulders, raising his rifle to the door again. "No, Sergeant."

"Good to hear." He strode away, using comms to order Stines and Hecate to the ladderwell.

There was one escape pod under the nose of the bridge, Ana knew from the briefing. It had been made to seat four people. They might squeeze eight in there, if they chose to. She felt like no one on that bridge was going to use it though. And there were thirteen of them—that she could see.

It was her turn to sigh. Pulling a black marker from her webbing, she strode to the blast door, confident no one was opening it from the pirates' side. She crafted her message quickly, writing backwards in large letters, then stepped back to watch the snarling pirates read it.

Ana read it too, aloud: "*Si vosotros deseais morir, adelante. Pero no decidais por ellos. Dejad que los niños huyan en la cápsula de escape.* That's for the adults," she told Chipper.

"What's it mean?"

"It says, 'If you have a death wish, go ahead. But don't make the decision for them. Let the children leave in the escape pod.'"

GREGORY HAD EXPECTED the mission to be concluded by now, but the evacuation of the Lobos ship was taking time. An hour in, Alpha and Bravo were placing the last of the prisoners on board to ferry back to *Assured*. Another trip would be required to pick up the Peacers staying back on the corvette.

Pan had ordered *Assured*'s Umaga-Morgen F380 Devilfly interceptor launched. Its pilot, a Lieutenant Berderhan, recommended a single missile strike to take out the bridge. It would cause further damage to the rest of the vessel, but there was nothing there that was essential to salvage. Gregory found that he understood Berdahan's professional matter-of-factness, but he was also a little appalled at it.

So far, there'd been no sign of the pirates complying with Jogianto's written request for the children's surrender.

Gregory was about to ask Chinyama whether it wouldn't be better to starve the pirates out, when the comms officer Sintopas suddenly called out across the bridge, his voice shrill.

"Captain! We're receiving a datapacket."

"From fleet command?"

"No, sir. Other direction."

"Other ...?"

Pan charged across to him, weaving around work stations while crew stepped from his path. For the moment, their attention had shifted from the viewscreen to the comms station.

What does he mean, other direction? Gregory wondered as he trailed the captain.

Pan leaned over Sintopas's shoulder, reading text data. The comms officer pressed his earpiece in tighter to better listen.

Gregory came up on the other side of the desk station. "What is it?"

"Well, there's audio as well as text, but it ain't English," Sintopas told him, releasing his hold on his ear. "Or Spanish, Mandarin, Hindi, or Nihongo."

"Tagalog?" Gregory asked, thinking of the strong Filipino presence in early migrations to Xerxes. Could the pirates have called in reinforcements?

"Not Tagalog," Pan said, straightening. When he faced Gregory, his expression looked startled, a look Gregory had never expected to see the captain wearing. "This transmission didn't come from human-settled space."

13

"MAYBE THE OTHER pirate ship will learn a lesson from this," Chipper said. He stood with Wepps and Jogianto behind the shuttle pilot's chair. They'd been the last to leave the corvette. At Chipper's request, the pilot had moved the skiff to a safe distance where the ship they'd just left was still visible through the forward viewport, but they'd have enough warning to evade debris from the looming explosion. The Devilfly had taken up a position six kilometers to their starboard, an object now too small for Chipper to make out with the naked eye. The fighter-interceptor was due to launch its missile in less than a minute. So in less than a minute, those kids in there would be dead.

Slaughtered.

"They'll learn nothing," Ana said beside him. "Clan Lobos ain't human, dude. Fireteam Charlie will probably go through exactly what we did. And they're gonna need to hold the ship and await our team reinforcing them for boarding, probably."

Chipper grunted. An anger he'd never experienced burned fierce behind his sternum. For the first time in his life, he felt like he'd be happy if someone died, namely those

Lobos animals refusing to let their children survive the adults' suicidal bloody-mindedness.

"Twenty seconds," the skiff pilot announced.

"They're really not going to do it," Wepps said, his tone brittle. Chipper and Ana both glanced at him and then each other. It was unlike the usually taciturn sergeant to allow any emotion to creep into his voice.

"I keep tellin' you all," Ana started, "they're—"

"Pod launch!" the pilot said.

Chipper's gaze snapped forward. A tiny flare—skating away from the corvette at high speed—marked the escape of the bridge pod.

Yes!

"Ohhh-kayyy," Ana murmured.

"Orders from *Assured* to chase and secure that pod," said the pilot.

Wepps put a hand on her shoulder briefly. "Give it a moment."

The Devilfly's missile launch was easier to see than that of the pod. Using a fossil-fuel drive, the missile's exhaust flame formed a pinprick of bright light flashing across kilometers of empty space in mere seconds. The corvette bridge vanished in a bloom of orange-white devastation, the rest of the ship reeling back like a prizefighter recoiling from a heavy punch.

"*Adios*, assholes," Ana whispered.

"Chasing pod," announced the pilot as the skiff wheeled to port, and away from the crippled pirate vessel. "Computer has control."

"To better dodge debris from the corvette," Chipper told Ana.

"Yeah, nice mansplaining, guy," she replied. "We have computers on Xerxian shuttles too, ya know."

He shrugged an apology.

"Does the captain want us to E-V to the pod, or hook it

and drag it back?" Wepps asked the pilot.

"Hook and drag," she replied.

"Question now," Wepps said to his subordinates, "is if it's three kids on board, or ten angry adults."

"BETWEEN THE YEARS 2123 and 2142, both CUSET and the People's Republic of China set up networks of leap-space relay stations. They're still in use today, and we have added to their numbers, of course, as well as repairing many of the older ones."

As he spoke, Pan shuffled back and forth across the end of the Ready Room, behind the captain's chair. The other personnel in the room—Gregory, Grace, and Fowler—listened with interest. *Bountiful*'s Captain Farahaji looked down at them from the wall screen. Chinyama had been left in command on the bridge while Pan became preoccupied with this new development.

A message from beyond human space. Gregory shook his head again in wonder.

The captain continued, "What's not well-publicized is that both superpowers sent automated construction-vessels to extend these networks far beyond the planetary systems they could settle at that time. And until now, we've had no information on where any of them went nor where they created relay stations. These far-flung stations would do what ours do: capture or record signals, compress large amounts of data into more manageable files, and accelerate the transmission of that data to FTL speeds. The general rationale behind building them out there was to provide for the future, to allow for further expansion of both superpowers. That was for the long term, at least."

Pan stopped shuffling and leaned on his backrest.

"In the medium term, they were expected to be useful

in situations such as exploration vessels sending an SOS message or a *we've-found-something-valuable* message back to established space within days, rather than decades ... or centuries."

It was incredible to Gregory that such artifacts still worked after almost a thousand years without maintenance or recharging. Humanity in its golden age before PBT had been more advanced than it was now. *We're still reliant on their tech and their creations!* To confirm he was understanding Pan, he asked, "And this datapacket has come from one of those relay stations?"

"No. This datapacket came *through* one of them. Many of them, rather. It had been picked up by six others beforehand and relayed along the chain. Then one that's parked only six light-years from here detected the leapspace antenna on our signal buoy and fired the message our way."

"The message originated beyond the network?" Farahaji confirmed.

"Correct."

"A human settlement," Fowler said. "Not in the records." He swore colorfully a moment. "Old Chinese. Refugees from PBT. Or an early post-PBT Xerxian mission."

"Again, no. The packet's metadata says it traveled for forty-two years *at* light speed before it hit the first relay station in the chain. From the metadata received, we now know that *that* relay station is two-hundred-six light-years from here."

Fowler pushed back in his chair and Gregory leaned forward in his, both men doing so in shock.

"Two hundred and six ..." Gregory couldn't finish it.

Farahaji said, "The message came from two hundred and forty-eight light-years away. From here. It's in a region we haven't even begun to chart. And neither the audio nor the text is in any human language."

"That we know of," Fowler said, rubbing his chin. "As you say, there were a *lot* of records lost during the dark age. When it comes to the CUSET-PRC period before it, we don't know what we don't know. Especially because good old Earth has forbidden contact with us."

Interesting use of 'us', Gregory thought.

Pan rubbed his chin. "For all we know, this could be a human language. Or, it could be encrypted."

Three people spoke at once ...

Farahaji: "Why bother sending us an encrypted message?"

Fowler: "How do we know it was intended for us?"

Gregory: "Was it actually sent toward human-settled space? Or did we just chance picking it up?"

Pan finally rounded his chair and sat. Answering Gregory, he said, "It was directed at the relay network. Here's how we know that. Colonel Fowler, you said we don't know what we don't know about CUSET and the PRC pre-PBT. But we do know a lot. One of the things we discovered early on and kept confidential was that both superpowers didn't only send out automated ships to plant relay stations. They also sent out unmanned probes with the specific mandate to discover and contact non-human life forms."

"Holy crap," Grace whispered.

"*Idiotas*," Fowler muttered. "What a great idea—attracting the attention of aliens."

"It's obvious what we need to do," Farahaji said. "Ambassador, you need to contact both Fleet Command and whatever ministry would be responsible for this. Suggest a response. Fleet and parliament will both get the alien transmission before your packet gets there. But it'd be good to have your suggestion arrive on its tail. We're the first to hear this. This could be very good for your career." *And ours*, her expression said.

"What suggestion?"

"That will depend on whether we can interpret the alien language quickly," Fowler said.

"Ah, now we have an interesting development there," said Farahaji and reached off-screen for her pad. "My senior comms officer pinged me a moment ago. She has discovered two phrases strewn throughout the audio transmission in three human languages."

"Your comms officer is obviously better than mine," Pan muttered.

"What phrases?" asked Gregory.

The *Bountiful*'s captain read from her pad. "'You come to us. You us friends.' The grammar isn't any better in the Mandarin and Spanish versions."

'You come to us.' God Almighty. Gregory said, "Can we hear that audio, please?"

"We'll have it ready for you in a minute."

"Captain Farahaji, are you saying I should recommend that we go investigate?"

Farahaji just smiled. Pan did not react other than to cross his arms.

"You seriously don't want to?" Fowler asked Gregory.

In truth, he had to admit it's exactly what he wanted to recommend. An alien transmission, proof of a space-aware species capable of responding to human languages in kind ...

Humans had dreamed of meeting such people for more than a millennium. And it was so much more positive than what they were doing here. More exciting.

The only problem would be ...

"What we're doing here," he told them all. "Our bosses aren't just going to let us let Lobos go."

Farahaji shrugged and opened her mouth, but Fowler beat her to it.

"I heard you negotiate for a living, Ambassador. If you want to be on the ships that investigate this transmission, then go to your yacht's comm station, hit record, and start negotiating." He paused a moment. "Sir."

Farahaji closed her mouth. It was what she'd wanted to say—though, doubtless, she'd have found a nicer way to say it.

Looking at the faces around the room—and remembering the fireteams away on mission—Gregory realized he already had the kernel of his argument to the ministry. And in his heart, he knew that this was what he wanted, what he'd always wanted and had given up hoping for.

"I'll see what I can do."

"Be certain," Pan said, uncrossing his arms to lean on the table. "Be very certain. If we go, we don't just have the lives of three fireteams at stake. All of us—"

The Ready Room door shot open. Chief Petty Officer Lindberg stood there, flushed after the short run from the bridge. "You need to come now, Captain."

Onscreen, Farahaji turned aside as someone interrupted her. Her feed cut off abruptly.

Pan was already halfway along the room. "What is it?"

"The pirates, sir." Lindberg stepped aside as he rushed past her, then completed her message to the other men in the room. "They've taken out Fireteam Charlie."

March 16-19, 3014, Old Earth Calendar

14

ONE OF *ASSURED'S* long-range cams had been tracking the pursuit vessel, capturing the episode clearly. The explosion blazed like a short-lived sun, a blue-white flower of radiation springing from the edge of the asteroid field and swelling out into empty space.

Empty except for the *Lioness*.

Standing in his customary place between the two helm consoles, Pan barked, "Repeat! Slow it down!"

Behind him, Systems Chief Lindberg slid her palm around her console. The bridge's forward screen replayed the recording. Gregory put a hand out to steady himself on Lindberg's desk, stomach churning. The eruption flared from a large asteroid on the belt's fringe, gobbling up those around and spreading to encompass the tiny *Lioness* too. Shockwaves rippled through the asteroid field, tossing around boulders as if they were cotton balls. It was the eighth time he'd watched this, and it was no less painful to watch in ultra-slow motion. Gregory dropped his head; he didn't think he could watch it another time.

"A goddamned nuke," Pan cursed. He spun on his heels, glaring at Fowler.

The colonel put a hand to his chest. "I didn't do that."

"But your government sent us here."

"Yours too."

"Good people on that T15, vaporized! A *Bountiful* pilot and masters-at-arms. Four Peacekeepers. A medic."

"Gentlemen," Gregory started.

Fowler leveled a finger at Pan, face darkening. "The other 'good' people you didn't count on that ship were Xerxians!"

Ignoring him and Gregory both, Pan snapped, "You couldn't have warned us they'd have traps like that?"

"If I'd known about it, you think I'd send Dayang and Olesco into one? Your prejudice against us is eating away at your ability to think!"

"*Gentlemen*!" Gregory hollered.

The two men fell silent.

Silent like the rest of the bridge.

Around the room, faces had paled, hands were on stomachs or heads or covering mouths. Some staffers stared at the captain and colonel, aghast at the flare-up between senior officers. Most stared at the freeze-frame onscreen depicting a blue-white phosphorescence occupying space where some of their colleagues had just been. Sintopas's head was swinging from side to side as if he'd started shaking it in disbelief and forgotten to stop. Grace stood near Chinyama, leaning on the balls of her feet, watching the room. Fowler and Pan continued to lock gazes.

No one, it seemed, was taking charge.

So Gregory said, "The skiff with the captured escape pod will be back soon. Commander Chinyama, are you taking charge of onboarding those prisoners? They may be the corvette's children."

"Yes, Ambassador," Chinyama said.

"Captain," Gregory continued. "You and I should return to the Ready Room and relay everything that's happened in the past thirty minutes to Fleet Command and to the ministry. They'll expect recommendations from us."

The captain gave him a terse nod. "I know what my recommendation will be," he muttered as he brushed past Fowler on his way out.

"Colonel," Gregory said, raising his voice to snatch the Xerxian's attention away from Pan. "You are of course welcome to join us. Not only because you're the Xerxian representative here, but because you lost people just now."

Fowler appeared to dial down his anger a notch or two, then gave Gregory a respectful nod. He gestured for the ambassador to lead the way. Grace followed them as far as the Ready Room door and accepted her boss's gesture to wait outside with a grimace of disapproval.

Inside, Pan stood by his chair, leaning over the small tab he always left there. He waited until the door closed behind Fowler before speaking. "The last corvette entered the asteroid belt further along from the blast point. It appeared unharmed, but they better hope their shields are up because there's a hell of a lot of debris coming their way. That bomb really churned up their area of the belt. Our final Mako missile is useless at this point. But *Bountiful* carries a payload of three *Orca* hunter-killer strike-torpedoes along with one moonslayer nuke. Captain Farahaji could pepper the region that corvette went into. It can't move fast enough to get out of the vicinity before *Bountiful* returns here. They used deadly force on us; we return the favor." He lifted his chin, awaiting rebuttal.

"I agree," said Fowler.

"Excellent. Ambassador?"

"As military commander, it's your right to respond as you see fit, of course, Captain. However, my position is still to err on the side of caution, given the potential for terminating the lives of young, unarmed children and infants."

"Lobos arm their children and infants," Fowler said.

"Nevertheless, I recommend seeking express authorization from Fleet Command before taking such action."

Pan gritted his teeth. "The datapack will take hours to reach them. Theirs will take hours to return. That's if they don't spend a day deliberating like they did before sending us here."

"Giving our enemy time we don't want them to have," added Fowler.

Gregory pressed on. "Meantime, we monitor whether any ships leave the asteroid belt by stationing fighters as well as our capital ships at key points around the belt."

"A belt by definition," the Xerxian replied, "is wide and long and deep, meaning they can move within it undetected. We can't cover the entire belt; it circles the star for god's sake. In the time it'll take our message to reach Foucault, and theirs to return, that corvette—and possibly other unknown ships—will be long gone from the section of belt we want to bomb."

"Doesn't *Assured* carry remote-piloted drones?"

Pan said, "No, but *Bountiful* carries five semi-autonomous ones, AI-piloted. I take your point, Ambassador."

Fowler took a step toward him, tone insistent. "Don't take his point, Captain. Don't take his *side*! You know what we have to do."

"Welcome to the Confederation, Colonel. As much as I'd like to bomb the absolute shit out of that belt right now, the ambassador is right: we must consider higher advice before indiscriminately murdering innocents in the heat of the moment."

"My god," Fowler said and ran his hand through his hair. "But if your superiors tell you to do it, it'll be fine? Your double-think is insane."

"Perhaps it is. And perhaps we just don't want to be rogues. I'll send our drones in there as soon as we're close enough, and I'll ask Captain Farahaji to return *post haste.*"

Fowler pressed his lips together into a thin line and folded his arms tightly across his chest.

"Then," said Gregory, "shall we take our seats and start recording? I recommend a joint message with the bare facts bullet-pointed and the three of us each making comments on them."

Pan pulled his chair back and waved the other two into theirs. Fowler dropped into his so hard, the chair gave a small crack of protest.

"Very well," said Pan. "First I'll hail Captain Farahaji in case she'd like to join in. Once we start, we'll let you do the bullet-pointing, Ambassador."

THEY EACH MADE their recommendations in succinct fashion.

On the topic of Clan Lobos's nuking of the *Lioness*, Pan, Fowler, and Farahaji endorsed rattling the pirates loose from the asteroid belt with hunter-killers and the moon-slayer. Gregory appealed for Fleet Command to develop a longer-term solution with the potential for a lower body count—but knowing the political pressure to shift Xerxes into the DCHC, he finished his statement by saying he would "unhappily support" whatever force was authorized.

On the topic of the apparent contact from an advanced and ostensibly friendly non-human civilization, Gregory argued that Fleet Command send replacement vessels to Pollyanna to take over the action. This would release *Assured* and *Bountiful* to investigate the alien signal's source. He argued that the two ships carried an experienced ambassador, two experienced captains, a representative of the Xerxian government, and a complement of experienced and recently-blooded soldiers and naval staff. They also carried versatile support craft such as starfighters, drones, skiffs, and shuttles. If the non-humans intended violence, they would be equipped to repel it. Fowler and Farahaji simply affirmed what he'd said without addition. It was Pan's turn to demur. He said they'd lost half their Peacekeeper and Tactical compliment, and had an existing mission to complete.

"However," he added, "if you're considering Ambassador Gregory's argument in favor of journeying into alien space, then I am willing to go. I will add that it need not be a prolonged mission, but could be a mission of initial contact and reconnaissance, informing a later and longer-term diplomatic initiative."

Gregory asked if anyone wanted to make a final comment. No one did. He closed off the message. Pan sent the file through to Sintopas for compression and dispatch.

Fowler stood. "I need to contact my personnel and inform them of the loss of their comrades." Without waiting for approval, he marched from the room.

Pan said, "Ambassador, if you don't mind, Captain Farahaji and I have some things to discuss."

It was Gregory's turn to stand. "Thank you for your support on the mission to the non-humans, Captain Pan."

"Don't thank me, Ambassador. Because if our superiors approve of us going—and if I don't have opportunity to avenge the lives of my people here—then I certainly won't be thanking you."

15

SINCE THE DCHC NAVY did not employ religious chaplains like some planets' surface forces did, Pan and Farahaji asked Gregory to facilitate the memorial service for the slain crewers and troops from the *Lioness*.

Nine hours after the meeting in the Ready Room and the recording of the joint message, he was sitting alone in his cabin with a coffee in his left hand and a pencil in his right, drafting a plan for the service. Three pieces of crumpled paper lay at the back of his desk, testimony to his first failed starts at the project. He'd never done this before. But his fourth attempt seemed to be working, at least on paper.

There'd been funeral templates and articles on his tablet and in the ship's servers. And he'd been to his fair share of funerals and memorials over the decades. The most difficult of which, of course, had been the one for his wife and daughter. And in the end, that service had been the inspiration for this forthcoming one—the key had been in remembering all the things that had irritated or disappointed him during that insipid, by-the-book ceremony and then thinking of ways to do the opposite for the surviving comrades of these fallen women and men.

Find a close friend for each to say a few words, he was writing when his tab chimed twice from the bed where he'd tossed it. He dropped the pencil, stretched, and scooped up the device. Two icons showed onscreen: one indicating an incoming data file, the other a vid-call request. He tapped for the vid-call.

Pan's face appeared with his own cabin's wall behind him. "Awake?"

"Drafting the memorial service."

"Have you eaten?"

Gregory checked ship time. 2106. Having banned Grace and Piers from interrupting him, he'd missed dinner. "Forgot to. What can I do for you?"

"Didn't want comms sending this via your pilot first. Thought I'd send it straight through to you."

Gregory's eyes shifted to the file icon that had slipped up into the top right of screen. "The file? Fleet Command got back to us?"

"Them and your ministry. I'll let you watch it. Once you have, come eat with me in my cabin. I'll have tea and san choy bow ready."

His image vanished, and the file icon slid to center-screen. Gregory's index finger reached for it, hesitated over it. What would be the official reply? Would they let them go seek out the non-humans? Or would they want them to stay and slaughter humans instead?

His stomach doing somersaults, he tapped.

PAN LAY a plate in front of Gregory and carried his own around his side of the table. The captain's dining table sprouted from a wall by the door, barely big enough to seat the two of them comfortably.

Gregory had never been in the captain's stateroom

before. Surprisingly, it was no larger than his own yacht cabin. Also, it was decorated sparingly: an acoustic guitar in a corner-stand by the bunk, a porcelain Buddha, a watercolor of a green-blue lake and snow-capped mountains, a small bench by the entrance to the washroom holding tea-making paraphernalia, and a polished wood barrel, the contents of which Gregory could only guess at. Also, three family holos—sisters and brother, elderly parents, but no partner and no children.

"This smells amazing," Gregory said. The two lettuce leaves contained a steaming mix of meat and veggies. Hints of ginger and garlic rose to tickle his nose, making his mouth water. There was no cutlery on the table, no chop sticks. Gregory assumed they would be eating by hand.

"Kitchen made it," said Pan, sitting. He poured tea into the delicate china cups and nudged Gregory's toward him. "But it's my father's recipe. Please. Eat."

Gregory got a hand under one of the cool, crisp lettuce leaves and curled it around the fillings like a tortilla. He took a bite. Flavors exploded in his mouth, and he couldn't prevent a moan of pleasure. The contrasting textures and temperatures of clean and cool lettuce leaf and warm, oily meat mixture were as interesting to his palate as the fresh, exotic tastes. It was enough to make him forget why they were meeting—almost.

Pan positioned his teacup so it lined up with the center of his plate and placemat, then turned it one quarter turn. "So. You got your wish. Wish*es*." He lifted a lettuce leaf and took a smaller bite than his guest, munching noisily.

Gregory put his food back on the plate, chewed and swallowed, lifted a napkin to dab at the dribble of juices under his lip. "That's ... one way to look at it."

"First envoy to a new alien species. That will look good on your curriculum vitae."

Gregory took the cup and sipped. He was glad green tea

always came in such tiny vessels. His wife, Tabitha, had loved the beverage and kept a stash, but Gregory had never grown accustomed to it—whenever he'd had it, he'd always felt someone had boiled grass and served him the juice. "Yours too."

Pan nibbled more food and spoke around it. "Not all Maoans are obsessed with status."

"Nor all Caultans."

"Still. You must be pleased."

"I am." *For the opportunity to do something worthwhile for once. And to distance myself from this whole sordid Pollyanna affair.* "You're not looking forward to meeting a race of potentially equal advancement?"

"As a military man, no. It's dangerous. But as a military man, I accept that someone needs to ascertain just how dangerous they are."

"And if they're not dangerous?"

"I can't see how they won't be." He nibbled again, then put the lettuce on the plate. "Every animate creature is dangerous to something else in some way."

"Rabbits?" As soon as he said it, Gregory flashed back to his daughter's hutch back home. Perhaps that was *why* his subconscious chose that particular innocuous animal.

Pan indicated their meal. "Dangerous to lettuce."

"That's a stretch."

Pan acknowledged it with a nod and a faint smile. "If the aliens *aren't* dangerous to us, we'll have the opportunity for trade and so forth. You will have a wonderful time, I'm sure."

"Captain. There's so much darkness in this life. Is it wrong to wish for an exciting new opportunity? A positive new era? Knowing that we are not alone, that we might have peers out there to share and explore this universe with? It excites me. It will shape our species for this new millennium and beyond."

"You say 'share and explore with'; I say 'compete with'." He popped the last of the lettuce leaf in his mouth and turned his plate to bring the second one nearer.

Gregory ate more of his own, thinking through what he should say next. He and Pan had never particularly been at odds, but the captain was understandably upset over the sudden loss of crew.

"I believe I know what I'm doing with the memorial," he said to change subjects.

"That's good."

"I was wondering if you captains could recommend a friend of each of the Confederation personnel. To say a few words about that friend."

"Nice touch. I'm sure we can."

"We lost Sergeant Ouw. Would you like to speak for her?"

"I make it a habit not to be 'friends' with my crew. I'd think the XO might do so. As her direct command. Or perhaps Wepps. Yes, I'll ask Wepps."

"I can ask him, sir. That's my job."

Pan nodded. "Thank you." He ate more san choy bow, face creased in thought. Swallowing, he said, "You'll speak too, I hope."

"Oh, yes. And I won't mince words, I promise you."

"Mince ...?"

"Ah. Sorry. Old Earth expression. I won't be diplomatic, is what I'm saying."

"Oh?"

"Your two ships have a right to anger. I'll acknowledge it. I'll express it. I won't try to reassure them that their comrades have gone to a better place."

"That's fine. Please add that they died as heroes, doing their duty."

"Of course."

"And that they contributed to the future health of the DCHC. Something like that."

Gregory gave him a wry smile. "Sounds like you could deliver this talk yourself."

"No, no. I give orders, not speeches. I think that you're good at comforting people and helping them make sense of things for themselves. Me, I'm good at telling them what to do, what to think, what to say. Not very useful during grief."

"I was also thinking that we could—unofficially—devote our new mission to their memory."

"Yes," Pan murmured after some thought. "Yes, all right." He ate some more, wiped his fingers on a napkin, then raised his teacup in toast. "To our new mission, then."

Gregory raised his. "To our mission."

They sipped and returned to eating in silence. Gregory's thoughts turned to the orders from their bosses back on Foucault's Moon. *Bountiful* would remain behind, keeping up the blockade using its own small ships and drones. The orders for *Assured* were short and simple: *reconnoiter, make contact if you can, leave quickly if you need to, act as you see fit since there will be considerable delays in communications.*

Gregory watched Pan over the lip of his teacup and hoped that the captain was wrong about the danger. That they would not be flying into another ambush.

AFTER THE FOLLOWING evening's memorial service, Gregory escaped the throng of mourners assembled in the Rec Hall as quickly as was decent, making his way to his yacht. Grace accompanied him, complimenting him on the service as they climbed the ramp.

"I only hope it meant something to *them*," he replied.

At the top of the ramp, she caught his arm. "It did, Boss. How many people pumped your hand afterwards, or touched your shoulder—or hugged you!—and you don't think you touched their hearts. Bloody good job, Boss. Bloody good job."

"Thanks, Grace."

She stepped back. "Can I lock you in here?"

"Why?"

"There's a number of wakes kicking off soon. I'd like to go to a couple."

He curled his hand into a thumbs-up. "Take the night off."

"Cheers. And what are you going to do?"

"Oh, I think I'll sink a scotch or three and listen to that non-human transmission a few dozen times."

"Wow. So exciting."

"It is for me."

She pulled her ramp remote from a pocket. "So, get off the ramp, then, if you don't want to be squished by it."

"Good night, Grace."

"Night, Chris."

In his cabin, with the first of the planned scotches in hand, Gregory powered on his tablet. The screen flickered with a dozen message icons, most audio files.

"What in ...?"

He opened one, from a Chief Warrant Officer Nanjillo. A voice with a Polluxan accent thanked him for being real and for giving words to her grief and anger. The next message, a text, told him he'd "done a good job," and that the new mission they were on would take all their minds off this horror. The next one he noticed, another audio file, came from Corporal Chipper Tukimatu ...

"Sir, I can't thank you enough for the way you ran the service. And for letting me speak about Mickey." There was a cough, the message clicked as if edited and Chipper continued. "Mickey Kumar was a damn good man, sir. He didn't deserve to go like that. He had a fiancé and a family and a dog. Oh, crap, I'm rambling. Just wanted to say thank you. Cheers, sir."

Gregory sent a *"You're all very welcome and our fallen will be sorely missed,"* reply to the three he'd opened. Leaving the rest until later, he called up the alien audio signal. He kicked off his shoes. Stretching his legs out on his bed, he raised his glass to his lips and hit the play icon.

The message played once, then again, and then a third time before Gregory stopped it, refilling his glass. The non-human language had apparently been garbled at first because the non-humans hadn't mastered human-compatible files. They'd also based their own file upon software conventions of the 22nd century. The better, cleaned-up audio from *Bountiful* revealed a lilting language punctuated with the occasional glottal click and huff. The huffs at first listen sounded like frustration, as if the speaker were getting their message wrong or becoming irritated with their hardware or something. But the accompanying written report from Farahaji's team indicated their belief that this was part of the language itself.

The report also said that deciphering the signal's written data had not been easy since it was not encrypted in binary fashion. *It seems*, read the report, *to be base-4 and not the now ancient and habitual human preference for off-on binary processing. But there are underlying paradigmatic assumptions on the non-humans' part that we don't understand with so little time to study them. And these make it hard to unravel how their computing works. However, they managed to crack some of* ours, *enough to use our system to record the voice file in three languages and send five images. The images represent star maps. Sadly, there are no images of the aliens themselves.* Gregory couldn't follow much else in the report since it was too technical for him.

"Star maps," he said and put his tab aside. "Pictures of the stars as seen from someone else's sky." He raised his glass to the aliens he had yet to meet. "Here's to your sky. And to us becoming friends under it."

16

CHIPPER WAS SHOOTING HOOPS.

He was the only one in the Rec Hall. Possibly, he thought, because it was midnight. Or possibly because everyone who wasn't asleep was either on duty, or dealing with their grief over lost comrades, or their anxiety—or excitement—over an impending two hundred light-year trip into the unknown. Those not asleep or on duty would no doubt be attending the various wakes in the mess, in the officer's bar, or in the unofficial enlisted bar behind a false wall on hangar deck.

He lined up, propelled the ball in an arc toward the hoop, and held his breath. It hit the ring, ran around it then flew out to the side, bouncing away toward the middle of the vast room. Chipper sighed and leaned his hands on his knees, catching his breath. Sweat soaked his regulation tee. He'd been doing this for two hours now, and though he'd missed more baskets than he'd scored, the activity was the only thing he could think of to deal with his feelings. He wasn't a big drinker. He wasn't the kind to pick arguments with others. He wasn't a journaler, a meditator, or someone who prayed. His only hobby was fishing, which he couldn't do on a starship in leapspace. Basketball was the only thing he could think of to deal with the churning emotion raging through his chest and inside his skull. He still felt devastated and angry in the wake of the deaths of the majority of Red Squad. And to a lesser extent, by the loss of life on the Lobos corvette. He could not get over the fact that those pre-teens—now in custody upon *Bountiful*—had been initially placed up against that blast door as a kind of human shield for the adults.

"How could they put machetes in the hands of *kids*?"

He didn't realize he'd said it out loud until he heard the footsteps approaching, until he turned and locked gazes with Jogianto. She was dressed like him: shorts, an *Assured* t-shirt, sneakers. She held his basketball. She said, "Those 'kids' *wanted* to kill us. They were probably already blooded. Hell, they were probably at *Heaven's Gate*. Someone was gonna have to stop 'em one day. We're just the lucky fools who got to do it." She tossed him the ball—hard! He caught it against his chest. "At least they'll live to be rehabbed."

"Not like the others on that bridge."

"See, regret's not real useful for us warriors, dude. Almost as pointless as morals. Because regret makes you sick over things you can't change. And morals ain't real clear." She came up close, close enough that she was looking up at him, shaking her head. She reached out and tapped his sternum and then her own. "You say 'right' but I think 'safe'. A few of them dying kept us safe. It made *space* safe for all the rich folk who wanna go scootin' around on their cruise ships in future. I'd like to tell you something that will make you feel better—"

He snorted. Empathy was not exactly any Tactical's strong suit, especially not this one.

"Believe it or not," she said, "I would. You did good on that corvette. *You did what they pay you for*. We all did. But, yeah, those Lobos assfaces put weapons in the hands of kids and indoctrinated them to kill anyone not in their clan. On *Heaven's Gate*, that included other kids, you know. Kids who *had* morals and nice lives, who didn't go around hurting other people. You and I are just the luckless bastards sent over to capture them. And shit went bad. Shit usually does, you know."

"So I'm learning."

"The best way to get over shit happenin' ain't by shootin' baskets. You need a couple of slugs of moonshine inside you, guy. There's a great setup on hangar deck. I'll pay."

"I'll pass."

"My God, you *are* a lily, ain't ya? Eesh." She stepped back and checked over her shoulder, suddenly edgy. "Well, listen, if you're not gonna accept a favor from me, maybe you can do one *for* me."

He raised his eyebrows in surprise. What in the world could she want?

"I know you Peacers got another code to send messages out, since they don't know when we're coming back. That's two in the last week. One for family, one for your sweethearts, I'm guessing?" She waited until he nodded. "So you used both?"

He shook his head. "Used one. Why?"

"One? Don't have family or don't have a sweetheart?"

"None of your business."

"Don't have a sweetheart. Right. Listen, I'll pay you for your second code."

This time, Chipper took a step back, his frown deepening. "What? Why? You got your own code."

"Nope. We didn't. We were allowed to receive messages. But Fowler doesn't trust us enough to let us send any."

"That's stupid."

"Stupid's one word for it. He thinks we'll either spill it about the aliens—out of spite for not staying around to avenge our lost brothers, or because we think our opposition party on Xerxes will pay us well for it."

"He told you that?"

She made a dismissive noise. "In his mind, he has no reason not to. We're not as ... diplomatic ... as you Confeds."

"That's for sure. He knows we have AI monitoring our messages during compression, yeah? They'd know if you were sending anything unrighteous, and they'd suspend it and flag it."

"I know that. But tell Fowler that. He obviously doesn't trust your AI to do that properly."

There came a pause while all of what she'd said rattled around inside Chipper's mind, along with the jumble of thoughts and emotions already in there from the past week's madness.

Eventually, she cleared her throat and jerked her head toward the callbooths. "So ...?"

He grit his teeth. "I dunno. Who you sending it to?"

She pulled her head back in a *you kidding me?* pose. "None of your business."

"Touché."

"Listen, you do this for me, I owe you. Big time."

"You gotta know I could get in a lot of trouble for this." *And you could be doing something wrong that I want no part in.*

"We're teammates, aren't we? Alpha team. Roo roo ra ra."

"You know it doesn't work like that. Xerxes isn't part of the Confederation yet. You technically work for a foreign power."

"I need this, guy."

"And I need to do the right thing."

"There's that word again. Right. How about what's right for me?"

"We talking philosophy now?" he asked.

She clenched her fist and half-turned, jaw working. Something was eating at her. And that was a feeling he recognized and understood.

"Look. Ana."

"Jogianto."

"Ana's easier."

She snorted a reluctant laugh.

He said, "I might still need that second code myself."

"There's no girlfriend," she said, eyes on the booth.

Her certainty about his single status rankled. More than a little. "How do you know?"

"Because you're so defensive and private about it. If you had a special someone, you wouldn't care what I thought."

"And you're not being secretive?"

Her fists curled tighter. She let out a small growl, took a deep breath, and turned back. "My parents," she said. "Gotta message my parents."

He gave her a little headshake. "Why not just tell me that?"

"It's ... complicated. You don't know our culture. You don't know me and my life. My parents, they're ... Well, let's say there's a reason I don't want Fowler knowing I contacted them."

He could have asked why not, but refrained since she seemed genuinely bent up over it. Then again, she could just be a darn good actor. "Our comms will know you contacted them."

"I've read the policies. Your comms guys don't eavesdrop on messages. They only read-watch-listen if the AI flags it. I'll be sending some 'friends' on Foucault a happy message."

Coded? Sheesh, I am an idiot.

Chipper bounced the basketball a couple of times. Why couldn't life—why couldn't one night—be as simple as standing here shooting hoops and not having to make a decision?

"Your parents, you say."

Jogianto pursed her lips and gave an unhappy nod.

"My problem is still that, tomorrow, my bosses could be coming at me asking why I let a spy use my account to slip a datapack out."

"You think I'm a spy."

"You just said I don't know you. I don't. And you might think I'm a dumbass, but actually I'm not." *Aren't you?*

"Never said you were a dumbass."

"Actually, ya did. Few days back."

"Maybe once, then."

"You argue about calling me a dumbass but you're not arguing about being a spy."

"We're all spies in some way, idiot—"

"Idiot's as bad as dumbass."

"—but it's *my* people I'm keepin' this from, not yours."

"You're spying on your own people? So you work for another faction?"

"I'm Sevens straight up. My whole career." She said it with her chin up as if inviting challenge. It sounded practiced, this statement. A creed to keep her own superiors off her back. There was definitely something she wasn't saying.

"You weren't born that way, though? You came from another faction?"

She swore and half-turned again, lashing out a punch at thin air. "Stop askin' me questions. Just answer one. Will you help me?"

Help people whenever you can, however you can, Son. His father's creed this time. One that Chipper happened to believe in too.

"I want to. I do, Ana. But I need more here."

Her lips pursed again. Chewing the inside of her cheek, she wrestled with something. After a minute, she checked the doorway for newcomers, then said, "My parents are enemies of the Sevens. They fled Xerxes in a purge twelve years ago when I was thirteen. If the party knew I was in contact ..." She drew a finger across her throat.

"The party would actually kill you?"

"I'd disappear. Hopefully, they'd kill me quick."

"The party don't suspect you're in contact?"

"God, I hope not."

"Wait. Your parents dumped you and ran? At age thirteen?"

She blew out a breath. "Yeah. Left me with my uncle. He's Sevens party to his DNA. Me, I've been loyal to 'em. But ... you know ... those two are my parents."

"How did they get back in touch with you? When?"

"Enough questions, guy. You helping or not?"

Chipper put his hands over his face and rubbed at his eyes. He was probably about to land himself in a world of trouble. "Dang," he said. "I guess so."

Jogianto punched the air again but this time in relief. "Yes!" She made an *after-you* gesture to the booths. "Can you speak the code in for me?"

"One condition. Door open. I get to listen."

Her relief turned sour, but she accepted it with a grimace. "You also get to watch the hall door in case anyone comes in."

"I'll stand in front of the booth. No one will see you past me."

She looked him over, up and down and side to side. "Probably not, big guy. Probably not. All right, let's get this over."

ONCE HER MESSAGE was recorded and sent, Ana leaned her elbows on the small callbooth shelf, her chin on her fists. The message had been a simple one, the coded phrases telling her parents to be patient, that things were moving fast now, that she expected to see them inside of a standard year. The last bit had been a lie because who the hell knew when she'd be seeing them. She wondered again if she even wanted to see them. Ever.

Behind her, Chipper cleared his throat gently. "Probably should come outta there now."

"Yeah," she sighed, rising. He stepped away to let her out. "Probably sounded weird to you, huh?"

"The whole boring message to some farmer friends? Nah, it was fascinating. I just gotta hope you didn't do something that'll land me in prison."

"I didn't, on my honor. And before you say anything, some Xerxians *do* have honor."

"I wasn't gonna say you don't."

"Mm. Do you realize how much *I* have to trust *you* here? Not to tell Fowler?"

"You can trust me."

She snatched the ball from him, bounced it a couple of times, then tossed it hard into his midriff. He caught it with an *Ooff!*

"You did do me a rich one, guy, but I gotta tell you ... you breathe a word of it to anyone—anyone—I'll castrate you. Slowly."

"It's always an incredible pleasure hanging out with you, Ana."

"Jogianto."

He threw the ball over her head to bounce away toward a corner of the hall. "Whatever. You said you owe me a favor? How about you start by buying me that drink."

Fair enough, she thought. *As long as he's not getting ideas. Just a drink, dumbass, that's all.*

"Most righteous thing I've ever heard you say, Corporal. Lead the way to hangar deck."

GENTLE MUSIC WAFTED from the speakers in the yacht's lounge. Acoustic guitar, soft electronic percussion, and a gravelly voice serenading in Spanish. It was after midnight shiptime, and Chris Gregory should have long since gone to bed. Instead, he folded his long legs under him and sipped at his martini. Piers was asleep in his cabin. Grace was out at the officer's bar. Gregory had peace. Quiet. A civilized drink. Exactly what the doctor ordered.

"Happy new day, boss man!"

Grace marched in, threw herself onto the couch opposite his, and reached for the music remote. "What's this crap?" She flicked through several options before settling on Polluxan manic-jazz. The rapid offbeat pounding and distorted horn stabs had Gregory wincing within the first three bars.

"It *was* relaxing," he muttered.

"That's relaxing," she said, nodding at his drink. "Mind if I get one?"

"Weren't you just drinking at the officer's mess?"

"I have room for exactly one more. And they're free here."

"Well, make yourself at home. Oh, that's right, you already did."

She laughed at that and launched from the chair toward the drinks station. Where the hell did she get her energy from? he wondered. She was only a year younger than him, spent all her on-duty hours in complete hypervigilance, had been awake as long as he had, if not longer, and it was now a little after one in the morning. Did she never tire?

Back in her adopted spot on the couch, she sipped the

froth atop a Centauran *Forest Fruits* ale and smacked her lips. "We're off to see the wizard, huh?"

"We're *what*?"

"Oh. Sorry. Modernist Era reference. I'm a fan of 20th century media, as you know."

"I do know that, and I still don't understand the reference. And—" he raised a hand to forestall her explanation. "—I don't want to understand it."

"Well, you did say 'what'. I was answering you."

"I take it back."

"You take back your 'what'?"

"I do."

"Nice negotiations there, Ambassador."

"I know when to avoid pointless conversational culs-de-sac."

Grace gulped ale and smacked her lips again. "God, that's good. Way better than the weak swill they serve in the O-club."

"You're welcome."

"So, conversation. All people are talking about around the ship is what they think we'll encounter when we get there."

"There?"

"The non-humans' system."

"Mmm."

"What's your take, Boss? Whatcha think we'll find?"

He lifted his martini, said, "Wonders," and sipped.

Grace's drink froze halfway back to her mouth. "Wonders. Wow."

"You object to that word?"

She gulped ale and set the half-empty glass down. "It's kind of a childish word. Maybe not childish. Just ... it's a little optimistic."

"I shouldn't be optimistic?"

She made a *not sure* face.

"I shouldn't be excited about this opportunity? This is an incredible moment."

"I get that. It is. But, you know, I'm paid to think about the dangers. The things that might go wrong."

"You sound like Pan."

She aimed a finger at him, grinning. "Well, you're acting like *Peter* Pan."

"And who on Foucault is that? Wait. Don't tell me. Another 20th-C reference."

She waggled her brows. "Means you're acting like the eternal child. Like everything's an adventure."

He found himself growing serious at that. "Grace, nothing in my life has been an adventure. Not for thirty years. Well, maybe parenthood was. But, if I'm acting like a Catholic kid at Christmas again, then let me have my moment."

Her face softened. "Sure, Chris. I can give you that." She tossed the remote to land beside him, then sculled the rest of her ale. And burped long and loud. "And with that, I'm done for the day and for the night. Play whatever crap music you want. Fantasize about your wonders and your adventure as much as you want. Drink as many of them martinis as you want. Coz seriously, you've earned it, Boss. You've earned it."

He waved her a good night and switched the music back, settled down again, and sipped more booze.

Fantasize, he thought. *Adventures. Well, why not? God, for the first time in forever, I have hope. I can actually be the diplomat I originally wanted to be.*

His thoughts turned a little sour at that last thought. It was pride, this desire to be and do something special, something memorable across the ages.

Sure, it is, Sourpuss, he heard Tabitha say. He heard it as clearly as if his wife were sitting there beside him, murmuring it to him. For a half second, he felt the brush of her hand on his. *Be happy for once in your damned life; be glad ... be optimistic.*

And the way he would have a few years ago, he murmured aloud to her, "You're right, hon. As usual."

This *was* an adventure. This *was* a great moment. And if he was remembered for driving it toward healthy and noble outcomes, then what was so wrong with that?

"Besides, hon," he said aloud again, "Grace told me I should spend more time with friends. Maybe a new friend or two is exactly what I'll encounter there."

A FLIGHT MECHANIC was leaning against the personnel ferry, pretending to polish a loose battery contact. Ana and Chipper both nodded to him. As the current lookout for *Assured*'s unofficial bar for enlisted personnel, he gave them a perfunctory once-over, then jerked his head toward the hidden entrance behind the stack of munitions crates. Ana and Chipper swung that way.

Inside, the small cargo compartment had been rearranged with six crates for tables, and smaller crates for chairs. A spare skiff inner-hull panel formed a bar, propped on more crates. Only six crewers sat at the tables, less than Ana expected: a pair of women chatting quietly, and a group of four intent poker players. No one manned the bar. An old-fashioned analog clock showed it was a few minutes after 0100.

She said to Chipper, "Pick a poison. I'm told they got homemade gin or rerouted scotch, beers, and red wine."

"Beer," he said. He didn't like any of the others.

"Good choice." She pointed at a makeshift table down at the back near the poker players. Proximity to them would mean they wouldn't think she and the big oaf were on a date; it would also discourage Chipper from trying anything if *he* thought they were. He trudged that way while she strode to the "bar." One of the chatting women rose and served her, scanning her retina implant to pay the bill.

A minute later, carrying four glasses, Ana glanced at the head comms officer, Sintopas, as he whooped loud and long, slapping the poker table. The heavily sweating man had placed himself in the seat in the corner of the room as if it afforded a commanding position. He scraped a pile of chips toward him, taunting the others. She peeked over a crewer's shoulder as they collected cards into a deck and started to shuffle. Looked like Sintopas was doing well out of the rest of them; his mountain of chips dwarfed theirs. She was sorely tempted to buy in and teach the asshole a lesson or two. Maybe after little Chipper went to bed ...

Chipper thanked her as he took his two beers from her hands. She put her scotch on the table and sampled her gin as she sat. "Ugh. Tastes like window cleaner." But she drank some more.

Chipper leaned closer, not drinking yet. "I ... I'm sorry things are the way they are. You know. With your parents."

She blew a raspberry, watching the woman near them deal cards. "You know, you're what they call in the stories a Nice Guy."

"Thanks," Chipper replied.

"Wasn't a compliment."

He scratched his nose. "It wasn't?"

"Drink your beer, *pare*," she said, using the Filipino term for 'pal'. It felt a little nicer now than some of the other terms she had been using for him.

He drank, nose wrinkling at it.

"You no like?"

"Prefer fruit juice," he said. "But it's fine. Thanks."

"Stop thanking me. Like you said, this is me repaying a favor."

"This is all I get in repayment? A couple of beers?"

She flashed him a warning look. "Better keep those thoughts clean, *pare*."

He flushed and his discomfort made her smile. "Oh! I didn't mean ..." He dropped his gaze, gulping beer.

"Relax, guy. Relax. Relaxing is kinda what this place is for." She jerked her head toward the game beside them, the men and women checking their cards and sizing each other up. "But I mean it about keeping your thoughts clean."

"Got it. Trust me. I am."

"Good man." She drained her remaining gin, grimaced, then followed it immediately with scotch to chase away the aftertaste. "Dunno what I was thinking trying that garbage. Whoever made it needs to be vented out the airlock."

Chipper was scoping the game now, neck craned to watch the bets. He seemed a lot like a big kid when he wasn't working. Innocent somehow ... harmless. His demeanor completely belied the skill he showed as a warrior.

"Why'd you join the Peacers?" she asked. "Like, you're good at it and all. But it seems like the wrong job for a Nice Guy."

He shrugged without looking away from the game. "It was either that or be a cop on Oceana. But nothing ever happens there, so I thought I'd try something more interesting. You know, see the stars."

"And the money's good?"

His smile returned, the one she'd only seen rarely and not for some time. It suited him, like his face had evolved specifically to display happiness. She envied that, she realized; her own face was no doubt the exact opposite.

He said, "Pretty good, yeah."

"You can buy the next drinks, then."

"Sure."

"I'm joking again, *pare*. Anything you want here, it's on me."

"I think these will be enough." He sipped at the beer and watched her hand turning her glass around.

"Was *Assured* your first posting?" she asked.

"Nah. Second, after the academy. I was with a disaster relief regiment for the first few years. Helping people after floods and wildfires and earthquakes and stuff."

"Sounds like a hoot."

"It was."

"That was sarcasm."

"Oh. Well, I enjoyed that anyway. Truth."

"And then you ended up on *Assured*."

"Yep. Thought it would be a nice quiet change for a couple of years." His expression captured the irony of that presumption.

"Didn't expect to get the job helping the evil Xerxians clean up their mess, uh?"

"Definitely not."

"So you think we're evil?"

He grinned again. "Some of you, yeah. That Hecate. Wow."

She raised her glass to him. "Yeah. Wow, all right. So would you have transferred here if you'd known all this was coming?"

He grew gloomy again, gaze dropping to his beer glass. "Killing people? No. No way."

"See, like I said, Nice Guy. The disaster relief makes a lot more sense for someone like you." He gave her another shrug at that. She sipped her drink, then thought, to hell with sipping, and swallowed the whole thing. The new scotch-burn was welcome, as was the beginnings of a slight head spin. Chipper just sipped at his.

"You send much of your salary back to your parents?"

"About half."

"Half. Sheesh. Well," she raised her empty glass in toast, "bending over backwards for your parents, that I get."

"Oh, no, they're not so bad. Oceana's just a pretty poor place, that's all."

"And us Xerxians certainly didn't help, dropping in for a past couple hundred years to sophie off your resources."

"Sophie?"

"Xerxian expression. Refers back to one of the people who got our civilization back on its feet by stealing from weaker people to build a stronger foundation for her own faction."

"Nice expression."

Ana tilted her glass and licked at the surviving drops of whiskey. "Xerxian," she said.

An eruption of groans and a winning cackle came from the poker table. Sintopas had won again. The last dealer shot to her feet and stomped away, muttering curses.

Ana said, "Anyway, your parents can't be that nice. They did call you Chipper, after all."

"Nah, some of the guys in basic gave me that name. It stuck. It's not so bad, actually."

Not so bad, she thought. Chipper had broken eye contact again, fidgeting with his glass. It looked to her like there was *something* bad he was avoiding here. Something to do with his name. And that was interesting. "They did, huh? Why that name? Why not ... I dunno ... why not Big Boy or Bear Whale?"

"Well, some of them who were from Centauri joked I'm as big as a wood chipper. Whatever that is. Still don't know. And the others liked the name coz I'm always chipper. Or try to be."

"You're always ...?"

"Chipper. Oh, you don't have that word on Xerxes either? Yeah, I'd never heard it before. It's like an old Earth word for *cheerful*." He waggled one hand and exaggerated a wide smile. "The cheerful soldier, that's me."

"Right. Like you've been real cheerful the whole time I've known you. That was sarcasm again, by the way."

"Yeah, I got it that time. And yeah, it hasn't been a great few weeks."

"But, still, *Chipper*? And you're owning it? It's a weird name."

"Let's forget that. I'll get you your next drink, ey?"

"More drinks can wait," she said, motioning him back into his seat. "I'm not giving up on this Chipper thing. What's your real name?"

His blushing deepened. "My real name? Tukimatu."

"Not your surname. I got that from the roster already. Your first name."

"Sheesh. Do I have to?"

"With this level of embarrassment, hell yes you have to. Spill it. What. Is. Your. Name."

Chipper's big frame bowed under the pressure, so much that his forehead sank toward the table top. When he first said the name, it was with such a quiet voice that Ana couldn't make it out over the hubbub from the poker table.

"Say again?"

He swallowed and glanced around them, then repeated it in a slightly louder voice. "Chippington."

"... *Chippington*?"

A sigh. A great, heaving sigh. A sigh that sounded a lot like the word *Yeahhhhh*.

"Your parents called you Chippington."

"Yeah."

"Did they hate you?"

"Sometimes I reckon they did."

"No, they didn't."

"No. They didn't."

"So. Were they brain-damaged?"

"No. Not especially."

"Is Chippington the name of someone famous on Oceana?"

"Nope."

"Someone from old Earth history?"

"Nope."

"Well, what does it mean?"

"I think they made it up."

"They made it up."

"I think, yeah."

"They never told you why they named you Chippington?"

His eyes slid to the poker game and back. "Can you ... please can you stop saying it?"

"Okay, but they never explained?"

"No."

"You never thought to ask them, 'Why the hell did you give me such a dumbass name?'"

"I asked. They avoided it."

"Then *why*? What's your guess?"

"I reckon they just wanted me to sound important. Like maybe if they gave me a rich-sounding name, I might turn out rich. Or a smart-sounding name, I might turn out smart."

There was an insult just begging to be made here, but she resisted. The poor dude really was suffering. She relented.

"Tell ya what, cheerful soldier. With history like this, you deserve a break." She stood. "You wanna try the whiskey?"

"Oh. No thanks. These are fine."

"Your loss." She pivoted and strode toward the bar, her face breaking into a grin now that he couldn't see it.

Chippington! And I thought I *had a bad childhood.*

INTERLUDE

Buoun

When the Domain Space mining cooperative had placed a datum station on the small asteroid, they had chosen to set it hovering eight arm's-lengths above the rock's knobby surface and tethered in place by a solid climbing tube. Buoun had never figured out why.

For the past ninety-something cycles now, the station had doubled as his quarters and workspace. It was furnished in the four corners respectively by bath-commode-stall, cot, computer work station, and cupboard-drawers-foodcooler unit. The middle of the roof held the hatch to where shuttles docked to replenish his supplies, to where one such shuttle would—in an orbit or two—take him on to his next assignment. The middle of the floor held the hatch for the climbing tube by which Buoun could traverse "up" and "down" between the slowly spinning rock and the datum station.

Whenever he was "down" there, he would take his measurements dressed in his envirosuit, sometimes converse with the three miners working its interior, occasionally travel to their *quarters bolted to the far side of the rock, before climbing back "up" to the datum center. These excursions into the asteroid provided welcome breaks from the confines of the little cube where Buoun spent most of his time. The box was the size of his bathroom back in the Human Exhibition and Research Facility.*

Returning to it this morning, climbing the tube with his envirosuit still on, Buoun felt the familiar constriction around his hearts, the feeling that he was about to reenter a prison cell.

This place *is* a prison for me, *he told himself.* Without a shuttle of my own, there is no way for me to leave without them willing it. They might leave me here forever! *Reaching the hatch, he pushed the button to repressurize both the tube and the datum center beyond it.* My body will be discarded into space to make way for a new worker, some other poor exile who has fallen into disgrace.

When pressurization was complete, a ring of blue light pulsed on the wall around a protruding button. Buoun slapped the button. The hatch irised open. Buoun climbed inside.

As he straightened, he gasped.

He was not alone.

Tapping the control on his suit made his helmet retract. He sucked in a lungful of recycled air, rich with the smells of old farts and the worm-sausage he had cooked for breakfast. With such a noble person standing opposite him, the stink caused him a twinge of embarrassment.

"Councillor Pi'yow't!" he said, hearing the rusty quality of his own voice. It had been four cycles since he had spoken aloud to anyone. "To what do I owe this honor?"

Auxiliary Councillor Pi was a finger taller than him, straight-backed and fuller-figured —as befitted someone younger and better nourished. Her trousers and tunic were of the practical type worn by leaders when traveling, light in color and fabric, missing a ceremonial short-robe's badges of office but keeping the brightly colored brocades of her rank. She stood with her back to the work station, hands clasped at her belly, returning Buoun's stare with a flat expression. The last time he had seen her had been the one time she'd visited him at the Facility. Newly appointed as Commissioner for Foreign and Diplomatic Issues, she had delivered the news of its closure and his impending reassignment in person. She had done it looking and sounding as emotionless as she did now ...

"Excellency Mu'ulkiinaat't would address you."

"He would?" Buoun leaned to the side, trying to see past her to the communications unit. No flashing lights anywhere there. "Shall I connect to—?"

Pi cut him off with a swipe of her hand, then jerked up her chin toward the upper hatch.

Buoun felt his throat and cheeks flush with color. "Up there?" The Grand Councillor awaited him in Pi's shuttle? The Grand Councillor had come to visit Buoun?! Here?!

Pi pressed the control for the upper hatch, causing it to slide aside and the lift tube to lower down to floor level. The tube was closed in on her side, open on Buoun's, large enough to transport crates of supplies, just large enough for two people to squeeze inside. From the other side of it, Pi's disembodied voice spoke again.

"You go up first, Buoun. I'll come up after you."

The Grand Councillor wore a short-robe colored the fiery orange of official duty. He also wore an expression of boredom, as though meeting with Buoun was some tedium he was forced to attend to.

Which is ridiculous, *Buoun thought as he adopted a deferential pose and appropriate distance on the opposite side of the shuttle cabin.* He is the one who called this meeting, who traveled out here to see me.

Councillor Naat was playing with his wristwrap, not looking at Buoun. His only acknowledgement of Buoun's presence had been to tell the shuttle's warrior-pilot not to bother searching him. That and a slight flaring of his nostrils at whatever stench Buoun had brought aboard.

More to prompt action than out of genuine respect, Buoun briefly covered his eyes with the palm of his left hand in acknowledgement of Naat's rank, his age and his person. "Tlela-huy, Shining One."

Naat grunted while the floor between them hummed with the rising of the tube bearing Pi. "Dispense with the formalities. I have a question for you."

He was forced to pause as the tube appeared between them, and Pi stepped out on Buoun's side. The tube retracted to its fitting above the datum center, and Pi moved around to stand by Naat.

A moment of silence passed, then Buoun said, "You said you had a question, Shining One."

Naat flicked an irritated glance at Pi, and it was she who took over the talking. "His Excellency's question is: Do you still speak Human, Buoun?"

"Nnnn," Buoun said, hedging so he had time to compose a correct response that would not sound disrespectful. "Just as we have many languages, the Humans also have many languages. So to ask—"

Pi cut him short with a curt gesture.

Buoun swallowed and stopped trying to correct his seniors. Answering the question, he said, "The Human languages I speak are called English, Guānhuà, Hindi, Nihongo, Hangul *and* Español. *I have practiced them every cycle for the past ..." He almost said* sixty orbits *but refrained —the length of time underlined his humiliation, his official status as a fool.*

Naat's rheumy eyes caught his own for brief moment, before sliding past to lock onto some other object over his shoulder. But it was enough to cause astonishment and joy to swell within him. There had been validation in that brief acknowledgement; there had been restoration of status.

What could possibly—? *he began to wonder.*

"Buoun," Pi said. "It is very good that you did so. Is there anything you need from your quarters below us?"

"Need?"

"You are coming with us."

In astonishment, Buoun forgot his manners and gasped, "Come? Come where?"

"You will be fully briefed aboard the Grand Councillor's personal ship."

"Personal ..."

"Gather your belongings and be quick about it," Pi said. "Your shame has ended."

She made a gesture of deference toward Naat, inviting the Grand Councillor to speak again in that dust-dry voice of his.

And he did. "We have visitors, Buoun," he said. "And you are the one to speak with them."

March 29–April 4, 3014, Old Earth Calendar

17

CHRIS GREGORY HAD BEEN NOTIFIED that *Assured* would emerge from leapspace at the emergence point tagged by the original probe—and that this would happen on Wednesday March 29, 3014 at 0511 hours. At 0500, he and Grace were seated in the captain's Ready Room, as invited, nursing mugs of strong Centauran tea and Gregory's personal tablet. Two stewards brought them a breakfast of ham steaks, scrambled eggs, mushrooms, and Oceanean seagrass. The cabin screen had split into two feeds, one from the ship's forward camera, the other from the side of the bridge. They had just started on their big breakfast when a chime sounded on the bridge and a helmsman called, "Exiting leapspace in three, two, one."

Gregory noticed that Grace braced herself slightly. But nothing happened. The transition in or out of leapspace was never accompanied by any physical sensation, and Gregory had long ago lost any sense of its novelty.

This time however, he put down his fork with his stomach churning with an almost child-at-Christmas excitement. He found himself leaning toward the wallscreen as the left side changed from gray static to depicting normal space ahead of the ship.

"We're here," he said to Grace. For once she returned his grin.

"Someone else's star system."

"Exactly. Someone else's home." He pointed at a dot of light onscreen, a dot slightly larger than the others. "Someone else's sun."

Pan's voice came from the wallscreen, issuing orders and questions to the bridge crew. Once more, Gregory heard Chinyama calling for an FTL-signal buoy to be launched to ensure a comms connection with the far-distant human network of buoys and signal stations.

He pushed aside the barely-touched breakfast and dragged his tablet over. Grace brought her chair closer to him and to it. They spent the next hour reading the data summaries that scrolled across it, fed directly from bridge stations, with ears cocked to the conversations on the bridge.

The new star system had twelve planets and a thin asteroid belt between planets VIII and IX. The home world, the only habitable planet, was fourth from the star. And G2V yellow dwarf could have been Earth's sun's twin. Entering the system from below the orbital plane, *Assured* stayed "down" there, taking their time as they passed beneath planet VII and angled toward planet IV.

At 0612, Sintopas onscreen announced, "Radio chatter increasing. None seems directed at us as yet. Hold that ... Just received signal ping from original probe."

Also onscreen, Pan said, "We've woken it up again."

"Look at this," Gregory said, pointing to and freezing one of the report streams on his tab. Grace grunted as she read it. Artifacts abounded around the asteroid belt, around the moons of the outer planets, in orbit around planets VI and VII, and around several clusters of rogue asteroids.

"Well-established space civ, then," Grace hummed.

Pan asked Sintopas, "Can AI decode any of that comms chatter?"

"No yet, sir," came the reply. "It does tell me that sixteen of these streams are in the same dialect or language as the message we intercepted. They are using familiar terms and grammar. We don't have enough to extrapolate a full meaning."

"I wonder when we'll be noticed," Gregory murmured.

At 1017, he got his answer.

Sintopas called across the bridge, "We've been hailed! Laser-signal has been timed perfectly to intercept our path. Putting onscreen now."

Gregory and Grace didn't need to squint at the scene on the wallscreen; the hail was conveyed to a corner window on Gregory's tab.

"It's English," he and Pan said simultaneously. The message welcomed them and invited them to change course toward the message's source—a ship half *Assured*'s size and escorted by five smaller craft the size of skiffs or fighter-interceptors. It then repeated in Mandarin and then in Spanish, Japanese, Hindi, and Korean.

"Korean? Japanese?" Grace blinked at Gregory. "May as well be Latin."

"Pretty popular languages at the time the probe was sent."

"Ambassador to bridge," Pan said, glancing into the camera.

"Time for the big show," Gregory said and preceded Grace out of the room and onto the bridge.

"When we're a thousand klicks away, slow to 0.09," Pan was ordering the helm as they entered. "Shields and weapons ready, but keep them powered down for now." He turned to Gregory. "Ambassador, good morning. Ready for this?"

"As I'll ever be. How long until we near their ship?"

"Ships," Pan corrected. "Pretty sure they have a group of small fighters escorting the bigger one. Three hours. Taking it slow, so as not to spook them."

"Sounds wise. Have we messaged them back?"

"Thought you might like that honor."

Gregory's answer was immediate. Turning to Sintopas, he said, "Reply message: We're approaching and intend no harm. We will stop the ship one hundred kilometers from theirs." He checked that with Pan who shrugged a *Fine with me.* "We'd love to open a dialogue."

"They'll understand all that?" Chinyama asked him.

"That probe's been here a long time. They've had plenty of time to learn our languages—although we should probably send them up-to-date dictionaries in English, Mandarin and Spanish."

"Right then. Sintopas, you got all that?"

"Yes, sir."

"Sent it?"

"Ready to."

"Then do as the man says. Let our hosts know we're coming over to say hi." To Gregory he added, "Let's hope they're friendly."

BRADLEY "WIDOWMAKER" Bradstock had been the first of the other Peacers to join Chipper in his mess booth. That had been at 0505, just before *Assured* dropped out of leapspace. He must have noticed Chipper hadn't made himself coffee, because he brought a second mug with him when he sat, pushing it across the table with a grunt in place of a *Good Morning*.

With an established reputation as a man of few words, Widowmaker had been even less communicative since the rest of his Peacekeeper team—who'd composed most of

Fireteam Charlie—had perished instantaneously in nuclear fire at Pollyanna. The two men sat silently side by side in their booth, watching the feed from the ship's forward cam on the screen shift from gray static to the black velvet of normal space, and glancing out the viewport beside them at the same void. Occasional snippets of information scrolled along the bottom of the mess screen: *Assured* had arrived inside the system's "Oort cloud," but had to course correct twice in the first ten minutes to avoid local comets; the system had twelve planets and one asteroid belt; comms traffic in alien languages was abundant; a single moving vessel had been identified one billion kilometers away, possibly a gigantic ore freighter ...

Stines and Westermann arrived at 0646, piling their breakfast trays high. Westermann still limped, but her leg was getting stronger all the time. The two newcomers brought lively conversation and conjecture to the table. And soon after, the mess began to fill with other curious off-duty crewers, hungry for information along with breakfast, their eyes glued to the screen above the serving counter.

"Not eating breakfast?" Westermann asked Chipper as she finished the final bite of hers.

"I will soon."

"Normally, I find half the servery empty when you get here first," she laughed.

Stines chuckled at that.

"You sick or something?" Westermann continued.

"I'm excited," he replied with a grin. "It's pretty zing, you know, being the first in an alien system."

"Oh, really?" she teased him. "Pretty *zing*, huh? What are you, a Thesian thud-poet now?"

Stines laughed harder. Widowmaker grunted acknowledgment of Westermann scoring a point on Chipper. Chipper poked out his tongue.

"I bet 100 francs that zing-boy here won't just be the

first Peacer to land on the alien planet," Stines chipped in. "He'll be the first to fall in love with an alien gal."

Westermann cackled at that. Widowmaker grunted again.

Chipper noticed Hecate, Manolo, and Umbrano collecting their meal then. They all shot glances at a side table, before heading for a table in back. Hunched over the side table was Jogianto. He hadn't seen her come in. Like Chipper, she only had a coffee, and she was staring out the viewport.

"Well, that's the rest of our team here, then," Stines grumbled, losing his good mood.

"How they working out?" Westermann asked this of Chipper.

"They're good operatives," he replied, "but they hate each other's guts."

"Evidently why they're not sitting together," Westermann replied.

"How are your two doing?" Chipper asked her and Widowmaker.

Bradstock shrugged.

Westermann groaned. "Painfully. The guy Umbrano thinks everything is a euphemism either for sex or for farts. He's worse than Stines here."

"Hey, don't compare me—"

"The woman, Manolo," she continued, "is so thick I wonder whether she sustained brain damage at some point in the past."

"Handle themselves fine in drills," Bradstock rumbled. "They follow orders."

"Seems like they hate Jogianto as much as Hecate does," Stines said. "They're eating together, and she's by herself."

"Yeah, they're not great buddies with her, that's for sure," said Chipper.

Stines replied, "Probably expect her to trip over and shoot them."

Widowmaker chuckled, causing Westermann to stare sideways at him. "Oh, *that's* funny? I've been cracking actually funny jokes for months, fella, and the first time I hear you laugh is at that lame effort?"

Widowmaker shrugged again.

"You know," said Chipper, "maybe we should reach out to these guys again and try to integrate better. Shall I invite them over? Table's big enough."

"They won't come," Westermann replied. "Why don't you try the loner, instead?"

"Yeah, your soul mate," said Stines.

"My ..." Chipper felt heat across his cheeks, the back of his neck. "What you mean by that?"

"Settle, Lover Boy, she's reasonably hot. I can understand."

"We're not—!" He had started saying it loud enough to turn heads around the Mess. More quietly, he said, "We are not lovers."

"Like to be though, huh?"

Chipper started to rise, his hands curling into fists, his scalp prickling with rage. "Take that back."

"Settle, mate, it's just a joke, just a joke. You're not that dumb. After all, that'd be about the most dangerous thing you could do, docking with one of them."

"Yeah," Westermann laughed. "Dangerous for your reputation and dangerous for your health."

Chipper dropped into his seat, grinding his fist into the palm of his other hand, chewing his lip, slow breathing his anger away. Jokes like this were standard banter, ribbing. He'd had worse, and it hadn't affected him. Why was he so touchy about this? "No more jokes like that, ey?"

Westermann leaned over and ruffled his hair before he could pull out of her reach. "Relax, Chip. Don't be so sensitive. You wanna invite them over, invite them over. Or invite her. We don't care."

"I care," Stines muttered, abruptly sour again.

Chipper turned his attention to the view screen. "Forget it."

The others took their conversation in another direction, musing about the aliens' military strength.

A glance at Jogianto—Ana—showed her face reflected in the viewport there. Her expression was as sour as his.

"WE'RE BEING HAILED," Sintopas announced. "Tight beam. Audio only."

"Quiet on bridge," the XO called, stilling the nervous chatter around the various stations.

They're all as keyed up as I am, Gregory thought.

"On speaker," Pan ordered. He tugged on the hem of his tunic, though no one but bridge personnel could see him. He faced the center of the room, though Gregory knew there were microphones all over it to pick up his voice. Human affectations were fascinating even in situations like this. Especially in situations like this.

Situations like this, he mocked himself. *You mean first-contact-between-species situations? The situations that have only happened twice in the past? That weren't anything like this?*

"This is Captain Pan Xinchun of the Confederation ship *Assured.* With whom am I speaking?"

Nothing came back at him but the faintest rattle and hiss of static. Pan exchanged glances with Chinyama and then with Gregory before raising his brows at Sintopas. The comms officer gestured to his controls and gave a thumbs up: *Everything's fine on this end.*

Pan opened his mouth to speak again and then came the

reply. "I am called surveyor-curator-envoy Buoun'nyimiun't."

The voice was cotton-balled by a poor quality microphone perhaps, or by some misintegration of the two species' technology. But the English words were clear—even if the jumble of syllables and glottal stops that made up this individual's name were not.

Gregory realized he'd been holding his breath. He released it in a rush and sucked in more. People were smiling at each other. Grace was actually grinning at him. He shook his head in wonder. The voice was the same one from the Pollyanna signal, the one that had said *You come to us. You us friends*. The same individual—or would all of these non-humans sound the same to human ears?

After a short pause, the voice continued. "It is correct for you to call me Buoun."

Bu-own, Gregory repeated in his head, practicing the pronunciation.

"I am standing with two more *Tluaanto*, Councillor Pi'yow't, who you can call Pi. Also her leader and my leader, Excellent One, Grand Councillor Mu'ulkiinaat't, who you can call Naat. Our councillors and our council are happy you are visiting us. They hope to make friends of your species."

"Species," one of the bridge weapons ratings snorted under her breath. She paled when Chinyama leveled a warning finger at her, and mouthed, *Sorry*.

Gregory found he was marveling at how well the non-human spoke English. Although, he remembered, the language and document banks on those old probes had been pretty extensive. Fortunately for them both, Standard English taught in Confederation schools for generations now was based on CUSET-era English.

Another pause had started, this one lasting a few

seconds. Pan asked Gregory a question with his eyes. *Do I speak here?*

Gregory pointed to him and then himself.

"This is Captain Pan again. We thank you for your welcome and for your ... kindness. The next voice you will hear belongs to Ambassador Chris Gregory." He gave the bridge a wry look and added, "You can call him Ambassador."

"Envoy Buoun," Gregory said. "Councillor Pi. Councillor Naat. We are indeed grateful for your welcome here, and for your invitation into your system. We received your message a short time ago, although the message has been travelling for more than forty of our years." He paused now, in case Buoun or some computer needed to translate for other people in Buoun's room. Would Buoun know all the words, would he understand the Earth-based units of time just mentioned? Gregory pictured three non-humans standing in an office, hunched around a comms console. For all he knew, though, they might be standing in a great council hall with a hundred listeners. A thousand.

When Buoun did not respond, he continued, "We would like to meet with you personally. We need to be careful not to contaminate you—" Pan nodded at this, and Gregory knew in the captain's mind this was code for *We don't want* you *contaminating* us. "—but we invite your representatives to come to our ship." He stopped there. It was enough information for the moment. This needed to be a careful and measured dialogue.

Immediately, Buoun responded. "We accept. I will be the Tluaanto *representative* as you call it. Is that word more acceptable than *envoy*? From the dictionaries aboard your probe, I had assumed the word *envoy* was best. But I am peachy to speak your languages correctly."

There were smiling headshakes all around the bridge now, women and men joining in with Gregory's astonishment at how well this Buoun spoke their language and understood nuance. Not to mention at his overt desire to "get it right".

"You speak English extremely well," Gregory said. "Although, we don't use the slang word *peachy* anymore. That's about eight centuries out of date."

A small noise that sounded like breath expelled through nostrils. And then, "Thank you for your compliment and for your correction of me. I have had a long time to learn human languages, Ambassador."

"*Envoy* is an appropriate title for you, Buoun. We will polish our use of titles and names once we meet. However, I am concerned for your welfare when coming aboard our vessel. Please communicate your needs in terms of atmosphere, sterilization, food, water?"

Pan was frowning now, his head down so others didn't notice it. He and Gregory had argued privately about the wisdom of bringing aboard a "creature"—Pan's word—and its "germs"—also his word. Gregory had dismissed this—humanity had almost a thousand years' experience bringing living matter from one planet to artificial environments and on to other planets without cross-contamination.

Except for PBT, Pan had responded.

"You may wear a suit if you need to," Gregory added.

"No need for concern, Ambassador," said Buoun. "But thank you. Judging by the data from the probe and the probe's atmosphere itself, I can breathe your air and you can breathe mine. If it is microorganisms that concern you, we anticipated this. We are unsure of your technology and procedures relating to them. *We* employ a biological technology, embedded in my body, that prevents potential pathogens passing from me to others and from them to me."

Curiosity rippled around the bridge, expressed in raised eyebrows and murmurs. If that were true, Gregory thought, the implications for human medicine were auspicious.

Never to worry about the scourge of PBT or its like again!

Pan was motioning to Gregory. It took him a moment to catch on. When he did, he said, "Buoun, we will still need you to undergo an examination by our machine, a robot, during the boarding process. This is to prevent the *accidental* transmission of pathogens on board. Is that acceptable?"

"Of course. We understand." For a moment there was nothing but that background static and perhaps faintly beneath it, the burble of subdued voices, people discussing something off-mic. If so, the recording could be enhanced, and once the non-human language was learned, it could be translated.

Non-human. We still don't know what they're called as a people.

"We would like to discuss arrangements in more detail," Buoun said. "Would it be acceptable for us to disconnect this transmission and reconnect with you in twenty of your minutes?"

Buying yourself time to chat with your bosses, huh?

"Of course. I look forward to continuing our conversation then, Envoy Buoun."

"As do I, Ambassador."

The faint static disappeared. Sintopas made a slashing gesture that indicated the connection had been severed.

People around the room continued exchanging looks, not daring to speak. Until Chinyama said, "You can make noise again, people."

There were chuckles and backslaps and even a handshake or two. Pan stepped closer to Gregory and Fowler came in from the other side.

The captain said, "Let's take the next transmission in the Ready Room."

"Agreed," Gregory replied.

"I want to be there," said Fowler.

"No one's stopping you," Pan said and led the way through the jubilant crewers, past Grace and Corporal Westermann flanking the doors and into the corridor.

Once they'd entered the Ready Room, Fowler slapped the door control and said, "No, I mean I want to be there for the meeting. The live meeting."

Gregory struggled for a polite way to say no.

Pan made that unnecessary by saying, "Absolutely not."

"I am the representative of my government."

"Yes," said Pan, coolly taking his seat at the head of the table. "A government that is applying for DCHC membership and not yet a member. On this mission, Ambassador Gregory represents all of us."

"But you'll be there. Won't you, Captain?" Fowler leaned against the wall by the door, clearly seething. Gregory wondered if the man had his hands behind his back to stop them from strangling Pan.

"I will be there," the captain said. "The ambassador needs a witness, he needs protection also, plus I am the military commander of this mission."

"And I can't operate as both a witness and physical protection for the ambassador if he needed it? Hell, why can't his bodyguard *also* come in? I don't see the problem."

"The problem is crowding."

"This room is plenty big enough. There's ten *mabaho* chairs in here."

"Sure, there are ten stinking chairs in here. But we won't be meeting in here. There's a smaller room close to the airlock on D-deck. Easier for sequestering the non-human by using that entrance. The main reasons for limiting people in the room are, first, to not overwhelm the alien since it will be alone, and second, to keep the alien's exposure to humans to a minimum so that it has as little intel to report back to its superiors with."

Gregory nodded in respect for Pan's responses. They were logical and well-put. They were also negative-minded and defensive.

"Folks," he said with a big, fat and very genuine grin on his face, "we're about to entertain a guest. Let's keep things civil. Between us and him. And between each other."

Pan and Fowler grunted in unison and looked away.

THE TLUAAN EQUIVALENT of a Human ship's bridge was a compartment called the Sailing Bench—for reasons Buoun had never bothered to learn. In a lifetime lived in space, he had rarely set foot inside a Sailing Bench. But he was in one now—that of the Grand Councillor's personal ship.

As his conversation with the Human envoy concluded, he mused for a moment that he had never felt such honor as this—but only half that honor belonged to being in the most exclusive room in the most exclusive ship. The other half stemmed from the moment he had just experienced.

I spoke with a Human. I, Buoun'nyimiun't, spoke with a *Human*!

Careful to maintain decorum, he slowly turned from the communications console to face the middle of the room and the personnel seated there: Councillor Naat, Councillor Pi, Naat's adjutant Councillor Hari, and the three ship's crew permitted to stay for the meeting. He had not been introduced to them, and didn't know their names.

When no one else spoke, Buoun thought that he may as well keep going. "An auspicious occasion, Shining One. Will you want me to travel to the Human ship immediately?"

It took the Grand Councillor so long to answer that Buoun had begun to wonder if the tension of the moment had given the old Tlu a stroke. Then he stirred and said, "I will return with my ship to Liberty Habitat. Councillor Pi and you, Buoun, will take my shuttle to the Human ship." He turned to Pi and directed the rest of his instructions to her. "You are to command the Human ship to remain where it is, not to venture closer to Suuchaat. We don't want the other domains catching whiff of this yet. Not until we have secured our own arrangement with the aliens."

"Yes, Excellency," Pi demurred.

"Let Buoun handle the first few meetings alone. But ensure you instruct him thoroughly before he does."

"Yes, Excellency."

"You are authorized to conduct up to sixty cycles of talks before being recalled to Liberty Habitat." He gave Buoun a brief glance, before standing, ready to leave the room. "I hope it will not take that long."

18

IT WAS at 0900 the following morning that Gregory stood at the image station, transfixed.

The non-humans, he now knew, were called Tluaanto. The hologram of this particular Tluaanto—Envoy Buoun—was sharply detailed, backed up by a flatscreen image of the room taken from above the door. The alien had seated itself —*himself!*—at the conference table, so it was impossible to tell his height. The Tluaanto transmission received back at Pollyanna had carried minimal data recordings and no images. The envoy's appearance therefore caused Gregory a mild shock. Seeing a new and sentient non-human, seeing a living and moving intelligent being, well, it was ...

Surreal!

Gregory's only regret was that he would not be the first to lay physical eyes on this representative of the species. That privilege had been bestowed upon Fowler, Wepps, and Hecate who had met Buoun at the airlock. They had then scanned his clothing and his carry bag as politely as possible. Then Hecate and Wepps had led him to this room before leaving him alone inside. Wepps had reported that the visitor was clear of any technology except for a kind of personal computer on his arm and a "choker" collar which scanning showed was a camera and recording device. The envoy had been allowed to keep them—he'd not be visiting sensitive areas of the ship, and it was perfectly reasonable that these people be allowed a record of their first meeting with humans.

The interaction with the two soldiers at the airlock had happened with little speaking, but it had been transmitted through three ECFs simultaneously. Gregory therefore knew that the Tluaanto spoke in understandable Spanish and English and that he stood at 1.65 meters in height.

Gregory drank in the alien's appearance with fascination. The individual appeared calm as he sat at the table and seemed comfortable in the human chair. His left hand played over the small personal device wrapped around his right lower forearm—it looked a little like part of a medieval human armor, what they'd called a bracer, and it sat over his tunic sleeve. His head was large compared to his shoulders and torso, the skull extending at the rear into a stumpy, downward-curving crest. It reminded Gregory of a picture of a dinosaur he had seen in grade school. The face was broad and not unpleasant to look at, the eyes children's-book large and widely-spaced with green irises and round pupils. He seldom blinked. His mouth was open and his lips moving as he read from his device, and Gregory caught glimpses of human-like molars and incisors, and a long slender tongue. The lips were thicker than most humans, the nose broad with huge, flaring nostrils and apparently—from what Wepps had told him—moist, like a dog's. The envoy's skin and fur were light tan and orange, respectively. His species seemed to carry head fur around the jaw like a human beard and down across the throat, as well as in a wide band stretching back from above the forehead to the end of the skull ridge.

Grace, standing at Gregory's shoulder, seemed more

conscious of the alien's fashion sense than its physiology. "Auburn and magenta tunic," she commented. "Light blue trousers. Doesn't really go with the orange hair."

Gregory turned a half-hearted scowl on her. "First of all, young lady, let's be thankful that our esteemed guest shares a human-like concern for modesty and actually *did* dress for the occasion. Secondly, perhaps Envoy Buoun sees in a different spectrum to us and these colors don't clash at all for him. And thirdly—"

"Let me guess, we should be respectful of other cultural standards, et cetera?"

"Actually, I was going to say you could follow his lead and wear a little more color yourself occasionally."

She glanced down at her gray and black suit and affected a look of mock indignation. "Color has been out since the last millennium. Modern up, old man!"

Behind them, Captain Pan coughed.

"Ambassador, I believe it's impolite to make the envoy wait much longer."

"Point taken, Captain. Just savoring the moment." He took a deep breath and let it out slowly. "Let's go make third contact."

ENVOY BUOUN LOWERED his chin toward his left shoulder and placed his right hand behind him. Gregory assumed it to be a deferential motion and reciprocated. When the Tluaanto spoke, it was in English and with a voice both throaty and somehow soothing.

"It is an honor to look into your eyes and to breathe your air, Ambassador Gregory. And thank you for returning my gesture of respect."

Despite himself, Gregory's own voice had a little tremor in it when he said, "You speak excellent English." The envoy's inflection was near-perfect for a native of Caultan's capital continent Yajnavalkya. In fact, the only thing that Buoun could be faulted on was a tendency to pronounce an *r*-sound more like a *w*. He also spoke with a slight tendency to lisp.

Gregory continued, "You could have come from my hometown!" He winced then, cursing himself.

Not exactly profound first words from one species to another.

Buoun blinked. "I confess I do not understand your second sentence. But yes, I speak your language. We hoped that would please you."

Gregory chose to maintain the informality for the moment. "I'm told you spoke Spanish also to our soldiers outside. How did you learn these languages so well?"

"Languages are a passion of mine," the Tluaanto emissary replied. "And I have had many *p'hushto*—or as you would say, years—to perfect several. The language recordings you sent on your probe were detailed and thorough. We could only presume they were meant for our learning." He paused and Gregory read mild concern in his body language. "Have I offended you? Would you have preferred to teach me yourself?"

"No, no. I am pleasantly surprised. You haven't offended us. Rather, you have honored us." He indicated the chair at which Buoun had been sitting. "Is it your custom to sit for discussions?"

"Yes. Is it yours also?"

"Absolutely," Gregory replied. "Please be seated." His trembling legs might give out on him any second now if he didn't sit.

He waited until their guest had sat down before taking his own seat, gesturing for the captain to sit beside him. Grace leaned at the wall by the door. "I hope you will not resent three of us talking to you, when you are alone. Grace there is my assistant–she records data for me, reminds me of things I have forgotten." A slight sin of omission, failing to mention she was mainly here for Gregory's protection. "And this is Captain Pan Xinchun, commander of this ship. You should address him as Captain Pan or Captain. But if you would prefer to speak with me alone, that is quite acceptable."

Pan stirred beside him—obviously, it was not acceptable to *him*.

Buoun blinked. "This ship is your domain. Feel at peace about all you do." He inclined his head to the side again, and Gregory thought he detected a note of wryness in the alien's tone when he added, "We are bound to make cultural errors, Ambassador Gregory. Let us not fear the offending of each other but instead enjoy the first intercourse of our cultures."

Grace stifled a laugh, covering it with a cough.

Gregory couldn't resist a smile himself. "Envoy, I think the word you were looking for was *interaction*, not *intercourse*."

"Ah. Thank you."

Gregory folded his hands on the table in front of him and, after another deep breath, began upon the speech he had prepared, dredging it up from his memory, refusing to read from the notes in his pocket.

"Envoy Buoun, I greet you in the name of the Democratic Confederation of Human Colonies. It is a great day in my species' history. We are joyful to meet a people with whom we can communicate easily. We are extremely grateful that you have permitted us to enter your territory on this diplomatic mission. You have shown us trust, grace, and friendship."

"We, too, are honored by your offer of friendship," Buoun interjected gently.

"Thank you. Before I speak of the purposes of our

mission, please allow me to give three assurances to you and to your government. First, our ship is armed with an energy shield for our own protection and with weapons. Those weapons are powered down. We are a peaceful mission. We in no way intend to attack your own vessels or habitats."

At this, Buoun whistled through his nose and inclined his head to the side. Uncertain of the meaning of this, Gregory paused but the envoy merely regarded him patiently.

"Second," he went on, hoping that he had impressed rather than startled his guest, "we are a peace-loving civilization." *At least, we'd like to be.* "And my government wishes to assure yours that we respect the sovereignty of your territory. We also plan to negotiate the sharing of whatever resources lie in the space *between* your territory and ours in the future."

Buoun repeated his behavior of seconds earlier, and this time Gregory felt unnerved by it.

"Envoy, may I ask why you make this noise and turn your head in this fashion?"

The Tluaanto blinked. "I ..." Lost for the right words, he tapped on his wrist pad until discovering the ones he wanted. "Ah, you refer to something we do when—" He read from his screen. "—pleasantly surprised and impressed by a discovery or revelation of great importance."

"Okay. Well, I guess having another civilization respecting the sovereignty of your own is a good reason to be pleasantly surprised and impressed."

"Very much so. And your third 'assurance'?"

"Ah. And third, we would like to assure your people that we come here seeking to understand you. We hope to slowly build the basis for an eternal friendship and bond between two peoples." He rested here and smiled.

Buoun took the cue well. "Again, we are grateful. The leaders of my domain issue similar greetings and commitments. They have instructed me to assure you of your safety while you are among us and of our interest in mutually beneficial trade, including information. A question they asked me to pass on early in our conversation is, Will you be requiring refueling for your 'starship'?"

Gregory looked to Pan who shook his head in mild irritation, as if Gregory should have known the answer. He hadn't. No one had ever bothered to tell him how starships work. He said, "Thank you, but no."

Buoun blinked hard. "You have travelled an extremely long distance. You won't require fuel for your journey home?"

This time it was Pan who said, "No. Thank you."

"That is ... surprising. But marvelous. Your technology is advanced, then. We knew this. But this fact remains surprising."

"May I ask," Gregory said, "have *you* travelled to other star systems?"

"Me personally or my species?"

"Both, I guess."

"For myself, the answer, sadly, is no." He scratched at his head crest and leaned forward. "Regarding our species, we are currently attempting interstellar flight."

THE TWO HUMANS *at the table exchanged a look at this disclosure. Buoun could not discern whether their reaction was born of pleasure, alarm, or some other emotion. The recording made by his collar would be pored over; decisions could be made on the information's impact at a later date. For now, he held with the instructions he'd been given. It had been decided for him that the Humans could know about some Domain Space (and broader Tluaan) advances, but not all. He agreed with the Council's opinion that the Humans should not yet know specifically about the currently-outbound vessel. Nor should they know about the one recently arrived at the Kh'het system—or what had been discovered there.*

In my lifetime now, we have learned of the existence of not one, but three intelligent alien species, *he thought before returning his attention to Ambassador Gregory.* What other marvels are out there, I wonder.

"YOU ARE ATTEMPTING IT?" Gregory asked. "That is exciting for you." In actual fact, he was surprised by this statement. He had expected greater advancement from the Tluaanto. Given the well-established settlement of their solar system, they should have been well on their way to others by now. But then it was a matter of how, always a matter of how. *Homo sapiens* would still be confined to theirs if it hadn't been for the accidental discovery of 'leapfrogging', as it had become known for the past nine centuries.

"Have you reached any other stars or star systems?"

"As I said, we are attempting it currently."

Buoun reached into one of his tunic's two breast pockets. He produced a sheet of what appeared to be plastic-paper. It crinkled as he unfolded it across the table top, but the folds vanished as if Buoun had ironed the fabric of a shirt.

Pretty neat tech, Gregory thought. From his side of the table, he could make out the curl-and-triangle scrawl of Tluaanto text on it.

Buoun said, "Forgive me if this is hurried ... the request I am about to present to you. We were unsure of how long ... *hzzz* ..." He consulted the wrist device for vocabulary. "We were unsure of how long these niceties were expected to take when you meet with someone. Is that the correct word?"

"Niceties? The word you're looking for is more likely to be *formalities.*"

"Ah. Thank you. While we are observing formalities, I am happy to postpone making requests if—"

Gregory interrupted with a wave and a smile. "We are more than happy to talk business. Please understand that *everything* we do and discuss here is novel, interesting, and helpful toward mutual understanding. What is your request?" He held his hand out for the document, but Buoun showed no sign of passing it over.

Instead, the envoy leaned over it and began reading. "'This document represents an official request from the Council of Domain Space to the envoys of the Democratic Confederation of Human Colonies and is dated the twenty-eight *Mlukh-it-kah* of *Hanshum* season in the one-hundred-twelfth *p'hush* of *Emmar Karaoun.*'"

There would come a day when such references and dating regimes were commonplace and boring. Gregory was glad again that he was here for the early stages of the relationship between species, when details like this were exotic and fascinating.

"'The Council of Domain Space,'" Buoun continued, "'formerly requests the exchange of knowledge or technology that is beneficial to our respective species.'"

"You're translating this as you read," Gregory said and felt Pan stir at his side, no doubt concerned that he was interrupting too much.

Far from seeming irritated himself, Buoun gave a little head cock that might have indicated pleasant surprise. "I would like to claim that I am so proficient. The truth is that I memorized the English, Mandarin, and Spanish versions of this so that I wouldn't stumble while presenting it. May I quickly check with you ... is it appropriate for me to continue in English, or would you prefer one of those other two languages?"

"English will be fine. Perfectly appropriate. Please continue."

Buoun steadied the paper and once more pretended to read directly from it. Perhaps that was a cultural thing. "'As the days pass and we know each other better, it may surface that there is knowledge or technology possessed by the Tluaanto which is desirable to the Human people. Domain Space of the Tluaanto desire the Human technology which enables inhabited vehicles to travel faster than the speed of light.'"

Pan had been fidgeting, but he grew still, hearing this.

Gregory said, "I understand."

The brief sent to him from the Office of Xenosentient Affairs had mentioned such a request as a possibility and Gregory had thought about it several times during the journey. His orders in such an event: stall. A spacefaring, non-human race posed a threat to humanity, no matter how some quarters might claim that as fear-mongering or prejudiced. Those quarters were rarely the ones who had to make hard decisions and live with the aftermath. Gregory agreed. He was in no hurry to hand the secret of FTL to a species he'd met mere minutes ago. The distrust was warranted, he felt. The "Tluaanto" could be at least as self-interested as Homo sapiens. For the moment, it seemed, humanity had an advantage its leadership intended to keep.

And so he stalled. "I will pass that request on to my superiors."

"Your superiors?"

"Those who govern our civilization."

"I understand. When can we expect an answer?"

"Not for some time, I imagine."

"Please, can you ask them to decide quickly? It is extremely important to us that—"

"They'll get back to you when they can," Pan interrupted. Gregory glanced at him; the man's jaw was set tight. He wondered how to gesture for him to remain silent without giving Buoun the sense of disunity.

Buoun folded his paper. "You cannot decide on this yourself. It is this way with my people also. In your language, I am an envoy. I am assuming that is the meaning also of the title Ambassador?"

"There are slight differences of context, but yes, please assume it means the same."

"Yes. I will pass on your need to await word from your leadership." He pushed his paper into the center of the table. "Please give them this. Or at least, send them images. Again, that is our custom and my leadership would greatly appreciate you following it."

Gregory heard Grace shift behind him as he stretched a hand toward the paper. Before he could touch it, her arm snaked over his and beat him to it.

"I'll take care of this," she said, her mouth close to his ear. She had worn gloves to the meeting. Gregory had wondered why but now he understood—it was her job to be suspicious and protect him. For all he knew, the paper was some kind of clever explosive, or loaded with nanites. The meeting room door opened. She said, "I'll be back in a minute."

Gregory exchanged a glance with Pan then smiled awkwardly at Buoun. The Tluaanto bared his own teeth in return.

What now? Gregory asked himself. Then told himself, *You talk. That's what diplomats do.*

"For the time being, Envoy Buoun, I wonder if we might confine ourselves to an exchange of basic information about each other's species. What we call in English *getting to know each other.*"

"That sounds wonderful," Buoun said, then added. "And appropriate."

Gregory nodded. "Then the next thing I need to offer you is refreshments. Er, food and drink."

"I understand," Buoun replied, perhaps mimicking the way Gregory had used the space-filler a minute earlier. "We have the same custom. Rather than impose on you, I brought my own. The container with my food and drink remains with your soldiers who are probably still testing it. I agree with that testing, by the way. I think it is wise that both our peoples employ care of, *hzzz*, contamination."

"Excellent indeed. I will ask Grace to check on your container as soon as she returns. Captain, she can also order us some refreshment too."

"Fine," Pan said. Gregory glanced at him again. He certainly wasn't enjoying this.

Spoilsport. You're settled enough during battle. This is real fun. And no one gets hurt.

Buoun said, "Half of the foods inside are a gift for your people to study. The other half are for me over the next three of what you indicated were hours. That is the limit my leadership set for our first meeting. I must make you aware also that, at the very least, I will need to drink the purified water inside by the time the first hour is completed. We are aware that many species do not need to drink as regularly as ours, so perhaps you don't know that we must take in liquid often to remain healthy."

"Humans can survive for three of our days without drinking under some conditions," Gregory said, risking Pan's annoyance at revealing so specific a vulnerability.

Buoun replied, "Tluaanto can survive one of our days. Barely."

Holy God, Gregory thought. According to *Assured*'s astronomer, one day on the system's home world was only about six hours longer than a standard human one. "And you came into space? Where the rivers and lakes are few."

Another head-cock. "Our recycling systems were well-enough advanced by that stage to attempt it. Water is not normally a problem for us. Also, we mine it wherever we find it in our system."

"May I ask, how long is it since you first sent an individual off your planet?"

"I am free to tell you that the first Tluaan team to reach orbit did so one hundred and twelve human standard years ago. Our population of the solar system has been slow in progress since then."

"Judging by what we have seen so far, it is actually quite fast. We are impressed."

"And you?" Buoun asked. "When did humans first enter Earth orbit?"

"Approximately a thousand years ago."

"A thousand! This ... is impressive. No wonder you are so much more advanced than us."

BUOUN TRIED *to quell the sudden upsurge in his blood pressure. He thought,* A thousand of their years. Fifteen hundred or more of our cycles. We only managed to spread amongst the asteroids and outer planets, while they spread across the galaxy!

His calculations passed onto the Council had estimated the possibility of one or two billion Humans in existence. But the figures had been rushed. Guesses based really upon nothing. What if Humans numbered in the trillions against the three-quarter billion Tluaanto currently alive?

Domain Space needed a peaceful agreement with them, and needed to capture it quickly. If the Humans made contact with Domain Surface, or Domain Moon, then the consequences for Domain Space would be dramatic, possibly catastrophic. A powerful species with numbers rivalling a pest-plague would make a fatal enemy.

Gregory was speaking again, his white teeth flashing as he did so.

"Well, advancement is relative," he said. "What you have achieved is no less impressive to us. And be assured that we do not consider you a lesser species or less-intelligent for not possessing a faster-than-light technology, or for having explored space for less time than we have."

The way Gregory constructed some of his long sentences was convoluted, and Buoun found himself racing to parse them and keep in step. He had developed practice software for conversation in Human languages, but its grammar had been guided by that of the probe's recordings and files.

The Human continued, "I reassure you that we are here as equals, as peers. Our civilization seeks to behave as sensible and sensitive custodians of the resources and ecosystems we find in space. We believe it is the responsibility of intelligent creatures to care for the universe, to cultivate its health, and live in harmony with it. We hope that you will be partners with us in that."

In his mind, Buoun flinched at this idea, though he kept his demeanor unresponsive. He had not come across the words harmony and custodians in any of the Human languages so far. But the inference was clear from context. The Humans viewed the universe as something to be cared for. More like a brood of offspring than a garden patch.

He raised a hand to forestall further speech from the Human envoy, giving himself a moment to think. This idea of nurturing the universe was the first truly alien concept he'd come across in Human thought so far. And the Council would not understand it easily. Ironically, lesser Tluaanto might, like those whose whole existence depended upon treating their family members and their domesticated *animals and their plot of farming land—as Gregory had said —with sensitivity. They might have enough similarity in values and lifestyle to grasp that way of thinking, extending to other planets and other ecologies. The Council of* any *Domain certainly would not. Another reason to hide the existence of those Domains from this Envoy and his ship crew.*

He said, "It would honor us greatly to be considered your partners, if I understand that term correctly. I interpret it as meaning equals and members of a team."

"Correct," said Gregory.

Buoun fervently hoped he meant that.

THE DOOR OPENED. Grace barely got a foot inside before Gregory asked her to chase down refreshments including the envoy's container. She nodded politely enough before leaving, but Gregory read clear displeasure in the narrowing of her eyes.

Well, that's what 'assistants' do, Ms. Renny.

"Ambassador and Captain," Buoun said, "would it be interesting to you if I briefly explain the history of our species as I know it?"

"Absolutely," Gregory said.

"Excellent. Then I will begin with one stage of our evolutionary ancestors, the *hignah'minto.*" Buoun leaned back in his chair and clasped his hands on his lap. "One point five million of your years ago ..."

BUOUN'S HISTORY lesson took most of the three hours allotted him. He started with the name of the Tluaan home world: Suuchaat.

They ate and drank together while he alternated between

the lesson he'd memorized and answering their spontaneous questions.

He left out any detail suggesting to the Humans that there were more domains than just Domain Space. The Council had wanted to convey the impression that Domain Space was *the representative of every Tluaan faction. Buoun had tried arguing that by naming themselves clearly as the domain that owned space, they were already giving a clue to Tluaan politics. This had been dismissed. The Council had stated they wanted their name on the agreement to make it official and binding.*

When his three-hour deadline was approaching, Buoun offered polite goodbyes and made ready to leave. As they stood together in the corridor outside the meeting room—with a Human warrior either side of them—the Human envoy promised to repay the history lesson with one of his own upon Buoun's return. Then Ambassador Gregory asked if it was possible in a day or two for him and Captain Pan to hold one of these meetings upon a Tluaan ship.

"It may be," Buoun hedged. "It will depend on a few factors."

"What factors?" Captain Pan asked, but Gregory interrupted before Buoun could find a diplomatic answer.

"We can discuss that another time. The Envoy needs to return to his ship. Envoy Buoun, it has been a true pleasure to meet and talk with you. I am eager to continue tomorrow."

"As am I."

Buoun crossed an arm across his breast in another polite goodbye. Ambassador Gregory mimicked the gesture. Captain Pan did not. Buoun was not yet clear on their ranking system and whether Captain Pan was an equal to Gregory, a subordinate, or a superior. The two males had interrupted each other frequently. Buoun's theory was that Captain Pan was an equal, here to observe and record and to debrief with Ambassador Gregory after. From his reading,

Buoun knew the word captain *designated the person in control of a vessel and could be used to designate both a civilian and a military person. There was some confusion or crossover in the way English used the term. "With your permission, Ambassador and Captain, I shall return to my ship now."*

The Humans along the corridor to the docking area all stepped aside to free a path for him.

The Ambassador said, "Please."

Buoun passed through the gauntlet of armed personnel who followed him to his small ship. A hundred heartbeats later, he watched the airlock sphincter close between him and the small crowd of Humans, then ran a tired hand across his face.

From the next compartment, he heard the scrape of fabric on wall as, presumably, Councillor Pi rose from her chair to come see him. He powered down his collar-camera with a gentle tap and—in a quiet voice lest the Council had other microphones in here—he said, "Buoun'nyimiun't, you just spoke with an alien species. And a friendly one at that."

He wanted to laugh.

He wanted to scream with joy.

He was standing in a Council runabout with a Council pilot and a Councillor. Buoun wished he was at home in his apartment right now; if he had been, he would be pouring himself a huge cup of his strongest vee'haat *to celebrate.*

19

THE ELEVATOR DOORS SWISHED ASIDE. Gregory stepped through and flinched when he noticed it was occupied by a Peacekeeper. He felt a mild blush creeping up his cheeks.

Guilty conscience. I'm out without my mom's permission.

He had managed to power down Grace's door alarm and sneak out of the yacht undetected. With luck, he'd be back long before she woke and discovered his absence.

"Plenty of room, sir," Corporal Chipper Tukimatu said brightly. The Peacer was unarmed, dressed in shorts, sneakers, and T-shirt. Even though he pressed his huge body into one corner, it still seemed like he took up a quarter of the space.

Gregory nodded politely and turned to the controls. He was about to tell the elevator "B-Deck" when he saw by the indicator that Chipper was already headed there.

"Going to the Rec Hall?" he asked.

"Yes, sir. Gonna shoot some baskets. After midnight, it's usually quiet."

"Quiet is what I was hoping for too."

"Oh." Chipper shifted uncomfortably. "I promise I'll give you space, sir. I just need to do something, ey?"

"I understand completely, Corporal. I can't sleep, and I figured I'd try some of this physical exercise people rave about so much. To stop my mind racing about the Tluaanto. And I wasn't saying I didn't want you there."

"Oh. Okay. That's good, sir."

Gregory adopted a conspiratorial tone. "Truth be told, Corporal, I'm out after curfew."

Chipper frowned. "Sir?"

"I snuck out of my ship without my assistant knowing."

Chipper got it then. A grin slowly transformed his polite expression. "Gotcha. She sticks pretty close, ey?"

"Well, it's no secret the main thing she 'assists' me with is security. Problem is, she thinks *everywhere* is dangerous. If I'm in the toilet longer than a minute, she checks up on me."

"Seriously?"

"Well, maybe two minutes."

Chipper's grin widened. "She check the toilet paper for booby traps?"

"Never know when it might explode just when you don't want it to," Gregory replied, and they shared a chuckle.

Chipper straightened in mock attention and snapped off a salute. "It'd be my honor to protect you while you're conducting your physical exercise, sir."

"Nah. Shoot your baskets—I'm guessing that's basketball, yes?—and forget I'm there. I'll walk at a sedate pace on one of the treadmills."

"You could play some basketball with me, sir."

"I recognize a hustle when I see one, Corporal. As I said, forget I'm there. I need to zone out anyway."

The elevator came to a stop and its doors opened.

"Let me go out first, sir," Chipper chuckled. "Make sure the corridor's safe."

"Excellent. After you."

Play-acting, Chipper mimed sweeping a rifle both ways, then gestured for Gregory to follow him. The Peacer continued along toward the closed red hall doors, his make-believe rifle still up and ready.

"Mind the carpet there, sir. Slight bubble in it. Could be a mine."

"Copy that."

Chipper tossed another grin over his shoulder. Gregory decided he liked this man very much. Not only was he a consummate professional by all reports, but he had an unexpected and endearing sense of humor. Peacekeepers and the various kinds of police Gregory worked with over the decades usually behaved with extreme rigidity or arrogance, sometimes both. Chipper, on the other hand, seemed a gentle soul. How did he reconcile that gentleness and light-heartedness with the violent actions his profession caused him to take, like those he'd taken recently? He let those thoughts slip away as he caught up with Chipper at the doors.

"I better stop acting like a kid, sir," the Peacer said. "In case anyone's in there."

"Copy that too," Gregory smiled back.

The Peacer threw open the doors.

Both men froze at what they saw inside.

The hall was unoccupied except for two female Tacticals. Dead-center of the hall, they were literally locked in combat on the floor, one with her legs wrapped around the throat and chin of the other. Blood ran from their noses and had smeared across their chins and cheeks. The pinned woman had one arm free, trying in vain to reach back and get a useful hold on her opponent.

"What the hell?" Gregory gasped.

Chipper was already moving, charging across the open space. "Break this up!" he snarled. "Let her go!"

"Not your business, *baka*!" This was from the one with the upper hand, Hecate. Jogianto, pinned and choking, wasn't saying anything. As Gregory drew closer, he could see the flush in her face was not just exertion—she was struggling to breathe.

"Do it!" Chipper snarled and circled them to get behind.

Hecate, stronger than she appeared, managed to crab-drag Jogianto around with her, keeping her opponent between her and the big Peacer. "You don't order me."

"But I do," said Gregory. "Release her now."

Jogianto's eyes widened, focused on him even as she clutched at her attacker.

Hecate hesitated, resisting his order, loathing all over her face.

"Corporal," he said, and Chipper started in.

Hecate released Jogianto, uncoiling from the grip she'd held and rolling backwards to put distance between them. She rose with her arms spread. There was blood on her hands, her blood or Jogianto's or both. More blood ran freely from her nose; it had spotted the flooring near them. How long had this been going on?

Hecate said, "Friendly sparring is all. Just practicing. Right, Jogi?"

Jogianto had folded over her knees, massaging her throat with her head down. "Right," she croaked.

"That's the story you're sticking with?" Chipper asked, suddenly sounding for all the universe like a military policeman. That tone plus his size would intimidate most people, Gregory thought.

The women nodded together. Jogianto hadn't looked up yet.

Hecate seemed to realize her hands were bloody, and

wiped them on her track pants. "Shower time for me, then." She swaggered past them towards the door. "Good session, Jogianto."

Jogianto flipped the bird.

After Hecate had left, Chipper offered to help Jogianto up. The Xerxian slapped his hand aside and rose swiftly. "Didn't ask for your help," she said, her voice hoarse.

"You were in trouble there," Gregory said.

She flashed him a filthy look and muttered, "Nothin' I couldn't handle."

"You weren't handling that," Chipper said. "You were about to pass out."

But Jogianto was already on her way to the door, leaving Gregory and Chipper shaking their heads at each other.

Once she'd gone, Gregory said, "What on Foucault was that?"

Chipper pulled a handkerchief from his pocket, squatted and wiped at the blood spots on the floor. "That, sir, was two Xerxians who hate each other's guts."

"The one who left last—Jogianto. At Luján's asteroid, she stated that the other one pushed her and caused her to stun Sgt. Wepps."

"Yep."

"My God. What is wrong with them?" Gregory wiped his brow. He'd done nothing, hadn't even started on the treadmill, and he was sweating.

"They're just people is all." Chipper rose, regarding his reddened handkerchief with a scowl. "People are stupid."

His eyes on the doors that had closed after Jogianto, Gregory nodded. "They sure are, Corporal. They sure are."

AFTER HIS OUTING the night before, Gregory was a little tired when Buoun returned for the second meeting.

He was also thanking God and all the saints that Grace hadn't found out about his midnight trip to the treadmills—especially the part where he'd walked in on two battling Tactical Enforcers.

If Pan—or Buoun—noticed his weariness, they didn't comment on it. In fact, it was Pan who kept yawning the whole time. The three-hour conference covered similar ground to the one before it, composed largely of history lessons from both civilizations. Perhaps Pan was merely bored.

In contrast to Pan, on this occasion and the two days following it, Gregory remained fascinated, learning a great deal about the Tluaanto civilization. Today, he was learning a little about their language ...

He learned that he should properly speak of Buoun as a *Tlu*—that word meant an adult man or male in their primary language. Adult females were called *Tlaa*. Both words together made the prefix *Tluaa* in the word *Tluaanto*.

"Something belonging to our species is Tluaan, as in 'a Tluaan habit' or 'a Tluaan device.' But the species itself, or groups of us, are named Tluaanto. The suffixes *'to* and *'nto*," Buoun told him, "refer to the full range or spectrum of a species, object or subject. Of course, it is an open ended noun; that is, it allows for the existence of unimagined or undiscovered mutations or versions of the subject. Asteroids plural are called *mehehmunto* since they are of different shapes and sizes. Your people in our language have become known as *humanto*."

The Tluaanto *n*-sound had a slight twang to it, as if it were made further back in the mouth than the English equivalent. Gregory attempted several words in their language and managed only to get a grasp on a polite greeting, the words for their species and for men and women, a phrase meaning *I like this food*, and the words for years and asteroids. In the interests of time—as much as languages had always fascinated him—he left it there.

During the third day's conference, he presented Buoun with a carved wooden stegosaurus.

"It belonged to my daughter," he had explained. "A creature from our prehistory, predating our earliest hominid ancestors by millions of years. They were wiped out by a huge *mehehm*."

Buoun took the small object with both hands, treating it as if it were fragile. "I am honored and grateful, Chris," he said. They had established a simple and informal naming protocol since the commencement of this meeting. "First, that you would give us such a precious thing, and second, that you used our word for asteroid."

"You are welcome. And it's not for you plural. It's for you personally, Buoun. I would like you to have it. I sense that you would treasure such an object."

"Indeed, yes. This *is* treasure. I do not own many personal objects of a decorative or instructive nature, so this is even more precious because of that. Did you say it belonged to your daughter, past tense? She has relinquished ownership?"

"She died," he replied.

Buoun's mouth dropped open for a second, then he clacked it shut and covered his eyes with both hands. "I am saddened," he murmured before dropping his hands again. "That must have hurt you very much." He pushed the wooden dinosaur into the middle of the table. "I cannot accept this. This bears significance for you and bears your daughter's *f'pae*."

"Please understand there is meaning in my gifting this to you, Buoun. My daughter, you see, was fascinated with non-humans. Most human children are. She loved dinosaurs—which no longer exist—as well as many pets indigenous to *our* planet. And then she was fascinated also with the other sentient non-human species we have met. She often spoke about visiting them and giving her old toys to their children." He laughed, though it was tinged with sadness. "As if Jarinyi and Anachromites had a use for such things. But I sense this is something you appreciate, and so it delights me to give it to you. On her behalf."

Buoun seemed stunned. He stared at the dinosaur without touching it. After a while, he said, "I accept it. With even more gratitude than I felt earlier. I am also shocked to hear that you have met other races. We are not the first to have interacted with you in this way, then?"

Pan stirred in that way he had of showing that he'd rather Gregory not reveal this information. Gregory ignored him.

"You are most definitely the first to have interacted like *this*. While you Tluaanto are not 'First Contact' for us—rather you are Third Contact—you are the first *Others* we have met who think and behave like us."

"The other ... other *Others* ... they are not like us?"

"The Anachromites are a hive species, as large as us in adult form but with segmented bodies and multiple legs and ... and other things. They are not bipedal like our species and yours. It took a long time before we recognized them as sentient creatures with a civilization and technology because they are so different to us. It is still almost impossible to communicate with them.

"The Jarinyi," he continued, "are more like humans and Tluaanto in that they stand upright like us, with two arms and two legs, a head, two eyes, two ears. But they also have two noses—well, kind of. And they speak through these noses. We cannot mimic their speech, but we can communicate through software. However, Jarinyi are what we deem a Stone Age race who do not show interest in advancing beyond that level of rudimentary technology."

And so, the conversation ran until the end of that meeting. Buoun parted company holding his dinosaur toy against his chest as a child might.

On the fourth day, he returned with gifts for Gregory and for Pan: Tluaan eating utensils, a polished gemstone, and a sample of an extinct Tluaan virus from the home world. "For research," he said, "and to show trust."

On the fifth day of negotiations, Buoun brought a friend.

Or rather, he brought a superior—judging by the way he deferred to the Tlaa.

The "auxiliary councillor" had been one of the other individuals introduced during the initial audio conversation. Her name was formally presented to Gregory and Pan in European and Mandarin script on the synthetic "paper" that Tluaanto seemed fond of. Gregory read it three times—it was a long name—and was immensely relieved when Buoun asked him to call her by the diminutive name Pi.

The female differed slightly from Buoun in appearance. She was a little taller and plumper. Her short robe—reaching to the knees of her trousers—was lined with expensive looking trim, and gemstones sparkled at her collar. Her eyes were slightly smaller. Occasionally, her facial and neck hair would ripple with other colors, reds and pinks. It was all Gregory could do not to watch her for these interesting changes. This had never happened with Buoun.

Pi remained an observer for most of that day's four-hour session. She refrained from eating during their time, though she drank regularly from the flasks of water Buoun had carried in. She spoke only twice: once upon first introductions when she greeted Gregory, Pan, and Grace by name and in that order. She spoke initially in slow and careful English and repeated it in Mandarin.

And then upon conclusion of the day's discussions when she said, again in two languages, "It has been pleasurable to learn from you and to see you with my eyes. I thank you for your ..." Here she had faltered until Buoun murmured the word to her. "Your hosp-itality."

"She was a piece of work," Grace muttered after the Tluaanto had boarded their still-attached shuttle.

"Now, now," said the captain as he turned away. But Gregory had seen his mild smile of agreement with Grace.

"Why do you say that?" he asked her.

"Just a feeling. Seems like every boss everywhere. Polite to others, but a pain in the ass to their employees." She smiled sweetly at him. "Paella for dinner, sir?"

20

IT WAS on the sixth day that Buoun made a revelation that had Pan asking for a recess.

Outside the meeting room and along the hallway, the *Assured*'s captain paced in a tight three-meter arc while Gregory leaned on the wall and rolled the cricks from his neck.

"They have interstellar ships," Pan said.

"So I hear," Gregory replied sarcastically.

"Earlier, that alien said they were *attempting* interstellar flight."

"Non-human," Gregory corrected. "Not 'alien'. And how does this new information contradict that statement?"

"He didn't tell us they already sent a ship out of their system thirteen years ago."

"Thirteen orbits. Their years are orbits." Thirteen orbits made it about nine human years.

"Whatever. And a second ship's halfway to wherever the first one went, apparently. This worries me."

"I see that."

"It doesn't worry you?"

"Why should it? Buoun didn't tell us on the first day they had a manned vessel on its way to the next star system. Big deal. Why should they? What if we turned out to be ...?" He huffed a laugh. "What if we had turned out to be Xerxian pirates? Tell us that and we'd be on our way to intercept and loot that ship."

"Intercept a ship now travelling at seven-eighths the speed of light!"

"Keep your voice down."

"You can't intercept a ship going that fast."

"Fine. I'm not as versed in the physics of spaceflight as you are. I was making a point. And you're way too suspicious—"

"After what we've been through, I can never be too suspicious. Ever again."

"I said, keep your voice down, Pan."

Personnel were gathered in tight groups at both ends of the short corridor. Pan caught his breath and stopped pacing. When he spoke again, it was controlled. "What else haven't they told us?"

"I'm guessing they haven't told us a lot. Same as we haven't given them data cubes with all our latest tech advances and political movements. The fact that they trusted us enough to tell us this at all is encouraging."

"They've told us to pressure us. They want our FTL tech."

"They're not leaning on us."

Pan affected a whiny voice: "Please help us, kind humans. Everything takes so long around here. It takes our poor starship nine whole years to reach the nearest system."

"Orbits," Gregory corrected mildly.

"If only there was a way to get there faster," Pan continued in the same mocking tone of voice. "The poor crew members of the second ship could be there and back in time for Christmas with their children."

"This is a side of you I've never seen before. Did you study theater at university?"

"Suspicion," Pan returned evenly. "With a minor in common sense."

"Captain, let's at least hear them out. They've told us this for a reason. And, sure, it's probably an opening to keep asking about the FTL tech. But let's hear what else they'll tell us."

"What does the ministry say about all this?"

"You know it'll take a month to get a reply. We'll ask the Tluaanto what they're offering on their side of a trade deal and see where that takes us."

"All right. But I don't like this. They drop a bit of information. They drop a bit more. How do we know that soon they won't reveal they've perfected ship cloaking and have us surrounded? Or their envoys smuggled nanoviruses aboard?"

"They were scanned intensively—"

"We're out of our depth here, Gregory."

"Yes, we are but not as badly as you make out. And we're going back in there and will be polite to them. You want to learn more about them? This is how we do it."

"By trusting what they tell us? And how much? We'd have done better to investigate and scan the system more extensively upon approach. Maybe we still should."

"We're *talking* with them, Captain. Like civilized beings. They have been cordial. And we shall be cordial as well."

ANA STOOD in the drill center's "muster" area—the room the Confeds called a "foyer." Hecate stood near her, but out of arm's reach. They had been summoned.

Twenty minutes of foot shuffling and zero conversation

passed before Fowler showed up, marching in dressed in combat gear with Umbrano at his heel. Ana and Hecate straightened, facing him as he came to rest with hands clamped behind his back with a face like thunder.

"Cut me out," he said.

A moment passed before Ana realized he wouldn't explain the remark. She asked, "Pardon, sir?"

"Confed bastards. They've cut me out. Of the negotiations. They let me search the envoy then whipped him away and ordered me off that deck. Haven't let me near him since." Umbrano remained standing behind him, looking, for once, quite uncomfortable. "If they think I'm the kind of man who sits on his ass while they play their games, they're bigger idiots that I thought they were." He poked a finger at them. "You two."

Ana felt her chin snap up—and saw Hecate's do the same.

"We've got drilling to do."

"Sir?" Hecate asked. "Are we ..." She gave a little snort. "Are we gonna take down the Peacers or something?"

"What? No!"

Ana took great pleasure from the flush of embarrassment spreading across Hecate's cheeks.

"No," Fowler continued. "But we're in foreign territory with reinforcements a long way away. While the Confeds enjoy high tea and crumpets with an alien, we are going to remain vigilant. We're keeping our edge."

"Yes, sir."

"I want you two to armor up." Ana noticed belatedly that Umbrano already had. "You two versus him and me."

Ana kept her thoughts to herself on that one.

But Hecate obviously couldn't. "Can I team up with Umby?" she asked.

Ana didn't think Fowler's mood could grow sourer.

Apparently, it could. He growled, "You two. You two worm brains. I've been hearing about nothing but childish squabbling between you two. Fist fights even."

Ana cursed inwardly. Someone had informed him about the altercation in the gym. Chipper wouldn't have snitched—would he?—so it had to have been that snooty ambassador.

Fowler's tone did not soften as he said, "You might hate each other—fine. There's no law against that. But you represent your Party here. Helldamn, you represent *me*! No more infighting. You'll work together, and you'll do it well. *Entiendes?*"

"Yes, sir," they replied.

"And it's not just the fact that we *represent* our people and Party." His voice did soften now as his eyes grew distant. "We *are* our people and Party here. There's five of us left. Us. Xerxians. The Confeds can say all they like about treating us as equals. But they've proved that's not true by the mere fact that they're in that conference room and I'm down here. So, when push comes to shove, if this vessel comes under attack, I'd rather trust you than them." He narrowed his eyes at Ana and Hecate once more. "And I'd rather you trusted each other."

"Yes, sir," they muttered.

He sniffed and checked the practice rifle strapped to his chest. "Armor up. You have three minutes."

As Ana preceded Hecate into the change rooms, Fowler's rhetoric rang in her mind. Along with one question: *If we're sticking together, then where's Manolo?*

"WE ANTICIPATE that a species who have inhabited multiple star systems for a thousand years may not require anything we have developed."

Buoun was translating what Pi was saying. The subject of FTL had been raised now. The Tluaanto wanted help with a drive, and Pi had begun to talk about what they might trade for it.

Buoun inclined his head toward her as she murmured again, then continued, "We believe we are advanced in many areas. Perhaps we are on the same level as you in some of that development. Perhaps even further since, as you have told us, you are still rediscovering many of your advances made in the period before what you call your dark age." She spoke again, he listened. "But perhaps the most useful to you is in the area of medical technology. Since you have relaxed some of your quarantine restrictions, and allowed us to enter and land via your cargo bay, we noticed one of your crewers who was working there was missing both of his legs."

Gregory looked to Pan who said, "Rating Weatherill."

"We can treat that condition," Buoun said.

"Well, that's kind," Pan said. "And impressive. But Rating Weatherill won't want that to be 'treated.'"

"Why not?" asked Buoun.

"It is a matter of honor, religion, and self-respect for him. He doesn't feel that *is* a disability and has lived that way his entire life. His particular religion also teaches that to change it would be against God's will."

Buoun translated that for Pi who looked less than impressed. She muttered something back. "We understand," he said, though he sounded like he didn't. "But the man in question has enhancements to help him. I believe you call them prosthetics."

"Not entirely true," said Pan. "To carry out his duties, he uses robotic limbs. He does not use these in his private life and time. They're not attached to his body. His religion accepts the robotics as a tool, the same way a vehicle, a hammer, or a computer are tools."

"Perhaps that is your way, to accept such restrictions. If his religion says it cannot be changed, am I correct in assuming that there are other religions that permit this? We have no religion, you see."

"There are plenty of systems of thought amongst us that would want to treat his condition," Gregory said.

"Ah." Buoun translated the conversation then said, "We can regrow the legs of people who desire that treatment."

"Appendicular regeneration," said Pan. "Our earlier civilization had that tech for a decade before ..." He pulled up short before he could say *PBT*, Gregory presumed. "Before circumstances intervened. We've lost it, but our scientists believe we're ten or twelve years away from cracking it again."

Gregory had read about that. They were also saying it would be incredibly expensive when it was redeveloped.

"We ... don't know the term *appendicular*. However, we could give that 'tech' to you now. Not in ten years' time." Gregory thought that perhaps the envoy had missed a calling in marketing. "We use a process of cellular repatterning or reprogramming. I have searched your words for the best term I could create to translate. These come closest. It is a technical process I don't have permission to reveal and, to be honest, don't personally have the expertise to understand. But if it interests you, and to be clear, if he wanted us to, we could regrow Rating Weatherill's legs on him. No need to grow a limb remotely before surgically attaching it as we used to do a hundred cycles back. We have other advances too. Food crops that thrive in zero gravity. Skin enhancements that resist burns. Enhancers that enable workers to live and work in low gravity for years without atrophy or other health problems."

Pan had gone quiet. There were some interesting ideas in here.

Focusing on transportation, engineering, and agricultural technologies as it regrouped following the dark age, the DCHC had not regained many of the medical advances of the 21st and 22nd centuries. In some respects, 31st century medicine resembled that of the 20th century. The greatest threat as always was the return of a strain of PBT—or some even hardier virulent organism out there awaiting contact with humans.

"This might be of interest to us," Gregory said in a slightly bored tone of voice. No need to tip his hand. "I will be passing what you've said to my leadership for debate as soon as possible."

He bit down on what he was about to say next as Pi's palm-held communication device blipped. She stared down at the stream of tiny multi-colored runes racing across it, her neck fur turning to a dark purple. She whispered something.

"W-we have an ... an emergency," Buoun explained, for the first time stammering and losing some of his excellent inflection. "In our home w-world's orbit. N-nothing you should—"

He startled. As did Gregory and everyone else in the room. From the ceiling, a klaxon blared. The room lights color-shifted toward red.

Gregory exclaimed, "What the hell?"

Grace had the door open from the outside and Pan plunged through it. "Boss," she said, her voice raised above the clamor.

Gregory rose from his chair, motioning for the Tluaanto to remain in theirs. "A moment, excellencies."

A hand clamped on his shoulder before he'd finished the phrase, and Grace yanked him out of the room, slapping the door button as they exited. At the T-junction to their left, crewers streamed past in both directions. Nearby, Wepps had his hand to his ear, concentrating on his comms.

Gregory didn't often see Peacers looking worried. Wepps looked worried.

"We're going to a safe room," Grace said.

"Why?"

"That—" She pointed to a nearby speaker. "—is an Approaching Vessel warning."

April 4, 3014, Old Earth Calendar

21

REGULATIONS STATED that at least one Peacer or security rating be stationed on the bridge at all times, standing to the side of the bridge entrance. This was a holdover from the earlier CUSET/PRC spacefaring era, intended to prevent acts of terrorism, criminality, or lunacy. On this shift, it was Chipper's turn. Normally, the four-hour stint was a study in complete boredom. This time, however, he was mere minutes into that shift when things began to get interesting—too interesting ...

The strained tone in Systems Chief Lindberg's voice was clear as she called across to Commander Chinyama. "XO, can you look at this?"

The lanky XO leaned low over Lindberg's console, a frown forming, before he faced the comms desk. Sintopas was off duty, replaced by an Ensign Meyers. Chinyama directed Meyers to hail the "approaching ship."

The workstation beside Chipper's position was one of the bridge's two sensor desks. With her eyes to glued to her monitors, the rating who manned it mumbled to herself, "It's coming like a bat out of hell." Chipper craned his neck to see but couldn't read the coded data that she was so easily deciphering.

"No response," called Meyers.

"You used the signal given to us by Envoy Buoun?"

"Aye, sir."

"On screen," Chinyama ordered. No tension had yet leaked into that calm voice of his.

The forward screen switched vistas from showing a distant stretch of asteroid belt to displaying the empty space above the Tluaanto home world. Empty except for a bright dot growing bigger. "Scans?"

The rating beside Chipper called back, "No shields, but heavily ionized hull plating."

The exact second she finished talking, another woman at another sensor station added, "Reading suspicious energy signatures, possibly particle beam generators."

"Get us moving. Evasive action. Raise shields, power up PC and MC."

Particle cannon and missile countermeasures, Chipper translated.

Chinyama continued, "Sound incoming alarm."

A chorus of *Ayes* came from various stations. A klaxon started up along the corridor outside.

Chipper found himself squeezing the grip of his slung rifle. As if that would help any. He swiped sweat from his upper lip. *What the heck is happening?*

"Envoy transport is detaching," the woman beside him reported. "Pulling away from us. And the bogey."

"Helm," the XO said, "change of plans. Screening maneuvers. Shepherd that transport, keep them in our shadow."

"Aye."

Systems Chief Lindberg asked him, "You think that bogey's coming for them?"

"Maybe there's an opposition faction we don't know

about. Either way, we're not letting that transport get away. Get a message to the envoy meeting, comms. Ask them for an explanation."

"Aye."

"Captain should be here any moment. Scans—"

"Particle generator energy build up!" one of them called.

"Here we go," said Lindberg.

Although an impact wouldn't affect the ship's gravity, Chipper automatically braced himself. *You said not to join the Peacekeepers, Da,* he thought grimly. *I'm beginning to think you were right.*

"AN APPROACHING …?" Gregory shook his head to clear it; the klaxon wasn't as loud and piercing out here in the hallway, but it was still annoying as hell. "There's probably vessels all over the place. What's the issue with this one?"

"If it didn't answer hails, and didn't shift course, it will have been designated hostile," Grace explained and tried to steer him toward Wepps. The sergeant had hurried toward the T-intersection and opened a hatch in a side wall.

Gregory resisted, pulling away and toward the meeting room's open door. Within, the two Tluaanto stared openly at him. "That makes no sense. Why would they attack us with their own envoys onboard? You don't think a Xerxian ship followed us?"

"Couldn't be. Xerxes didn't receive our encrypted course heading, and Fowler couldn't send one without us knowing even if he'd tried. But let's keep you safe until we know." She reached for his arm, and he dodged her.

"I'm not leaving them." Gregory stabbed a finger at the Tluaanto. "Our priority is preventing harm to them."

Relenting, Grace slapped the door jamb. "Follow us. Now."

The Tluaanto rose.

Buoun gathered their two water flasks under one arm. "What is it?"

Pi's neck hair continued to ripple with dark purple. She hissed questions at Buoun.

Gregory improvised, "A collision warning."

"Exactly," Grace said. "And you need to come to a safe room."

"Safe room?"

"With harnesses and a gel bubble. Keeps you safe if there is a critical event."

"I don't—"

"Just come, Buoun!" Gregory said, louder than he meant to. The klaxon was getting to him. As was the mystery of the danger to *Assured.* What on Foucault was going on? "Please. It's ten meters away."

Buoun hesitated one second longer, then nodded and took Pi's arm.

THE HUMANS HERDED them into a small circular room. The Ambassador's guard actually laid hands on Pi to hurry her through the entryway. He and Pi were strapped to uncomfortable seats, fittings that hadn't been crafted with Tluaan hips and spines in mind. If he hadn't glimpsed the message on Pi's device a moment before the alarm sounded, he might have wondered if they were being imprisoned for some reason.

Then again—he got his breathing under control and with it his thoughts—the Humans attending them were now similarly strapped and seated—Gregory and the warriors called Grace and Sgt. Wepps.

Worse than the mild pain from the awkwardly fitted restraints, and the terror of the emergency itself, Buoun knew he was close to the four Human-hour limit of their visits. His food was all gone. He and Pi would need some form of sugar within the next two of those "hours" or they would grow faint. Their water would last longer if they rationed, but it was not enough to see them through a ship's night—meaning Pi would need to trust Human water.

His anxiety piqued again, a wave of terror carrying him upward toward panic. He brought his focus inward, acknowledging the instinctive nature of most of the stress—deep-seated genetic-racial memories had flared to life, eons old, telling him that the combination of small space and being trapped within the chair's straps meant he was in fact caught in a sheh'shagun web.

The sheh'shagun are exterminated, *he reasoned with himself*, and the Humans are my friends. I am not in danger here. I am not in danger here.

To his left, Pi's coloring suggested not only alarm but deep suspicion. In rapid subtle hand signing, she said, Is the emergency out there some kind of Human trick?

Buoun shifted the water bottles he'd been gripping between his thighs and passed one across to her. Pi accepted it, the movement preventing further hand signs for the moment. Those graceful hands of hers were shaking. When she raised the bottle to her lips, water spilled and ran along her chin to drip onto her tunic. The bottle froze halfway back down when, from the floor center-cabin, a communications dome rose like a fast-growing fungus-cap. Thin strips of English, Spanish, and Mandarin text raced around it. Images flickered to life between these text-strips, showing their Council transport in one and a very different ship in another.

The design of that second ship, it wasn't Domain Space. From front-on, it looked like ...

"Domain Moon!" he said, speaking his own language.

"I see it too," Pi replied. She handed back her bottle and began signing again: Avoid specific terms when speaking. These creatures may understand our language better than they pretend.

If they were pretending, *Buoun thought,* and if they also understood sign, then they won't appreciate being called *creatures.*

He jammed the bottles between his thighs again and sent his own string of gestures. They are not stupid; we must tell them of the other domains.

She huffed and turned her face to the roof, clasping her hands together for the moment.

"This is bad," he heard Grace mutter.

Onscreen, the Moon ship fired, twin beams flashing past the camera position.

Across the small cabin, Wepps hissed words Buoun recognized as "swearing."

Pi glanced at Buoun long enough for him to sign to her, They missed.

Yes, but it's not this ship they're aiming at. *She indicated the other feed.*

Our transport? But why?

Buoun, you're good at Human things. But not Tluaan. Domain Moon were once the J'k'tek and Mujajamom nations, and they always lusted after space. They envy us. They want a star drive as badly as we do. If they destroy the transport, they can cripple the Human ship while awaiting reinforcements.

Are they insane? How can they think our forces won't respond and wipe them out?

"Don't underestimate them, Buoun," she whispered. Then, switching modes yet again, Our fleet is scattered throughout the system. Busy. Grown lazy. And the message that came to my communicator was an alert. Our satellites on this side of the planet have all gone silent. The

Council, including Naat, are more than three billion *shunagto* away from us. The message won't have reached them, and they'll only be just starting to discuss reasons for that satellite failure. But for the time being, they are blind and deaf.

She held out her hand for the water again.

And spoke.

"For the moment, we are completely alone here."

PAN MARCHED ONTO THE BRIDGE, taking command. Whereas Chipper was amazed at how calm Chinyama had remained through this emergency, he was equally amazed at Pan's energy and the enthusiasm the man seemed to have for the game that was afoot.

"Report!"

"Bogey has fired twice upon the envoy transport," Chinyama reported. "Whenever it slipped out of our shadow."

"Why's it slipping out of our shadow?"

"Its pilot is either not cooperating or panicking."

"Or both," Pan grumped. "Bogey has shields?"

"Ionized plating only."

"Weapons, ready."

"Aye, sir," returned the weapons station.

"Target aft sections. Short bursts until you hit something good." He placed himself before the forward screens, legs spread as if riding a high sea on the bow of an ancient whaling ship. Growing up on Oceana, working fishing fleets throughout his adolescence, Chipper had seen many a captain adopt that same pose. It inspired nothing less than complete trust within him. Pan added, "Let's see how tough they are."

The hostile vessel was easily definable now. Onscreen,

rapid bursts of laser fire stuttered out into space, tracking in the bogey's wake.

Mother lobster, Chipper swore in the Oceanean fashion. *We're shooting at aliens!*

The bogey made an error, attempting a hard turn to starboard. The turn slowed them enough for the laser targeting to catch up. A series of bolts slammed into the back of the vessel before the weapons officer took his finger from the button. The little ship was knocked into a lateral spin as flame jetted momentarily. Debris spread behind it. Continuing to spin, it caromed out of control on a trajectory that took it past *Assured* and would continue taking it out across the star system's orbital plane.

The helmsman asked, "Retrieval, sir?"

"Let them end up where they end up," Pan said. "Not our problem." He turned back to the room. "Comms, a channel to wherever those envoys are. If they're not in the meeting room, they'll be in the safe room down the hall."

Chipper's fists had curled tight, as tight as his chest felt. Though the two scan operators had high-fived each other when the bogey was disabled, Chipper's emotions were far more sober. Celebration seemed childish. This was not a happy moment. This was a possible prelude to a greater set of troubles than the pirate campaigns had ever been.

"WHO ARE THEY?"

Gregory eyeballed Pi as he asked her this. Her hands had been twitching for the past two minutes. Buoun's too. They probably thought he wouldn't notice they were signing to each other. He repeated the question.

The Tlaa glared back for a moment, then looked away.

So Gregory shifted focus to Buoun.

The envoy's shoulders slumped in a very humanlike gesture. "Enemies," he said.

Grace snorted quietly. "Duh." It was a complete lapse in diplomacy on her part, and an indication of how quickly she had come to accept the Tluaanto as people.

The klaxon had finally stopped a half-minute ago, leaving his ears ringing in the aftermath.

"We must know *exactly* who they are," Gregory said. "Threatening our ship might make them our enemies also. And we did not travel here to make enemies."

From the corner of one eye, Buoun watched Pi's twitching fingers a moment before his gaze returned to Gregory. His pupils were dilated. He opened his mouth as if to speak, closed it again, opened. No sound came out. His fur tended toward purple again.

Into the awkward silence, the room's comms channel flared to life.

"This is the captain for Ambassador Gregory's party. Be advised, immediate threat eliminated. And now I have a question for our visitors."

"We're in safe room ten," Wepps replied.

Gregory added, "Proceed with your question, Captain."

"What the hell was that?"

"Captain, language please," Gregory replied. "Envoy Buoun was about to explain this event. Envoy, we require clear and precise answers. Was that ship Tluaan? And, if so, to which Tluaanto did it belong?"

"Ambassador, Captain, yes. That vessel is Tluaanto. But it is not one of my people's. That ship belongs to another domain."

22

THE SMALL GROUP formed a rough circle in the corridor outside the safe room: Gregory, Pan, Pi, Buoun. Grace and Wepps watched from back near the meeting room door. Gregory's head pounded with a tension headache and swam with questions. But it was Pan who asked the next one.

"All right. Tell us. What is a domain?" Pan said this as he locked his hands behind his back and bobbed on the balls of his feet.

"Please, Captain," Buoun said. "We will educate you about all of this soon. But first we need to know if our shuttle survived the attack. And if we can restock our food and water from it."

"Your damned shuttle is fine—" Pan began then got control of his tone and volume after a gesture from Gregory. "And Sgt. Wepps can escort one of you to restock your supplies in a little while. But not until you explain yourselves."

Pi said something that Buoun appeared hesitant to translate.

"What did she say?" Gregory insisted.

"She ... she says you are guests in our space. You don't give us orders. I'm sorry. She should not have said that."

"She understands us, then?"

"Pi is a leader. She understands your tone, not your words. She understands the situation."

"We're guests that were fired upon." Pan brought a hand around to point at Pi. "We're guests that were forced to disable a Tluaan ship in order to protect your shuttle. Remember that. And answer our questions. Now."

Buoun gestured to shift Pan's attention back to him. "A domain is best defined as an area of ownership. In the past we had nations as you did. Our history was filled with warfare—and yours must also have been, since your vessel and your warriors carry such powerful weapons. Our nations eventually reached a point of ..." He consulted his wrist-device for a few seconds, then continued: "Of rationality. Across our world, we agreed to divide the realms of our planet and solar system among ourselves. This allowed for trade and for clear boundaries, avoiding dispute ... and for each group to retain some form of dignity."

"What were these realms?" Gregory asked.

"Domain Ocean. Domain Surface—who control only the land masses upon the planet. Domain Moon. Domain Space. Councillor Pi and I are from Domain Space. It is with us you have been speaking, and it is we who are the most peaceful and sophisticated of the—"

"Spare us the propaganda," Pan sighed. "If you're so peaceful, why are your fellow Tluaanto firing on you?"

Pi was openly signaling for a translation, but Buoun hurried ahead in English first. "As you say, they fired on us. You have not observed us initiating hostility this way, have you?"

"We don't know what we're observing," Pan said. "And what we're not. There could be all kinds of things happening on that planet that are relevant here. For all we know, Domain Space, as you style yourselves, have enslaved entire continents down there, and this is Domain Surface fighting back against their oppressors."

Pi's signals became more insistent and Buoun conceded, rattling off long strings of Tluaan words and hand signals. Pi said something more, and Buoun returned his attention to Gregory and Pan.

"She says we have done nothing of the sort. We are peaceful and interested only in exploration and in expanding the reach of our species."

"Said imperialists throughout the ages," Pan muttered.

"Please, Captain, Ambassador. Allow us to restock our food and water and we will sit down again and discuss this further. We also need to access data from our domain to ascertain what is happening. This data would be of use to you too."

"When I left the bridge, we were drawing close to your shuttle again and signaling it to dock. But we are not letting it leave with you on board until we have a clearer understanding of what is transpiring here and how it might affect us in future." Pan looked to Gregory who nodded unhappily.

Much as I hate to admit it, you're right, Captain.

Buoun consulted his device where Gregory this time could see human writing in multiple languages. The envoy put it away and said, "You intend to keep us here as hostages? I believe that is the term."

"Not hostages," said Pan. "Advisers."

Wanting to minimize Buoun's alarm, Gregory added, "We can't send you out there in an unarmed shuttle if more attack ships are coming for you."

But Pan was disinterested in conciliation. He continued, "Envoy Buoun, I want you to hear me clearly here—and you can pass this onto your superior in a moment. Ambassador Chris Gregory is polite. And compassionate, gracious, fair, and optimistic. I am none of those things. He came here to assess your potential to become our friends. I came here to assess your threat as enemies."

"But we—" Buoun started.

Pan cut him off. "The DCHC are now aware of a space-faring species whose motivations may threaten us. This sudden outbreak of ... internal politics ... has only elevated your threat status, in my opinion. You can stay on *Assured* willingly and cooperate with us in this matter—this might demonstrate your nature as our friends. Or you can be detained here against your will and answer our questions anyway."

Gregory's gut felt leaden. He could see the opportunity for that interspecies friendship evaporating the longer the starship commander spoke. He pointed toward the open meeting room door and said, "Captain, might I have a word?"

"There is no need for you to 'have a word,'" Buoun said. "And no need for threats. You are right in thinking our shuttle will be vulnerable if we leave now. And we are eager to prove our intentions as allies to you."

Pi again signed for a translation, and Buoun again ignored it.

"So, you'll explain all this to us?" Gregory asked.

"My human friends, it is your turn to listen carefully. To use a human phrase, I want to cooperate *one hundred and ten percent*. For my own safety. For the sake of a friendly alliance between your human faction and our Tluaan one. And because Domain Space—my domain—may depend on your assistance to survive this threat against us."

"And?"

"And," Buoun took a deep breath. "At this moment, I need you to assist me in a necessary lie. I need you to pretend to separate us, Pi and me. I cannot help you while she is here because she will understand enough of our interactions to misunderstand my actions as being—" He thought for a moment. "—not loyal. You could ... you could detain her and our pilot in our shuttle and stop it from detaching from your ship. You could calm her suspicions by allowing her to receive data feeds from our domain, so she doesn't feel completely isolated."

"And you?" Gregory asked.

"Take me back to the meeting room. Bring me some of our food and water. Send the same Domain Space data feeds in there so we can remain informed as we speak."

"Buoun, what are you going to tell her? About us separating you?"

"I'll tell her that you suspect me of first attracting your ship into our territory and second of inviting this attack on your ship. Then I will say that you are—" he checked his device quickly for another word "—interrogating me. I'll say you don't suspect her but want to protect her from further enemy attack for the moment. Later, you must tell her any information I gave you was given because of duress you put me under."

"You want us to present ourselves as torturers?"

Another dictionary consultation, then Buoun replied, "I understand the concept, of course. Our history is far from bloodless. And no, when everything settles—as I'm sure it will with your help—we will present this as a cultural misunderstanding. I thought you would torture me and divulged information to avoid it, then later I realized that you don't torture people—"

"We don't."

"I am very glad to hear it."

"You're not worried about being seen as a coward."

"Coward?"

"Weak. Scared."

Pale shading rippled across Buoun's neck and cheeks.

His ears flickered. Gregory could read none of that. The envoy replied, "But I *am* weak and scared. A warrior might be expected to resist pain, but not an envoy or scientist."

Pan and Greg exchanged a look. *Good to know*, Pan's expression said.

"She won't try to fly away?" Gregory asked Buoun.

"Can you not keep the shuttle hooked?"

"Tethered," Pan corrected. "Yes, we can. But answer the ambassador's question, please— she won't try to escape?"

"Captain. The closest base to us is in orbit where things are no doubt highly dangerous right now. Our satellites all went dark on that side of the world moments before your alarm started. She cannot head in that direction. We maintain bases around and on the next planet out from our star, but it is currently on the far side of the sun. Our shuttle—your *Assured*—are over a hundred million of your kilometers away from our next-nearest base. That is a very long distance for her to fly safely in a small shuttle. We maintain small numbers of other larger vessels around the system. But our main fleet of defensive ships are guarding the station in the asteroid belt upon which our council resides."

"Guarding it against ...?" Pan asked.

"Well, against you."

"Us?" Gregory asked.

"We did not know what to expect of you. Or rather, the council did not. You are much as *I* had hoped."

Pan snorted at Buoun's apparent fawning. To Gregory, he said, "If this is how we get intel, then by all means let's play bad cop."

Gregory had no idea what that term meant, but he nodded in agreement that they follow Buoun's plan.

Pan called down the corridor. "Sergeant Wepps, escort the councillor to the shuttle dock. Ms. Renny, I assume you need no assistance accompanying the ambassador and Envoy Buoun."

"I got this," she replied.

Pan caught Buoun's eye and gestured toward Pi. "If you please."

Buoun nodded and passed the "message" on. Pi appeared angry, eyes narrowing, throat fur cycling to a deep red. Her jaw worked, but she made no objection. And when Wepps gestured for her to precede him toward the shuttle dock, she complied—without so much as a backward glance toward Buoun.

The Tluaan envoy watched her go. Once she was out of sight, he turned to Gregory and bared his teeth in imitation of a smile. "I thought she'd never leave," he said.

Pan stomped off in the opposite direction, barking over his shoulder for them to follow him.

As they did, Gregory murmured to Buoun, "Nice joke."

"That is gratifying to hear. I wasn't sure it would translate."

23

CHIPPER WAS SO FOCUSED on bridge activity that he actually jumped when Captain Pan strode in past him again, barking at the XO for an update. The captain took up his customary position between the two helm stations, but faced back into the bridge. While the XO explained they were withdrawing from the planet now that the shuttle was reattached, Chipper heard more movement and voices in the passageway outside and turned in time to see Ambassador Gregory enter the Ready Room ahead of—

Chipper's breath caught.

Alien!

The Tluaan person at Gregory's shoulder was short with a large head which had a crest at the back. The fur on his head was orange. These people must've loved vivid color because this one had dressed in a light purple robe over a deep red tunic and trousers. He wore dark gray boots with rounded toes.

The Tluaan had passed him now, leaving Chipper to gape at the back of its head and think manic thoughts. A non-human! He'd just seen one, live! What was it doing up here? *It*. Was it male or female? Nothing in the head or face, its posture, the clothing, its bearing had given its gender away.

Mother lobster! This'll be something to tell my folks about. Mum, Dad, the moment I saw a non-human with my own eyes.

That made him remember the Tluaan's eyes in the split second it had glanced his way. Its eyes!

Sorrowful, piercingly intelligent.

And Chipper should have been watching the entire bridge, but he couldn't keep his eyes off the newcomer. He noticed now that it had left in its wake a faint sweet-bitter scent like Oceanean sea cloves.

"Stations, report," Pan called, and Chipper snapped his attention back to his surroundings.

"Ship, undamaged. Shields at one hundred percent."

"All weapons on standby."

"No vessels within thirty million klicks of us."

"No incoming hails. Plenty of chatter around the system though, sir. Running it through translation programs but not much luck following it so far."

"Keep on it," Pan said, interrupting the flow of reports. He focused on another sensor operator. "Esana, what's happening at the planet?"

"Sir," the woman replied, "on this side of the planet, it appears that surface-to-orbit missiles were launched from on-world and impacted a number of orbital installations. Several others have been snuffed out, and we're not sure how—possibly orbitally-launched missiles from other satellites. There was a massive explosion on-world we suspect came from an orbital laser, though we missed the actual firing. Big news is there's activity from the moon, which is still far side of the planet. It looks like five vessels, all about one-seventh the size of *Assured*, on an outbound heading."

"Toward what?"

"One could be on its way toward us. The others' targets

are unclear, but we know there are several massive artificial habitats around the asteroid belt. Those four ships could be on a heading toward this one." Esana cast a graphic up onto the main screen showing a mock-up of a sphere along with distance and position markings.

"Domain Space's council base," Pan said. "Most likely."

"Yes, it is," the Tluaan envoy said sadly. Heads turned toward him. Even Chipper gasped at the clarity of the words coming from a non-human mouth.

"Excuse me, Captain," said the XO, taking attention from the visitor. "'Domain Space'?"

"I'll explain soon, XO. Esana, there are Tluaan ships already near that habitat, right?" He glanced at the envoy as he asked.

The rating leaned over her station for a few seconds. "Traffic has been abundant along all visible points of the belt since we arrived, sir. Three ships of significant size are stationed right by the habitat, maybe a half dozen more within six thousand klicks of it."

"Any moving?"

"Three appear to be accelerating toward planet, sir. Might be an intercept course with the moon-origin vessels." At these kinds of distances, Chipper understood, specifics were difficult and bridge crews were often left to educated guesswork and computer projections.

"People," the captain said, "we are in a war zone. Eyes, ears and instincts sharp. Helm, move us around to get the moon in full view. Keep us away from any hot zones for the moment. But not too far away that we can't intervene if it becomes necessary. Comms, sensors, text me in my Ready Room with anything of interest. *Anything*. I want all camera feeds available in there too."

A chorus of "*yes, sir.*"

"Chief Lindberg, you have the bridge. XO, with me."

As the captain and Chinyama neared the exit, Pan drew

up short and eyeballed Chipper. The big Peacer gulped under the scrutiny.

"Where's Colonel Fowler?"

"Er, dunno," said Chipper. "Sir."

Pan swung around to address the bridge. "Fowler. Where is he?"

No one knew.

"Well, ping him. If he doesn't respond, send the Peacer to find him for me." He slapped Chipper's shoulder on the way out.

Chipper relaxed half a notch as other personnel trudged past him. He felt glad to be out of the captain's scrutiny, reassured to be in capable hands, along with a terrible feeling that hunting down the Xerxian colonel might be the easiest assignment he'd be getting in the near future.

ANA SHUFFLED her feet while Hecate beside her remained statue-still. The two of them stood at Fowler's shoulders as the elevator whisked them to F-deck.

What's on F-deck? she asked herself and conjured up a mental map of the ship. Officers' compartments, vessel list-and-trim-management system, back-up storage servers for the instrumentation, power and lighting networking systems. And a small hydroponics section. *What are we doing?*

The lift slowed to a stop, the doors opened, and Fowler exited fast with his head down, deep in thought. In the wake of the alarm—which had gone quiet several minutes ago—he'd said nothing to them beyond the command to follow. She and Hecate exchanged an unhappy glance before hurrying to keep up with him. Their commander stalked forty meters along the main arterial, turned one corner, then another. A moment later, they found themselves following him into his stateroom.

Ana knew it was Fowler's the moment she stepped inside ...

The aroma of Xerxian catfrog stew lingered from where Fowler had been cooking on a corner pot-and-burner.

The only clothing hanging neatly on the rail by the single bunk were two other clean-and-pressed versions of his normal uniform and a set of exercise clothes.

And the work desk held a 3D still-image of Fowler's home town of Juarez Falls as seen from the other end of the valley.

The desk and the floor beside it also played host to five paired tablets. The small network of devices was manned by Enforcer Manolo, slumped in Fowler's chair, fingers tapping at one of the tabs. She or Fowler had jacked one of the devices into a wall port using ceramic-fiber cable.

"Is that Confed data?" Hecate gasped, drawing nearer.

Ana scrambled to get in front of her, the better to see.

Manolo glanced up and grinned. "Some of it's alien too. Can't read it, but we can decrypt it someday soon."

Fowler had moved to stand by his bunk. He asked, "What do we know?"

Manolo's grin turned his way before she refocused on her tabs. "This is glorious, Colonel. The aliens are fightin' amongst themselves. Some shitty little unshielded gunboat came over and tried to hit the alien shuttle we got docked. Chinyama took it out with lasers; it's spinnin' out of control toward the edge of the star system. Whole thing gets better too. Orbital artifacts are snuffin' each other out. The moon just launched a bunch of big ass bogeys that might be warships. There's been some kind of explosion at a facility on-planet, probably payback from one of the orbital platforms." She slapped her thigh. "I'd pay to watch action like this."

Hecate chuckled. "Think it's us arrivin' here that kicked this off?"

"Or did we fly into a war that was already happening?" Ana added.

Fowler didn't answer. Rather, he began pacing and they had to retreat to Manolo's side to keep out of his way in the tight compartment. "Those Confed bastards cut me out of meeting with the alien envoy. They're planning things now, and I'm still uninvited. No explanation for the alarms and ship maneuvers. Any idiot could feel that *Assured* was firing laser cannons, but still no explanation for it from Pan. That *cabrón* thinks he can leave me out completely? Manolo, he's probably in his Ready Room by now. You tapped in?"

One of her big hands flashed across to another tab and tapped something. "Here ya go. No one in there yet, but we'll hear it when they is."

Ana startled at this. If the Confeds found out what was happening ... "The Ready Room, sir? And they won't detect it?"

Manolo laughed, sweeping her arm around the various tablets. "Have they detected any of this yet? I'm better'n any of 'em."

Not as good as me, you armpit itch. Shoulda been me here doing this. Properly.

"Some Confed tech is better than ours," Fowler smirked. "And some of ours is better than theirs. Now get to work. Jogianto, those two are yours. Hecate, you got that one. Start analyzing. Text my tab with anything important."

"People comin' into the Ready Room," Manolo said.

Fowler put an earpiece into his right ear and tapped it. "Manolo, patch their feed in here."

"I AM NO MILITARY TACTICIAN," Buoun was saying,

"but those white markers there will probably be collections of what we call prone-fighters."

Gregory followed the line of Buoun's finger onto the Ready Room's wall screen. An animated tactical mock-up showed Suuchaat's western hemisphere facing *Assured* and the orbital region around it. The planet showed blue; the black space around and above it was awash with light-purple, yellow, white and green speckles and dots, as if someone has dusted it with an exotic spice powder. Tiny letters marked height above the surface along with their headings. Buoun's "prone-fighters" moved in a tight cluster of minute dots with one set of lettering accounting for that cluster, headed right to left across the screen. They did not appear to be moving quickly, but then they were very small —no doubt much smaller than the dots intimated—and even low-orbit space covered vast distances.

Pan immediately seized on Buoun's explanation, approaching the screen from the opposite edge. "Fighters? Whose fighters?"

Buoun was also standing—in fact, no one in the room had sat yet. He touched a nearby section of display with one brown fingernail. "This yellow dot will be one of our stations."

"Yellow means it's damaged," Chinyama explained to him. "Missile-damaged?"

"Yes, possibly. Or laser. But not enough to prevent the launch of those craft."

"Why 'prone'?" asked Gregory.

"Their pilots lie forward to steer their vessels."

"And this is another set of fighters here?" Pan asked, indicating a similar configuration of white dots on the left-hand edge of Suuchaat, also moving right-to-left. If his interpretation of the mock-up's distance key was accurate, they were about twenty thousand kilometers from the first cluster.

"I believe so," Buoun replied. "Domain Surface maintains one minor orbital platform in geosynchronous orbit on Suuchaat's far side with two automated satellites defending it. Legally, they are not supposed to keep combat vessels in orbit, but these dots probably originated there."

Gregory marveled at Buoun's use of such technical language—then marveled that his own brain bothered thinking about the Tlu using words like *geosynchronous* when there were bigger issues here.

Pan studied the display. "Their home station is certainly not visible from here. So, at that speed, they must have been launched at least fifteen minutes ago. Right when all this trouble started.

"A preemptive move," said Chinyama. "And look, your fighters are turning back toward the others."

"This is terrible," Buoun muttered miserably.

"Sir," the XO continued, "I'm concerned about that moon-origin ship launched our way."

Pan nodded. "Computer, shift tactical mock-up across to moon, full view." Obligingly, the display swung left and up to where the full sphere of the moon was now visible over the planet's shoulder. The satellite appeared the size of a golf ball onscreen, painted a different shade of blue to the planet, though in real life it was as gray as old Earth's. There was a green marker angling out from it and toward the left side of the screen. "They've changed their mind about attacking us."

"That ship *has* changed course," Chinyama confirmed. "This heading appears in line with that of the others we saw."

"They're not all stupid, then."

The Ready Room door slid open and Wepps entered, carrying an insulator bag. Without pausing, he placed the bag on the table and straightened. "The envoy's resupply, sirs. Councillor Pi is safely aboard her shuttle with Peacekeepers Bradstock and Stines watching over her."

"Excellent," Pan started, before something onscreen drew his attention away. Red dots had begun flashing from three locations on the lunar surface. Pan swore when he saw them.

"What are they?" Gregory asked.

"Launch sites." He brushed past Buoun on his way to his customary end of the table, tapping at a keyboard as he sat. The wall screen split into two displays, the new one running lines of text within nine separate boxes.

Pan jumped up again to pore over the text up close. Chinyama joined him to do the same, blocking Gregory's view of the tactical mock-up so that the ambassador had to step left to see. Buoun had backed away to make room for the two officers.

Pan said, "My bloody ghost, that's bad."

And Chinyama said, "Rockets."

"Big ones," Pan added.

"Accompanied by a fleet of ... forty-five smaller craft. A fighter escort perhaps. Wait ... Sensor readings indicate nuclear warheads."

"Oh, my God," Gregory said as Buoun exclaimed something in his own language. "Headed where?"

"Give it a moment," said Pan. Several seconds later, new white markers appeared moving outward from the red launch sites and in different directions. "These two are outbound—and see here that the five Moon ships headed for the belt have changed course abruptly, perhaps with new targets now—but this nuke's headed for the planet. Wait!" He leaned close, his head swinging between the lettering under the marker to one of the text boxes and back again. "More likely something in high orbit farside."

"We have several populated stations in orbit on the far side," Buoun moaned. "Please stop that missile."

"We have time," Chinyama advised. "If we hurry."

Pan shook his head. "No doubt the battle's going on over there too. If they're throwing a nuke at his guys, then Space is probably kicking their asses over there."

"Kicking their asses?" Buoun asked.

"Winning," Gregory explained. "Idiomatic."

"Oh. That is not certain. And there are many lives on our stations there. One in particular—"

"I'm not intervening," Pan growled. "We are not your servants. And we are not your allies."

"Captain," Gregory said. "Destroying that nuke would be an act of mercy."

"Any intervention is an act of war. We only fired on that runabout because—"

"We could be buying time for a resolution of this conflict."

"Or escalating it!"

"They're firing nukes! It can't get much more escalated than this."

Teeth gritted, the captain got his own voice under control. "Ambassador, hear me. I don't want people to die any more than you do. But as I keep saying, we have no formal treaty with Envoy Buoun's faction. They're just the first ones we met. They might be the bad guys; the ones firing the nukes might be the ones we should buddy up to. We are weeks away from receiving orders from either Fleet Command or the Parliament, and we don't have enough intel yet to advise them."

Buoun reached out both hands as he continued to plead. His throat fur did not color-shift as much as Pi's had, but the distress was evident in his face. "Captain. There is a balance at work here, and Domains Surface and Moon are seeking to upset it. Our history has taught us one thing—the balance must be maintained or there will be catastrophe. If things become bad enough, my council might even consider maneuvering a small asteroid to use in response."

"Holy Christ," Gregory hissed.

"They'd throw an asteroid at their own planet?" Pan asked, eyes wide.

"War has led to nothing but madness for thousands of our planet's orbits. But we conquered that madness. Or thought we did. The establishment of the domains achieved the longest period of peace between us in history. We must conquer our madness again—and quickly, with your help—or there will be nothing left of our species."

"Envoy, I have my orders, and I have my rules of engagement. The best I can offer you and Councillor Pi is sanctuary aboard my starship. But we are unfortunate observers at this stage."

Unrelenting, Buoun turned one outstretched hand toward Gregory while the other began worrying at his ear as if massaging stress from it. "Ambassador. You don't know us. But you know me. You know I admire your species. Deeply. And it is not just that you are new and unfamiliar, unique, exotic. You represent not just the possibility for my domain to advance further technologically. You are our way forward morally. As a species. We have poor qualities, yes. We also have fine ones. A thousand years ago, as you were climbing off your world for the first time, we were leaving our medieval-analog era behind and with it rejecting religion. When we did so, we abandoned many barbaric practices along with practices that had held back science. But we also lost some of our better morals."

Perversely, Gregory's thoughts shifted suddenly to wondering at the envoy's command of English—and at the way he suddenly didn't need his dictionary as much. Did heightened emotion sharpen the Tluaan mind?

Was he playing us earlier?

Buoun continued, "Those morals have been preserved

largely among the poorer classes whom also I admire greatly. Across all domains, some of our simplest people live selflessly while practicing prayers to gods and ancestors, to ethereal beings who can help them magically. What if … what if, in a way, you are those beings. Not gods. But, in a way, saviors. You can help us do what we can't do for ourselves. You can save us. From ourselves. Please help us re-effect the balance. And please, please, stop that rocket!"

Pan growled as he shook his head in obstinacy and returned to his seat, where he slumped over his tablet and entered commands Gregory couldn't see.

Buoun's plaintive gaze remained locked with Gregory's. But before the human ambassador could say anything, Chinyama spoke again.

"The other two nukes may be headed for those asteroid habitats. Or the fleet near the council one. At this speed, and if I'm correct in their target—"

"You probably are," Pan interjected.

"—they will reach the closest in one hundred-twenty-three days. Plenty of time to evacuate those habitats or move them."

"Our habitats cannot be moved," Buoun said, palms against his cheeks once more. "Including the orbital one on the far side of Suuchaat. And it cannot be evacuated in time. Please, that rocket headed into orbit must be stopped." He gripped both ears fully now, wringing them. He made such a distressing picture that Gregory felt actual tears welling in his eyes and had to blink them away, had to look away.

"This is your war," Pan told Buoun.

"And it's your presence that provoked it."

Voice rising, Pan said, "And you invited us here. Invited aliens here! Without informing the rest of your species!"

"Please. Please, Captain. Please, Ambassador. I'm not asking you to kill anybody. Just to stop that rocket. I do not know if our habitats have sufficient defenses to stop it. And if it hits the largest one—" He swallowed what sounded like a sob. Every human in the room frowned at that. Buoun's hands had left his ears alone, but they'd moved to his cheeks, patting, rubbing, self-soothing.

Gregory made a calming motion. "Buoun. What is it?"

"Sixteen thousand lives. That is how many people are on that station. And my younger sibling and her family are among them."

Pan wasn't arguing with him now, nor was he slumping in his chair. Buoun had the ear of every human in the room, judging by their expressions.

He certainly has mine, Gregory thought. *Jesus, his sister!* "Captain. Rules of engagement be damned. He's asking us to prevent deaths, not cause them."

Pan looked to his XO who gave him a small nod. Pan wrinkled up his face at him. "*Et tu,* Mr. Chinyama?" He sighed. "This could be the end of my career."

"Or it could be the end of sixteen thousand lives," Gregory said.

"You do not fight fair, Ambassador. Nor do you, Envoy Buoun." He growled in exasperation as his fingers played over the keys on his control board. On the tactical, an orange ring appeared around the rocket in question. It was nearly at the point where it would pass behind the planet from *Assured*'s perspective. "Helm, note the target I've just marked and commence an intercept course, close enough to destroy it with missiles within the next three minutes. Chief Lindberg, I'll be there in a moment." He released the button, rising. "Envoy, follow me onto the bridge."

"Thank you, Captain. Thank you."

"Seriously. Don't thank me. I can only hope that we're about to make matters better and not worse."

AS ANA SCOURED the data coming her way, Colonel Fowler's door alert chimed.

"Shit," the colonel muttered and punched an intercom beside his cot without opening the door. "What?"

"Ah, Colonel, this is Tukimatu."

Shit, all right, Ana thought. All the Enforcers' eyes flicked between the door and Fowler.

"What?" Fowler repeated.

"Uh, Colonel, the captain wants you on bridge. Now."

"I'll be there in a few minutes."

"He said now, sir."

Rather than scowling, Fowler smiled. "Finally invited to the party, am I? Go hold the lift for me, Corporal, I'm putting my boots on."

He let go of the button, checked the camera to ensure Chipper had left, then grunted happily and went to the door. "Message Umbrano to meet me on bridge level," he said and marched out.

"That was close," Manolo murmured.

Tellin' me, Ana thought.

"Why are you looking at Tluaanto signals?" Hecate asked her.

Ana scowled back. "Why you looking at my tabs and not your own?"

"Hack you."

"Likewise."

The stream of alien symbols was hypnotizing, and was probably pointless, though Ana had software helping her look for patterns of interest. One string kept repeating, and the software kept flagging it: three symbols, identical, buried in a radio signal from the far side of the planet. Amongst everything else, Ana couldn't see why the software would think that string important ... and it still had no way of translating any of it into a human language.

She sighed and turned her attention to the human data flowing in.

PRECEDING FOWLER ONTO THE BRIDGE, the first thing Chipper noticed was the alien envoy. The delegation had returned to the bridge, and the Tluaan envoy had been placed at the back where he leaned against a railing near Chipper's official position. As Fowler lingered in the doorway beside him, Chipper found it hard to tear his gaze away from the Tluaan visitor.

He's right there again!

Ambassador Gregory stood beside Envoy Buoun. Sgt. Wepps and Ms. Renny had moved along the bridge to Chipper's right to find standing room between workstations there. Captain Pan stood in his customary place between the helm stations while XO Chinyama had relieved one of the sensor operators.

"There it is, sir!" a helmsman said.

Chipper's attention snapped to the tactical mock-up onscreen, instantly locking onto the red-ringed bogey they must have been chasing around the planet.

What's going on now? he wondered.

"Particle beam, sir?" asked one of the weapons cons.

"Belay that. Might hit any one of a dozen other artifacts in orbit. XO, am I right in thinking that rocket's not following a simple predictable course?"

"It's firing retros in random spurts, corkscrewing erratically."

"To throw off orbital defenses. Weapons, set Mako missile to avoid gravity well and launch at full speed."

The weapons controller was already battering his keyboard before Pan's orders were finished. A second after the word *speed*, the rating tapped his final key with a pianist's flourish and called, "Missile away."

Over his shoulder, Pan told the two diplomats, "Should make it in time."

"Continue pursuit, sir?" asked the helmsman.

"Until I say otherwise." Pan's words came out harsh, and he patted the man's shoulder as if to make up for his tone.

Chipper stiffened when the captain spun around and addressed him directly. "Where's Colonel F—?" His gaze snapped to the doorway. "Never mind."

Fowler ventured inside, coming to rest beside Ambassador Gregory.

A male Tactical took up position in the doorway, blocking it—the one called Umbrano, a fellow almost as big as Chipper. He must have come up in the next lift after theirs, probably at Fowler's request. Chipper checked his wrist-scanner which showed the man was unarmed, as would be protocol for non-DCHC personnel on a starship bridge. Nevertheless, he kept Umbrano well within his peripheral vision. The big Tactical's jaw worked as he chewed gum of some sort, his focus entirely on Buoun as Chipper's had been only a moment earlier.

"Any chance I'll be told what the hell's happening?" Fowler snapped.

"If you'd been available, you'd already know. Where were you?"

"Even Xerxians take showers sometimes. Despite Confederation beliefs."

Just after a klaxon had been sounding? Chipper wondered.

Apparently just as skeptical, Pan shot back, "Long bloody shower."

Fowler ignored that, turning toward the Tluaan. "We

met upon your first arrival. But perhaps you don't remember me?"

"Envoy Buoun," Gregory said, "this is Colonel Fowler of Xerxes. Ranking, Colonel. Name, Fowler. Colonel, this is Envoy Buoun."

The envoy and the colonel nodded to each other, then Fowler faced forward again. "So nice of you to finally invite the Xerxian representative to the p—"

"Enough, Fowler," Pan growled. "Open your ears for a very fast update. There was an attack on the envoy's shuttle by a foreign Tluaan power which we repelled; we are now attempting to take out that red bogey onscreen with a Mako."

"Our last Mako?"

"You have something else you'd like to use it on?"

Fowler ignored that. "And why are we attacking a Tluaan target?"

"The rocket is unmanned but bears a nuclear warhead. We're attempting to prevent the destruction of a populated habitat."

"Things are never dull around here, are they?"

"Not so exciting that we need your man there." Pan pointed at Umbrano.

"I might him need him. To run an errand or two."

"Then he can wait back by the elevator."

Fowler hesitated before sending Umbrano down the corridor. With a huff and muttered imprecation, the Tactical vanished from the doorway. Chipper craned around to make sure he went where the captain wanted him—which he did. With two Peacekeepers, two envoys, the ambassador's assistant, and now two Tacticals, the bridge was beginning to run out of places where people not manning workstations could stand and keep out of the way. One less person made a huge difference.

Chinyama cleared his throat. "Captain, I'm designating

an artifact in gold onscreen. Believe this is the rocket's target." Chipper saw a small gold flashing triangle just in view around the arc of the planet. "Object is a cube, approximately four hundred by four hundred by four hundred meters."

"That is it," Buoun said, and Chipper marveled at the rich tone of the creature's voice.

Person's voice, he corrected himself.

Onscreen, the rocket corkscrewed closer to its target. Uncomfortably closer. *Assured's* missile narrowed the gap quickly, but Chipper couldn't have been the only one wondering if it would make it.

"Rocket distance to impact, one hundred and three thousand klicks," the XO called.

Someone swore but the officers ignored the break with discipline. Chipper could see the envoy's hands tightening around the rail.

"Ninety-six thousand."

The other sensor operator piped in with: "Mako distance to impact, thirteen hundred klicks."

"Come on, come on," Chipper heard someone mutter. A moment later, he realized it had been him.

"Eighty-five thousand."

"Six hundred."

"Sixty-five thousand."

"Three hundred."

"We're going to make it," Gregory told Buoun who did not respond.

"Fifty thousand. Rocket accelerating."

"Mako compensating. One hundred ninety klicks now ... Impact in twelve seconds. Ten."

The last few seconds played out without commentary and ended with a brief bright bloom of color onscreen.

"Rocket destroyed," said Chinyama, and the bridge erupted into cheers—though most people perhaps had no idea of the true importance of the event. Chipper certainly was still guessing.

"Captain, I am very grateful," Buoun called out above it all.

The captain acknowledged him with a distracted flick of one hand. "XO, have we gotten a datapack off to Fleet Command?"

"I sent my report across to Mr. Meyers moments ago, Captain."

"Compressing now, sir," the second-shift comms officer said. He added, "Sir, I'm not picking up as much comms traffic as I'd expect in space this well populated."

"But you're picking up some?"

"Low UHF traffic, sir, and computer's still having difficulty translating all of it."

"Some will be in languages other than mine," said Buoun. "If you like, I could translate parts of it for you."

"Maybe some other time," said Pan. "Right now—"

"Sir!" Meyers interrupted. "Incoming signal from planet. Tight beam audio-visual."

"Ah. This is where your translation skills may come in handy, Envoy Buoun. But be precise, please, and remember we are recording everything that happens here."

Posture deferential, Buoun replied, "Of course, Captain."

"On screen, Mr. Meyers."

What followed was yellow pixelated static on the monitor accompanied by a screeching-like microphone feedback. Hands went over ears all around the bridge.

"Kill it, Meyers, kill it!"

Meyers did, cutting off the static and screeching immediately and leaving a dull ringing in Chipper's ears and Fowler swearing a blue streak.

"What was—?" Pan never got to finish his question.

Before he could, everything went to hell.

24

ONE MOMENT, Chris Gregory was standing perfectly stable and secure on a starship bridge as he had done a hundred times before. The next, he was pitching sideways to land in a tangle of limbs, with Buoun beneath him and Fowler on top. All three of them continued slipping sideways along the floor, which made no sense whatsoever. It was as if they were being dragged by an unseen force. A force like—

Gravity!

Shipgrav's gone haywire, he realized. It had realigned the bridge floor at a dangerous angle. Other people had fallen, were falling, were gripping for dear life to panels and railings.

And then the floor swung back to where it was supposed to be. Bridge lighting kept dimming and brightening, dimming and brightening. Fowler sprung away, allowing Gregory to climb off Buoun, making apologies for something that wasn't his fault. He was surrounded by gasps and groans and more undisciplined imprecations as others got to their feet. The Peacer, Chipper, was rubbing his shoulder where it must have struck console or floor. His weapon had twisted behind him on its strap and was making a low beeping noise. He frowned at it, confused.

What happened?

"Report!" Pan hollered, appearing from behind the port helm desk.

As people swiftly called out their lack of serious injury, Meyers shouted over the top of them all. "Possible virus embedded in that signal!"

Back on their feet, primary and backup helmsmen reported simultaneously, "Helm unresponsive!"

"Partitions!" Pan barked.

"Erecting," one after another station called back as personnel returned to their controls.

"Rifle malfunction," Chipper called, turning heads. The corporal looked up from studying the tiny screen on top of the weapon. "Control chip fried."

"Here," Chinyama called to him and equipped him with a ballistic sidearm from a locker under one of the work-stations.

"Chief Lindberg," Pan continued, "systems status."

"Terrible. Systems unresponsive or compromised are: propulsion, radiation monitoring, water cooling, shields, and comms." She paused to wipe sweat from her eyes. "A.I. intervened to recover gravity quickly. Partitions appear to have protected other systems."

"In-ship intercom?"

"Patchy, sir, but working."

Pan glanced at the main screen which was currently blank. "Start feeding priority reports, including medical, into the corner of the main screen. Comms, get me forward camera visuals as well as navdata displays."

"Trying, sir."

"Try harder. Sgt. Wepps, alert all Peacekeepers to equip ballistic weapons while replacing pulse rifle chips." Wepps put his hand to his earpiece to pass the message on. "Ms.

Lindberg, get A.I. to extrapolate its solution for the shipgrav situation to repair other systems. Helm, what's our heading?"

"Moving in a mild lateral spin, sir, but we're lucky," the backup helmsman replied while her partner was busy. "Current vector and speed take us past the planet's gravity well and out between it and the moon."

"Not so lucky if those moon bases fire a nuke at us while we can't evade it."

"Helldamn," replied the helmsman. Then, "Sorry, sir."

"Ms. Lindberg, once intercom's restored, warn all decks to equip themselves with magboots against the threat of losing gravity again. Corporal, you're healthy?"

Chipper clipped his new handgun holster to his vest. "Yes, sir."

"There are magboots in the corridor closets. Start finding the right size for everyone on bridge. XO and Sgt. Wepps, take the ambassador and envoy into the Ready Room and strap in again until we're confident of stable grav." From a pocket, he produced a tiny comms device and squashed it into his ear. "Keep the intercom on open mic."

"Aye, sir." Chinyama gave over his station to its original operator and signaled for Gregory and Buoun to precede him.

"Fowler," Pan was saying as Gregory left, "go with them or stay here? Your choice."

"The bridge is far more exciting," the colonel replied.

"Yeah, thanks for mentioning *my* name," Grace muttered from just behind Gregory. "I'm the invisible woman, am I?"

"That's kind of your job," Gregory said, unsurprised that his voice came out in a tight rasp. This situation was by far the most danger he'd ever been in. Breath was coming in short bursts and with effort as his body tried to tell him there wasn't enough oxygen—but that wasn't true, he knew

—no one else was suffering that way. This was fear. And he had to control it before it controlled him.

"And I'm not paid nearly enough for it," Grace was saying. "Or any of this crap."

Gregory forced air deep into his lungs, concentrating on inflating his ribs up under his armpits. He held it while flashing Grace a *that's enough* look. Then released it slow. He was not giving in to fear. He was not giving in to fear. He was not—

He felt better already, he realized.

Down at the far end of the corridor crouched the Tactical who'd come in with Fowler, his back pressed against a bulkhead, flexing his left wrist. Blood ran from his nose and had smeared across one cheek.

"All right?" Wepps called out to him.

The hulking man shook his head, scowling. "Swallowed my helldamn gum!"

AS WEPPS BUCKLED Buoun in to his Ready Room chair, Chinyama asked the Tluaan, "What is Domain Space?"

Gregory recalled then that the XO hadn't been present the first time Buoun had explained it.

"In our current historical context, what you think of as cultures or nations have become four 'domains.' Each owns or manages its own area of our world or system. Space, Moon, Surface, Oceans."

"And now they're at war."

From his chair beside the envoy, Gregory asked, "Buoun, all this fighting. It's over us?"

Buoun looked rather dejected as he answered. "Probably. My council did not inform the other domains of your presence here."

"Bloody politicians," Grace sighed from her chair. Wepps gave her a quick grin of agreement as he buckled himself in to the chair closest the door.

Gregory continued, "But you—they—the Council must have known that the others would detect us. You've already said the others have satellites and space stations."

"And surface sensors and telescopes. Yes, they knew. And as you were arriving, Domain Space sent messages to the other councils that your ship was actually our ship. A new science vessel returning from investigating the space between our system and others. They promised to eventually share the research they were still collating."

Feeling his heart sinking, Gregory put his head in his hands. *So much for my dream of noble aliens ...*

Grace said, "They lied."

"Forgive me for saying this. But your politicians do not?"

"Touché," she admitted. "The captain might say that's more proof that we shouldn't trust you rather than should."

"Grace," Gregory warned. As his protection detail, it was hardly her place to enter such discussions nor to represent Pan's opinions.

"Just sayin'," she muttered.

Buoun made a placating gesture in her direction and then Gregory's, perhaps distressed by the appearance of conflict between them. "My council lied for many reasons. But they were honest in their intention to share knowledge with our other domains. We anticipated learning much from you and then passing it on."

"All of it?" Gregory asked.

Buoun's gaze dropped to the table. "Much of it," he replied.

Grace snorted again.

On the wallscreen, the tactical display showed several white or yellow rings with seemingly nothing inside them.

Were those artifacts or ships too small to display ... or was this signaling their complete annihilation, the circles indicating debris fields?

"Envoy, I understand trade. I understand holding out on the other party. For you to create and maintain an advantage is not criminal in our eyes." He shot a warning look at Grace to forestall any reaction from her. "What we're not sure of is your intention to use your advantage to bully or dominate your rivals."

"Forgive me for interrupting," Chinyama said. "There seems to be activity at an inner asteroid. Sensors show it shifting from its previous trajectory and turning."

"Turning?" Ice trickled through Gregory's innards. "Buoun. Tell me your people wouldn't seriously weaponize an asteroid?"

"I ... I don't know."

"You really would hit your own planet?" Grace sighed in disbelief.

"That's what the captain's asking," said Chinyama, pointing to his tab. "The asteroid's course is changing toward Suuchaat. He has sent a message to your shuttle demanding Councillor Pi order the asteroid's course to its original one. He also asks that you use my tab to translate it for her." They'd set up a stylus-function for the envoy to handwrite messages in his own script. "The full message is onscreen here."

"I'll tell her," the Tlu said miserably, reaching for the tablet as Chinyama passed it across. He waved away the XO's offered tutorial in its use. "Your probe carried similar-enough communication interfaces. I press the orange circle to record a voice message?"

Chinyama nodded.

The humans in the room exchanged worried glances while Buoun spoke rapidly in his own language. A full minute later, he pushed the tab back across to its owner.

"You may send that. I also added a recommendation of my own."

"What was it?" Gregory and Chinyama asked in unison.

"That our council accept any advice or directives that Ambassador Gregory and Captain Pan may offer for winning this conflict."

"But your cover story for being up here alone is that we are interrogating you. Your council will think you've made your 'recommendation' under duress."

"Duress?"

"Pressure."

"Oh," Buoun said, and then: "Oh!" as the full meaning if Gregory's statement registered. "I am a fool." Buoun's hands went to his ears again, twisting them.

"No, no," Gregory said placatingly. "A mistake is only natural. You're desperate. Like we all are."

Reading from his screen, Chinyama said, "The captain heard what you said. And he approves of the sentiment. But he reminds you, Envoy, that we are still observers here. Also that we're currently crippled."

Buoun let out a very human sigh, but for the moment, he put his hands in his lap and gave his poor ears a break. "Has Pi replied at all? If she does, whether in audio or text form, I'm happy to translate for you again."

Chinyama checked his screen. "Captain says not yet."

"It is what you might call, er, posturing," Buoun told them. Then, perhaps because he remembered Pan could hear everything happening in the room, he raised his voice and his chin and repeated it to the air around him. "We would never damage our planet with an asteroid. It is our origin. Also, we are friends with Domain Ocean, and they don't deserve this."

"How about damaging your *moon* with it?" Chinyama asked. He hadn't checked his tab, but this was his question.

Buoun faltered and looked away.

"That's answer enough," said Grace.

Another sigh from Buoun. "You must listen. Please. The clans or nations that became Domain Moon were historically the cruelest and most aggressive our species ever produced. It took concerted effort from a coalition of the rest of the planet to bring about the conditions that led to the founding of the domains."

Chinyama said, "Are you saying that they were the cruelest and your domain was the most enlightened?"

"We were not perfect—we still are not—but our clans and those comprising Domain Ocean were certainly the most progressive at the time, the most interested in ideals such as compassion and the good of the species. At the end of the war, Ocean and Space's nations were somewhat more powerful technologically. We also had trust between us. And one of the reasons our nations chose Space for our domain was to put distance between us and Domain Surface."

"Surface? You were talking about Domain Moon?"

"Yes. Because they were even more aggressive, they were awarded the moon. Where they could cause less threat, it was thought at the time."

"So why is Moon on Surface's side now? Why is Surface on theirs?"

"I cannot tell you that with certainty, but I can guess. Moon has always held resentment that they inherited what they see as a lesser version of Space. Domain Surface allowed Moon to keep a small island as farming land on Suuchaat. But the moon has water-ice and minerals and we provided them with artificial gravity technology to help them there. I have always had some sympathy for them in that, as their poets say, they have been banished to the poorest land on Suuchaat and the smallest world in space."

"Buoun," Gregory asked. "Why were you not happy to tell us this with Pi present?"

"Because my council did not want you to even know there were domains until much later. Until we had secured agreements, trade ..."

"And what do you want?"

"I? I want friendship. I want an end to conflict." Buoun's gaze touched on each of theirs. "From the moment I stepped into your probe, I felt not only wonder, but hope. Hope that there might come a new *age* of wonder. Where all of the Tluaanto could leave primitive instincts and conflicts behind."

A hush fell across the room. Chinyama read something from his screen, his usually reserved expression turning sheepish as he then relayed the captain's message: "And that worked out really well, didn't it?"

"MANOLO," Ana said, having to clear her throat to engage her rusty voice, "are you seeing many repeated patterns in the Tluaan codes?"

Manolo's only reply was a terse shake of her head. Her attention didn't budge from her own screens.

Ana hummed unhappily. Neither their Xerxian software nor the Confeds' was making a lot of sense of the Tluaan data. This data arrived from multiple sources, sometimes in streams, more often in fragments. Apparently, Envoy Buoun had just entered some Tluaan script into the system, script which the Confederation software was now hungrily pawing at—but the only concrete result from the analysis so far was to decide that certain signals were the identification markers from various vessels.

"These transponder signals," she said, more to herself

than the other women. "They're all six characters long. Except for ..."

This one, she finished in her head. Her finger traced a border around the pattern in question, freezing it onscreen for further scrutiny. *All the others are six characters. This is* —she counted them—*eighteen.*

What in a pirate's hell would be three times the normal length of the others? Another virus? A virus-blocker?

"Stop focusing on one thing," Hecate snapped at her.

"It's called analysis, bitch."

"It's called not knowing what you're doing, *bitch.* Feel free to ask for help."

"The day I need your help is the day I'll—"

She never finished the phrase. An idea hit her and hard.

Ask for help. Help! *What if that's what* they're *doing?*

She zoomed on the three characters that always repeated after the initial six, hacking the signal to morph it back into its original databits.

And there it was! As *actually* transmitted, stripped of the Tluaan alphabet and encryption overlays, the sequence was a simple series: three long, three short, three long.

She sat back with a huff, staring into nothing. Was it possible? Would the Tluaan have learned such an archaic and obscure *human* code?

She dialed up the audio version and there it was again. Stark, clear, obvious now that she knew what she was seeing and hearing. A thing she'd only ever heard in old talkie-novs and twodees.

Three beeps, three pips, three beeps.

She tapped the comm in her ear. "Umbrano, you near Fowler? ... Who cares about your wrist? ... Or your hacking gum! Listen. Tell him there's a code buried in the signal from that approaching shuttle. It's in Morse and it's in English. It's SOS. They're saying SOS!"

"SHOE SIZE?" Chipper asked the assistant helmswoman.

Her forehead was pebbled with blood seeping from a graze or carpet burn. And yet, although she was banged up and under enormous pressure, she flashed him a smile. "Six. I got baby feet."

He waggled his brows, raising one of his giant boots from the floor. "Lucky you. Try finding this size in most stores."

She chuckled as he turned away and asked the size of the prime helmsman.

The man said, "Ten," distractedly.

Behind them, Chief Lindberg told Pan, "Nav and tactical displays active, sir. Cameras still offline."

"Is this data reliable?" Pan shot back.

"Yes, sir."

"Then what is that object on an intercept course with us?"

Chipper's heart went to his throat, remembering Pan's words minutes before about nukes, remembering the fate of Charlie Team at Pollyanna.

"Small craft, possibly a small shuttle. Point of origin appears to have been mid-to-high orbit. Emissions trail indicates use of fossil fuel drive."

"Low tech," Pan said. "Maybe the same signal that hit us also hit these habitats. Question now is: friend or foe? Are they hailing us?"

"Comms still down, sir," replied the comms officer.

"Dammit. Did that datapack get off to Fleet before the virus signal?"

"Yes, sir. Only just."

Chipper was halfway to the door when Tactical Umbrano darted through it and whispered in Fowler's ear.

He stopped and watched them. Everyone else was too busy to notice them.

Fowler blinked, gave Umbrano a *really?* look then shooed him back out into the corridor.

What the heck was that? Chipper wondered. No one else had noticed the exchange.

"Captain," Fowler called. "Mind if I look over some of the signals your comms have been recording?"

"What? Why?"

Good question, thought Chipper.

"Might be clues as to who that ship is. Fresh eyes can be useful."

The comms officer flashed Fowler a dirty look that only Chipper saw, probably thinking Fowler's request was an insult to his own ability.

"You think you can read Tluaanto, go for it," Pan said. "Meyers, give him room beside you."

Meyers complied. But he didn't look happy about it.

As bridge hubbub continued, Chipper went out to the corridor closets to retrieve the magnetic boots that crewers had ordered. Umbrano was at the closet already.

"All you Confeds have small feet, huh?" he said.

"Not me," Chipper said as Umbrano made room for him.

"True. Got something in your size for me?"

Chipper reached into the very back and dragged a pair of size thirteens close. He held them up. When Umbrano went for them, he pulled them back and said, "What'd you tell Fowler?"

Umbrano's face darkened, "None o' your bangbang, hombre. Gimme my boots."

"You guys know something the rest of us should?" How that was possible, Chipper had no idea. But he had to ask.

"Us guys?" Umbrano smirked. "No us. We're you." Maintaining the smirk, he held out a hand for the boots.

Chipper dropped the strung-together laces over it. Umbrano winked and headed for the corridors' far end.

Wise guy, Chipper thought and returned to the bridge. He was handing the third crewer their boots when Fowler shouted from the comms station.

"Captain! I have a feeling I know what this signal is!"

Pan strode around to him and looked where he was pointing. "It's just slashes and dots."

"No, Captain. Not slashes. Dashes. Dashes and dots."

"Dashes and ... SOS?!"

"Exactly."

"You can't be serious."

"I am. The Tluaanto have had select records of our history for a generation. Why wouldn't those 22nd century probe designers include Morse? If this *is* Morse, then this code following it might relate to numbers."

"My God, if this is true ..." Pan turned his attention to Meyers. "You think it's possible, son?"

Meyers nodded, chewing his lip. "Could be."

"If they're numbers," Fowler continued, talking fast, "they could be coordinates."

"To what?" Pan slapped the console and spun to march toward the door. "Perhaps I dispatched the envoy too early. Meyers, patch this data thru to the XO. Colonel Fowler, please join me in the Ready Room."

"Nice to finally be invited to a meeting," said Fowler.

Chipper looked on as the senior officers departed, convinced now that Umbrano had passed on something that promoted Fowler's discovery.

Which would mean that the Tacticals had their own analysis going on.

Which would mean that the Tacticals were tapping into *Assured*'s data.

Oh, crap, he thought.

25

"I WAS ORIGINALLY TRAINED IN SURVEY," Buoun told the Humans assembled in the Ready Room, "and I had a natural interest in your navigational frameworks and your history of travel and charting. I studied Morse code as well as your various systems of coordinates. In the early days, where expectation of a human visit was high, I was able to teach a small proportion of our people to understand your coordinate system as well as Morse—and then to translate our coordinates into it. I thought this might be useful if we had trouble communicating in other ways, and my superiors at the time agreed. One of the people I taught was my female sibling, Ahn'chonmek."

In mentioning Ahn's name, Buoun was momentarily awash in fresh and conflicting emotions: childhood nostalgia; the shame of his family's eventual spurning of the 'crazy human-lover'; terror at the prospect of her death if Domain Moon or Surface attacks had reached her habitat; hope that these Human coordinates he was reading—transmitted in a very Human code—originated with his sister.

Sister, *he thought, and his emotion turned to amused*

self-deprecation. I'm thinking of her by the Human term! I really am a crazy human-lover.

"What's wrong?" Gregory asked from beside him, staring hard into his eyes. "You seem suddenly upset again."

"This time I am affected by many emotions at once. Some of those are positive ones. This signal, you see, is indeed Morse code as Colonel Fowler suggested. The signal must originate from the station you saved. Very probably my sister is safe. If this is the case, I can never display the gratitude I feel toward you all."

"And this may be her in that approaching shuttle," Pan said, "using Morse code to tell us she needs help?" He settled in his customary chair and cleared his throat. "That would settle the friend or foe question." Buoun didn't understand the remark, but nodded politely. "Although, isn't it possible one of your enemy Domains has intel on things like Morse, and this is a ruse by them?"

"Anything is possible. But that is very unlikely."

Pan touched the intercom. "Ms. Lindberg, any chance of scanning that approaching vessel for weapons or anything indicating explosives, overloading nuclear cores, that kind of thing?"

"A moment, Captain." Lindberg had a brief discussion on mic with a rating. "Thirty seconds, sir. Stand by." Buoun counted Human seconds in his head while the Humans in the room exchanged nonverbal communication. At thirty-three seconds, Lindberg spoke again. "Nothing hazardous to Assured *detected."*

"Thanks, Chief." Pan released the intercom. "Envoy Buoun, if I give you control of our signal laser, could you signal that shuttle to use the docking mating cube on the opposite side of Assured *from where your shuttle is docked?"*

Buoun's cheeks swelled with pride at the level of trust this request intimated. He straightened in his chair. "That is something I am well able to do, sir."

"Mr. Wepps, how are those chip replacements going?"

Wepps checked a display on his wrist. "My team is all good, sir. Westermann has a replacement rifle to bring Chipper." He shot a quick look at Fowler which Buoun couldn't read.

Pan continued, "Wepps, Fowler, I want four troops in that docking lounge. I don't care which ones."

"We'll make that work, sir," Wepps said.

"Two each?" Fowler asked the sergeant.

Wepps nodded. "You and Umbrano, me and Stines." He looked to Pan, "Unless you want me with Envoy Buoun, sir?"

Pan shook his head. "The XO can escort him. Commander, take a sidearm from the weapons safe."

Chinyama nodded and indicated for Buoun to unbuckle his belt. "We'll find you some magnetic boots that best fit you, sir."

Buoun began fussing with his belt as his cheeks flattened. An armed escort. The Humans didn't trust him all that much, then. But he could continue trying to earn their confidence.

It was then that it occurred to Buoun that he was playing a dangerous game—to side with and work with these aliens might seem like the best path to serving his Domain's interests, but if he didn't act carefully, his Council might not see it that way.

"XO," Pan was saying, "if the envoy's use of the laser is successful, please convey him to the docking lounge to meet our new guests."

WITH GRAVITY CONTROL STILL UNCERTAIN, Gregory watched Buoun shuffle awkwardly into the service lift wearing his ill-fitting and heavy magboots. Wepps and

Fowler followed him while the beefy Tactical named Umbrano waited inside.

"Good luck," Gregory told Buoun through the gap in the closing doors, and caught Fowler's eye roll before those doors clamped shut. He turned to Grace and, since it was only them left in the corridor, he gave her an eye roll too. The relaxation of self-control felt good.

"What's that for?" she asked.

"That is for Xerxian Tactical Colonel Fowler. Who is a total pain in the—" He broke off, catching Chipper Tukimatu watching them from the doorway of the bridge twenty meters away. "Let's return to the Ready Room."

They had only walked a few meters before Chipper came striding toward them, his expression grave.

What now? Gregory glanced down at his shoes. *Don't tell me he's going to make me wear magboots too.*

"Ambassador, sir. I need to tell you something. Bridge staff and Sgt. Wepps are all too busy."

Phew, not boots then.

Gregory tugged his tunic straight, matching Chipper's solemnity. "Go ahead, Corporal."

"It's ... er ..." Chipper faltered, scratching at the back of his head.

"Spit it out, guy," Grace muttered, not so invested in solemnity.

Chipper blew out a frustrated breath. "It sounds dumb, sir, ma'am. But that idea that Colonel Fowler got about the SOS. Well, I ... Oh, maybe it's nothing. Sorry, sir—"

"Oy!" Grace barked, getting right in Chipper's face. The Peacekeeper went rigid, not withdrawing but clearly fazed. "I'm a little sick of me and my boss being yanked around today. You've already wasted half a minute of our lives. So, satisfy the curiosity you now have piqued in us. What *about* the idea Colonel Fowler had?"

Chipper kept his focus on Gregory, peering past Grace

at him. Grace Renny might have been half a head shorter than the big Peacer, but she was damned intimidating when she wasn't pretending to be invisible.

Chipper said, "A minute or two before he had his bright idea, that other Tactical—Umbrano—he came onto the bridge and whispered something in the colonel's ear. A few seconds later, the colonel asked to study the Tluaan comm signals."

Gregory felt his eyes widening. Grace gave a huff of surprise and backed off, returning to her employer's side.

"Probably nothing," Chipper said, scratching at his head again and edging away.

"Nothing, my ass," Grace said.

"She's right, Corporal," Gregory said. "That's not nothing. So, all you saw was him whisper in Fowler's ear? Couldn't hear it? No? Fowler's reaction was what?"

"He, the colonel, he seemed a little surprised for a half a second. Then he covered it and sent Umbrano back into the corridor here. Almost straight away he was asking to jump on the comms station."

Gregory looked to Grace who grinned a dark grin.

Grace told Chipper, "You have good instincts. Back in my old precinct, we had a saying. If it looks like crap, and smells like crap, try not to step in it."

"Sorry?" Chipper said, confused.

"It's a profound saying, isn't it? It means if something seems off, it usually is."

Gregory took over again. "Thanks, Chipper. That is very useful information. Better return to your station. We'll take it up with the captain when we get a chance."

CHIPPER HAD TURNED to go back to the bridge when his earpiece chimed.

"Tukimatu? Wepps, here."

With his back to the ambassador and his assistant, Chipper put his index finger print to the earpiece to accept the signal. "Yes, Sergeant?"

"Change of plans. Stines is on his way up to relieve you on the bridge. But don't wait for him. Come down to Docking Lounge C immediately."

"But there should be someone on bridge at all times."

"I'll clear it with the captain. You just get down here."

"Copy." With his hand to his ear, he pressed between Ms. Renny and the ambassador, ignoring their curious stares. At the lift, he stabbed at the wall button and asked Wepps, "Still there, Sergeant?"

"Yes. There a problem?"

"No. No problem. Just wondering, Sergeant. Why me?"

There came a pause before Wepps gave an uncharacteristic chuckle, followed by an even more uncharacteristic frank remark. "Because the situation here will require a Peacer with more tact and sensitivity around non-Confederation people than Stines has. Now, is your ass moving in my direction?"

"Sergeant, it and the rest of me are currently awaiting the elevator."

"See you soon. Out."

CHIPPER ARRIVED at Docking Lounge C to find the contingent had grown. Westermann, Hecate, and Jogianto had joined Umbrano. Wepps and Fowler stood at the far end of the rectangular lounge, leaning over a datapad. A monitor above the airlock showed the Tluaan vessel still a few minutes out. Buoun gazed up at it from below, his long-fingered hands clasped behind his back.

Stopping ten meters out from the cluster of enlisted

personnel, Chipper offered Westermann a nod and a wink. Westermann winked back then returned to quiet conversation with Hecate. Unwatched now, Chipper crooked a finger at Ana Jogianto. She flinched and glared back, taking a stubborn sideways step in the other direction. He pointed to her and pointed to the floor at his feet and mouthed "Now."

Jaw working and fists clenched, she stomped over to him. "*What?*"

"Any idea how your boss came up with the idea that the Tluaanto embedded a human Morse code signal in their comm streams? Because that was a really random thing to suspect." He stopped talking because he realized she had flinched at the question and was looking away. *Oh, now I* know *there's something up here. If it smells like crap ...* "You do have an idea. Donchoo?"

"You're an idiot. He's a colonel because he puts random things together to come up with random ideas like that."

"Yeah. Maybe. Or maybe he's a colonel because he has other people doing the work for him. I got some ideas of my own starting to take shape. Starting to—" He mimed fireworks. "—pop! Like maybe it was the woman on Fowler's team with some computer and comms tech savvy who actually discovered that SOS signal." He dropped his voice to a stage whisper. "Like maybe Fowler's team has found some way to tap *Assured*'s systems."

"No *way*."

"If that's true, if I'm right, that's big trouble for you guys."

"It's not true. And you can stop all this shit right now."

"If it's not true, why aren't you walking away from me with your nose at its normal haughty angle, stuck straight up in the air?"

"Hack you."

"Because you're scared that what I know is gonna get you all in the brig."

She glared at him, eyes afire. He couldn't help noticing that she looked more beautiful than the universe itself, and Chipper found his shoulders dropping, his stomach turning to mush.

Damn, lady. I wish ...

"Look," he whispered. "Ana, I don't want you getting in trouble. I ..." *I care about you? Can't say that.* "I respect you. You're good people. You are. Not him." He looked down the passage to Fowler who was saying something making Wepps scowl. Then Chipper stared at Hecate who was throwing curious glances their way. "Not her, definitely. But you are, Ana. I had to tell someone what I saw—"

"What you saw?"

"Umbrano whispering in Fowler's ear right before your boss jumped on the comms desk and pretended to discover something important."

Ana groaned then. Her palm made it halfway to slapping her forehead before she regained control and forced the arm back down. "Just great."

"Look." He swallowed while he got his words straight, then couldn't believe he was saying them. "If you need to go cover your tracks somehow, go. Now. I'll cover for you here. I'll say you had—I dunno—diarrhea."

She gaped at him. "Diarrhea."

"Or food poisoning. I'll say that. Not ... not diarrhea."

"I'm going nowhere. There's nothing to cover up, guy."

"Please, Ana. You just about admitted—"

"I *didn't* admit *nothing*. But if anyone like me, like us, did a thing like that, they would have already covered their tracks."

"Oh."

"So you can keep your crazy ideas to yourself. Keep

your *charity* to yourself. I don't need some Peacer crossing the line for me."

"I wasn't. I just ... I wish there weren't lines at all."

"You say you respect me? Well, respect this. I don't need your help." She had her finger in his face now. Five minutes ago, it had been Ms. Renny's face in his face; now Ana's finger.

I have such a way with women.

"Don't need it," she said with emphasis on each word. "Got that?"

He brushed her finger aside and leaned closer, his own indignation returning. The Xerxians had betrayed trust with the Confederation. And Ana had betrayed his trust in her.

"Oh, yes, Tactical Enforcer. I sure do got that."

She spun on her heel and marched back to her former position. Chipper leaned his back and shoulders against the wall and started some breathing exercises to calm down.

HE AND GRACE were wearing magboots now; Pan had insisted on it and finding them had been Stines's first task when he'd reached the bridge.

Gregory now loitered in the position he'd occupied during the assault on Asteroid CP11X. The little alcove made him feel like he was out of the way. Although the room was not as overstaffed as it had been that day, there were a couple of extra techs crawling around between open console panels, running diagnostics. Grace had found a similar position on the far side of the door.

Pan and Chinyama had been locked together for a couple of minutes in one of their regular head-close-to-head consultations when Comms called, "Message from Sergeant Wepps."

Wheeling around, Pan barked, "On speaker." Then: "Bridge here. Report."

Wepps's calm voice came through as clear as a bell. "Captain, I'm using the wall intercom down here. The Tluaanto passengers have disembarked and they report to be from that Domain Space habitat. One of them is Envoy Buoun's sister. They are currently embracing, sir. Please hold while I attempt to bring the envoy over here."

In the background, Gregory could hear the chatter of multiple voices, rapid-fire Tluaanto words and urgent cadences.

Eventually, Wepps came through again. "Captain, the envoy's sister has an urgent message for this vessel's commander. Envoy Buoun, please speak into this and the captain will hear you."

"Ah, Captain?" Buoun said. "Can your Ready Room hear me?"

"We're on the bridge. Just go ahead."

"My sister says, 'Do not accept any signals from the surface of the planet. It carries hidden programs designed to disrupt and destroy other computer programs and data'."

Pan drew a hand down his careworn face. In the drollest of tones, he replied, "Now she tells us."

26

A FEW MINUTES BACK, Ana had found a stray length of softwire dropped and forgotten by some harried, careless technician. Standing in the corner of the officers' mess, she coiled the wire around and around and around the fingers of her left hand.

Across the room from her sat the five Tluaan newcomers. With them sat the captain, the XO, Envoy Buoun, Ambassador Gregory, the ambassador's assistant, Renny, and Fowler. Tluaan faces, she thought, looked like a cross between a cat and an orangutan. Four of the newcomers were Buoun's size, but the fifth would rival Chipper and Umbrano for height and weight.

This one was a warrior, dressed in a thin bodysuit which accentuated their impressive musculature—a musculature that gave no hint of gender, if the idea of binary gender even applied to all Tluaanto. They had willingly handed over weapons upon arrival—but not water flasks, since Tluaanto needed regular hydration—and sat back from the rest of the table, unspeaking, watchful. Wepps, near Ana, had barely taken his eyes from the warrior since arrival.

She'd reached the end of the softwire, so she unfurled it and started again but in the opposite direction. This was the only way she could think of to keep her mounting anxiety under control. In the last month, things had not gotten better as she'd hope they would in joining this mission. No, things had gone from *crap* to *crap-meets-fan*. Half the team she'd joined were dead; the rest of them were adrift in a damaged starship in the middle of an alien war, a gazillion kilometers from resupply and reinforcement.

Worse, if what Chipper had reported about Fowler was believed, the very allies they had arrived with—the Confeds—could turn on them at any moment. There was no guarantee her efforts and Manolo's would keep evidence of their spying concealed. Even worse than that perhaps, she seemed the only one on that team who felt conflicted over it. And what did that make her? Weak? Soft?

Same thing, you tulalâ.

Uncommitted, then.

Reaching the end of the softwire, she pulled it taut, turning the flesh of her left-hand fingers dark with trapped blood. *Uncommitted. No one is more committed to dragging Xerxes out of the dark age and into the light than me.* That was all she'd hoped for since turning thirteen: that there would come a day when a young Xerxian woman could live without fear of kidnap and attack from rival clans; a day when she would not face rejection and abuse because of her *parents'* political decisions; a day when she would be judged on the merits of her intelligence and on skills that were *not* the ability to kill and steal and sabotage and cheat and sneak. Those were skills her superiors were happy to employ for their sake, never for hers.

One year ago, when it had been announced that popular Sevens Party Colonel Andre Fowler was assembling a team to work alongside Confederation personnel, Ana had been the first to apply. When she was accepted into the training program, she'd been ecstatic. This was her chance to do something about making that bright future day come early. This was her chance to be free: free to travel, free to see her parents again, free to reach for a future in which she was not Ana Jogianto Tactical Enforcer, but Ana Jogianto *woman*. In the first few weeks of their assignment, she'd found Confederation personnel to be more accepting of her than she'd expected. Although there were always those—like Stines—who were only too happy to express their spite. Exposure to Confed culture and subculture, to their gossip, their senses of humor, their values, had buoyed her. *One day soon*, she'd told herself, *one day soon*. And yet, being part of a Tactical team required her to display the very parts of herself she hated most, the toughness that kept the bullies and the doubters at bay.

Pain in her fingers forced her to release the tension on the wire, to commence uncoiling it again. A glance around —none of the other four soldiers shuffling their feet near her had noticed. The soldiers stood in a cluster by the entry to the glassed-in mess, on guard duty for the conference, though surely there was nothing to protect anyone from *inside* the ship.

Nothing besides us damned Xerxians, she thought bitterly.

No, none of these guys had noticed her thing with the wire. They weren't interested in her. Not Wepps, not Peacer Westermann, not Hecate—

And not Chipper.

The big guy hadn't so much as glanced her way since their whispered altercation two hours back. Why did that bother her so much, she wondered. He certainly wasn't another Olesco—her casual lover murdered by Clan Lobos —who had been svelte and man-pretty, the way she liked 'em.

So why did she want him to be cool with her, then?

Deep down, she suspected she knew the answer, though she struggled to deny it. Chipper Tukimatu was kind of an embodiment of everything good the Confederation represented. And for the last few weeks, he'd been the closest thing to a friend she had had since Uncle James died. That uncle had been the only person she'd ever been able to trust, the man who'd protected her throughout her vulnerable adolescence.

And then he was gone.

And there'd been lovers and allies and comrades since, but never a friend. Never someone to drop her guard around, to joke with. Until Chipper came along.

And you blew that, she accused herself. She threw an angry glance across the mess to where Fowler sat in council with ten others. *No. Not me. That bastard blew it for me.*

The wire had unwound. This time, she dropped it on the thin carpet and ground it beneath her boot. If she didn't find a better control for these strong emotions and soon, she felt she would come apart.

Beyond the window closest her, a dozen meters away and near a corridor junction, a gaggle of *Assured* staffers had congregated, muttering amongst themselves and trying to catch a glimpse of the non-humans.

"Ass-heads," she muttered. If Tukimatu embodied the best of the Confederation, these *bulalas* embodied the dumbest, the most childish.

Hecate followed her gaze, then sniffed, adopting a tart tone of voice. "You gonna tell me you weren't a little curious yourself? Your eyes were bugging out your face when that big one came through the mating tube."

"Well, I saw them first," Chipper joked half-heartedly, saving Ana from having to reply to Hecate.

"You saw *one* of them first, Chip," said Wepps. "Up on the bridge. Now, stop yabbering on about trivialities, all of you."

"Yes, Sergeant," Chipper said.

Hecate rolled her eyes.

Outside, a middle-aged man in a nurse uniform had ignored the gestures of his buddies and was creeping a few meters closer, neck craned.

"That's *it*," Ana hissed. She ducked through the mess door and advanced on the man. The rest of the guard detail would probably interpret her words as reaching breaking point with the rubberneckers; in actual fact, she'd hit upon the very therapy she needed to let off some steam. Hearing the door seal behind her and unworried about making noise that would disturb the conference, she barked at the suddenly rigid male nurse. "What in hacking hell do you think you're doing?"

He began retreating long before she reached him, stammering gibberish.

Behind him, a female flight tech spoke up, affecting nonchalance. "No one said we can't take a look."

Reaching the nurse, Ana grabbed his collar, whipped him around, and dragged him to the junction. "They didn't, huh? Well, how about I say it?"

"You? You're not even DCHC personnel." The flight tech checked her colleagues for support. She wasn't getting it; they were backing off, leaving her alone and out in front.

Ana released the nurse after shoving him past the tech. The tech was tall, so Ana got right up under her nose and gave her the stinkiest stink-eye she could summon. She tapped the weapon strapped to her vest. "I'm DCHC when I report to Sergeant Wepps back there. And Sgt. Wepps says I'm authorized to stun the complete shit out of *anyone* who steps into this corridor."

The tech gulped, but stood her ground. Behind her, the rest of the group were fast vanishing around the corner.

"Your friends are way smarter than you."

The tech risked a glance back, swallowed again, then let

out a feeble "Hack you," while scampering to catch up with them.

In the mess, her colleagues frowned at her. When she was back among them, Wepps said, "And what was that about?"

"That was about doing my job and maintaining security around this conference." She nodded at the tables at the far end. "Sir."

Wepps snorted. "Fair enough. Just don't call a Peacekeeper sergeant "sir." We're not officers—*we* work for our supper."

"Fair enough," she echoed and adopted an at-ease pose. She felt better, she had to admit, and all it had taken was a little bullying of some dumbasses. That thought brought a mild pang of guilt: *You're a true Xerxian, Jogianto.*

She caught Chipper looking before he snatched his gaze away.

And doesn't he know it?

BUOUN HAD BEEN TRANSLATING *for a while now. The Humans made assurances for the safety of the newly arrived Tluaanto; the Tluaanto heaped thanks upon the Humans for the rescue and dealt out what news they knew.*

Currently, it was his sister speaking and passing on more information, information that she as Habitat Registrar had been well-placed to know.

"... our satellites and habitats destroyed all of Moon and Surface's satellites this side of Suuchaat, hence their desperate behavior launching the nuclear rocket. The last thing we heard was that Domain Surface have satellites from the far side of the planet moving around, following a lower orbit, evidently coming to finish off our habitats. We know of three Domain Moon fighters who've survived the far side

battle and are also advancing around this side to join them. This was the last we had before the signal disguised as a Domain Ocean signal infected our network."

"And Assured's,*" Buoun replied before passing on the information. He went on to backfill information about the Surface signal, that while* Assured *had been able to block it, all Domain Space assets within range were still affected, the virus a mutating code which was still being transmitted and which would constantly reinsert itself at every opportunity.*

Seizing control of the conversation then, Fowler turned to Pan. "We're fighting blind here. Not much better than their Domain. We have a single fighter aboard. Have you launched it? It could provide vital support and data."

Pan was already talking before Fowler had stopped. "We can *think for ourselves, thank you, Colonel. The Devilfly has been out on patrol for an hour now. We also have a tech on both Tluaan shuttles marrying their sensors to ours."*

Sensing none of this was meant for the ears of the other Tluaanto, Buoun held his lips together and his fingers still. Across from him, his sister Ahn's expression and coloring indicated intense curiosity, as did that of the warrior seated behind and to her left.

The warrior was a female in keeping with ancient traditions of the nations forming Domain Space, introduced to him as Vazak, a commander-of-sixteen, possibly an equivalent rank to that of the Sergeant Wepps. Possibly higher. Although there hadn't been a war in her lifetime, she had a chunk torn from the tip of her right ear, and a bright pink burn scar across the knuckles of her left hand. Presumably, they were from combat training, which Buoun heard was frequent and brutal for Domain Space warriors, keeping their skills honed and instincts clear for if the day ever came.

The scars gave her an attractive appearance, he had to admit, feeling a swell of interest he hadn't experienced for decades. He shook the feeling off. Vazak was signaling him subtly for a translation, but he gave her a slight flick of his ears to indicate polite refusal.

Pan and Fowler continued to squabble. Buoun continued to wait. Of course, his sister Ahn had learned enough English during her adolescent life-phase that she could probably follow at least a tenth of what was being said.

Buoun became aware of silence descending on the table. All Human eyes were on him, as were those of Ahn and Vazak. Someone expected something of him, but he couldn't tell who. "I'm sorry. Could you repeat that?" he asked Pan, guessing.

Ambassador Gregory spoke instead. "We need to speak privately with you. Can you ask our guests if they would prefer to be returned to their shuttle, or if they would like to stay here? In which case, our conversation will relocate."

Buoun's heartrate increased slightly. What did they want with him now? Some new subterfuge they didn't want the others witnessing his part in? He had only just been reunited with Ahn, and now they were separating him again.

It's your own fault, Buoun, *he scolded himself.* It was your idea and your offer to deal with them secretly.

He passed on the question, knowing already which choice his sister as leader of the party would take.

"We will return to our shuttle," she said, eyes shifting between Gregory and Pan. "We have food and water there for fifteen cycles if necessary."

"It is my hope it won't *be necessary," Buoun replied and made a sign of familial affection to her, touching the middle knuckle of his left thumb to his lips. She returned the gesture. The other Tluaanto including Vazak pretended not to see, as was polite. To Gregory, Buoun said, "Please return them to their shuttle. I must ask, will they be allowed out again soon?"*

The Ambassador and Captain exchanged glances.

"That depends on circumstances," Gregory replied.

Pan added, "These people are as safe with us as your Councillor is. Their shuttles are attached to the sides of Assured *and within our energy shielding."*

Buoun hemmed. "Another technology we would be eager to trade for."

"And the topics of trade and technology are what we want to talk to you about. Privately."

Buoun halted his own gesture of query halfway through. It was not a Human signal.

To Ahn and the staff she had brought with her, he said, "They wish to speak with me alone."

"Why?" This was the first time Vazak had spoken since coming on board. The warrior's rich voice resonated within her large chest cavity, and the word caused Gregory to flinch.

"I have been their ... advisor for some time now."

Vazak straightened in her chair, causing it to creak—it was only now that Buoun noticed she dwarfed it. "You are under duress."

"A small amount. Please do be not be alarmed," he hurried on as the other Tluaanto stirred, concern-colors rippling his sister's fur. "Once the emergency has passed, I am certain it will all resolve itself as a misunderstanding. They have not harmed me. Far from it. But it's clear they fear for their lives, and I am the only one who speaks their languages well enough to help them resolve this."

"Is it their place to resolve this?" Vazak asked.

Buoun watched for the Humans' reactions in his peripheral vision, but all of them sat still, allowing the conversation to play out.

"Is it not the place of the Council?" another Tlu added, one who had not been introduced to him.

He replied, "Wasn't it this ship and its leaders who allowed your shuttle to berth here? Earlier, they protected Councillor Pi's shuttle from a different Domain Moon attack."

Vazak huffed and looked away, capitulating. Buoun's chest and cheeks swelled with pride: the act of forcing a warrior to back down ...

Be careful of overreaching, *he warned himself, the pride-reflex deflating as quickly as it had initiated.* Winning one short argument does not make you her equal. *He looked to Ahn, whose head had also bowed in acceptance.*

She said, "We will leave now." Her party rose to their feet. Pan signaled the soldiers by the entryway, and one of them slapped the control to open it. Coming to his side of the table, Ahn gripped Buoun's sleeve and murmured, "Please be careful, sibling-dear-one. We do not know what these creatures ultimately want from us, nor what they can do to us."

"But we do know what the other Domains will do, sibling-dear-one. For the moment, I feel safer under the control of these people*—" He stressed the word. "—than I do under threat from Moon and Surface aggression."*

She bowed her head again and moved away, the others trailing after her. Vazak gave him a sidelong look as she went; Buoun was sure he saw surprised respect in it.

What a long way I have come in the last few cycles. From a living joke and embarrassment, to the one Tlu who, by his cooperation with aliens, may yet save his domain from this conflict.

Another prospect occurred to him then, that history might yet mark him as a traitor.

Perhaps *that* is why Vazak respects me, *he thought.* Because she knows that no matter which way I turn, I face potential enemies and personal disaster. And yet I persevere.

For a brief time, he had been back among his own people. Now that they had exited the eating room to vanish into a side corridor, Buoun felt a twinge of loneliness and abandonment. Three Human soldiers had left with Ahn's group; the tallest and the shortest of them had stayed, staring at him from across the room. All eyes here were staring at him.

He thought, I am either braver than I thought I could ever be, or else I am an incredible fool.

ONCE THE NEWCOMERS HAD GONE—WEPPS, Hecate, and Westermann escorting them—Gregory took his seat and leaned toward Buoun, waving him back to his own chair. "The captain and I have agreed on a plan. But it requires your cooperation."

"A plan? To end this conflict?"

"Yes."

"I will do anything."

Fowler snorted, a non-verbal signal Buoun still had trouble interpreting.

"Don't make that promise before you've heard us out," Pan said.

Gregory was nodding. "You won't like this, I promise you."

"Hnnh," Buoun said. "What do you need me to do?"

"To translate. Again. And to help us find the right way to signal your enemy domains' leadership." The envoy nodded. "Because our comms are down, we are patching a transmitter into your sister's shuttle and routing it through a smaller craft we launched which is currently circling us." He broke off to ask the XO, "How long until we're ready to try?"

Barely glancing up from his tab, Chinyama replied, "Any minute now. Tech's running tests, pinging the receiver at the councillor's ship and the patrol fighter."

Focusing on Buoun, Gregory continued, "We'll return to the Ready Room now so the captain and XO are close to the bridge again."

"We can stay here," Pan interrupted. "For the sake of time. Commander, perhaps leave your tab with us and *you* can head back to the bridge."

Chinyama pushed the device across the table and rose. He gave all assembled a farewell nod. "Godspeed."

Gregory leaned toward Buoun, picking up the explanation. "The captain and I will work with you to speak to the hostile domain leaders. We presume there's a common language you can use?"

"I am fluent in it. This all sounds acceptable."

"Mm. So far," Fowler muttered.

"Oh," Buoun said again, as one of the details seemed to hit home for him. "You are not 'patching' your comms into *Pi's* shuttle?"

"Right," Pan said.

"Because she would not approve of the message you want me to relay?"

"You got it," Gregory said.

"What will be your message? If you can please put it in a short—" He consulted his wristwrap for the English word. "—short version?"

Gregory hesitated, gathering his own words. Pan and Fowler cleared their throats simultaneously, hinting for him to hurry. With a nod toward Fowler, he said, "As representatives of two Human factions, we will offer friendship, dialogue, and *potential* trade to all domains."

Buoun startled, one hand twisting at an ear for a few seconds as his head dropped and his gaze turned inward. He made a small humming sound—to Gregory, it sounded like the moan of an anxious child. Then he dropped the hand and raised his head.

"You must say to me, 'You have no choice but to work with us'."

"Pardon?" Gregory asked. Then he understood. "Ohhh. All right: Buoun, you have no choice but to work with us."

"Say to me 'If you desire our continued friendship and trust'."

Gregory repeated it.

Buoun gave a human nod. "If you have the capability to —" another dictionary check. "—edit the record of this conversation, please do so. It must indicate that you made those remarks so that I can claim to have misunderstood those statements to be threats, placing me under duress. Any Tlaa or Tlu or my station would instinctively capitulate in that circumstance without later penalty. Later, I will realize my error when reporting to my superiors, emphasizing your second statement about friendship so that my leaders continue to trust you."

Pan and Fowler gaped at Buoun as if he had grown another head. What he'd said was certainly convoluted, to say the least.

But Gregory replied, "I completely understand." And he did.

Deception. Games. Complex societies always have their social and political machinations.

The tablet chittered.

"We have outbound comms," Pan told them.

BUOUN'S SENSE *of helplessness was back, and growing. Although they had made multiple attempts to contact a variety of ground and moon installations, none had responded.*

Colonel Fowler eventually spoke up. "They distrust us. They suspect a cyberattack similar to the one they hit us with."

"Agreed," Pan replied. "Leaving us no closer to ending this conflict."

"We're the lucky ones here, remember," Gregory said.

"We'll repair our ship's damage in time to escape the system if need be, and—"

"Don't be so sure," Pan interrupted. He tapped his tablet, presumably referring to the reports streaming across its surface. "Each time we try to reboot sensors and comms, that damned Surface signal is there waiting for us, mutating constantly so that we can't erect effective defenses against it. Eventually, if they don't launch ships or missiles against us, we'll drift far enough away from the source to reboot, reorient, and get the hell out of here. But that might take a week, and who knows what will happen between now and then."

Gregory nodded. "To us. And to their domains."

"I understand the stakes, Ambassador. And I'm still not sure we shouldn't just leave them to it."

"Please," Buoun said. "There must be another way."

"There is," said a voice from the back of the room.

Heads turned. The smaller of the two soldiers had taken a few steps closer.

"Jogianto, no one asked for your opinion," Fowler said in what seemed to be a Human snarl.

Pan silenced him with a gesture and caught the soldier's attention. "If you have something to offer, let's hear it."

"Well," the soldier said. From her general shape and higher-pitched voice, Buoun guessed she was female. "That signal is originating somewhere. Why not do what we've been doing with the pirate factions? End the problem at the source."

Buoun didn't know the word pirate. But it certainly provoked a moment of thoughtful silence from the leaders at the table.

"Cut off the head ..." Pan murmured.

"A ground action?" Fowler asked the soldier. He seemed to have lost all sign of the irritation he'd initially displayed toward her.

"We've got the Confed fighter circling out there, unaf-

fected by the viral signal. I think those craft can hold two extra personnel?"

"Not enough," Pan said. "Ambassador, your yacht was unaffected by the virus?"

Gregory nodded. "Our systems were—and are—sleeping."

The soldier ventured closer to the table, rubbing her hands together in what Buoun interpreted as excitement. "The yacht could keep computer systems dormant and navigate the old-fashioned way. And if our comms picked up any enemy transponder signals before the blackout, the yacht could mimic them using radio only."

"To mask the approach of our ship so it doesn't get shot down," Pan said. His eyes had widened with what Buoun took to be enthusiasm. Or perhaps blood lust.

"Holy mangos," said the large soldier at the back of the room. When they turned to him, he added, "If we find that transmitter, we could destroy it, or *we could repurpose it to transmit a virus back at the enemy."*

"Excellent idea," said the smaller soldier. She and he locked gazes for a moment and nodded to each other before facing their leaders once more.

Fowler rubbed his chin in thought.

Gregory squeezed the top of his nose.

Pan's fingers flew across his tablet. After two dozen heartbeats, he sat back and grinned at them all. "The signals carrying the virus left one hell of an easy trail to follow. Buoun, do you think either your superior or your sister will assist us with further information?"

Buoun wasn't sure about Pi, but if he enlisted Ahn's help to petition her ...

"If it will stop continued warfare, then yes, I will find a way."

"Then this is worth a try."

27

CHIPPER UNDERSTOOD why Pan and Gregory had chosen the ambassador's yacht in place of a skiff: as a diplomatic vessel, it had decent shields, and it was faster and more maneuverable in atmosphere than a boxy runabout. But it wasn't really made to carry troops.

For example, he thought to himself, the cozy confines of the yacht's circular lounge accentuated Warrior Vazak's bulk rather than accommodating it. The Tlaa seemed to think the semicircular couches too narrow for her, forcing her to stand. Leaning against the wall beside her, and bulked himself with rifle and combat vest, Chipper had to agree with her.

The remainder of the six-person fireteam filed into the room and slumped onto the couches. At the far end of the small ship's forward passageway, the ambassador and his assistant squeezed into the cockpit hatchway, chatting with the pilot, Piers.

Chipper caught Vazak's eye and gave her a nod. A moment later she returned it, the movement a little wooden. It was probably alien to her.

In a thick voice, she said to him, "We go planet. We will fun. My life all want fun one day."

Envoy Buoun had taught her a handful of English words and gestures during the briefing, so the team could communicate with her on a basic and functional level. But Chipper couldn't imagine where she had picked up the word *fun*. And did *My life all want fun one day* mean she'd waited a lifetime for battle? If so, how had she sustained the burn scars across her left knuckles and the piece taken from her right ear's tip?

From the middle of the starboard couch, Hecate broke up laughing—perhaps it was at Vazak's poor grammar, perhaps at her blood-hungry sentiment, perhaps both. Chipper gave the Tactical a scowl and Ana elbowed her, but if Vazak minded, it didn't show in any body language Chipper could read. Maybe the human form of laughter didn't translate to her; maybe her kind were unaffected by mocking. He gave the warrior a thumbs up, and she squinted at it before returning it.

"We will fun," she repeated.

"Fun all right," Stines said from one end of a couch. He patted his PR19 beside him. "Little bit o' seek 'n destroy."

"Amen," Hecate grated, her laughter subsiding.

"Just keep it professional," Wepps warned. He sat at the other end of the couch from Stines, the portside couch. "Do your jobs. Get in, get out. Keep the body count as low as possible, as the captain ordered."

"Tell her that," Stines said, flicking a finger toward Vazak. "Looks ready to *eat* the first bogey we come across."

Hecate snorted.

Well, Chipper thought, *that's it. A comment from everyone in the away team so far. All except ... her*. Ana was studying the backs of her hands, quiet as usual, contained. Chipper felt bad about the words they'd exchanged in the docking lounge. She wasn't a bad person. Was she?

Spying on Assured! *For God's sakes.*

But then she'd seemed so conflicted over it. Not arrogant or dismissive—not even cagey. She had seemed ... guilty. That was a good sign, wasn't it? A conscience was the mark of a good person.

Also, this mission might result in a solution to *Assured*'s situation. And it was Ana's idea. While the last thing Chipper wanted to do was end up killing some Tluaanto, her idea was a damn *good* idea. Surely that made up for any past sins.

Approaching footsteps drew the group's attention along the passageway. Ambassador Gregory stopped at the top of the ramp, halfway between them and the cockpit.

"Be successful and come back safe," he said. A few mumbled *thank-yous* rolled back his way as he passed out of sight down the ramp.

Past the ramp, Chipper caught Grace Renny by the pilot's chair, planting a kiss on the man's forehead. There was an exchange of words, and then she came hurrying back up the passage, with a face like thunder. She gave the team no good bye, no good luck. No one else it seemed had been in the position to see the kiss, no one but Vazak. If she'd witnessed it, she wasn't reacting to it.

As the ramp rose and Piers warmed up the engines, the Tluaan warrior slid a long, keen blade from one thigh sheath, a tiny bottle of oil from another. She squirted oil on the knife then polished it against the fabric of her bodysuit. The suit made the Tlaa seem underdressed for a firefight. It was all she wore beneath a chest holster holding her handgun and some kind of grenade, and the thigh strapping that held the sheath in place on one leg and a flattened water flask on the other. Was the suit as tough as armor? Or did Tluaan warriors not care about things like personal protection? Chipper ran a palm over his own combat vest and wondered if it made him weak in Vazak's eyes.

"See, Sergeant?" Hecate said, eyes on the long knife. "Furball's ready to carve herself some steaks."

Stines chuckled while Ana blew out a breath in disgust.

Wepps's expression darkened. "Warrior Vazak is prepping her weapons the way I saw you doing about ten minutes ago. She is a soldier like you. I hear any of you using derogatory terms about her again and mission or no mission, it'll mean twenty-four hours in the brig."

"Most Peacers get a call sign, Sergeant," Hecate complained. She raised her hands in surrender as Wepps's brow furrows deepened. "But we're not doing that with any Tluaanto. I get it."

"She gets it," Ana muttered.

"Well, that's sugar to my ears, Enforcer Hecate," Wepps said. "So now we can all act professional, keep our words and actions on task, and our thoughts on mission."

He received a chorus of "Yes, Sergeant", causing Vazak to scrutinize them for a moment.

The yacht lifted, its deck shifting almost imperceptibly beneath Chipper's boots. Though gravity adjusted immediately, he still shifted his stance a little, as if he was back home aboard a boat hitting a wave, or aboard an aircraft taking off.

And here we go, he thought with lead in his gut.

The hand that had caressed his body armor dropped to his strapped-on rifle. If he had to fire on hostiles, he would. He'd behave professionally, as Wepps had said. His teammates depended on it, as did everybody aboard *Assured*.

But Chipper didn't have to like it.

THIS IS like being in the back of a troop carrier, Ana thought, though they were all in the back of a rich man's vessel. *No vidfeeds back here. No viewports*. They had been off *Assured* for almost an hour now and had only the pilot's infrequent updates over the cabin intercom to keep them informed.

Beside her, Hecate had her eyes closed and her fingers tapping a beat on the table. The rhythm no doubt came from the audio implants she knew the woman owned, subcutaneous stereo speakers with a tiny data chip loaded with music. Ana could never stomach the thought of something like that.

From the other side of the cabin, Stines' gaze ranged around the yacht's interior, alighting mostly on Vazak and Hecate. Did he have a thing for Hecate now, she wondered, or did the Thesian see both Tluaanto and Xerxians as different species to himself, ugly and untrustworthy?

Wepps was quiet, composed, his hands folded on the table, his eyelids hooded, his breathing deep and even.

Vazak was finished with her knife. She had dropped into a squat where she, like Hecate, had her eyes closed. As if also to a rhythm only she heard, the warrior's head moved side to side. Then again, it may have been self-soothing. Or even some form of prayer or meditation. Did Tluaanto do that? Ana vaguely remembered some of the information filtering out of the Gregory-Buoun sessions indicating Tluaanto were entirely without religion.

And there was Chipper, his back against the wall by the short hallway into the personal quarters area. Fidgeting. Wringing his hands. Flicking pieces of dust off his rifle, scratching at his scalp, rubbing his eyes. He kept his gaze turned down and inward. What was he thinking? He hated combat—she knew that about him now. But he was damn good at it, she also knew. She wondered then what he'd rather be doing. Did he have plans for after his Peacekeeper tenure? Was this a means to an end, rather than a career in itself? She rarely gave a thought to what motivated others, what secret plans they might harbor the way she harbored hers.

The intercom crackled. The pilot Piers said, "Apologies again for the delay. We had to travel the long way around the South Pole to avoid visual sighting from orbital assets. We're descending over the correct continent's landmass now. So far, no one's challenging us. I'm heading for cloud cover to get us closer, and I'll give you a heads-up when we're ready to land."

"How long?" Wepps called down the corridor.

Through the speakers, Piers replied softly, "Taking it slow. Maybe ten minutes."

The intercom fell silent. The human soldiers had already run through weapons checks, tightened straps and pocket covers on their vests, patted those pockets to ensure they had remembered everything they needed. But they all did it again.

It's just keeping busy, Ana thought as she ran an unnecessary diagnostic on her PR19. *What else do you do when you got this much nervous energy, but ya can't use it yet?*

A glance at Vazak answered that question: the Tluaan warrior was rolling shoulders, flexing her muscles beneath that crazy bodysuit, arms then legs, then back it looked like. The stubby pistol she carried was sheathed, along with her knife.

"So hungry," Stines muttered, putting away the cutting laser both he and Hecate carried in place of sidearms. The stocky Caultan eased off the couch and searched his pockets. "Forgot to grab meal bars. Anyone got a meal bar?" He received nothing but grunted negatives, prompting a grunt of his own. "I actually feel like popcorn anyway. Maybe they got some in the galley here."

"Forget that," Wepps muttered. "Food later."

Stines sighed, then smoothed his pocket covers closed. "Rich guy probably doesn't eat it, anyway."

Wepps came off the couch and out from behind the table. "Gonna stand with the pilot. I'll let you know when we're close." Vazak stepped forward, as if to accompany him. Wepps stood nowhere close to her height. She towered over him. He made a *wait here* gesture and told her slowly, "Be ready."

"I ready," she assured him, patting her knife sheath.

"I'm sure you are," he muttered. He headed for the cockpit.

When he was gone, Stines said, "Glad there's only one of her. Imagine if we had five of the buggers, and they turned on us?"

"She's not gonna turn on us," Ana said.

"We're helping her side," Chipper agreed.

The group fell silent again. Ana checked the time. She checked it again six minutes later when Wepps stomped back down the corridor.

He raised the large tactical tab he'd brought along. "Huddle up."

They complied as best they could in the cramped space between lounge tables. He positioned the tab so all could see the aerial photograph on it. It depicted a cross-shaped facility with some kind of communications dish on its roof at the nexus of its four wings. Outbuildings and tarmac spread around it, and a single road led to and from it. Blobs along the road and in the compound were no doubt vehicles of some kind.

Wepps said, "Our target. Buoun's sister gave us this intel before we left. This image is about twenty hours old now."

"It's out in the middle of nowhere," Hecate said. And the facility was, surrounded on all sides by the red-browns of a desert landscape. "That's good."

"What about air traffic?" Chipper asked. "Air threats?"

"Nothing active nearby. Only one of the objects in the

compound looks like a landed flier. Remember this is twenty hours old; we're still approaching through cloud cover, so we have no current visual as yet. Piers said there *is* something that might be a small airbase five hundred klicks north. We have the Devilfly inbound now from *Assured* for air cover."

"Nice," Stines whispered. "They ain't got nothing that's a match for that little fighter."

Hecate snorted but said nothing.

Wepps continued, "There are two things we do need to worry about. One, maybe there's a large garrison stationed inside this main building or around those outbuildings. Two, Domain Surface might target this ship from orbit once we land and they realize what we're up to."

"Shit," Stines said.

"And that's why—" Wepps slid a finger around the screen to change the angle and zoom on the image. "—we're landing inside there."

The new perspective showed a large opening in the south end of the main building; sunlight revealed empty space inside. Still, it was hard to gauge exactly *how much* empty space or even how big the opening was.

Wepps had obviously had the same thought. Already he was tapping up a short animation set on a loop and showing the yacht passing through the door. "It's high and wide enough. But, Vazak, will this work?"

"She won't understand that," Stines muttered.

But the tall Tlaa was leaning forward, eyes narrowed at the animation. "Yes," she said, straightening and tapping data into the wristwrap on her right forearm. After reading something, she looked up at him. "Hen-Ger."

Hecate snorted again. Stines said, "*What?*"

Ana signaled the warrior to show her the relevant screen on her wristwrap. Sure enough, she had a Tluaanto-English dictionary like Ana had seen the envoy using.

"She means hangar," Ana told them. As one, their mouths became wide Os as they understood. Enunciating the syllables, Ana told Vazak, "*Hangar*."

"Hangar," Vazak repeated and pointed to the looped animation.

"So, it's okay?" Wepps asked her, tapping the animation to confirm it.

"Hangar good okay."

"Sugary," Wepps said.

"Why do they have a hangar inside a data center with a transmission dish and all of it out in the middle of nowhere?" Chipper asked.

"Domain Space suspects Surface use this place to program unmanned drones as well as develop cyberwarfare," Ana replied. "I picked that up from the Tluaanto while we were programming the virus."

Wepps continued, "Once we're inside, Vazak has her orders to lead us to the data center. Then it'll be over to you, Jogianto, while the rest of us keep an eye out."

"Make it bloody quick," Stines grumbled. "No stuffing about."

Ana glared at him. A half dozen possible retorts occurred to her, but she held her tongue. In the moment's pause, Chipper spoke up anyway.

"Same side, brother," he said. "Remember?"

Stines made a noise in his throat and looked away.

"We are cleared for lethal force—"

Hecate and Stines smiled at that, Ana noticed, while Chipper actually winced.

"—with one exception," Wepps added. He returned the original aerial image to the tab's screen and zoomed in on a certain spot, revealing what appeared to be a grounded aircraft. It was broad across the "shoulders" with large fan housings or turbines on either side, white with a painted sigil or glyph on the roof between turbines. The sigil comprised three intersecting green ovals with a blue chevron at the outer point of each oval.

Vazak gesticulated toward the image. "Con-cill!" she said. "Con-cill!"

"What the bloody hell?" Stines hissed.

Wepps chuckled humorlessly. "She means council."

Ana got it immediately. "That flier is a Domain Surface Council member's aircraft?"

Wepps raised and lowered his brows in confirmation.

"Con-sill." Vazak mimicked a human nod. "Vazak-us-you kill con-sill."

"Whoa—" Chipper started before Wepps interrupted him.

"Vazak, not kill, *not* kill council," the sergeant said.

Her sudden frown was easy to read. This was an opportunity she was not going to pass up. To kill an enemy leader or two ...

Wepps groaned, "Jeebus Crumpet. I thought Buoun made this clear to her." He passed the tab off to Stines then mimed getting his hands around something. "Not kill. Catch. You understand? *Catch*! Gods, she's not getting this. Her and Buoun have dictionaries on their devices. Why can't we?"

Ana clicked her fingers for attention. She made the shape of a gun with her hand and pointed it at Hecate. "Kill. No." Then she reached across and grabbed Hecate by the arms. Hecate glowered, but didn't resist. "Catch." She tugged Hecate into the middle of their huddle and held her fast. "*Catch*."

Vazak's frown cleared, her ears flattening. As Ana released Hecate, Vazak's arms shot out and grabbed the much shorter Xerxian woman around the torso, hoisting her onto one broad shoulder.

"Hey!" Hecate yelled. She'd been fortunate that the ceiling was quite high here in the lounge.

"Catch!" Vazak said.

Stines and Chipper burst out laughing.

"Yes," Ana said, feeling her own face melting into a big grin. "Catch."

"Put me the hell down!" Hecate squealed, not sounding anything like a tough Enforcer.

Ignoring her, Vazak said, "Catch con-sill?"

"Catch council, yes," said Wepps. To everyone else he said, "Hopefully she won't go hunting them. Make it a lot easier for us if those council members are in the data center."

"How do we even know they're still there?" Ana asked. "The intel's twenty hours old."

Wepps shrugged. "We don't. And the main mission hasn't changed." He nodded up at Vazak. "If she sights a domain leader and they're easy to stun and bag, we bag 'em."

"As long as I don't have to carry them, I'm fine with it," Ana said.

"Put me the *hack* down!" Hecate growled, making her voice deeper.

"Reckon she can carry a couple," Wepps replied.

"Catch con-sill." Vazak finally put Hecate down. "Good okay."

The Enforcer scrambled over a table and stood up on the couch. "Jesus, she ever does that to me again ..." She tugged at her vest as if to straighten it.

Sobering, Chipper asked, "Should we really be capturing enemy leaders? Won't that create political complications?"

Wepps eyeballed him. "Since when did political complications become a soldier's concern?"

"Yes, Sergeant."

"Okay." Wepps checked the time then hooked a thumb toward the yacht's exit. "Get ready for go time."

He headed for the cockpit while the rest of them piled up around the hatchway. Stines, Hecate, and Vazak fell into introspection again, bouncing on the balls of their feet. Ana found herself exchanging a look with Chipper. The big guy's eyes were wide, his face flushed, his jaw clenched tight.

She gave him a brief smile. "It's gonna work," she told him.

"Absolutely," he said.

"And we're all coming back," she told him and then turned her gaze on the others. "All of us."

Stines nodded. Hecate grunted. Vazak didn't react.

Her gaze lingering on the Tlaa, Ana thought, *I agree with Chipper. Capturing enemies and dragging them back here? Sister, you just made this way more complicated than it needs to be.*

MUCH OF THIS chatter between soldiers was piped into *Assured*'s bridge, via an old-fashioned radio pick-up worn by Wepps—and then via an uncompromised analog-radio link routed through the yacht's comms panel. This time, there were no ECF feeds filling the bridge main screen since they operated digitally—they'd see no visual, and hear only Wepps's audio.

Gregory had taken up position by Buoun at the railing. Fowler stood on the other side of Buoun. In a lull in any conversation coming through from the yacht, Buoun pointed toward the screen, since that was also where the audio speakers lay. "The human named Jogianto: she is the one who had the idea of attacking the facility?"

"Yes," Fowler replied.

"Her name ..."

"Yes?" Gregory prompted him.

"Well, it has the *-nto* suffix. Tluaan. *Tluaanto*. Does this mean there is something plural about *her*?"

Gregory gave him a sidelong look, catching Fowler doing the same thing from Buoun's other side. *What the hell kind of question was that for a time like this?* "Er ... no."

"Hm. Good to know."

The envoy fell silent again, and Gregory allowed himself a small shake of the head as his attention returned to the screen. As was their custom, Pan and Chinyama stood shoulder to shoulder below it, talking quietly. The bridge was also quiet—nothing like the craziness during the Warlord Luján away mission almost a standard month ago. At Gregory's back, an older Peacer was on security duty by the door—the one with the callsign Gregory considered rather ugly: Widowmaker.

A new voice crackled from the speakers, that of the Devilfly pilot, also resorting to radio since *Assured*'s laser-comms and leapspace comms were still down.

"Commencing low orbit pass over enemy airfield." Earlier, she had reported the results of a sortie through Surface-held space: she had extinguished a relay station, six unmanned drones and two weather satellites. No loss of life; a show of force, only. And, they all hoped, a distraction from the ground assault. The Devilfly's cameras and other sensors worked fine. A moment later, Berderhan reported, "Airfield appears civilian. No threat there and nothing approaching on sensors. Returning to mission target airspace."

Other voices spoke over the tail end of her message.

"Landing," was all Piers said.

And Wepps called out to his team, "Coming in hot! Hatch opens in twenty seconds."

The knot in Gregory's gut tightened.

Here we go again.

28

THE FIRETEAM'S formation around the hatch was the same as they'd adopted when boarding the pirate corvette—back before Chipper had imagined meeting non-humans, let alone shooting at them. He and Stines stood behind a kneeling Ana and Hecate respectively, weapons ready, riding out the mild bumps as the yacht settled to the hangar floor. In contrast, Vazak rested against the bulkhead opposite the hatch, one hand on her shoulder-holster, the other on her hip, the very picture of unfazed. Chipper swallowed against the lump in his throat, but couldn't budge it. His eyes fell to the selector switch on the side of his PR19: it was set to *AP*, "anti-personnel" being the clean way of describing a lethal setting.

Do what you have to. Do what you must. You're a soldier, damn it.

He raised his chin, and the lump in his throat dissolved as acceptance flooded through him. A click announced the hatch lock disengaging. The rustle of cloth and creak of gloves announced the fireteam's grips tightening on weapons. Chipper heard Wepps coming up beside him from the cockpit.

"Five bogeys sighted," the team leader said. "They fled down a passage to your ten o'clock."

The hatch slid open, the ramp already engaging, lowering from the ship's hull before rolling out like a rug. *Unlike* a rug, it hardened immediately into a stable surface as it touched the hangar's concrete floor. Without hostile contacts out there, Ana and Hecate shot to their feet and charged down, the male Peacers at their heels. Ana curved left toward the cockpit as Hecate and Stines veered right to the tail. Perched atop legs 1.8 meters high, there was space beneath the yacht's belly for them to cut under it rather than around. They didn't stoop; Chipper had to. He glanced behind him, to where Vazak jogged out into the middle of empty space, without cover, turning in circles, seeking an enemy.

Cripes alive!

He faced forward again, putting her out of mind. His nostrils now prickled from the smell and bite of petrochemicals and concrete dust. To his right, patches of sunlight breaking through the hangar's opaque window panels formed warm yellow rectangles across the floor. That was the only color here apart from the paint job on the yacht—the hangar design was utilitarian, grays upon grays. No other vehicles were in here, but a network of gantries, small derricks, and catwalks laced the perimeter, and beams crisscrossed the ceiling. Now that he looked more carefully, the roof seemed to be shifting a little from the outside breeze. Some kind of shade cloth? A kind of insulating fabric, more likely. It was cool in here while the glare beyond the hangar entrance hinted at a very hot day.

Through the stink of chemical and construct, Chipper could discern something else now, a native musk left by the beings that had been working here perhaps. Or by something in the atmosphere. He thanked God for the booster shots he'd received against germs ...

Wepps pointed to a doorway eighty meters off the yacht's nose. Ana already had her rifle angled that way; Chipper did the same.

"Straight through there," Wepps said as Hecate came around from their left. Stines had stayed by the tail with an eye on the open hangar entrance. "Tluaan intel says the data center's where the building's four wings meet." He pointed at Hecate. "You're on point, then me, Ana, Stines."

"What about her?" Ana asked, jerking her shoulder at Vazak. The huge warrior was pacing now, nose in the air.

"She's meant to stick with me," Wepps sighed. "I'll guess we'll see about that."

"What about *me*?" Chipper asked.

"Watch the ship," Wepps said simply. He whistled for Stines. "Go, Hecate."

Hecate bounded away at a sprint. A second later, Ana did too, but Chipper snared Wepps's armor to hold him place as Stines raced over and past them.

"Sergeant, if it's what I said about not capturing an enemy leader—"

Wepps's surprised expression softened. "It's not, Chip. I need someone here who can actually do what they're told and keep this ship intact for when we get back. I'd like to leave here when I need to."

"Right, Sergeant," Chipper replied, caught between relief and the shame of feeling relieved. He let Wepps go, and the sergeant cuffed him affectionately before he, too, raced away.

Hecate was almost at the door before Vazak seemed to notice and follow. Despite her bulk, the Tlaa was *fast*, those long legs eating up the space at twice a human's speed.

"You need me?" a voice asked from behind him. Piers. Halfway down the ramp and ashen-faced, but steeled for the worst.

"Cockpit," Chipper told him. "Keep the engines warm. Be ready to go at a moment's notice."

With a nod, Piers scampered inside.

Chipper glanced down at the stubby grenade launcher under his PR19's muzzle. *Hope you guys don't need this.* He took a knee under the vessel and kept his head on a swivel, watching both the hangar entrance and the door—the door through which his team was fast disappearing.

A GAGGLE of Tluaanto awaited them, one hundred meters along the corridor. Ten of them, all unarmed, none anywhere near Vazak's size. From a hundred meters away—most of the way to the building's hub—they stared at the alien interlopers coming through their door. They reminded Ana of the gawkers outside the mess when the Orbital delegation had been inside.

What is this, show time at the zoo? she wondered.

Without warning, Hecate burst-fired from beside her. Ana flinched. The EM rounds slammed against the ceiling above the crowd, showering them with fragments and dust and sending them packing.

Passing her human teammates, Vazak jogged ahead, her pistol out of its holster. She squeezed off a shot of her own, the energy bolt sizzling just over the heads of the fleeing. The group broke into two, vanishing behind side doors. As the fireteam jogged after her, Vazak looked over her shoulder and called, "Fun!"

"Christ," Stines grumbled to Hecate. "She's crazier'n you are!"

Hecate made a crass gesture.

Wepps snapped, "Secure those doors," indicating the ones the civilians had gone through. The cutting lasers carried by Hecate and Stines were also good for melting metal, melding doorframes to doors. When they reached the rooms the Tluaanto personnel had gone into, Stines stayed behind, putting his cutter to work. The others continued on, Wepps and Hecate checking the other side rooms as Ana and Vazak kept on at a walk toward the open space another hundred meters further. The data center. Despite the permission to use lethal force, when Ana heard Wepps's weapon go off behind her, the sound was that of stun bolts.

Can't bring himself to kill non-combatants. Well, fair play to you, Sergeant. That's exactly why I wanna join you Confeds.

"Seal this one too," he shouted back to Stines.

Nearing the open area mid-building, Ana saw movement in there. More civilians? Or—

Her instincts saved her life. A shaggy head and broad shoulders appeared above a work station just inside the main chamber; Ana ducked right and into the final office doorway of the corridor. An energy bolt crackled past her left shoulder. Another hit the wall above the doorframe, forcing Ana to jiggle at the handle until it opened. Outside, Wepps and Hecate had gone to ground, Hecate pulling something from a hip pouch. Vazak appeared mid-corridor right outside the room Ana was in, firing from the hip. She heard an agonized shriek from the data center, and Vazak sauntered into the room with her to take cover at the door, unfazed.

Making eye contact, Ana said, "Still fun?"

"Fun," the big Tlaa confirmed.

"Roachbot active," Hecate called out in the hall.

Ana risked a peek. From a prone position, Hecate had the tiny controller for the bot in her hands while the robot scuttled along the hallway floor at great speed.

"Careful of collaterals," Wepps called to her. "We want those leaders if they're there."

"Trust me," Hecate replied. "Dialing it down."

Several more energy bolts flashed past, forcing Ana to retreat. Vazak returned fire, but without a resulting cry of pain this time.

"Two bogeys only, eleven o'clock," Hecate called, and then blue-white light flashed once followed by a thick *whump* of sound. She'd used the flashboom setting on the bot, Ana realized, rather than H.E. A half second later, she also realized that her crew was moving. She followed after Vazak as fast as she could, but the Tlaa quickly overtook Hecate and Wepps, entering the chamber ahead of them and to the left of the doorway. The warrior was one meter inside—with Wepps coming up mid-corridor and Hecate far-right—when something huge dropped on her from the ceiling and she rolled sideways and out of Ana's view. Wepps and Hecate swore, Wepps with rifle high and sweeping the roof, while Hecate's swept the maze of work-stations around the room. Satisfied there was no further threat from above, Wepps leaped onto a console and fired stun-bolts at the point Ana figured the flashboomed hostiles were.

"Two down," he called and jumped to the next console, tracking his rifle left for new threats while Hecate focused right.

Reaching the entrance to the chamber, Ana threw herself on the floor. All of the desks appeared to be set up off the floor with a meter of space beneath them—this allowed her to check the room from a prone position. A quick glance to her left revealed Vazak grappling with a warrior of similar size, with bushier head-fur and more formal clothes. They scuttled around on one hand and two knees, both with knives drawn and teeth bared. They came together in a tangle as Ana forced her focus ahead of her.

There!

"Contact forward!" she yelled. "Mid-room. Four, maybe five bogeys. Could be civs." The knot of Tluaanto were bowed low, with knees, hands, and heads all touching the floor. None appeared as big as the warriors she'd seen so far.

"Got 'em!" Wepps yelled from above and forward. "Ana, you're free to move. Hecate—"

"Still clearing," the Tactical called back.

Ana got up and slipped down an aisle between desks, bringing her close to the sergeant's position as he hopped to the floor. She smelled charred flesh and fabric: over to the left, two enemy warriors were down with smoking holes in their torsos and heads.

"Hack it, I missed all the action!" Stines whined, entering the chamber late. He pulled up short, captivated by the two grappling warriors.

"They're yours to watch," Wepps told him. When he noticed Ana trying to pick out the council members from the five Tluaanto cowering on their knees mid-room, he whistled at her. "Forget them." He stabbed a finger at a nearby data terminal as he closed on the frightened huddle of non-humans.

"Right," she said and bent over the work station. She slipped her folding keypad and smartwire from a vest pocket and got to work, recognizing the data port she'd been shown back on *Assured*. The port was a configuration of three slim holes arranged in a tight triangle. Squeezing the smartwire's end to activate it, she pressed it against the metal between the holes. While she caught her breath, the wire's end parted into tiny filaments that snaked their way against and into the input apertures. She fit the other end of the smartwire into the keypad.

"Clear!" Hecate called.

With one hand training his rifle on the group of cowering Tluaanto, Wepps waved the other at the door on the far side of the chamber. "That's front door. Hecate, that's yours to watch." He stabbed a finger back the way they'd come. "That's back door. Stines, that's yours—and keep an eye on ... them," he added, meaning the warriors down behind the bank of work stations.

"Bloody oath, I will," Stines replied.

Ana checked the keypad, waiting for the green light and bright alert tone that would signal contact had been established. It wasn't coming fast, and she found herself bobbing up and down on the balls of her feet. "Come on, *porquería*, come on!"

Ahead of her, Wepps pulled items from the largest pouch on his vest. Three cakes of high explosive. Then the detonator.

Once the virus was on its way out to the rest of Surface's settlements and installations, Wepps was going to turn this place to atoms.

Yes! she thought as the keypad bleeped confirmation of a connection. Suddenly, nothing mattered so much to her as uploading the data virus and getting the hack out of here. She hoped Piers still had the yacht engines running. She hoped Chipper wasn't facing any contacts back there—

Joyful whooping from Stines turned Ana's head: Vazak had risen from behind the bank of desks, wiping dark blood from her knife onto her suit leg. There didn't appear to be any tears in that suit. From his position covering the entryway, Stines flipped the Tlaa a thumbs up. She ignored it, vaulting over consoles to get to Ana's station faster. Although Ana knew Vazak was on her side, watching that mighty body approaching at full steam, her ape-cat face flushed and her throat fur dark, with that huge blade drawn —holy Christ, it was *scary*.

At Ana's side, Vazak considered the ovular monitor screen at the back of the work station. Ana clipped a datawafer to the keypad—the wafer containing the mutated virus—and started typing. All of this had to be by memory and with a precise touch since none of the right-to-left gibberish running across the alien monitor screen made any sense to her. It didn't need to, she reminded herself. She'd programmed the virus with a little help from that gambling addict Sintopas and one of the Orbital's crew; it was solid. As long as her typing was accurate, the program she unleashed would bridge human and Tluaan systems to send that data-virus racing out into Domain Surface networks at lightspeed.

Vazak grunted something, and it took Ana a few moments to recognize it as the English word *Good*. The warrior was already moving away and toward the seated captives before Ana could respond.

Vazak pointed at one of the trembling Tluaanto—Ana couldn't tell their gender at a glance, especially not when distracted and awaiting a confirmation bleep from her keypad. *Come on, come on*, she thought. Vazak barked commands at the Tluaan individual. The individual stood up. Ana noticed that this one wore a short robe over the normal Tluaan tunic and trousers, a garment with silver embossing along the sleeves and hem. After a moment, the individual crawled along the floor until they were two meters from the rest of their group. They glared back at Vazak, covering their fear with an exaggerated hauteur.

Vazak said to Wepps, "Con-sill."

"Copy," Wepps replied. He raised his voice. "We're not taking these other four. Or incinerating them. Vazak, tell them to run." He mimed it with his fingers and pointed to the front door.

Vazak frowned a little and watched his lips as he repeated the words.

Her expression cleared. "Run. Yes." She turned to the four civilians and snarled three syllables at them. Nothing happened except that they drew tighter in on themselves. Vazak drew a deep breath. This time she roared the phrase at them. And this time, they didn't hesitate, rising as one and bolting hard toward the entry Hecate was guarding.

The Tactical slapped her rifle barrel against the backside of the last one leaving and cackled.

Wepps approached the last enemy individual—the Surface council member—waving them closer to Vazak. They complied—grudgingly. Immediately, the warrior stepped in and scooped the individual onto her shoulder then retreated around the desks at a trot.

Ana's comms crackled—they'd been able to rig them to operate in a closed system away from *Assured.* They could communicate amongst themselves but not with their capital ship.

"Fireteam, this is Chipper. Pilot marks three aircraft inbound fast and low from the north. Devilfly is distracted and can't engage."

Wepps hit *transmit* button. "Close?"

"Very."

"Troop carriers? Bombers?"

"Can't be certain."

"Copy." Wepps whistled to Hecate and gestured for her to come back. He hit the detonator timer and set out after Vazak. "Two minutes till boom-boom, boys and girls, let's frog it!" He slapped his comms again. "Returning hot, Chipper. Vazak has one enemy prisoner."

Ana squeezed the smartwire, telling it to withdraw.

Chipper's voice crackled through their comms again. "Radar indicates first enemy aircraft has landed, north end of compound. First enemy aircraft has landed."

Ana tugged out the data wafer and pocketed it, folding the keyboard as Hecate arrived at her side. She gave the wire a tug, but it wouldn't detach. What was taking it so long?

"The man said boom-boom," Hecate told her. "You know boom-boom?"

"Go if you have to. I'll be done in a sec."

"Leave it!"

"Can't! Captain doesn't want traces of human tech left here."

"Screw him!"

Ana wondered if Hecate would have said that aloud if her ECF had been sending to *Assured.*

Hecate continued, "The tech's about to get evaporated. Let's *go.*"

"They're orders. Just leave. I'm almost—" A deep-throated shout from the direction of the "front door" sucked the breath out of Ana's lungs. Warriors? Where the hell had they—? "Oh, shit."

She trained her rifle on the door a split second after Hecate did. The very next second, two enormous Tluaanto came barreling through it. They wore clothing closer to human combat fatigues than to Vazak's bodysuit. Their head-fur was shaggier than hers. And they were bigger. Both carried long knives, their rifles slung. Seeing the humans, they ululated and cut toward them, hurdling the first desk in their path.

Ana and Hecate fired simultaneously, a sustained volley that blew both hostiles off their feet and back onto the desk.

"Now will you go?" Hecate asked her, turning her head for a second.

In the second that followed, an energy bolt whipped by, centimeters overhead. Ana had the impression of three or four more warriors crowding the doorway before she dropped into cover.

"Holy mother!" Hecate hissed, collapsing next to Ana.

"You hit?"

"Nah, just pissed off."

"Bad timing, huh?"

"Damn right." A barrage of energy bolts swept overhead, turning patches of the next desks past them into molten slag. "What now?"

Ana's keypad and smartwire were still up on the desk.

She wished she'd listened to Hecate and left them thirty seconds ago—she was going to have to anyway. She jerked her chin at the "back door".

"Head for the corridor. I'll cover you. Then you cover me while I catch up."

"So they can hit me while you hit them?" Hecate sneered.

"God! I'm trusting *you* not to run and leave me here!"

"It's a dumbass idea, whoever goes first."

Both women recoiled when fresh fire pounded the back of the desk they'd sheltered behind.

"That's gonna punch through real soon," Hecate said.

Ana pulled a grenade from a vest pouch. Hecate nodded and followed suit. They scooted to opposite ends of their cover, coming around into a crouch to face it. Ana slung the rifle over her back and pulled her sidearm—the Xerxian 12-mm felt a lot more comfortable than the Confed rifles, and it would be easier to fire blind over a desk. There came a temporary lull in the shooting, and with it the scuff of footsteps as hostiles repositioned themselves.

"Me first," Ana said. Hooking her forearm over the desk, she fired four wild shots. When return fire hammered home near her, Hecate lobbed her grenade then ducked back. Ana quickly twisted the top of her grenade and depressed the timer. Enemy fire swung Hecate's way, allowing Ana to lob her grenade too, careful to send it far past Wepps's charges. The two women jammed hands over ears and opened their jaws wide against the pressure wave to come.

The twin explosions shook the floor and rattled the desk. Rubble peppered the room and smoke boiled quickly up toward the high ceiling.

"*Now* I'll go first!" Hecate said and launched herself in the direction of the back door.

Ana popped up, handgun ready ... But there was zero enemy contact. And judging by the mess they'd caused, there wouldn't be. Her anxious gaze fell to Wepps's explosives, sitting undamaged where he'd placed them. How much time had elapsed?

Ana turned and sprinted after Hecate. The other Tactical had paused by the door to offer cover if needed, so Ana passed her easily and heard her fall into step a few meters behind.

They were fifty meters out of the data center when Wepps's charges ignited.

The resulting pressure wave threw them off their feet. Ana tucked herself into a roll as she landed, coming to rest face up and in perfect position to watch the network of cracks race along the ceiling above her.

"Shit!" she cried and hunkered up tight again, arms over her head as the roof caved in.

29

THEY ARE RISKING THEIR LIVES, not only to free their ship, *Buoun thought,* but to end the war between our domains. To save our species. To help us to rise above a half million generations of conflict. *Truly, these humans were noble, brave.*

And they have killed warriors! They are strong!

But would they be strong enough to get back off the planet?

BRUSHING DUST and detritus off her vest and her legs, Ana rose shakily to her feet. Most of the fallen rubble around her was small, although one of those chunks of metal or concrete had gotten through her arms to glance off her head. Her skull still rang with the impact, and she put her palm to the egg that was starting to rise there. The hand came away spotted with blood. Not much blood for a head wound.

Not so bad.

Then she looked around for Hecate.

Hecate was in trouble. The Tactical's upper torso lay face up and dusty—but her lower half was stuck beneath a huge mess of debris. Her eyes were open, and for a moment, Ana thought Hecate was dead. Then the eyes tracked toward her. And Hecate blinked. Ana hurried over, stumbling on fragments of roof. Part of the wall had come down to her left revealing the office behind it. She slapped at her comms but got nothing for the effort. Something must have hit her rig—or had it been the pressure wave from the explosion?

Hecate coughed dust from her lungs—it had congealed with her sweat to form a muddy sheen on her face. "Don't think mine's working either," she grated.

"I'll get you out of this."

"We've ... got more hostiles incoming. You need to leave." She coughed again. "Feel like I've told you that before."

Ana squatted, fumbling for a grip on a hunk of concrete. She strained at it, arms burning.

"That ain't gonna work," Hecate told her. There was a little blood trickling down through the muck on her face from a head cut. She chuckled. "Well, girl ... Looks like you get your payback after all."

"Payback?" Ana straightened, gaping at her in disbelief. "*Now* you admit you tripped me!"

"Satisfied, bitch?"

"You're the bitch."

Hecate shrugged her eyebrows, accepting. She turned her head back toward the obliterated data center. "I've got a grenade. I'll take as many of these hair-asses with me as I can."

Ana shook her head and was about to reply when she heard the scrape of footsteps at her back.

Stines. Standing forty meters back toward the hangar.

"A little help," she called to him.

He gave her a sad shake of the head, then a wink, then a quick salute. And then he sprinted away.

Ana stared after him, disbelieving.

"Who ya gabbin' to?" Hecate grated.

"No one, I guess," Ana sighed. She crouched to study the arrangement of rubble to the side of Hecate's position.

"What are you doing?"

Ana didn't answer. Cross beams and spars had fallen on knots of hard-fabric and concrete and tiles in a jumble. But there was one particular steel spar—it hadn't fallen all the way down, caught against a wall-stud.

"Might work," she mused. "Can you reach your cutting laser?"

"The Confeds won't wait, Jogi! Just go!"

Ana bent over, reaching for the exposed pockets on Hecate's vest. The woman slapped at her hand, then grimacing in pain, reached into one herself and withdrew the laser for her. "What the hell you gonna do with that?"

Ana took it, stepped aside and took aim, running the line of concentrated light vertically along the center of the wooden stud, evaporating a channel as wide as two fingers. Some of the wood around it sparked, smoked, caught fire.

Hecate continued to rail at her. "Don't do that. What are you aiming at? You'll make it come down and hit me in the head ... Ohhhh, I get it. That's what you want! You *are* an opportunist bitch! No witnesses. Just shoot me and get it over with!"

The main spar shifted, dropped a few centimeters into the channel. Hecate, mercifully, quit jabbering. Then Ana heard shouts, down past the mess of the data center. At least one aircraft had landed outside, delivering warriors.

No, no, no. Gimme a little more time.

She kept on with the laser, widening the channel. The shouting got louder as Tluaanto picked their way through the other side of the field of destruction.

And the spar dropped!

It fell fifty centimeters, landing on one of the cross beams fallen across Hecate, jamming the farthest end down and against the floor, raising the other end twenty centimeters above Hecate's thigh, freeing her.

"You—" Hecate started in a surprised tone. Then she started scooping smaller debris off her.

Ana tossed the laser and moved in to help. "Basic leverage," she told her with a smirk.

"Great," muttered Hecate, yanking at a strand of steel cable. "And if the whole thing had swung around and clamped down harder?"

Ana dropped the chunk of concrete she'd moved and took hold of Hecate under the armpits, dragging her free. "Then ... I could still have ... shot you in the head. Win-win."

Hecate actually laughed at that. Or perhaps it had been a grunt of pain. Either way, she was free now.

"Can you walk?" Ana asked her, checking the data center. Figures were visible now, smudges amidst the smoke and dust. Their voices were louder. There might have been ten of them. Maybe twenty. And she had no doubt now they were warriors.

"Can you look pretty?" Hecate replied. "Of course not. Check it." Ana looked. Hecate's right thigh was bleeding heavily through the material of her pants. "You can still shoot me."

"Thinkin' about it," Ana said. She kicked a sheet of ceiling panel closer. It was lightweight but tough, about two meters by a meter. "Drag yourself onto that."

Hecate's expression was dubious but she complied, using her hands to lift the bottom half of her onto the makeshift sled. The voices in the data center were closer, as were the smudges moving there.

Hecate had lost her PR19, so Ana passed hers over. "You're covering our retreat."

"Fine with me." Hecate sat up straighter. "Not sure what the point of this is. The Confeds have obviously left us here."

"While there's life ..." Ana said, quoting a Confed poet she'd heard somewhere. But she feared Hecate was right.

The ceiling panel had snapped away a little uncleanly so that the metal edging formed a strong enough lip for Ana to take hold of. She turned her back to it, faced toward the hangar. Hopefully not an empty hangar. Ana bobbed down, took hold, and started dragging.

It was goddamn harder than she expected. And rougher, the panel catching and snagging, slowing them down. "Hang on back there."

"Already thought of that. I'm smarter than you, remember?"

"Heavier too. Ever think about goin' on a diet?"

"Ever think about shuttin' up?"

Ana had to lean forward more, driving from her thighs. Her calves were killing her, her shoulders and forearms screaming. Part of the edging she was holding was beginning to bend outward with the pressure, and if she lost a hold on that ...

She kept up the banter, taking her mind off it. "Seriously. How'd you get so fat, Hecate?"

"It's all muscle, girl."

"Not around your ass, it isn't."

Another grudging chuckle from Hecate.

And then a shout of discovery from behind them. Hecate fired a volley. And another.

Emerging from the cloud of dust, Ana stared down the corridor ahead, dismayed to find she had at least one-fifty meters left.

"Got one!" Hecate crowed.

Something sizzled over Ana's shoulder, so close she dropped the plaster—making Hecate swear. Ana swung around in a crouch, feeling for her sidearm. She'd lost it. For the first time in her life, she was in a fight without a weapon in her hands. More energy-blasts punched into the walls and debris around them. "We're not gonna make it," she muttered, then kissed the St. Mary tattoo on her wrist.

Tipping onto her side, Hecate passed her the gun. "Then we die with honor."

"May as well." She got the new rifle stock against her shoulder. "That bastard Stines probably told 'em we're already dead."

Figures were coming out of the haze now. Three, four, five of them. Ana brought one down with a burst of fire. She steeled herself for return fire. With these odds, there was no way—

A grenade launcher thumped from behind her. Ana actually caught sight of the projectile sailing through the space between her and the enemy before it exploded against a chunk of ragged ceiling panel and sent the enemy scattering. Ana kept Hecate's gun pointed at the data center.

Hecate craned her neck around. Beneath the grime, her face was ashen with pain and perhaps with shock. There wasn't much expression there. But she managed a faint smile at whoever was coming up behind them. "Thank God for that. Someone strong enough to actually help me here."

"You're welcome," Ana said, risking a glance backwards. Chipper was twenty meters back, running hard with Vazak sprinting up from behind him.

Chipper came to a stop at her back and fired a few rounds down the corridor. Nothing came back at them. Vazak arrived, lifted Hecate in her arms like a child, and headed off the other way. Though it must have hurt, this time Hecate didn't complain.

Ana was sighting along her weapon again when a big hand took hold of her vest and yanked her upright.

"What the—"

"You run. I'll cover," Chipper said. He fired a sustained burst from his own PR19, then glared at her. "Are you *deaf*?"

She set off then, hearing him jack a grenade into the slot beneath his rifle muzzle and fire it. The race back along the corridor felt like it went on forever, her running with one hand pressing against the lump on her head, expecting any moment to get cut down by hostile fire.

And then, she was on the ramp, *up* the ramp, collapsing on the floor between the two couches and tables. Seconds later, Chipper came tromping up the ramp, shouting "Go, go, go!" Ana turned her head to look around: Vazak and Stines were standing in the passageway to the yacht's personal quarters and amenities. Vazak pointed back toward the toilet door and said, "Con-sill." They'd put the prisoner in there, obviously. Stuck back there, with nowhere to go, Stines wore a fierce glower, but had his eyes down, his head down.

Yeah, best you don't make eye contact with me, cabrón.

She got up on one elbow and faced the front of the yacht. Wepps was visible in the cockpit entry. Chipper sagged against the wall by the closed hatch.

"Hey ... thanks," she called to him.

He gave her a weary thumbs up then sank onto his haunches, losing himself in his thoughts.

Laying back, resting her head on one arm to avoid pressure on the contusion, Ana murmured to herself, "That was some fine work there yourself."

From close by on her right, a voice replied, "You're supposed to let other people tell you that."

She turned her head. Hecate. Visible beneath the table, lying on the couch with a wad of gauze pressed to her thigh.

"Ha. Didn't see you there."

"I figured."

"Well, *you* won't be telling me what a great job I did, I'm damn sure."

"Of course not, *baka*. And you tell anyone I thanked you, I'll call you a damned liar."

Ana nodded slowly. "And anyone asks why I saved your ass, I'll tell 'em you owed me money from a poker game."

"Copy that."

They turned their heads away and, in total harmony, both women murmured the same relieved cussword.

INTERLUDE

Buoun

"The war is not over," Pi told Buoun. They sat together in the meal area aboard their shuttle. The small craft was still attached to Assured. *Pi had a pot of haktulu worm stew in front of her and two plates. So far, she had served herself, but hadn't indicated whether Buoun was welcome to eat from it.*

No doubt, *he thought,* I'll be eating nothing more interesting than fruit for my next meal.

Pi sipped from a cup of ve'haat before adding, "Rather, the war has paused."

"Paused, Councillor?" Buoun replied. "But surely—"

"Surely," she interrupted, "the intervention of the Humans surprised and terrified our enemies. Surely, they miscalculated. Surely, Domain Surface won't dare resume hostilities while one of their Councillors sits soiling his trousers in the starship's prison cell."

"Actually, I believe the Councillor is being held in a stateroom. As a guest."

Pi grunted. "A guest who can't leave is a prisoner. And surely," she added, returning to her point, "Domain Moon are rethinking their next moves while their ally is out of the game."

Buoun signaled agreement, being polite. He had hoped that the war would indeed be over. The Humans were walking a fine line. But, as Pi said, the shooting had stopped. Domain Moon's poorly thought out nuclear missile fleet still churned toward Liberty Habitat, but there was plenty of time yet to recall them.

But if hostilities did resume, if Moon and Surface completely lost their minds ...

He hid his fear response by pretending to look up data on his wristwrap.

If the war escalated, the Humans might live up to their military designation as Peacekeepers, forced to call in more combat vessels from the extensive fleets he presumed they owned. That was not something Buoun wanted to see happen.

Pi made an impatient noise low in her throat, irritated perhaps that Buoun was not paying full attention to her. He lowered his wrist, offered an apology.

She indicated the ladle poking from the stew pot. "Eat," she said. "You have had a worse time than I have, this last cycle and a half." Blinking in surprise, Buoun thanked her and reached for the ladle and bowl. "Obviously, your contribution—and that of the Orbital personnel—was instrumental in not only protecting your own domain, but in helping the Humans get back control of their systems, placing them deeper in debt to us."

Buoun tried not to let his disagreement with this point show in his body language as he plopped the first ladle-full of stew into his bowl.

"Buoun, it is my strong suspicion that you effectively lied to me and colluded with the Humans in this matter. Hzz," she hissed in mild amusement when he almost dropped his meal on the table. "Put your bowl down before you spill it all.

And swallow your fear. I am of the opinion that results are all that matter. If you lied and colluded, then your judgement in the matter has been proven sound. And do not fear that I will mention this to Councillor Naat or others; it is no one's concern but ours. I may not approve in principle *of colluding with a foreign power, but in matters concerning Humans, you are indeed an expert, and I will trust your judgments from here on."*

"I ... am grateful. Councillor."

"Just be sure that—if it is to happen again—you include me fully. Trust must move both ways, Buoun."

"Yes, Councillor." Hardly believing he had gotten away with it, Buoun slurped and nibbled at his stew. When he had first boarded, the food had smelled incredible; now he barely tasted it. Swallowing, he ventured a question, "What is to become of the Domains? The accord? While you know that I admire and trust the Humans, I am *concerned that their arrival provoked such a sudden and dramatic flare up between us. We finally achieved a workable political and cultural homeostasis. But now we see it threatening to crumble—"*

"Buoun, if you had ruminated upon your own species' history more than that of aliens, you would know that such accords, such balances, are always in flux. Every kind of homeostasis exists only as an illusion. An illusion can only be maintained by viewing it from a distance. The body, an ecosystem, a political arrangement—look closely and you will see that these are the product of ebbs and flows, micro-change and micro-management."

She reached beneath the table for another cup and poured him a ve'haat, nudging it toward him.

"Besides," she said, "if you fear for the well-being and ascendency of your own Domain, you can rest your mind. Do not be alarmed for us. The Humans have not conquered us yet. And they do not know all that we know."

April 5-10, 3014, Old Earth Calendar

30

FOR THE HUMAN crew and Tluaan guests of CNV112 *Assured*, the week after the away mission passed in a haze of crazy-busy periods and prolonged and boring downtimes. System repairs took most of the attention with priority focused on restoring the ship's mobility, shields, comms, and defenses.

For Ana and the other members of the mission team, the first 48 hours after their return meant a stint in quarantine. During it, Ana shook her head frequently since she knew that Envoy Buoun and the other Tluaanto hadn't faced anything like that when *they'd* boarded *Assured* for the first time. The quarantine sequestered the women in one "zoo tank"—*not* its official name—and the men in another. Vazak was not invited: 'women' did not include Tlaa apparently. After those two ship-days were up, Ana discovered that the warrior had been escorted to one of the docked Tluaan shuttles to remain there until further notice.

When the ship's surgeon and two corpsmen arrived to set them free, Ana was first one out. Standing in the passage, stretching and breathing in air that seemed lighter than that of the tank, she glanced left to see Chipper coming out his door. He waved; she returned it. Stines emerged next, noticed her, turned white and hurried off the other way. Wepps and Piers passed Ana with a cheerful "good morning" and vanished up a ladderwell, chatting about showers and real sleep.

Ana and Chipper watched as Hecate was stretchered out by the corpsmen, destined for the sickbay. The surgeon had said her prognosis was good. With accelerated-stem and nanite therapies, she'd be walking—limping, probably—by the end of the week, and running by the end of next month. When Hecate's stretcher vanished into a nearby lift, Ana and Chipper discussed their own next steps: they were looking at a lot of downtime now the crisis was over. Both agreed that they'd slept enough during quarantine, and that showers were overrated when you could no longer smell your own stink. After two days of liquid diet, the thing they were looking forward to more than sleep or showers was solid food.

And that was where Ana's emerging good mood had stalled—when they'd arrived in the mess and she'd seen what was served up as breakfast. It hadn't seemed to bother Chipper at all.

Now they sat in a booth hunched over their bowls of stewed fruit and protein gruel.

Ana said, "I seriously don't get why we had to put up with two days of quarantine. With modern air sampling and those hacking booster shots we all got, you'd think they'd just give us the once over. Like Vazak obviously got."

Chipper nodded, using his spoon like a shovel, already on his second bowl of fruit-*n*-gruel. Halfway through her *first* bowl, losing interest in it, she nudged it across the table to him and picked up her mug. Confed Navy food was bland and unimaginative, but at least the coffee was good.

She slurped some down then said, "All the Tluaanto walk around no worries while we heroes get stuck in a glass box for two days. It stabs, dude. Totally stabs. Doncha think?"

The question forced him to swallow early, and his face screwed up for a few seconds as he waited for the big lump to work its way down his esophagus. "Don't I think what?"

She stared at him a moment then said, "And I thought Confeds had manners."

"Huh?"

"Nodding that big dumb head over and over like you're listenin' to me. And you ain't listenin' to me."

"I was. I heard ... You said ... Gimme a sec ..."

She kicked him under the table.

But not hard.

LATER, they strolled out and toward a lift, the one furthest from the mess—the direction of their stroll had been by some unspoken agreement, giving them more time for conversation.

That conversation was nothing more than small talk. Same as it had been for the past hour—once Chipper finally got his fill of mess crap. It was nice, she decided; *this* was nice, the walking, the talking, the spending time with someone she trusted. It was nothing like she'd had with Olesco, of course—that poor, gorgeous, dead asshole—nothing like with *him*. If she'd been with Olesco, right about now they'd be finding some outa-the-way place together to do *The Thing*, as Olesco had called it.

She didn't want *The Thing* with big-lug-Chipper here.

Did she?

Walking beside her, he was telling some story about

hunting for wolf crabs back home, oblivious to her thoughts. Ana glanced at him. He was well-proportioned, he had a symmetrical face, and his smile was actually a thing of beauty.

Well, maybe a physical relationship wasn't *entirely* out of the question, she decided. Yeah, maybe. Maybe one day she'd want *that*. Maybe.

But for the moment, it was nice to enjoy something she'd only read about and watched in Confed comic books, on Confed holodramas.

It was nice to have a friend.

When they finally reached the end of the corridor and approached the lift, it opened.

Out stepped Stines.

Invective gushed from Ana's mouth. She lunged, fists curled, ready to take out some teeth, but was held back only when Chipper threw an arm in front of her. Stines retreated behind the bigger man, backed against the wall.

"What's this about?" Chipper demanded, facing her.

"This *cabrón* left us to die."

"He ...? *Really*?"

"Damn right, really."

Chipper half-turned, studying Stines. "Now you mention it, I did wonder why he told us you were both lost. When you weren't."

"I didn't know they were buried under that mess," Stines said.

"You—!" Ana lunged again, but Chipper caught her easily.

"Now, now, I'm sure if we run this by Sergeant Wepps, he can get to the truth of it." His words and tone said *Peacekeeper*—but Ana noticed with interest that the suspicion and anger beginning to smolder in his eyes said *Tactical*.

"Hack you both," Stines snarled, pressing himself

against the bulkhead, edging away from the lift. "She already told him this bullsweat." He lifted his chin toward Ana. "Wepps is sending me to an inquiry because of you."

Chipper had his back fully to Ana now, his front to Stines. He rubbed his chin. "An inquiry. Wow. I've heard they're pretty rough. Lots of talking and answering questions and things. Hey, Ana?"

"What?" she ground out between gritted teeth.

"You know you can't strike this man, ey? Not only because it might undermine your case against him, but because you're Xerxian. It would have political implications ... and probably get *you* called up to a hearing too."

"I don't care about no hearing." She took a deep breath, trying for calm. Stines was in her eyeline now, backed up into the corner made by the passageway's end. She could probably get to him if she tried, but Chipper was making sense. And he was in the way.

"However—" Chipper said with a small groan as he stretched overhead. His right hand made busy with something on the ceiling as he continued. "—his eye-cams aren't working. And I don't reckon the corridor cam is either." He dropped the arm that had been reaching overhead and stepped half-inside the elevator with one shoulder holding the door. He raised a hand to show Stines the lens from the security camera above them and winked.

Stines gaped.

And Ana darted in before he could react, launching a lightning-strike punch into the man's gut. Stines folded and collapsed, gagging and gasping.

Chipper withdrew into the lift as Ana entered, his face a picture of peaceful innocence. He tapped a button. "Basketball court might be free. You feel like playing some basketball?"

"Sure," she grinned back. "I'm a little amped for some

reason. Need to burn it off." She whipped out a hand to catch the door as it tried to close. "Hey, Stines?"

Stines's screwed-up face rose; he squinted at her.

"If you were headed to breakfast, it ain't that great today. Then again, you probably won't miss it." She let the door go. "I don't think you'll be eating for a week."

31

LIBERTY HABITAT, Ambassador Chris Gregory thought. Seen through the *Assured* skiff's forward viewport, the gargantuan spherical habitat grew more and more immense until there was nothing else for Gregory to see out there. *Home to Domain Space governance and 68% of their population. And with room for plenty more population as they grow in the future ...*

The view through the window shifted as the shuttle angled "down", as Piers followed a smaller Tluaan runabout into the appropriate dock.

Gregory said, "Twenty-one-point-one kilometers in diameter," and shook his head in amazement. "Almost nine and a half million cubic meters."

From the rows of seating behind them, Buoun piped up. "That habitat is our domain's crowing achievement."

"Er, you mean *crowning*," Grace told him.

"Oh. Thank you."

As the skiff came in close to the habitat surface, giant steel doors retracted to reveal a hangar bay beyond. The runabout darted inside, but Piers entered more carefully and eased the craft onto the floor.

"Atmosphere rising outside the ship fast," Piers told them all. "Give it another thirty seconds and you should be right to disembark."

"We'll wait until we see Tluaanto walking around out there first," Wepps said from one of the rear seats. He was seated beside Vazak, who'd no doubt found her seating for the journey uncomfortable but who'd made not a single noise about it.

"I agree with the sergeant," Grace said.

Buoun whispered something in his own language, snapping Gregory's attention back to him. The Tlu was transfixed, seemingly unable to tear his eyes from the view through the window.

Gregory touched his arm. "You okay?"

Buoun blinked, glanced at him with an unreadable expression. "Yes. Oh, yes. I am very okay. I never thought I would see Liberty Habitat again."

Gregory exchanged a frown with Piers. "You never—?"

"It is, as you say, a long story. But this story, as you also say, has a happy ending." He nodded forwards. "See there?"

Gregory looked. An interior door had opened thirty meters from the yacht's nose. Two warriors Vazak's size came through first. Then Councillor Pi, who had departed *Assured* to the habitat mere hours after the resolution of the away mission. And after her, a trio of gray-furred Tluaanto.

Buoun added, "I believe it is safe to disembark. Come, come and meet our leadership."

AS THE RAMP engaged and started lowering, Gregory had his pad out, with Tabitha's image onscreen smiling up at him. *Here we go, love,* he thought, *back to work for me, and let's hope the Tluaanto listen to me.*

He strode down the ramp, putting the pad away inside

his vest. The first thing that hit him about the Tluaan port terminal was the odor. The air tasted strongly like musk and, weirdly, curry. The strange olfactory combination was as disorienting as the curved angles of the hangar's side walls.

However, the floor looked and felt like a human artificial habitat floor: some kind of ceramic tiles joined together with sealant. And the delegation standing halfway to the doors looked like any of a hundred other delegations he'd met in his career.

Yeah, except for the fur. And the ears. And the head crests...

He paced over to them with Buoun at his side, and Wepps, Vazak, and Grace at his back. At five meters away, Buoun murmured for him to stop here and then made introductions.

"Human emissaries, you know Councillor Pi." The Tlaa nodded to Gregory, then dropped her gaze. "I introduce you all to Councillor Klep, Councillor Hari, and Grand Councillor Naat. These names are their diminutive epithets, since our full names are much longer. But in all meetings now and in future, you may call them by those.

"Naat," Buoun continued, "is our senior leader, policy maker, and decision maker. Klep and Hari are here as observers, and you should direct all your communication to Naat. He speaks some English phrases, he understands more than he can say, and he will learn it quickly by using it. But for the time being, he will rely on me to accurately pass on his messages and to pass yours back."

Buoun then made introductions in the Tluaan dialect, and Gregory could make out the names of each person in the party, as well as what he thought might be the Tluaan word for warrior when Buoun introduced both Wepps and Grace.

Interesting. How does he know Grace is a fighter?

Naat spoke at length to Buoun. Appearing sheepish about it, Buoun then translated for the humans present.

"The Grand Councillor wishes to forgo lengthy formalities including food you can't eat and liquid you can't drink and seats that aren't made for your ... bottoms. Shortly, he will lead you on a tour of some of our facilities and places of interest. He hopes you will be pleased by the honor and trust he is offering you by this."

"Indeed, we're honored," Gregory replied.

Naat made twin gestures Gregory understood to mean he understood the human remark and was impatient for Buoun to continue translating his original message.

As expected, Buoun continued, "But first, the Grand Councillor has an urgent question he would like to ask."

"What is it?" Gregory asked, folding his hands at his waist.

"Will you hand over the Domain Surface councillor?"

Gregory had half-expected this. He answered immediately, tone measured, face calm. "We will not. That councillor is not a prisoner; he is under our protection. Instead, we invite you aboard our ship to negotiate peace. With him and then with the other domains."

Buoun translated this, then translated Naat's response. Things continued this way for a short while.

Naat said, "Peace? Yes, both Councillor Pi and Buoun told me that a comprehensive peace was your intention. We are not opposed to peace."

Gregory replied, "Then you will return to our ship with me, Grand Councillor?"

Naat: "I will not. But Pi will go. It is the responsibility of her role to negotiate with foreign powers. We will also send Councillor Hari here as surety."

Gregory studied both Tluaanto named. Even an idiot would be able to see in the body language of both non-humans that they were displeased at this directive and more than a little anxious about it.

"Our intentions *are* peaceful, I assure you all," he said. "And we know from our own history that a united species is a strong and progressive species."

Naat dipped his head at this, but said nothing. Did he agree, disagree? Would discussions take a day, a week, a decade?

We're only at the beginning of this thing, Gregory thought. *We have a long,* long *way to go...*

But it was working. It would work. And the violence committed by *Assured* and her crew: it had been perhaps worth it in the end; it had been necessary, ethical.

Naat was speaking again, with Buoun translating as his leader spoke. "We will begin our tour then. As we walk, perhaps you will explain how you intend to include Domains Moon and Ocean in your peace discussions. In two of your hours, we will expect you to carry our representatives with you to commence those discussions. The Council and I would like to see this resolved as quickly as possible. Because we have another matter that we would like you to be part of."

As Naat kept talking and Buoun kept translating, Gregory's eyes grew larger. His companions stirred uneasily as the revelation became clearer.

"At my direction," Naat said, "Buoun hid some knowledge from you. Until such time as we could confirm you were a trustworthy species. It is clear now that you are. In the closest star system to ours, a Tluaan ship is there. A Domain Space ship. It has been there for some time. A second ship is on its way and will arrive in three of your years."

The humans glanced at each other, speechless.

Naat took a deep breath and continued. "It takes these ships many years to travel there, and many years for their messages to return to us. We can only travel at fractions of the speed of light. And we cannot communicate faster than light speed. It was only seventy human days before your arrival that we received our ship's first transmissions. These transmissions relayed two facts: first, that the expedition had run into difficulties and needed assistance—assistance that would take us many years to provide; and second, that they had discovered an artifact. A type of vessel. And aboard it, living there, another race of intelligent creatures."

A more noticeable ripple of surprise went through the humans assembled. Gregory's heart was pounding.

Are you kidding me!

The leader waited a moment, presumably so all of that could sink in. Then he chattered something else as Buoun listened.

Buoun straightened, faced Gregory fully, and translated. "Ambassador Gregory, we invite you to take us to the Kh'het system in your ship, to provide assistance to our current expedition, and explore what we have found there, as partners with us."

Buoun's posture relaxed a notch and—as Gregory tried to gather his whirling thoughts—the Tlu affected a human smile, something that was beginning to suit him.

"In other words, Ambassador, we were wondering if you would like to come and make fourth contact."

EPILOGUE

Buoun

STANDING at a window on Liberty Habitat's ninetieth level, watching the Human shuttle leave, Buoun glanced at the Grand Councillor standing beside him. They were alone here. Perhaps because of this fact, or perhaps because the Humans had changed the nature of everything forever, Buoun felt brave enough to adopt a frank and informal tone. He asked, "So, now we will disclose everything to the Humans? We will tell them the true nature of Project Kh'het? We will change our policy toward the Qesh and the Xenthracr?"

"No," Naat said and affected such a breathy sigh that for a half-heartbeat, Buoun thought he was speaking with a Human. "We will continue to let the aliens see us as their clan-cubs, as friends*." Here Naat used the English word. "They will not understand what is happening in Kh'het System. Since they trust us and rely on us for information, they will believe what we tell them. They will see us as*

offering the Qesh mercy. And this will gain us more goodwill and accelerate their decision-making when it comes to handing over the stardrive technology."

The Grand Councillor took a step closer to the window. Beyond it, the shuttle dwindled to a dot among the pinpoints of the stars.

Buoun hoped that Naat was not watching his reflection in the glass, not noticing the shock that he couldn't keep from his posture and his face, the shock he felt at what he'd said.

After this, *Buoun thought,* after all this, we will continue to lie to them. To use them as our resources.

A dull misery began to spread through his insides.

We will risk their friendship. We will risk everything.

Naat put a hand to the glass. And he said, "We will get the Humans' drive from them, Buoun. And then they will not be the most powerful species traveling among the stars."

***

GUIDE TO HUMAN-SETTLED SPACE

Anticus: DCHC name for the home world belonging to the apparently sentient race called Anachromites (or "mound-builders".) In the past eight hundred years, human scientists have not found reliable ways to communicate with Anachromites, and this is part of the reason that the Anachromites' status as sentient beings is still debated today. Humans had research settlements and a religious settlement on Anticus that were unaffected by the PBT Crisis

Bona Vista Station: artificial habitat in space

Castor and Pollux: two habitable planets of the Dioscurin system (not to be confused with the stars originally called Castor and Pollux in the constellation Gemini)

Centauri: agricultural world with two continents and three archipelago chains, third of the original worlds to form the DCHC in 2982

Drop-in-the-Ocean: remote starbase in interstellar space; refueling station

Earth (and the Sol system artificial habitats): status largely unknown

Eventide: home world for the sentient stone age race

who call themselves Jarinyi. Humans have established three research facilities on Eventide with Jarinyi permission. A branch species of Jarinyi known as Nguwuu also inhabit an area of Eventide but remain hostile to humans

Foucault's Moon: Capital of the Democratic Confederation of Human Colonies (DCHC)

Landfall Island: Oceana's second largest island, Chipper's home

Nakayama Station: A habitat orbiting one of Centauri's moons; an old CUSET-era multi-corporation server-base and storage facility

Oceana: DCHC world with a small population

Pride of Mao: originally a Chinese world before the dark age, Pride of Mao was one of the three original worlds to form the DCHC in 2990. ("Mao Kuo" is the official name for people from Pride of Mao)

Theseus: DCHC world, Earth-like but with fewer oceans and uninhabitable around its equatorial zone because of extreme daytime temperatures; Theseus's highest urban and commercial centers are around its poles

Xerxes: in 3014, Xerxes' fledgling government is negotiating to join the DCHC. First settlement and mining/farming established in 2131. First urban center established in 2138. Three waves of settlement arrived on Xerxes between 2131 and 2140, its settlers predominantly Spanish, Filipino, Central American, Mexican, Scottish, US, and Irish

Yun Dao: isolationist world, status largely unknown

SHORT LEXICON OF TERMS USED IN THIRD CONTACT

Auxiliary CIC: a starship compartment serving as a backup processing and control center for ship's systems and information in case its bridge or flight deck are compromised or damaged (CIC, an old term meaning Command Information Center)

baka: *cow* (origin Filipino)

bulala: *an idiot*; evolved Filipino low-level insult (originally a Tagalog-language adjective meaning *star-struck* or *stupid*)

CUSET: A late-21st to mid-22nd century union of corporations formed to venture into Earth's solar system and to colonize beyond it

cycle: the Tluaan term for a day (approx. 30 Earth-hours long)

Devilfly: 1) predatory insect-analog indigenous to Pollux; 2) an Umaga-Morgen F380 Devilfly is a single-occupant fighter-interceptor capable of operations in space and in atmosphere and armed with laser cannons, countermeasures, and two ship-to-ship high explosive missiles

fifteenth: the Tluaan equivalent of an hour, the

Suuchaat day being divided into fifteen segments of approximately two Earth-hours long

frog it: slang for *running fast, leaving fast* (reference to the Faster-Than-Light technique known as leap-frogging)

glitchy: dangerous, changeable, uncontrollable (Thesian slang)

hack: an expression of profanity; a swear word referring to the hacking of another person's data or personal systems (which was the ultimate antisocial act in the 22nd century when the term is thought to have originated)

heartbeat: Tluaan version of human seconds; approximately 1.1 Earth-seconds

hún dàn: scoundrel; bastard; hoodlum; wretch (Mandarin phrase)

Kh'het: The Tluaan name for the closest star system to theirs

Liberty Habitat: Huge artificial habitat where most of Domain Space's population and governance resides

Lioness: 1) extinct Earth predator; 2) a Mumford T15 *Lioness* is a "pursuit runner" class of space vehicle, with fast acceleration, long-range fuel-tanks, one forward-firing laser emitter, and a ship-to-ship missile bank

mabaho: Filipino word for *stinking* or *rotten*

ngeh: *no* (Tluaan Domain Space dialect)

orbit: the Tluaan term for a year (i.e. one orbit of Suuchaat around its star), approximately 242 Earth-days (in Domain Space language, one orbit is a *p'hush* while *p'hushto* is the plural form)

PBT: A virulent disease originating from a colony world in the mid-2140s. The virus quickly spread among humanity's colonies, decimating populations and initiating the collapse of civilization. In the early 31st Century, the human race is still recovering from the resultant interstellar dark age.

PRC: People's Republic of China, a former "superpower" political civilization of the 20th-22nd centuries who were CUSET's main competitor in colonizing other star systems

porquería: *piece of crap* (31st century Xerxian Spanish idiom)

retinaid: Xerxian tech, a cyber-neural enhancement sending electronic images direct to the brain's visual cortex

sahsah/sahss: *yes* (Domain Space dialect)

shārén bù zhǎyǎn: stone-cold killer, one who kills without blinking (Mandarin phrase)

sophie off: to *siphon off* or *steal* (also the word sophie is sometimes used on its own to mean *steal*)

sugary: *excellent* (Polluxan slang)

Suuchaat: Tluaan home world

Tlaa: female Tluaan

Tlu: male Tluaan

Tluaan: collective adjective for things to do with Tluaanto; (e.g. *this object is Tluaan in origin*)

Tluaanto: collective plural for a group of Tluaan individuals where gender is not specified; (e.g. *Look at the crowd of Tluaanto over there*)

tulalâ: *vacant-brain* (Xerxian slang) (evolved Filipino phrase originating from the Filipino/Tagalog word for *staring into space* or *astonishment*)

weaners: Xerxian slang for weaklings, referring to babies newly weaned from their mothers

EXCERPT FROM ASSURED (ENVOYS BOOK #2)

BEYOND CHIPPER'S E-SUIT FACEPLATE, the corridor was a sea of bodies, some still smoking from grenade blasts or multiple EM pulses. The visor gave him a sense of separation from the carnage, making it seem strangely unreal as if he were watching a violent streamie. Another reason to be glad for the environment suit.

Something jostled him. Stines slipping a spare air recycler into a suit pouch for him. The sour-faced Peacer tossed another spare up to Warrior Vazak waiting on the *Lioness*'s roof. Chipper grabbed him before he could return to his firing position.

"You really wanna follow my lead?" he asked.

Stines shrugged one shoulder. "Why not? I ain't got any ideas."

Chipper nodded, then thumped on the hull of the *Lioness*. "Lieutenant Catanno, you hearing me?"

"Yes." The pilot's reply was cut through with static, another sign that the vessel's comms were in bad shape.

"Where you at with repairs?"

"I need a code-jockey in here to look at this mess. Man, I can't even tell if it *was* a signal that screwed everything up, or if it's some kind of virus. Maybe some fragment left over from the Domain Surface attack."

Chipper frowned. The Domain Surface virus attack had been two weeks earlier, and still it was causing problems. "Why didn't you say that before?" This new possibility could undermine the sketchy plan he'd just come up with.

"Just thought of it."

Chipper put a finger to his helmet and mimed pulling a trigger. Stines actually chuckled. "Catanno, you're a navy lieutenant. You fly ships for a living. You make important life or death decisions as part of that job."

"What's your point, assface?"

"Make a decision now. Is it a virus shutting you out, or is it a signal?"

Almost grudgingly, the pilot said, "I think it's a signal."

"You think?"

"It's a signal, all right? It's a jamming signal or a scrambler or something."

"All right, then. I'll tell you guys my plan. None of us are gonna like it." He thought about that a second. "Except maybe Vazak."

While he got his thoughts in order, Chipper wondered, *How in the hell did we get into this mess?*

WHAT ELSE HAS ALDIN WRITTEN?

Books by Peter J Aldin

Scrapper

Eventide

Assured (Envoys #2)

The Stars Remain (Envoys #3)

Chasing Hell (a 4HU novel)

Books by Pete Aldin

Doomsday's Child (series)

Black Marks

Nine Tales

ABOUT THE AUTHOR

Peter J Aldin writes action-adventure in sci-fi or fantasy settings. An Aussie, he lives in his homeland. From there he supports Chelsea FC in the English Premier League. He is a fan of rums, whiskys (and whiskeys), as well as board games.

He also writes under the pen name Pete Aldin: these stories are darker, more brutal thrillers in paranormal or other fantasy settings. They contain more gore and a *lot* more swearing.

For a free ebook and newsletter updates:

Or connect with Peter J Aldin at www.petealdin.com

Printed in Great Britain
by Amazon